NORTHERN IRISH LITERATURE, 1975–2006

Volume 2: The Imprint of History

Michael Parker

palgrave
macmillan

First published 2007 by
PALGRAVE MACMILLAN
Houndmills, Basingstoke, Hampshire RG21 6XS and
175 Fifth Avenue, New York, N.Y. 10010
Companies and representatives throughout the world

PALGRAVE MACMILLAN is the global academic imprint of the Palgrave Macmillan division of St. Martin's Press, LLC and of Palgrave Macmillan Ltd. Macmillan®is a registered trademark in the United States, United Kingdom and other countries. Palgrave is a registered trademark in the European Union and other countries.

ISBN-13: 978-0-230-55305-7   hardback
ISBN-10: 0-230-55305-2   hardback

This book is printed on paper suitable for recycling and made from fully managed and sustained forest sources. Logging, pulping and manufacturing processes are expected to conform to the environmental regulations of the country of origin.

A catalogue record for this book is available from the British Library.

Library of Congress Cataloging-in-Publication Data

Parker, Michael, 1949–
    Northern Irish literature, 1975–2006. volume 2, The imprint of
    history / Michael Parker.
        p. cm.
    Includes bibliographical references and index.
    ISBN 0-230-55305-2 (alk. paper)
1. English literature—Irish authors—History and criticism.   2. English
    literature—20th century—History and crticism.   3. Literature
    and society—Northern Ireland—History—20th century   4. Northern
    Ireland—Intellectual life.   5. Northern Ireland—In literature.   I. Title.
    II. Title: Imprint of history.

PR8753.P37 2007
820.9′358—dc22   2007023071

10   9   8   7   6   5   4   3   2   1
16   15   14   13   12   11   10   09   08   07

Printed and bound in Great Britain by
Antony Rowe Ltd, Chippenham and Eastbourne

Also available:
NORTHERN IRISH LITERATURE, 1956–1975
(Volume 1): 0-333-60415-6

NORTHERN IRISH LITERATURE, 1956–2006
(2-Volume pack): 0-230-55326-5.

To Philip Hobsbaum (1932–2005)

Contents (Volume 2)

List of Maps

Abbreviations

ACNI	Arts Council of Northern Ireland
ANC	African National Congress
BBC	British Broadcasting Corporation
CRA	Civil Rights Association
CSJ	Campaign for Social Justice
DUP	Democratic Unionist Party
DCAC	Derry Citizens' Action Committee
DAAD	Direct Action Against Drugs
DPP	Director of Public Prosecutions
FF	Fianna Fáil
GAA	Gaelic Athletic Association
GOC	General Officer Commanding (British Army)
HMSU	Headquarters Mobile Support Unit
HU	*Honest Ulsterman* (Literary magazine)
IICD	Independent International Commission on Decommissioning
ITV	Independent Television (UK)
IMC	International Monitoring Commission
INLA	Irish National Liberation Army
IRA	Irish Republican Army
IRB	Irish Republican Brotherhood
LVF	Loyalist Volunteer Force
MEP	Member of European Parliament
MP	member of Parliament
NAIJ	National Association for Irish Justice
NP	Nationalist Party
NATO	North Atlantic Treaty Organization
NICAT	Northern Ireland Committee against Terror
NORAID	Northern Aid Committee
NICRA	Northern Ireland Civil Rights Association
NILP	Northern Ireland Labour Party
NIO	Northern Ireland Office
OED	Oxford English Dictionary
PD	People's Democracy
PSNI	Police Service of Northern Ireland
PUP	Progressive Unionist Party

PIRA	Provisional Irish Republican Army
RTE	Radio Telefis Eireann
RIRA	Real IRA
RP	Received Pronunciation
RC	Roman Catholic
RAF	Royal Air Force
RIC	Royal Irish Constabulary
RUC	Royal Ulster Constabulary
SF	Sinn Féin
SDLP	Social Democratic and Labour Party
SAS	Special Air Service
SSU	Special Support Unit
UCDC	Ulster Constitution Defence Committee
UDA	Ulster Defence Association
UDR	Ulster Defence Regiment
UDP	Ulster Democratic Party
UFF	Ulster Freedom Fighters
ULC	Ulster Loyalist Council
UPV	Ulster Protestant Volunteers
UUC	Ulster Unionist Council
UUP	Ulster Unionist Party
UVF	Ulster Vanguard
UVF	Ulster Volunteer Force
UWC	Ulster Workers Council
UKUP	United Kingdom Unionist Party
UR	Ulster Resistance
UUAC	United Unionist Action Council

Acknowledgements

In writing this book over the last 11 years, I have received support from a wide range of individuals and institutions. Thanks to colleagues in the University of Central Lancashire, I have benefited from several invaluable periods of research leave between 1999 and 2005. Their support and generous funding from the Arts and Humanities Research Council enabled me to undertake a full year's research in 2000. As a result of Fellowships awarded by the University of Liverpool and the University of Ulster I have had access to excellent library facilities. Staff at the Linenhall Library Belfast, especially Robert Bell, John Gray and Yvonne Murphy, and the Public Record Office of Northern Ireland have assisted my work greatly, as have librarians at the British Library, the National Library of Ireland, LLRS (the University of Central Lancashire), the John Rylands Library (University of Manchester) and the Sidney Jones Library (University of Liverpool).

Many individuals have provided immensely helpful critical feedback and encouragement, or by answering queries, or by supplying me with access to rare literary or historical material: these include Malcolm Ballinn, Csilla Bertha, Rand Brandes, Scott Brewster, Ophelia Byrne, Ruth Carr, Neil Corcoran, Marianne Elliott, Kelvin Everest, Sarah Ferris, Robert Greacen, Richard Greaves, Adolphe Haberer, Brendan Hamill, David Hammond, Liam Harte, Seamus and Marie Heaney, Hugh Haughton, Philip and Rosemary Hobsbaum, Eamonn Hughes, Jerzy Jarniewicz, Richard Kirkland, Maria Kurdi, Harry Lane, Paul Livesey, Michael and Edna Longley, Bernard Mac Laverty, Aidan Mac Poilin, Sean McMahon, Deirdre Madden, David Marcus, John Montague, Donald Morse, Shane Murphy, Bernard O Donoghue, Frank Ormsby, Martine Pelletier, Ondrej Pilny, Glenn Patterson, Thomas Dillon Redshaw, Stephen Regan, Shaun Richards, Marilynn Richtarik, Anthony Roche, Neil Sammells, Bruce Stewart, Christine St Peter, Rufus Wood and Una Woods. Particular thanks go also to the artist, Nicola Nemec, for allowing me to use her painting 'Transient Land' as the cover illustration, and to Whitney Standlee and Liz Hodgson for help in preparing the final typescript. The greatest debt is owed to my wife, Aleksandra, and daughters, Judith, Juliet and Catherine. This book is dedicated also to the memory of three other women: Eileen Bond (1913–2005), Lucy Hughes (1881–1972) and Elizabeth Dunleavy (1838–1927).

Earlier versions of some sections have appeared in *Essays in Theatre, Honest Ulsterman, Hungarian Journal of English and American Studies, Irish Studies Review, Irish University Review, New Hibernia Review, Symbiosis*, and in *Irish Encounters* eds Alan Marshall and Neil Sammells, and *Contemporary Irish Fiction: Themes, Tropes, Theories* ed. Liam Harte, all of whom have generously granted permission for me to use this material.

I would also like to acknowledge formally the following individuals and publishers for granting me permission to use quotations from:

There is a House by Ruth Carr, published by Summer Palace Press, reprinted by permission of the author

The Irish for No and *Belfast Confetti* by Ciaran Carson, by kind permission of the author and The Gallery Press, Loughcrew, Oldcastle, County Meath, Ireland, and Wake Forest University Press

Reading in the Dark by Seamus Deane, published by Jonathan Cape. Reprinted by permission of the Random House Group Ltd. US copyright © 1996 Seamus Deane. Used by permission of Alfred A. Knopf, a division of Random House Inc.

The Way Paver and Other Stories by Anne Devlin, by kind permission of the author and Faber and Faber Ltd

These Days by Leontia Flynn, published by Jonathan Cape. Reprinted by permission of The Random House Group Ltd and the author

Translations by Brian Friel, by permission of Faber and Faber Ltd and The Catholic University of America Press, Washington DC

Somebody, Somewhere by Alan Gillis, by kind permission of the author and The Gallery Press, Loughcrew, Oldcastle, County Meath, Ireland

The Spirit Level by Seamus Heaney, Copyright © 1996 Seamus Heaney. Reprinted by permission of Faber and Faber Ltd and Farrar, Straus and Giroux, LLC

Shadows on our Skin by Jennifer Johnston, by kind permission of the author

Proxopera by Benedict Kiely, by kind permission of AP Watt Ltd on behalf of the author

To a Fault by Nick Laird, by kind permission of the author and Faber and Faber Ltd. US permission: Copyright © 2006 by Nick Laird. Used by permission of W.W. Norton & Co., Inc

The Ghost Orchid by Michael Longley, published by Jonathan Cape, reprinted by permission of The Random House Group Ltd and Wake Forest University Press

Hidden Symptoms and *One by One in the Darkness* by Deirdre Madden, by kind permission of AP Watt Ltd on behalf of the author and Faber and Faber Ltd

slitting the tongues of jackdaws by Eilish Martin, published by Summer Palace Press, reprinted by kind permission of the author

The Force of Change by Gary Mitchell, by kind permission of the author and PFD

Biting the Wax by Peter McDonald, reprinted by kind permission of the author

Captain Lavender by Medbh McGuckian, by kind permission of the author and The Gallery Press, Loughcrew, Oldcastle, County Meath, Ireland, and Wake Forest University Press

Observe the Sons of Ulster Marching Towards the Somme by Frank McGuinness, by kind permission of the author and Faber and Faber

Cal by Bernard Mac Laverty, by kind permission of the author, published by Jonathan Cape. Reprinted by permission of The Random House Group Ltd

There Was Fire in Vancouver (1996), *Between Here and There* (2002) and *The State of the Prisons* (2005), by Sinead Morrissey, by kind permission of the author and Carcanet Press

Why Brownlee Left and *Quoof* from *Poems 1968–1998* by Paul Muldoon. Copyright © 2001 Paul Muldoon. Reprinted by permission of Faber and Faber Ltd, and Farrar, Straus and Giroux, LLC

The Ghost Train by Frank Ormsby, by kind permission of the author and The Gallery Press, Loughcrew, Oldcastle, County Meath, Ireland

Pentecost by Stewart Parker ©1987, reprinted by permission of Alexandra Cann Representation for the Stewart Parker Estate. All rights strictly reserved

Burning Your Own by Glenn Patterson, by kind permission of the author

Fivemiletown by Tom Paulin, by kind permission of the author and Faber and Faber Ltd

The Billy Plays by Graham Reid by kind permission of the author and Faber and Faber Ltd

Banjaxed by Grainne Tobin, published by Summer Palace Press, reprinted by kind permission of the author

Dark Hole Days by Una Woods, by kind permission of the author

Every effort has been made to contact copyright holders. If some have been inadvertently omitted, please inform the author or the publisher at the earliest possible opportunity so that the matter can be rectified in any future editions.

Michael Parker is supported by the Arts and Humanities Research Council.

 Arts & Humanities
Research Council

Introduction to Volume 2

> Works of literature do not simply reflect or are not simply caused by their contexts. They have a productive effect in history ... the publication of these texts was itself a political and historical event that in some way changed history.
>
> J. Hillis Miller[1]

Northern Irish Literature, 1975–2006 (Volume 2), like its predecessor (Northern Irish Literature 1956–1975 (Volume 1), provides a detailed picture of the changing political and cultural contexts from which the poems, plays and novels emerge, and encompasses the work of several generations of accomplished writers from a range of cultural traditions. The literary texts discussed here do often reflect particular historical moments, yet also offer what Declan Kiberd has termed 'anticipatory illumination',[2] possibilities of alternative futures and states of being. Two instances of literature's capacity to imagine otherwise and ways are Seamus Heaney's play, *The Cure at Troy*, whose closing Chorus senses 'a great sea-change / on the far side of revenge', 'a further shore / ... reachable from here',[3] and Michael Longley's sonnet, 'Ceasefire', composed in the period preceding the IRA's declaration in late August 1994 that they were suspending military operations.[4] Longley's poem implies that the barbarous cycle can only be ended by extraordinary acts of imagination, gestures of magnanimity, mutual respect and trust. Northern Irish writers over the years have shown themselves to be well ahead of their political counterparts both in such acts and gestures, and have thus contributed much to the altering of perceptions which has brought resolution within reach.

The principal turning-points which frame the texts examined in Chapter 1 are the crisis leading up to the hunger strikes of 1980-81 and surrounding the signing of the Anglo-Irish Agreement of 1985. Violence escalated alarmingly in the aftermath of these events, yet both proved to be critical *nuclei* in Northern Ireland's history since they prompted the participants in the conflict – republicans and loyalists, nationalists and unionists, the British and Irish governments – to reassess their long-term strategies. The literature of this phase bears witness to significant shifts in terms of genre, content, perspective and mood. Before the mid-1970s, the predominant literary genres were poetry and drama, and most texts were authored by male writers. In the years between 1975 and 1985, however, there was a surge in the number of literary novels published, many the work of gifted women writers such as Jennifer Johnston, Una Woods, Anne Devlin and Deirdre Madden. Not surprisingly, issues of gender come increasingly to the fore in this fiction, as for the first time since the Troubles began the voices and perspectives of women characters gain sustained attention.

Another constituency frequently under-represented in the literature of the province since the late 1960s has been that of urban working-class Protestants. As a result, emphasis is given at this juncture in the book to writing depicting their lives and struggles. When first broadcast on BBC television in February 1982, Graham Reid's play, *Too Late to Talk to Billy*, made a tremendous impact. Viewers found Reid's portrayal of the tense, bruising relationship between Billy Martin, his father and sisters, deeply moving and recognised that the kinds of problems encountered by this fictional working-class Belfast family seemed not so dissimilar to those faced by families everywhere. Frank McGuinness's *Observe the Sons of Ulster Marching Towards the Somme* had a similarly transformative effect. Like the New Ireland Forum, *The Crane Bag* and the Field Day pamphlets which preceded it, the play did much to enable reconfigurations to occur in cultural and political discourse. It broke the consensus maintained by Irish political, historical and literary texts since the founding of the Free State that the sole defining event of 1916 was the Easter Rising. Instead, like Michael Longley's poem 'Wounds', McGuinness memorialised those caught up in a different sacrifice, that of the men of the 36th Ulster Division who fell at the Battle of the Somme. His drama served as a reminder for audiences in Ireland, Britain and further off, that the unionists' history is integral to the island's narrative and that any future settlement would need to take full account of Northern Protestant readings of the past, Northern Protestants' anxieties about the future, Northern Protestants' sense of identity.

This focus is maintained at the beginning of Chapter 2, which opens with a sequence of literary works strongly affected by the post-Agreement climate. The conviction that art and artists might still play a potent, transformative role in healing the riven individuals and cultures of Northern Ireland lies behind Stewart Parker's play, *Pentecost*, whose recurring symbols are light and music. However, much of the writing considered next is less sanguine about the prospects of art banishing the sectarian darkness and discord. Tom Paulin's, Peter McDonald's, Ciaran Carson's poems and Glenn Patterson's first novel may be preoccupied with the fragmentation, disorientation, and instability they find all around them, yet nonetheless offer salutary moments of remembering and remembrance. Not so long after *Fivemiletown*, 'Sunday at Great Tew', *The Irish for No* and *Burning Our Own* appeared, history took a momentous, unexpected turn again. The sudden implosion of the Soviet empire during the latter half of 1989 had unforeseen consequences for Northern Ireland. It gave credence to the Northern Ireland Secretary's and the SDLP leadership's assertions that in the absence of a Soviet threat Britain no longer had any 'selfish strategic or economic interest'[5] in remaining in Northern Ireland and so helped convince Sinn Féin to alter its policy and direction. At this very same juncture the political landscape in the Republic was transformed utterly. On 9 November 1990, Mary Robinson, a 46-year-old liberal feminist lawyer, was elected President, ushering in a period of radical change. Pluralist and internationalist in stance, Robinson's Ireland quickly distanced itself from its narrow nationalist past and, even more alarmingly for the northern republicans, exhibited increasing empathy for the unionists and their plight. At the centre of this penultimate chapter is an examination of the negotiations leading up to the August 1994 ceasefires and the quickenings in poetry and fiction that accompanied what came to be known as the peace process. Alongside its recognition of the achievements of high profile figures such as Medbh McGuckian, Michael Longley and Seamus Heaney, it pays particular attention to the work of less well-known poets, such as Ruth Carr, Eilish Martin, Gráinne Tobin and Frank Ormsby, and the emergence of a new generation of writers.

Chapter 3 traces the lack of significant political progress that followed the ceasefires, and then how the momentum for change at the time of the Good Friday Agreement was all too quickly dissipated. The unease and hostility with which the Agreement came to be viewed by large numbers of unionists are much in evidence in Gary Mitchell's *The Force of Change* (2000). Like people in both communities in the province, Caroline, the central female character in the play, feels distaste at having to compromise her ideals and temper her expectations for justice.

The issues of decommissioning and policing, and the slowness with which the main political parties have addressed them, have proved a major source of disillusion in Northern Ireland today. My account of the province's political history concludes with the St Andrews Agreement of October 2006, when the British and Irish governments set a deadline of March 2007 for the restoration of devolved government. Volume 2 ends celebrating the work of an emerging generation of Northern Irish poets who, like their literary forebears, seek to re-inhabit the private domain, but remain susceptible to the pull of a changing politics, albeit one that is now more often international than local.

Since continuing shifts in the historical, political and literary narratives in Northern Ireland over the past five decades are the principal object of my attention, it seemed appropriate to choose for the books' cover a painting entitled *Transient Land*. This is a work by Nicola Nemec, a talented, young painter, born in North Belfast in mid-April 1972, into a working-class community, to a Protestant mother and Catholic father. Like the artists whose work is examined in the main body of the text, she has had a lifetime of questions about her cultural and political identity, and experienced irritation at attempts by others to ascribe to her a.nd her work a fixed position. In an interview, she spoke of her distaste at the notion that there is 'No in-between'.[6] Her paintings thus resemble the finest writing discussed below, which similarly attempts to establish in-between, inclusive spaces, to find in Art an alternative to the fractured, shattered, urban spaces of the province.

Painted during the New Year of 1994, at a liminal moment in Northern Ireland's history, *Transient Land* conveys perhaps through its multiple shades of blues and browns a sense of energy, a clash and meeting of indeterminate elements, a violent resolution. In it she appears to be striving after something both material and transcendental, her aim being to encourage people to see things differently, to transform vision. In less awesome fashion than Picasso's *Guernica*, but like the poems, plays, novels and criticism examined here, her painting reflects an art which attempts 'to change the perceptual angle' within and between people, and so 'represents a blink of liberty'.[7]

Finally, following the Index, contents of *Northern Irish Literature: Volume 1* are listed, including titles of core texts discussed.

1
Name upon Name: 1975–1986

I   A changing map (July 1975–December 1979)

High levels of violence continued in the province throughout the second
half of 1975 and most of 1976; the toll for 1975 (267 fatalities) was 40 less
than the previous year, but in 1976 killings again reached 1974 levels. The
fact that the majority of these casualties were civilians, murdered in paramilitary and sectarian attacks,[1] is strongly reflected in the literature of the
period, particularly in its poetry and emerging fiction. Amongst the most
notorious killings were those of three members of a Dublin group, the
Miami Showband in late July 1975; their murder by the UVF near Newry
prompted a moving, angry elegy by Paul Durcan.[2] A fortnight later five
Protestants were killed and 60 were injured in a PIRA bomb and gun attack
on a pub in the Shankill Road. The republicans' intended targets were the
UVF, whose members were said to frequent the bar. None of the dead were
linked to the loyalist paramilitaries, however. Although the Provisionals'

leadership repeatedly claimed that their organisation was above sectarianism, the fact that the gang involved, while making their getaway, shot at women and children waiting at a taxi rank suggests otherwise.[3]

Throughout the autumn of 1975, tit-for-tat killings and bombings occurred almost daily, and reached a deadly climax on Thursday, 2 October, when the UVF launched a wave of attacks which left 12 Catholics dead. One of those responsible for four of these murders was Lenny Murphy, the leader of the Shankill Butchers; seven of the 19 Catholics for whose deaths this gang later stood trial were slaughtered with butcher's implements.[4] Not surprisingly, as a consequence of the horror these crimes evoked, abattoirs and allusions to butchery feature frequently in Northern Irish literary texts.[5] By the close of the year a further 70 people in the province and in England perished in the violence; 130 of the year's 267 fatalities are estimated to have died at the hands of republican paramilitaries, 121 at the hands of loyalists.

Multiple killings in Armagh and Down marked the beginning of the new year. On 4 January 1976, six men from two Catholic families were shot in their homes by the UVF. In retaliation, the following day, a local IRA group calling themselves Republican Action Force ambushed and then massacred ten Protestant linen-workers at Whitecross, South Armagh. On their way home from work, their minibus was flagged down by a dozen figures wearing combat gear. At first the workers believed they were British soldiers, since the man addressing them had 'a pronounced English accent'.[6] Having asked each of the occupants to state his religion, the paramilitaries told the driver, the only Catholic on board, to 'run up the road'. The remaining 11 men were then lined up by the road and machine-gunned down; amazingly, though struck by 18 bullets, one man survived to give an account of the killing.[7]

From the spring onwards, the British government initiated a policy which would be later dubbed 'ulsterisation', and which saw responsibility for security passing increasingly to an expanded RUC. This strategy, pursued first by Merlyn Rees and then his fiercely anti-IRA successor, Roy Mason, resulted in a decline in the number of Army deaths and in loyalist paramilitary membership.[8] Throughout the summer, meanwhile, sectarian assassinations continued unabated, along with murders of RUC officers and reservists. In late July, at Sandyford, Co. Dublin, the Provisionals planted a 200lb mine which killed Christopher Ewart-Biggs, recently appointed as British ambassador to the Irish Republic, and Judith Cook, a 27-year-old civil servant. Their original target was Merlyn Rees. A last minute hitch led him to postpone his visit to Dublin, otherwise he would have been travelling in the ambassador's convoy.[9]

In late summer 1976, hopes were raised that the carnage might be brought to an end. The emergence of the Women's Peace Movement (later called the Peace People) came in the wake of an appalling incident that occurred on 10 August in West Belfast. Three children, Joanne Maguire (aged 8) and her brothers, John (aged 2) and Andrew (six weeks) were tragically crushed to death when an IRA getaway car careered into them; its driver had been shot dead at the wheel by soldiers. Within days, in what Bernadette Devlin termed 'an explosion of female rage',[10] thousands from both communities were marching through Belfast to demand a cessation of violence. Peace rallies were held on 12, 14, 21, 28 August and 4 September, organised by the children's aunt, Mairead Corrigan, and Betty Williams, both of whom had witnessed the deaths, and Ciaran McKeown, a journalist who wrote for the *Irish Press* and *Fortnight*. The scale of the Peace People's success can be deduced from attendance figures at their events; a rally at Ormeau Park on 21 August drew an estimated audience of 20 000; 25 000 people marched from the Shankill Road to Woodvale Park on 28 August; the 4 September rally in Derry attracted another 25 000. Hardline republicans and loyalists were disturbed by the movement's popularity and its cross-communal bridge-building, and as a result increasingly resorted to intimidation to deter its supporters. In a letter to the *Irish Times* in the late autumn, the poet Robert Greacen describes how at one rally in Falls Park the Peace People were spat upon and had mud, stones and eggs thrown at them.[11] Hostility towards their campaign grew in republican areas, according to two histories of the IRA,[12] when Corrigan and Williams encouraged Catholics to inform on the paramilitaries, and described 'instances when members of the security forces may have stepped beyond the rule of law' as only 'occasional'.[13]

A sudden, steep decline in killings in December 1976 persisted into the following year and beyond, leading McKittrick and McVea to conclude that this period marks 'the end of the most violent phase of the Troubles', though 'no one could know it at the time'.[14] They attribute this in part to the appointment of Roy Mason as Northern Ireland Secretary. Formerly a defence minister, Mason adopted a simpler, military approach to the province's problems. Rather than expend energy on grand political initiatives 'that might lead to failure and leave people in deep despair again',[15] he concentrated primarily on security policy and economic redevelopment. Promising to roll up the IRA like 'a tube of toothpaste',[16] Mason implemented a range of rigorous measures: intelligence-gathering was improved, along with co-operation with the Gardai; arrests increased, and detainees held for longer periods; new interrogation centres were set up, like the one at Castlereagh, where terrorist suspects were subjected to intensive grilling by rotating teams of detectives often for up to eight hours and throughout the night; the rate of convictions rose, many as a result of confessions made during 'protracted questioning'.[17] Mason's period of tenure also saw an expansion in SAS operations, particularly in South Armagh.

The political parties responded in very different ways to the new Secretary of State's approach. Faced with Mason's scepticism about the value of reviving inter-party dialogue, and disheartened after the collapse of power-sharing, SDLP did all they could to promote collaboration between the Westminster and Dublin governments in the hope that this might stimulate political change. With the same goal in mind, John Hume courted leading Irish-American politicians, such as Edward Kennedy and Tip O'Neill, convinced that they might not only intercede with Britain on behalf of constitutional nationalism, but also help in curbing the flow of funds to the terrorists.[18]

Unionist politicians, meanwhile, were divided and uncertain as to what line they should pursue. Four unionist parties (UUP, DUP, Vanguard and the Independent Unionists) had banded together to fight the Northern Ireland Constitutional Convention election as the United Ulster Unionist Council (UUUC). The Convention's failure in November 1975 and again in March 1976 to achieve cross-community agreement over the province's future governance created the political vacuum that Mason had inherited.[19] Whereas the UUP welcomed the Secretary of State's robust strategy for dealing with the IRA and unwillingness to indulge in political experiments, DUP-supporting working-class loyalists were impatient and demanded an immediate return to majority rule. Determined loyalists had triumphed over the British government in the spring of 1974, and could do so again. In the teeth of opposition from the UUP, Vanguard, the Orange Order, the trade unions and the Protestant business community, a new strike body was formed in April 1977 from a coalition of forces which included Paisley's DUP, the UWC, the USC, the UDA. On 3 May 1977, the United Unionist Action Council (UUAC) launched its strike, setting up roadblocks, intimidating individuals, shop-owners and businesses.[20] Unlike Rees in 1974, Mason deployed the military and the police to keep the roads open; an extra 1200 British soldiers were flown in on 1 May for this very purpose. This time round workers at the province's main power station refused to back the stoppage. On the eighth day of the strike, Harry Bradshaw, a 46-year-old Protestant bus-driver was shot dead by the UDA while picking up passengers. That evening, John Geddis, a 26-year-old Protestant, and part-time member of the UDR, died in a UVF fire-bomb attack on a strike-breaking filling-station where he had stopped to buy petrol. Instead of castigating the people responsible for his son's needless death, Geddis's father, a member of the UUAC's central committee, blamed those who failed to support the strike.[21] Two days later, on 12 May, the strike was called off. Despite Mason's and moderate unionism's victory in this battle of wills, Paisley and his party made major advances in local council elections held on 18 May.[22] These results demonstrated not only Paisley's 'extraordinary resilience', as McKittrick and McVea have pointed out, but also the unionist electorate's reluctance to reject those they perceived as taking a strong stand on their behalf.[23]

Major transitions were afoot within the republican movement at this same juncture. A younger generation of republicans, including Gerry Adams, Martin McGuinness and Danny Morrison, were now in the ascendant and taking a lead in overhauling its political ideology and structures. Obligatory references to 'the colonial yoke', British 'vested interests' and 'armed struggle' persist, but Adams's writings start emphasising the role that grass-roots *political* activism might play in liberating Ireland. This change in inflection is evident from as early as October 1975. While still in prison, Adams wrote an article for *Republican News* in which he promotes the concept of 'active abstentionism', encouraging local republican communities to create their own agencies and support systems as alternatives to those of the 'Brit administration'.[24] In an address jointly scripted by Adams and Morrison for the Bodenstown commemoration in June 1977, republicans were informed, albeit in coded fashion, of the need to extend their theatre of operations into the political sphere.[25] Many commentators have rightly detected in such pieces 'the germ of his later emphasis on building up Sinn Fein into an organisation in its own right'.[26]

On the military front, similarly, the Provisionals could not afford to stand still. The security forces' increasing success in recruiting informers and breaking detainees forced them to reorganise themselves and to train members in techniques to thwart future interrogators. Confirmation that Mason's measures were hitting hard can be seen in a confidential PIRA report, seized in December 1977, following the arrest in Dublin of Seamus Twomey, their Chief of Staff:

> The three-day and seven day detention orders are breaking volunteers, and it is the Irish Republican Army's own fault for not indoctrinating volunteers with the psychological strength to resist interrogation. Coupled with this, which is contributing to our defeat, we are burdened with an inefficient infrastructure of commands, brigades, battalions and companies. The old system … has to be changed.[27]

The memo went on to advocate the restructuring of the PIRA into cells, each consisting of no more than four volunteers, specialising in robberies, bombings, shootings or executions. In order 'to confuse British intelligence', they were urged to undertake operations 'as often as possible outside their own areas'.[28] The creation of small, tightly-knit units meant that the paramilitaries became less dependent on local people's support and limited the damage inflicted by informers.[29] Another important, but controversial move made at this time was the decision to divide the PIRA into two commands, a Northern Command consisting of the six counties of Northern Ireland and five adjoining counties in the Republic, and a Southern Command whose function would be to supply logistical support for the northerners' struggle.[30]

Under intense pressure from the security forces, increasingly, from 1977 onwards, the Provisionals struck at what they termed 'soft targets', such as members of the RUC or UDR, living in remote, rural areas, like the fictional Robert Morton in Bernard Mac Laverty's *Cal*.[31] Typical of such victims was William Gordon, a 41-year-old, part-time UDR officer, who died along with his ten-year-old daughter on 8 February 1978, when the PIRA booby-trapped his car; one of those police sought in connection with this killing was Francis Hughes, who, three years later, would become the second of the hunger strikers to die.[32] Just nine days after those killings the PIRA committed one the worst atrocities of the Troubles, when they planted an incendiary device at the La Mon House hotel to the east of Belfast. A warning call from the bombers was received by local police at 20.57 hours, but before the hotel could be evacuated the bomb exploded. Twelve people attending a dinner dance, seven of them women, were killed, their bodies burnt beyond recognition by the fireball that swept through the dining-room; over 30 others were injured. Condemnation of this despicable attack was universal, forcing the IRA first into an admission that their warning had been 'totally inadequate', then an expression of sympathy for 'relatives and friends of those who were accidentally killed'.[33] Despite the fact that all of the dead were Protestants, loyalist paramilitaries did not retaliate. Over the next eight days, 25 republicans were arrested in West Belfast, including Gerry Adams, who remained in jail for seven months, facing charges that he was a member of the IRA.

The appalling state of the casualties and widespread contempt the La Mon bombing engendered left many republicans deeply demoralised; there was even speculation that a unilateral ceasefire might ensue.[34] What would help restore morale, however, were developments in the unfolding crisis in Northern Ireland's prisons. Protests and ill-feeling had intensified in the mid-1970s as a result of the policy of 'criminalisation' under which convicted paramilitaries were denied special category status. Initiated by Rees and continued by Mason, the policy aimed at countering perceptions of gunmen and bombers as anti-colonial freedom-fighters, seeking rather to promote a view of them as unprincipled, sadistic thugs. A requirement that all paramilitaries sentenced *after* March 1976 dress in prison clothing, like other lawbreakers, prompted the 'blanket protest' in the autumn of that year. Inmates in Long Kesh (The Maze), supported by a small group at Armagh Women's Prison, wrapped themselves in blankets rather than wear prison issue. The authorities' reaction at Long Kesh was to attempt to coerce the prisoners into submission, by confining them to their cells, halting remission, suspending family visits, and denying access to radio, television, books, newspapers, letters, writing paper and pens.[35] Although by mid-1977 over 140 republicans were 'on the blanket', and prison officers had begun being targeted by the IRA,[36] public sympathy and interest in the protest was negligible. Drawing attention to the blanket protest in a *Fortnight* article from September 1977, Tom Hadden argued that the British government's treatment of the prisoners breached Article 3 of the European Convention of Human Rights.[37]

Tensions escalated in April 1978 when prisoners embarked on a 'no wash' protest. Complaining that prison officers frequently beat men on their way to the showers and toilets, they started refusing to leave their cells to empty their own chamber pots. Once the prison authorities made it clear that they had no intention of ordering warders to 'slop out' for them, prisoners began smearing their cell walls with excrement in order 'to dissipate the stench'.[38] This came to be known as the 'dirty protest', and attracted considerable media attention, particularly after a visit to the prison by Archbishop Tomás Ó Fiaich, the Catholic Primate of Ireland, on 30 July 1978. In a statement in early August, the Archbishop denounced the disgusting conditions in which prisoners now existed, which he said were analogous to those 'of people living in sewer-pipes in the slums of Calcutta'.[39] His declaration that 'these boys' should not be looked on 'as criminals' infuriated Mason, who, later that month, came under further pressure when an Amnesty International Report criticised the maltreatment of terrorist suspects at Castlereagh.

Keen to demonstrate that their commitment for the struggle remained undiminished, the PIRA ended 1978 in a flurry of violence. On 14 November a series of synchronised car bomb attacks left considerable damage in six different Northern Irish towns; the following week, 50 more bombs detonated. On 26 November two IRA gunmen shot dead in his North Belfast home Albert Miles, the Deputy Governor of Long Kesh, who had special responsibility for the H-blocks. On 1 December bombers targeted 11 towns in the province, and just over a fortnight later Liverpool, Manchester, Bristol, Coventry and Southampton. Finally, four days before Christmas, a PIRA unit machine-gunned a foot patrol in Crossmaglen, killing three young soldiers (aged 18, 20 and 22).

In 1979 the British Army would suffer a steep increase in casualties, over half of them on 27 August, when 18 soldiers lost their lives in an ambush beside the border at Warrenpoint. Earlier that same day Lord Louis Mountbatten, Queen Elizabeth II's cousin and a former Viceroy in India, had been killed by a PIRA bomb on board a boat at Mullaghmore, Co. Sligo, along with his 14-year-old grandson, his daughter's mother-in-law, and a 15-year-old boatboy from Enniskillen. These killings caused a major crisis in Anglo-Irish relations, and a surge in sectarian assassinations carried out by the UVF and UDA.[40] Mountbatten was the third high profile victim that year. On 22 March, two PIRA gunmen had murdered the British ambassador to the Hague, Sir Richard Sykes. Eight days later, during the General Election campaign, Airey Neave, the shadow Northern Ireland Secretary and a key figure in Margaret Thatcher's Conservative team, had been killed when the Irish National Liberation Army (INLA) bomb exploded under his car as he left a House of Commons car park. Undoubtedly this personal loss affected the Conservative leader deeply, and played no small part in her attitude to republicanism once she acceded to the position of Prime Minister on 3 May 1979. The IRA hoped that their late August killing spree might provoke Mrs Thatcher into taking precipitate repressive measures which might boost their support in the nationalist community. She, however, resisted pressure from the Army to return primary responsibility for security to them, and instead sanctioned the recruitment of a further 1000 officers to the RUC. Believing that there were no sensible or viable alternatives to the policies of 'ulsterisation' and 'criminalisation', and seeing little point in mounting a significant political initiative, Mrs Thatcher's initial strategy was simply to maintain a 'holding operation'[41] in Northern Ireland.

Fleetingly, in late September, a chink of hope had again appeared that the killings might be brought to an end. Addressing a crowd of over 250 000, during his visit to the Republic, the newly-elected Pope, John Paul II, appealed for change on the other side of the border:

> On my knees I beg you to turn away from the paths of violence and to return to the ways of peace. You claim to seek justice. I too believe in justice and seek justice. But violence only delays the day of justice ... do not follow those who train you in the ways of inflicting death. Those who resort to violence always claim that only violence brings

about change. You must know that there is a political, peaceful way to justice.[42]

In their reply, issued 48 hours later, the IRA stated their conviction 'that force is ... the only means of removing the evil of the British presence in Ireland'. With the historical precedents of 1916 and 1921 in mind, they expected that the Catholic Church which now condemned them would 'upon their victory ... have no difficulty in recognising us'.[43]

Benedict Kiely, *Proxopera*; Jennifer Johnston, *Shadows on our Skin*

Two of the earliest examples of serious literary fiction to address Northern Ireland's political crisis were by established writers who had spent most of their lives outside the province. Benedict Kiely, born in Co. Tyrone in 1919, had settled in Dublin in 1944, where he had already written nine novels before the publication of *Proxopera*, in 1977.[44] Jennifer Johnston, born in Dublin in 1930, had come to prominence in the early 1970s with a succession of novels dealing primarily with Ascendancy families around the time of the First World War. In the years preceding her composition of *Shadows on our Skin* (1977), she had moved from the Republic to Northern Ireland to live, settling in Brook Hall, outside Derry.

Dismissed by Jennifer Johnson as 'dreadful', 'romantic rubbish',[45] and characterised by Joseph McMinn as 'wholly sentimental in its appeal and deliberately naïve in its imaginative response',[46] *Proxopera* is more interesting a text than these comments imply and merits more sustained consideration than it has thus far received. A preliminary examination of the story's characterisation, plot and narrative perspective might seem to confirm McMinn's two main charges. Its central character, Mr Binchey originates from the nationalist community, and is a retired teacher and a widower with heart problems. Somewhat surprisingly for a history teacher, he appears to have little interest in or grasp of the political, economic and social factors that have led to the crisis in Northern Ireland. After his family are taken hostage by the IRA in their own home, he is forced to drive his bomb-laden car to the nearby town. Intense love for his native places, along with profound loathing for the paramilitaries, lead him to abandon the car close to a lake away from the town, despite the potential repercussions for his son, daughter-in-law and their two children. In the closing pages readers discover that the paramilitaries take their revenge by kneecapping his son and setting fire to his home, the white three-storeyed house he had idealised as a child.

For most of the novella's first half, third-person narration is employed, with past and present events focalised solely through Binchey's eyes. Once he sets off on his deadly task, however, the story is entirely narrated by him and the illusion of a separate, structuring intelligence abandoned. This latter section contains perhaps the most successful writing in *Proxopera*, employing as it does a stream of consciousness technique; real tension is created as Binchey negotiates the hazards on the road and in his memory, and there is a welcome lessening in his self-obsession as the fate of actual Troubles' victims are called to mind. The text alludes specifically to the Miami Showband massacre (67) and to the killing of a judge 'in the presence of his seven-year-old daughter' (78).[47]

That the novella is primarily an elegy for the North's lost innocence is a view which understandably has gained currency.[48] The defamiliarising, ominous sequence of images with which the text opens immediately alerts the reader to the idea of an all-consuming violence, all-destroying change:

> *Sea-lions and sharks, alligators and whales with mouths that would swallow a truck …*
> That lake would never be the same again.
> *… oh the sights that we saw as we waited for death on the treacherous waves of Lough Muck*
> Yet the birds, they say, sang around Dachau (3)[49]

Given that the lake is not the site of a mass atrocity, and that Northern Ireland's carnage is in no respect comparable to that of the Holocaust, the allusion to Dachau must be regarded as appropriative and wholly inappropriate.[50] In the ensuing lines, Nature and humanity are depicted oppositionally in traditional Romantic fashion. Tranquil ('the still surface', 'the silence'), reflective of timeless continuity ('still', 'the circle of hills'), the lake, with its fertile environs ('harvest-coloured') and hidden depths, is clearly privileged over the beings that disturb and observe it. The text's tendency to represent the world in terms of dualities and hierarchies can be further illustrated by the disputed reading of the lake in the opening pages. Whereas the unidentified son states simply that 'The water never knew what was happening', the father develops at some length his Wordsworthian/Coleridgean vision of a sentient nature. Indeed, his assertion that 'That lake would never be the same again' creates a precedent to which the text frequently returns.[51]

Certainly, some of the narrator's boyhood recollections, 45 years before, seem Edenic in their simplicity. The taste of 'clear ice-cold' water from a spring near the lake he describes as a primal experience, an initiation into the enduring world of myth: 'That, for him, had been the well at the world's end mentioned in the old stories' (5). In contrast to the contemporary landscape, which is tainted and uncertain, the terrain of his childhood years appears physically and morally solid and orderly:

> The walk from the town to the lake switchbacked over rolling farmland, root crops and oats, *heavy* black soil, *solid square* slated farmhouses, a *well-planted* Presbyterian countryside. (5; my emphasis)

Yet, claims that the novella treats the past *only* as 'a lost golden time' or that its 'backward look' is merely 'nostalgic'[52] ignore a number of troubling elements to which attention is drawn. Melancholia, suicide and sexual abuse are all alluded to as part of his growing up; in his earliest account of his home region, he mentions a small lake used regularly by 'demented old ladies and others' (6) to drown themselves.[53] Midway through the story Binchey provides a disturbing thumbnail portrait of an abusive, homosexual 'Christian' Brother, who, while 'on the Chinese mission' (39), interfered with boys, and subsequently drove two other priests to suicide. And at the novel's close, he remembers how one of his best friends, Tony, went mad at the age of 18, bringing an end to 'the laughter of the water' and the 'dream' (92). The causes of madness, like the reasons behind the paramilitaries' deeds, are, however, not something which engages the narrator's interest; he appears to accept misfortune and evil deeds as the way things are.

The most malign feature from the community's past which continues to haunt its present is sectarianism. In the opening pages, it is cited as the cause of the 'bloody row' which ensued when a 'guileless, love-deludhered' young Protestant took a Catholic girl to a dance at the Orange Hall (6). Shortly afterwards the narrator goes on to pinpoint when and why his attitude shifted towards the Twelfth of July celebrations. 'Up to the age of twelve or so the band and the banners' were 'fun things', he states:

> Then after twelve or so you began to think the thing wasn't funny any more ... and the giant drums were saying something ... What it was all about was hate, which as always bred hate, and suddenly you were sick of the town. (8)

Segregation is a fact of death as well as life in the community Binchey cherishes. Generation after generation of Catholics and Protestants lie separate from each other in the graveyard. Its emblematic significance is enhanced by Binchey's disclosure that his late wife, who was 'born and died a Protestant' (32), is interred there *next to* his Catholic parents. The fact that he and his wife married across the sectarian divide is intended not only to increase empathy for him and enhance his liberal credentials, but also to present the Bincheys' marriage as a paradigm of what relationships in Northern Ireland might be.[54]

In furtherance of both these aims, the narrative contains a sketch of the pair's all-too-brief time together, which has considerable bearing on the text's class and sexual politics. Education provided the common ground on which they met; her father, 'a tea and whiskey salesman' (34), had approached Binchey to ask him to tutor his daughter in Latin to help her pass her senior certificate. Both Binchey, then a second-year college student, and the girl's father, recognise education's potential as a vehicle through which social and economic aspirations can be realised and status in this unequal, divided society secured. The acquisition of a prestige discourse, like Latin especially, differentiates its holders from others, and in *Proxopera* is employed to distinguish Binchey from his 'half-educated' (43), 'stupid' (45) captors. (From their first entry, *their* language is characterised by clichés and obscenities.)

Latin also figures in the text at this juncture, however, as a source of pathos and subtle eroticism. The section discussed above begins with Binchey contemplating driving past the graveyard the next morning, 'bearing the bomb, an angel of death' (31). Suddenly, the text becomes strewn with untranslated, aptly italicised fragments from Catullus. Joined together they read, *'Soles occidere et redire possunt. / Nobis cum semel occidit brevis lux, / Nox est perpetua, una dormienda / Da mi basia mille'* ('Suns may set and rise again/As for us, when the brief light has at last set,/we must sleep one endless night. / Give me a thousand kisses').[55] A man not noted for his modesty, Binchey boasts how Catullus proved a 'great friend to me' (33) in his wooing and winning of his schoolgirl-bride. Subtlety departs, however, once Kiely's ageing narrator offers an account of the courtship. It is revealing in the light of the novella's gender politics that the woman he so valued lacks the benefit of a name.[56] Pruriently, and all too convincingly, Binchey recalls his adolescent excitement seeing her skirt ride up or glimpsing 'the white northern slopes of her breasts'. The translation of woman into landscape is, of course, a recurring trope in male-authored, Irish literary texts,[57] yet this is immediately followed up by an allusion to Keats's 'Ode to a Nightingale', in which he sexualises the English poet's lines, imagining the girl's 'warm south, the true, the blushful Hippocrene' (33).[58] In terms of the text's *cultural* politics, his constant references to a plurality of texts, from a range of traditions signal a refusal to be defined and confined by a single national narrative.

Perhaps the text's least impressive feature is its simplistic representation of the republican paramilitaries. Close to caricature, partly as a result of the cartoon-like names used to denote them (Corkman, Gasmask, Soldier's Cap), they do not merit Laura Pelaschiar's description of them as 'incarnations of evil', 'from beginning to end'.[59] In fact, from the moment they first appear, the narrator depicts them ambivalently, as both sinister and slightly ridiculous. 'Granda, there's a funny man in the hayshed' (13), says Binchey's little grandson, the first to discover them; 'ex ore infantium' (19), indeed. As a man bearing a shotgun, wearing a gasmask '*slashed* at the mouth' steps out 'into the open', the narrator compares the sound he makes to that of 'somebody with laryngitis … trying to talk through tissue paper and a comb' (13). Shortly after emerging from the laurels where he possessed 'a sharp clear voice' (14), the cell's leader develops a speech defect, a symptom, presumably, of his defective ideology; repeated references to Corkman's 'hissing' (18, 19, 20, 21, 22, 23, 31) are designed to foster a view of him as satanic, but ultimately serve to subvert the very real menace he is meant to embody.[60] In a not untypical moment from later in the novella, when Gasmask has 'snored and rocked himself' out of his seat and onto the floor, Corkman orders him to go 'and relieve Charlie Chaplin', warning him not to 'frighten the birds' (39). Binchey concurs in Corkman's assessment of his accomplices, dismissing Gasmask as an 'imbecile' (51) and comparing Soldier's Capto Quasimodo (53). In so doing, he de-individualises them, just as they de-individualise their victims.[61]

When not exposing their propensity for comedy and grotesquerie, Kiely's proxy attempts to convince us that the paramilitaries are uneducated, illogical, evil, lunatics. Corkman's careful planning of the operation, knowledge of the teacher's background ('I do my homework', he quips (37)), and familiarity with Spenser's lesser-known works (37) suggest that he possesses some intelligence, yet Binchey refers to him as a 'madman' (19, 28, 49, 51), as just another of the many 'brainless bastards' and 'morons' in the Provisionals ranks (51, 60). On the rare occasions that it is acknowledged, the paramilitaries' political motivation is exposed as bogus or deluded. Thus, when Corkman explains that their targeting of the town hall/post office/house of Judge Flynn is in reprisal for the loyalists' murder of a PIRA-sympathising publican, the better-informed Binchey retorts that the PIRA had shot him 'because he spoke against murder gangs at a town council meeting' (27). After being recognised by him, Gasmask (Bertie) confides to 'Mr Bee' that he became 'a soldier of the Republic' to protect 'our oil' (44) from the Brits.

Although at first it seems that Corkman has no moral qualms about inflicting pain – he threatens to kneecap the children (15) and the housekeeper (18) – he exhibits amazing restraint given the frequent insults directed at him by Binchey father and son. To quieten them down, he relates a story about three UVF men, who, after failing to find a Catholic to kill, shot 'One of their own. Think of that' (30).[62] Yet the contempt he expresses for these loyalists, 'the sort of animals we're dealing with' (29), turns out to be not dissimilar to what he feels for his fellow-activists; of Mad Eyes Minahan, he says, 'Jesus, I could shoot him … The dung I have to work with' (52), and then he kicks him in the privates while he is down (53). Like some latter-day Iago, Corkman is presented as taking a sadistic delight in the exercise of power, and a pathological obsession with sex. Several times he speaks of the bomb as a 'she' – 'She'll do the job' (49), 'She's as delicate as a virgin' (51), 'The virgin's in the boot. Waiting to be bust' (53). 'She's as delicate … as a virgin' (62) – and predicts technology will be 'the way we'll bugger the Brits' (49). Yet it is Binchey who initiates this virgin imagery, first by playing on Derry's name as the Maiden City, then comparing the IRA men unfavourably with the Cambridge rapist (35–6).[63] These insistent sexual allusions point to the prevalence in Irish masculinity of machismo, but equally reflect how traditional nationalist political discourse tended to use and abuse gender.

Binchey's reading of Northern Ireland's political narrative is conditioned primarily by local perspectives and allegiances. In another tellingly inexact, inept analogy, the history teacher compares the state of Derry, with its 'riots and ructions and bombs and bloody Sundays', to 'Dresden on the morning after' (35). By employing lower case and pluralising 'bloody Sundays', he appears to deny the particularity of that event, seeing it, as some contemporary British and unionist accounts of it did, as a single episode in a larger sequence of atrocities. The following morning, however, just before his departure with the bomb, Binchey describes Gasmask, down on one knee, 'in a perfect imitation of a British paratrooper shooting down civilians on Bloody Sunday' (52). The implication is not simply that the PIRA is no better than the murderous Paras; by the mid-1970s, as statistics demonstrate,[64] the Provisionals had far superseded the British Army in their responsibility for deaths in the province. As Kennedy-Andrews points out, the novella works on the premise that it is 'militant Irish Republicanism, not the forces of British colonialism'[65] that constitutes the biggest threat to Ireland, a premise that the Dublin government had also come to endorse. For Binchey, the revisionist, there is little distinction between loyalist and republican paramilitaries, and at one point he tells his captors, 'More of you should kill each other. Go to the Greenland Cap and settle whatever it is between ye and leave normal people alone' (31). His Mercutio-like, 'plague upon both your houses' stance mirrors a widespread attitude in Britain and Ireland at the time and since, an attitude born of frustration but often also of a profound disinterest in the political and economic factors fuelling loyalist and republican violence.

What energises *Proxopera*'s second half is the uncertainty over the story's outcome, the immediacy generated by the present tense, and the intimate access to Binchey's inner world gained as we accompany him on his solitary journey.[66] A mass of different, private and public considerations, texts and memories jostle for attention, his and ours. In this deeply intertextual text, narrative serves as the means by which the militants' 'brutal effrontery' (51) and evil intent are countered and thwarted. Of major significance to Binchey's and the fiction's resolution is the catalogue of attempted killings and paramilitary 'successes' that he calls to mind;[67] these include failed proxy bombings near Kesh (58) at Belfast's Europa Hotel (59); the murder of an RUC officer in Binchey's home town (68); the devices left at the Tower and at the Ideal Home Exhibition in London (70); the booby-trapped wreath left in a graveyard at Scarva, Co. Down (71). Remembering how recently a Belfast judge had been murdered on his own doorstep (78), Binchey recoils from the thought of being responsible for such a crime. To destroy either the courageous Judge Flynn or the Town Hall where he took part in amateur theatricals[68] becomes unthinkable.

Another crucial influence in Binchey's decision is the 'presence' of father, and his attitude to militant republican tradition. Memories of a wartime exchange involving his and Bertie's father temporarily distract him from his anxieties about 'what is now happening in my white house'. Significantly, Binchey's father is placed in a domestic setting, cooking porridge, when Gasmask's father breaches his peace, 'collecting cash for Caithlin ni Houlihan, the Hag of Beare and Caith Ni Dhuibhir, and Patrick Pearse and the sainted dead who died for Ireland' (65). Binchey Senior's sardonic reactions to fundraising for republican MPs who will refuse to sit at Stormont or Westminster ('That'll save train and boat-fare') and the declaration of an Irish Republic ('Oh la dee da') clearly act as a precedent for his son. Tellingly, in terms of the reading of republicanism *Proxopera* provides, Bertie's father is depicted a few pages later grasping a copy of Hitler's *Mein Kampf*, under the illusion that anyone planning to march against and invade England 'had to be a republican' (74). For Binchey Junior, as for Conor Cruise O'Brien,[69] the Provisional IRA are virtually indistinguishable from fascists.

Proxopera ends poised somewhere between hope and its absence. Like the Peace People, Binchey longs for ordinary northerners from both communities to band together to renounce violence; like so many others at the time of the text's composition, he cannot envision a political process which might stop the carnage. Blame for the desecration of his homeland he apportions widely, 'Ireland. A long history. England. Empire. King William. The Pope. Ian Paisley. Myself' (84), but this hardly constitutes a major advance on that of Haines in *Ulysses*.[70] Like Cruise O'Brien, Binchey has clearly developed a deep antagonism towards the heroic ideology perpetuated by the Free State's and Northern Ireland's founding fathers. Fifty years after the treaty and the Civil War, people on the island are still killing, maiming and imprisoning each other. One of the text's bitterest outbursts interweaves quotations from Bryant's 'The African Chief'[71] and T.D. Sullivan's patriotic 'God Save Ireland',[72] in order to forge a link between a particular[73] and general state of enslavement:

> His son stands silent, chained in the market place amid the gathering multitude that shrank to hear his name, men without hands, girls without legs in restaurants in Belfast, images of Ireland Gaelic and free, never till the latest day shall the memory pass away of the gallant lives thus given for our land, images of Ulster or of a miserable withdrawn corner of O'Neill's Irish Ulster safe from popery and brass money and wooden shoes. These mad dogs have made outrage a way of life. To the wheel, to the wheel, to the wheel, time's ticking away, in the town the churchbells are ringing, Catholic, Church of Ireland, Presbyterian, Methodist, Baptist, all calling people away from each other ... but why not unite here and now and not wait for then'. (55)

Given that he cannot right the past, Binchey's reiterated references to 'the wheel' and 'time ticking away' contain an appeal to the text's primary audience on the island to end cultural and denominational apartheid and so help write a different Irish future.

Self-reflexivity figures within Jennifer Johnston's *Shadows on our Skin* from the outset. The novel opens with a schoolboy, Joe Logan, apparently composing a sentimental elegy for his father, imagining how it might appear in the obituary section of the *Derry Journal*. It soon becomes apparent as the poem moves through its second and third drafts that the boy's father is very much alive, and that rather than it being act of *pietas*, it expresses a longing for his father to die: 'You've lived too long already, Dad/And when you go I won't be sad' (8). Joe's first attempts to give voice and form to his feelings of oppression take place within the context of a mathematics lesson, as his teacher introduces the class to the abstract beauty of equi-lateral triangles. These geometrical structures embody a symmetry, har-mony and equality entirely absent from the boy's domestic and street life. It soon emerges that the text will itself be preoccupied with a shifting pat-tern of triangular relationships, those between Joe/his mother/and father, Joe/Kathleen/Brendan, Brendan/the Movement/Kathleen.

Intermittently Joe's subsequent, far more skilled efforts to 'make words dance' (140) are recorded, as, like his creator, he tries to construct an alternative order in which he can feel at ease, at home. Shadowing his literary efforts are the lyrics of a Horslips song, 'Time to Kill', employed as a vehicle for commenting on both characterisation and action.

> Now we have time to kill
> Kill the shadows on our skin.
> Kill the fire that burns within,
> Killing time my friend. (56).[74]

The first occasion on which the words surface in the text comes when Joe visits the home of Kathleen Doherty, the young teacher who befriends him. When read simply as metaphor, they underline the fact that Joe's and Kathleen's association is likely to be temporary; Kathleen is on a one-year contract, and plans to leave Ireland in the summer, and so is killing time before marrying her soldier-boyfriend who is stationed in Germany. The shadow and fire images suggest how spectres from the past (public and private) loom over the younger generation's present, frus-trating their desire for individuation, their progress towards political and sexual maturation. What instigates violence and vengeance in the novel is invariably deferral and denial in both these spheres.

At times *Shadows* appears too deeply haunted by other texts, Irish and British. The unremittingly gloomy, colourless, urban landscapes it presents are barely distinguishable from those in Alan Sillitoe's, Stan Barstow's and David Storey's north-of-England-set novels; tellingly, perhaps, the houses in Johnston's Derry are described as having 'the look of cardboard cut-outs' (9). Joe's unhappy, divided family circumstances similarly resemble those in many working-class British fictions and films from the late 1950s onwards. His mother, an embittered, desperately hard-working woman, and his father, an archetypal, feckless malingerer, who kills time smoking, drinking and gambling, could both have stepped out of O'Casey plays. Endlessly harking back to his supposedly glorious past and the physical sacrifices he made for Ireland, Mr Logan appears to combine elements of both Captain Boyle and his crippled son in *Juno*. Like Billy Casper,[75] Joe constantly lands himself in trouble at school because of his inattentiveness, but grows in self-belief partly as a result of a relationship with a supportive teacher. Both Hines's and Johnson's novels conclude with their child-protagonists distraught, following the cruel interventions of an elder brother.

By focalising the novel primarily through a child's perspective, Johnston manages to direct a great deal of empathy towards the vulnerable Joe, caught up as he is in cross-fire on the streets and in his home. In one of the most effective, immediate scenes, Joe and his friend, Peter, are passed by two members of an army patrol, just as they are leaving school. Seconds later, just around the corner, the soldiers are struck down by a sniper:

> The two shots were loud and very close. The sound of them echoed down the street for a moment and then there was total silence ... Peter seemed to be the first person in the whole city to break the silence. 'Wow'.
> 'Armalite', said Joe.
> 'Yes'.
> They stood where they were, uncertain what to do. (149–50)

Equally well-realised is the section detailing an army weapons search, during which Joe discovers a gun which his brother, Brendan, has stupidly concealed amidst the bedclothes (157). Displaying considerable initiative, courage and loyalty, Joe hides the pistol in his school-bag under his English books, and later drops it into the river at the quayside he had recently visited with Kathleen (166). A weakness in this strategy, however, is that the child character has little or no political grasp of what is happening, and is merely a spectator, rather than interpreter of events. The arguments that rage between his mother, father and Brendan just go over his head; on one occasion, his only contribution before going to bed is to opine lamely that 'Life is very obscure' (69). The child's eye perspective results in greater emphasis on domestic conflict in the novel's first half than on the violence in Derry. Consequently, the war fought out in the city is reduced to background noise and pictures for much of the time. Given that gunfire and explosions were recurrent features of life in Northern Ireland's major cities by the mid-1970s, Joe's responses may not be untypical, and could be seen as reflecting the extent to which violence has become 'normalised'.[76] When, during one of Kathleen and Joe's excursions, a waitress in Donegal asks the teacher about the situation in Derry ('Is it desperate?'), she receives an extremely blasé reply: 'You get used to it' (142).

The novel seems about to acquire a sharper political edge following the return of Brendan, Joe's elder brother, from England. His 'involvement' with the Provisionals is presented as arising from loyalty to his father, antipathy towards the British, and a desire to help in the community's defence, particularly following an Army raid (59–62). The ground is prepared for this well before his homecoming, when readers are informed of his father's success in initiating him into republican mythology:

> Brendan knew those names as well as his own: Liam Lynch, Ernie O'Malley, Liam Mellows, Sean Russell ... all heroes, dead heroes, living heroes, men of principle, men of action ... The world was peopled with heroes, with patrols and flying columns and sad songs that used to drift down through the floor to Joe below, songs about death and traitors and freedom and more heroes. (21)

The narration here positions Joe at a distance from his father and brother. 'Below' them he may be, yet his indifference towards the repetitious, simplistic, maudlin, version of history they espouse is privileged in the text, and aligns him with his mother's stance towards 'the struggle'. Responding to Brendan's report of how 'Five were lifted last night', she comments, 'They ask for it. If you go round creating destruction you ask for what you get'. To categorise Mrs Logan as 'non-political', as Kennedy-Andrews does, and claim that she does not understand 'anything about political freedom and social justice'[77] is perhaps an over-statement. What has made her sceptical about republican politics, North and South, is its attachment to violence and to a rhetoric of violence, *and* its failure to deliver practical, material improvements to the quality of people's lives. She questions, for example, the freedoms people in the Republic enjoy long after the expulsion of the British there: 'Is there a job for every man? And a home for everyone? Have all the children got shoes on their feet?' (154). She blames her own inability 'to live a decent life' – like the constant feeling of being 'tired' (66) – primarily on her husband, however, rather than on the system and state which contain her.[78] In contrast to her menfolk, who regard the current conflict as unfinished business left over from the 1919–21 War of Independence, Mrs Logan is unconvinced by the idea of history as a seamless continuum: 'Does it not enter your head that there's a rare difference between sitting round and listening to a bunch of old men telling their hero stories and what is happening now. I've learned a bit of sense' (67).[79] That Mrs Logan's function in the text is partly to give voice to a non-partisan, humanist perspective[80] – one which echoes that of the Peace People – is evident from the later clash with her husband:

> 'Two of the enemy are dead.'
> 'Two children.'

'What do you mean children?'
'That's all they were. Younger than Brendan.'
'Enemy soldiers. What sort of traitor do you think you are to moan over enemy soldiers?' (153)

The level of confrontation here is not replicated in exchanges between the principal representatives of the younger generation, Kathleen and Brendan, though they too respond very differently to the violence. Like Friel's in *Translations*, Johnson's characterisation and dialogue seem intended to demonstrate the heterogeneity of the northern nationalist community, and thus problematise received, and often polarised views of that community amongst audiences in and beyond Ireland.[81]

After the novel's midway point, issues of allegiance, accusations of treachery and acts of betrayal progressively come to the fore, primarily as a result of Brendan's increasing profile in the narrative. Following their excursion to Grianan, Brendan unexpectedly arrives to meet Joe and Kathleen at the bus-stop, claiming that he has been sent 'to see he got safely home. The wain'. Embarrassment at having his secret friend discovered quickly gives way to outright hostility as Joe observes his brother's obvious sexual interest in Kathleen. An early indication of his proprietorial attitude towards her is his attempt to withhold her name from Brendan:[82]

'Have you been waiting for us?'
'Well ... sort of ... Miss ... Miss?'
'Doherty', said Joe without much enthusiasm.
'Oh, call me Kathleen'. (98)

Despite having only just met, Brendan is in a hurry to ascertain where Kathleen's political sympathies might lie. After informing her that a couple of soldiers had been killed during rioting that morning, he adds, 'I won't weep any tears. Will you?'. Her political and cultural allegiances cannot be easily defined, given that she is the product of a 'mixed marriage',[83] is not from the North, and is engaged to a British squaddie. Consequently, she deflects his question, and replies ambiguously: 'You could spend all your life crying' (99). Marginalised for most of this extended first meeting between Brendan and Kathleen, Joe expresses his resentment in childish gestures, such as when he deliberately stamps in a puddle and drenches them all (99). Though a very minor misdeed, it presages the spiral of violence he will later set in motion when he tells Brendan about Kathleen's forthcoming marriage to Fred Burgess (182–3).

Joe's betrayal of confidences leads directly to Brendan's decision to flee to England and the retribution visited on Kathleen by his 'friends', the 'Boys', who cut off her hair and beat her up (189). In effect they translate her body into a text, to warn others of the price exacted on those who transgress the sexual code of the tribe.

The very decision to close the novel with the ritual humiliation inflicted on Kathleen is indicative of Johnston's desire to demonstrate how private and political domains intersect in 1970s Derry. Yet her principal concern, one senses, is not with politics, but with the dynamics of emotion affecting her younger characters. The intrusion of history on Joe, Kathleen and Brendan's lives is only partly responsible for their indeterminacy, their status as inner émigrés.[84] At our very first encounter with Kathleen, the then anonymous girl confesses, 'I'm not quite sure what I'm doing' (23). Even after she has been named, she remains a curiously elusive, enigmatic figure, whose vulnerability, like her chain-smoking, may be attributable to the recent deaths of her parents (89), or to a sense that she 'belongs' elsewhere, or to a fear of her relationship being exposed. Profoundly alone, like Brendan and Joe, she eagerly embraces opportunities for companionship. Repeatedly an object of the male gaze (22, 73, 84, 86, 99), she generally responds warmly to male attention, such as when she waves to a foreign seaman by the dockside, recognising that, like her, he is far from home (147). Despite being frequently depicted as 'hunched', inward-looking and full of self-doubt, Kathleen emerges as the most intuitive, sympathetic and prescient[85] individual in the text. She is equally perceptive diagnosing Joe's over-determined view of the world ('You mustn't be too rigid about things. Look at every object with an open mind' (51)) and Brendan's bewildered state: 'He's in a state of great confusion. That always appeals to me' (176), 'I think he'll go away. He's not very strong. His mind is too open to suggestion' (177).

Johnston's characterisation of Kathleen and Brendan may well reflect to some extent the reconfigurations in gender positions already underway in Ireland.[86] Although at the close translated into a victim-figure, the young teacher is a more assertive, independent character than any of the women in Kiely's *Proxopera*; and thus prefigures Colette in Una Woods's *The Dark Hole Days* or Finnula in Anne Devlin's 'Naming the Names'. Similarly, Brendan might be read as exemplifying the crisis in masculinity that intensified in the course of the Troubles.[87] Desperate to acquire a sense of identity by committing himself to the republican movement, and 'carry on' where his father 'left off', he finds himself unable to function when faced with the actuality of a gun: 'I was not the right person any more … I wouldn't be any use to them' (181). Much as she tries to 'ground' her narrative in contemporary political and social realities, Johnson does not succeed, as she herself acknowledges.[88] The novel does not contain a single allusion to actual events in Derry's recent history, and ignores entirely the sectarian dimension to the conflict. Instead of delving into the experiences and ideology which contribute to the making of a PIRA activist, *Shadows* presents us with an impressionable young man, driven merely by 'some sort of dream' (181). Even its resolution contrives to turn away from the brutality and injustice exacted upon Kathleen, by placing greater emphasis on Joe's penitence[89] and the partial absolution he receives as she presents him with a copy of Palgrave's *Golden Treasury of Verse*. As one reviewer wryly noted, that 'may not do much for his talent as a poet'.[90]

Michael Longley, *The Echo Gate*

In earlier phases of the Troubles Northern Irish poets had often turned to elegy as the most apposite of forms with which to explore and make public their responses to events. This period, however, witnesses interesting shifts in poetic practice, including an increasing number of commemorations of recent individual casualties of the violence.[91] Paul Durcan's 'In Memory: The Miami Showband' has already been cited, while Seamus Heaney's *Field Work* (1979) includes three such elegies, 'The Strand at Lough Beg', 'A Postcard form North Antrim' and 'Casualty'.[92] Writing in a context in which the numbers of victims and their devastated families continued to mount, the form provided 'a sufficient space'[93] in which personal loss could be acknowledged publicly, and tragedy re-individualised.

   One of the most accomplished elegists of this time was Michael Longley, whose fourth volume, *The Echo Gate* (1979) contains a particularly moving poetic triptych entitled 'Wreaths'.[94] The first of these, 'The Civil Servant', was prompted by the murder of Martin McBirney by the PIRA on 16 September 1974, on the same day and around the same time they shot and killed another prominent man-of-law.[95] McBirney was a greatly-respected public figure in Northern Ireland, a man of wide-ranging interests and talents. A close friend of Louis MacNeice and Sam Thompson, he had written several plays and documentary programmes for the BBC, including one on Daniel O'Connell aired shortly before his death.[96] Given that he had repeatedly defended civil rights' activists in his work as a barrister, had stood for the NILP in three Stormont elections, and was married to a Catholic, he could hardly be considered a credible enemy of the nationalist community and its working-class.

Like 'Wounds' before it, Longley's elegy makes much of quotidian domestic details in illustrating how even the home was now a site of brutal violation by Northern Ireland's dysfunctional politics. Its opening line depicts the civil servant in his kitchen 'preparing an Ulster fry for breakfast'; the tense is imperfect, the mood active. The matter-of-fact manner with which the killing is recorded adds to the poem's chill, and to the empathy it generates for its victim. In a rapid, progressively invasive sequence, the poem's subject is intruded upon, ousted grammatically ('He' becomes the object, 'him'), penetrated physically ('entered', 'pierced'). In his mouth, the bullet displaces his breakfast, destroying that which had culturally sustained him ('The books he had read, the music he could play'). Trespass follows trespass. Next to encroach upon the family home is the forensic team, whose impersonal efficiency almost matches that of the gunman. To them, he is something to be dusted around, until the time of their departure when they unceremoniously remove his body ('rolled up like a red carpet'). What remains, however, as a sign of the crime and of his now permanent absence is 'a bullet hole left in the cutlery drawer'.[97] For his widow, the object which most symbolises him is his piano, to which she turns to mark the devastation of her loss, the division the killers have opened up. Systematically, she removes its black keys, rendering it, like her, their marriage, their home, a desecrated thing. Throughout the poem, Longley maintains an austerity of utterance, conscious of the responsibility the poet bears to the bereaved, neither to exploit their grief, nor to proffer to them false solace.

The second poem in 'Wreaths' recalls an even more unlikely target of the paramilitaries, a greengrocer, murdered because of his religion. James Gibson, a 42-year-old Catholic and father of five, had a shop on the Stranmillis Road. One Saturday afternoon, on 8 December 1973, the penultimate day of the Sunningdale Conference, two masked UDA gunman walked into his shop, one of them repeatedly firing bullets into his body. The dominant images in Longley's poem are apposite, but ironic ones, associated with celebration and the plenitude that accompanies Christmas. As a result of those whose business is death, the greengrocer's shop becomes a site of crucifixion, its evergreen symbols of nativity (the holly, the fir trees) out of place.[98] Like the previous elegy, this is a poem without consolation, yet one which embodies and urges a gesture of redress. It ends urging members of both communities to 'pause', and to patronise in a positive sense 'Jim Gibson's shop', buying 'gifts' of 'Dates and chestnuts and tangerines' (12).[99]

The sequence's final and most complex poem, 'The Linen Workers', establishes a loose contiguity between three narratives, in each of which a victim or victims are represented metonymically by their teeth. It grips the reader from the outset with its bizarre preoccupation with the state of Christ's dental health. Although images of transcendence ('ascended ... into heaven') and wholeness ('with him') are to the fore in the opening line, the rest of the stanza is preoccupied by an imperfection 'in one of his molars', a space as telling as that in the cutlery drawer. Countering the movement embodied in the poem's first verb ('ascended') is the timeless stasis depicted in lines 3–4, which picture Christ 'fastened for ever', not with nails, but by his canines. In stanza two strategies of 'reversal' and defamiliarisation are again deployed, as the speaker's dead father displaces Christ as the poem's presiding figure. It begins affirmatively, with a double, blazing epiphany induced by 'that smile', this 'memory', but then the genre shifts into comic-gothic once the 'false teeth' of the father hove into view, 'Brimming in their tumbler'. These in turn are supplanted in stanza three, in which moving images of the Whitecross killings[100] take centre screen:

> When they massacred the ten linen workers
> There fell on the road beside them spectacles,
> Wallets, small change, and a set of dentures:
> Blood, food particles, the bread, the wine.

Whereas the references to the scattered spectacles, wallets and dentures originate in one kind of discourse (journalism), the allusions to 'blood', 'bread' and 'wine' derive from another (Christian theology), specifically the sacrament of the eucharist. As most critics note, the actual bodies of the linen-workers are 'absent' from the poem, yet these latter, supplementary images partially sacralise them, linking their brutal fate with that of Christ.

The fourth and final stanza makes explicit the elegy's function as a rite of mourning, as Longley again assimilates the profound grief and shock of his community by revisiting personal loss. The need to bury his father 'once again' implies that this latest horrific multiple killing, like that of the three Scots soldiers in 1971,[101] has created a 'breach in nature'.[102] Ultimately the poem's speaker strives to effect a measure of closure by seemingly picking up each of the strewn items listed in stanza three, all of which could well have been belonged to his father.[103] The intimate, restorative rites he imagines performing in the private sphere are analogous to the whole endeavour of the poem, which is to clarify, balance, recompense, articulate.

Brian Friel, *Translations*

Writing from a very different geographical, cultural and political position to Longley's, Brian Friel's attention in *Translations* centres upon Irish identity, and the complex, painful, plural legacy of Ireland's past. This past is viewed primarily from a nationalist perspective,[104] as shaped primarily by experiences of poverty, dispossession and disorientation (linguistic, cultural, political, economic, spiritual) endured prior to and during the period in which the play is set, and in the intervening years up to the time its composition. Set in 1833, in a fictional Donegal townland called Baile Beag, *Translations* traces the advance of the English and the English language into the smallest recesses of Ireland and Irish consciousness, and alleges that following its military success against the risings of 1798, a success consolidated politically through the 1800 Act of Union, Britain pursued a policy of linguistic and cultural colonisation. The principal manifestations of this strategy presented in the play are the work of the Ordnance Survey team, which mapped and renamed Ireland's geographical features between 1833 and 1846,[105] and the introduction of the National School system which 'encouraged use of the English language' and 'the exclusive use of English textbooks'.[106] In contrast to other postcolonial literary texts and traditional nationalist representations of pre-colonial Ireland, however, *Translations* does not offer an idealised portrait of the indigenous community. Rather it presents it as confused and divided in its responses to the English and the cultural impact of anglicisation.

Interviewed three months after its first production, and asked whether *Translations* is a 'political, polemical play', Friel replied, somewhat disingenuously, 'I really do not know. I am the last person to ask, really'.[107] Notes from an occasional diary he kept while at work on the script reveal that in fact Friel was extremely anxious about its political freight, and how that might impact on the play's aesthetic qualities and reception. One entry from 1 June 1979, five months before the text was completed, insists that 'The play has to do with language and only language ... if it becomes overwhelmed by that political element, it is lost'.[108] Another from the previous month registers 'the thought ... that what I was circling around was a political play and that thought panicked me'.[109] Yet as *Translations* itself exemplifies, language does not exist in a sanitised, timeless, ideology-free zone, and so the subject of the play could never have been '*only* language'. Friel's later account of the play's inception, written two years after the successful first production, during the highly-charged period that ensued after the hunger strikes, discloses that from the outset his interests were leading him into contentious political and cultural territory. The very terms he deploys when referring to the role language plays in identity are in themselves oppositional. 'Irish' and 'death' are tellingly linked together, and countered by 'English' and 'acquisition':

> For about five years before I wrote *Translations* there were various nebulous notions that kept visiting and leaving me: a play set in the nineteenth century, somewhere between the Act of Union and the Great Famine; a play about Daniel O'Connell and Catholic Emancipation; a play about colonialism; and the one constant – a play about the death of the Irish language and the acquisition of English and the profound effects that change-over would have on a people.[110]

For most of Friel's lifetime, and long before the establishment of the Irish Free State and Northern Ireland in 1922, issues of languages held an intense significance for nationalists. Gaelicisation was a key policy of Sinn Féin from the first Dáil onwards, and successive governments in the South placed great emphasis on linguistic restoration as a means of cleansing Ireland from the contamination of its colonial past. In the vanguard of attempts to revive Irish were the Free State's schools, which sought to counteract what Father Timothy Corcoran described as the 'baneful influence on the Irish language of the British-imposed National School system of the nineteenth century'.[111] However, as early as 1927, academics sympathetic to Irish, like Professor Michael Tierney, realised that the government's strategy of trying to consolidate Gaelic-speaking areas in the west (the Gaeltacht) and impose compulsory Irish lessons elsewhere had relatively little prospect of success:

> The task of reviving a language ... with no large neighbouring population which speaks even a distantly related dialect, and with one of the great world-languages to contend against, is one that has never been accomplished anywhere. Analogies with Flemish, Czech, or the Baltic languages are all misleading, because the problem in their cases has been rather of restoring a peasant language to cultivated use than that of reviving one which the majority had ceased to speak.[112]

By Friel's teenage years, the 1940s, it had become apparent that Irish-speaking was continuing to decline, or to quote the words of *The Leader* newspaper, 'the last reservoirs of living and vigorous Irish ... in the Gaeltacht are vanishing before our eyes'.[113] The inadequacies of government policy towards the language and the Gaeltacht were savaged in

Flann O'Brien's *An Béal Bocht* (1941). Centred on the fictional village of Corkadoragha, O'Brien's satire lambasts the tendency of nationalist ideologues to romanticise peasant life and poverty, rather than take the necessary drastic economic measures needed to halt rural misery and depopulation. Acquisitiveness and exploitation, it emerges, are not solely an English trait:

> The advent of spring was no longer judged by the flight of the first swallow, but by the first Gaeligore seen on the roads ... Of course, they carried away much of our good Gaelic when they departed from us each night, but they left few pennies as recompense to the paupers who waited for them and had kept the Gaelic tongue alive for such as them a thousand years. People found this difficult to understand; it had always been said that accuracy of Gaelic (as well as holiness of spirit) grew in proportion to one's lack of worldly goods and since we had the choicest poverty and calamity, we did not understand why the scholars were interested in any half-awkward, perverse Gaelic which was audible in other parts.[114]

Thus, in Friel's *Translations*, Maire's demands to be taught English and rejection of 'the old language' reflect not only Daniel O'Connell's and the Catholic hierarchy's 'progressive' attitudes in the 1830s and 1840s, but also those of a century later when 'Irish was increasingly being associated with rural impoverishment and deprivation'.[115] From the late 1940s onwards, it was recognised that Irish might survive if people in towns and cities *sought* to learn it as a means of understanding more of their collective past; the post-war period saw the founding of such organisations as Gael-Linn in 1953 which, through its sponsorship of literature, music and film, did much to restore its pride and prestige.[116]

During the period immediately preceding *Translations'* composition, interest in the Irish language quickened in Northern Ireland. Much to the dismay of enthusiasts who for years had promoted the language as a cultural resource for *both* traditions, the republican movement started to encourage the learning of the language for their own political purposes. Their strategy replicated that of their predecessors, the IRB, at the beginning of the century, in seeking to deploy Irish as 'a territorial weapon'[117] within the struggle to decolonise. Learning Irish became almost obligatory for the expanding numbers of republican prisoners in Long Kesh in the mid- to late 1970s, a complementary expression of 'active republicanism'.[118] While it would be foolish to regard *Translations* as evidence of Friel's support for Irish language revival, the playwright is clearly picking up on current discussion of the language question within Northern Irish culture. Since 1970, through their poetry and prose,[119] first Montague, then Heaney had demonstrated how effective even traces of the old tongue could be in affirming the distinctness of Irish cultural identity, particularly at times of acute political and cultural threat. Friel's own views on the language question seem to accord with theirs and those of Flann O'Brien, who argued that 'a continued awareness here of the Gaelic norm of word and thought is vital to the preservation of our peculiar and admired methods of handling English'.[120] In a piece for *Magill*, Friel himself stressed the necessity for Irish people and writers to embrace wholeheartedly the English language and its words in order to make them 'distinctive and unique to us', 'identifiably our own',[121] echoing the sentiments of Hugh, who, at *Translations'* close, concedes, 'We must learn those new names ... We must learn to make them our own. We must make them our new home' (444). Apart from the inter-mittent use of deeply resonant words and quotations from Latin and Greek, Friel's play is written entirely in English. Although the audience quickly falls in with the illusion that the characters are speaking in Irish, the Irish language features in the play solely in the form of place-names and names from myth, survivors of a discourse whose future is tenuous.

Claims that *Translations* is steeped in a 'pervasive nostalgia', presents the old home as 'a kind of Eden',[122] or valorises 'the absolute priority of the (patriarchal) family unit'[123] are wide of the mark, as stage directions, characterisation, action and dialogue all make clear. Signs of economic decline and emotional deprivation are there to be read in the dramatist's description of the set; the O'Donnells' hedge-school is held in '*a disused barn ... where cows were once milked and bedded*'; '*Around the room are broken and forgotten implements*'; '*The room is comfortless ... there is* no trace of a woman*'s hand*' (383; my emphasis). A huge gap in the text and the family is the absence of the mother, as it is in Friel's earlier play, *The Gentle Island*; the sole reference to Caitlin Dubh (Dark Kathleen) comes in Hugh's late speech where she is translated into the 'goddess' he hero-ically abandoned to go to war (445). Her loss has meant that Manus ful-fils the role of '*unpaid assistant*' to his father, it soon emerges; as well as being tasked with the bulk of the teaching, he takes on the menial domestic chores.

When the curtain rises, the audience is confronted with a distinctly un-Arcadian scene and community. A lame young man, Manus, is attempting to cajole the '*waiflike*' Sarah into speech. Sitting at a distance from them is the filthily-dressed, 60-year-old Jimmy Jack, whose fluent utterances contrast with her halting ones. The Infant Prodigy can be heard translating and revelling in *The Odyssey*, a somewhat ironic choice of text, given that the sole excursion he ever made was an aborted one; like Manus's father he set off to join the 1798 Rising. If Sarah can only manage to get her tongue and lips working, Manus promises a 'wide world' will open up for her, and a feeling of liberation once she is able to share 'the secrets in that head of yours' (385). Like the trapped figures in Sartre's *Huis Clos*, however, each of the three voices romantic yearnings which will never be realised.[124]

With the arrival of the next triad of characters on stage, Maire, Bridget and Doalty, bringing news of events from beyond the O'Donnells' barn, the diverse nature of the community – in attainments, ambitions and attitudes towards the Strangers – becomes even more apparent. In several respects like *The Gentle Island*'s Sarah, Maire is an assertive, and at times acerbic young woman, eager to flee the domestic drudgery,[125] emotional, economic and spiritual limitations of life in Baile Beag. Characterised in the text as both '*strong-minded*' and '*strong-bodied*' (387), she brings a sexual frisson to the stage from her first entry, when she flirts playfully with Jimmy Jack (388) in revenge for the chaste kiss Manus gives Sarah ('Well, now, isn't that a pretty sight' (387)) and, more importantly, his neglect of her and her desires:

> MANUS: I can give you a hand at the hay tomorrow … If the day's good.
> MAIRE: Suit yourself. The English soldiers below in the tents, them sapper fellas, they're coming up to give us a hand. I don't know a word they're saying, nor they me; but sure that doesn't matter, does it? (389)

Although capable of laughing briefly at Biddy Hanna's letter detailing 'All the gossip of the parish',[126] she becomes infuriated by the fatalism in the local mindset. When Bridget relays rumours of a mysterious sweet smell, and mentions the possibility of blight, Maire erupts:

> Every year at this time somebody comes back with stories of the sweet smell. Sweet God, did the potatoes ever fail in Baile Beag? … There was never blight here. Never. Never. But we're always sniffing about for it, aren't we? – looking for disaster … Honest to God, some of you people aren't happy unless you're miserable and you'll not be right content until you're dead. (395)

While the text presents evidence of personal tensions, marked differences of perspective which predate the advent of the English, it is equally

keen to demonstrate how destabilising their presence is. The establishment of the new, free National Schools directly threatens the O'Donnells'
main source of income, as both Biddy Hanna (389) and Maire (394) grasp,
as well as the primacy of the Irish tongue. It also serves as a factor in the
break-up of Manus and Maire's relationship, when she learns of his
unwillingness to compete with his father for the post of principal. The
work of the Ordnance Survey team similarly generates divisions. Doalty's
account of his mischief-making, shifting the surveyors' poles to ruin
their calculations, provokes laughter from Bridget, sarcasm from Maire,
but an endorsement from Manus; for him, Doalty's act is politically symbolic, an expression of non-violent resistance, a reminder to the colonisers
of the indigenous 'presence' (391).[127] In sharp contrast to the Donnellys,
whose resentment initially takes the form of a campaign of theft and
sabotage (393), Maire has adopted an accommodating attitude to the
Redcoats, by allowing them to house their theodolite overnight in her
byre. Prior to Owen's arrival, it is she who embodies the clearest proof of
the reconfigurations taking place in early nineteenth-century Ireland.
Her willingness to stand up to Hugh and contest his choice of curriculum is symptomatic of a younger generation's unwillingness to acqui-
esce unthinkingly to the old order. Significantly she '*turns away impatiently*'
when asked to give the principal Latin forms of that very verb:

> (*MAIRE gets to her feet uneasily but determinedly*)
> MAIRE: We should all be learning to speak English. That's what my
>   mother says. That's what I say. That's what Daniel O'Connell
>   said last month in Ennis. He said the sooner we all learn to
>   speak English the better. (399)[128]

Her confrontation with Hugh is intimately linked to frustration with
Manus and with the ignominy of her economic and social position,
which she imagines marriage will partially amend. Earlier, while outlining
a 'Map of America', she had signalled her intention to emigrate, informing
Manus that 'The passage money came last Friday' (394). Maire's interest in
cartography, especially in places far removed from Donegal, predates her
meeting with Yolland, and prefigures that of Owen.

Following the arrival of Hugh's younger son and his English 'guests',
fragmentation in the parish becomes even more pronounced. Already a
successful Dublin-based entrepreneur, Owen has taken on the role of
'part-time, underpaid civilian interpreter' (404), presumably in order to
ingratiate himself with the authorities and secure future army contracts.
Economic self-interest underlies his anglophile, unionist sympathies – he

speaks early on of 'the King's good English' (404) – and his gross mistranslations of Captain Lancey's speeches quickly confirm that his lack of loyalty to his family, culture or community of origin. Tellingly, he refers to the latter as 'you people', when requesting a hospitable reception for 'Two friends of mine' (402); these 'friends', it emerges at the end of Act One, are not even aware of his real name.[129] When Yolland later questions him about Manus's lameness and private circumstances, he breaches family confidences by relating how the disability was a result of his father's drunkenness, concluding his account by smugly affirming, 'I got out in time, didn't I?' (413).

As the play moves into its second act, however, the presentation of Owen becomes more nuanced, reflecting no doubt Friel's deeper understanding of the character's historical 'original', John O'Donovan (1806–61), one of Ireland's foremost Gaelic scholars and a contributor to the Survey.[130] There are still speeches which confirm Manus's reading of him as a collaborator; Owen does not merely 'consent'[131] to cultural assimilation, he facilitates it amongst others. Unaware of her prior attachment to his brother, Owen acts again as a 'go-between' when Maire eagerly invites Yolland to the dance (425), having earlier introduced the pair to each other (408).[132] Whereas Act One demonstrated his skills in 'spin', Act Two reveals a genuine enthusiasm for and commitment to the survey, which contrasts with Yolland's diffidence and unease; ironically, it is the Englishman who emerges as more sensitive to the damage anglicisation inflicts and more attuned to the hostile mood in the locality.[133] Like O'Donovan, Owen *believes* the renaming exercise possesses merit in itself, bringing a measure of accuracy and rationalisation after years of linguistic confusion and neglect.[134] To him there is little point in retaining a name like Tobair Vree (Brian's Well) when knowledge of the minor tragedy behind it has, like the water, all but dried up. And when he speaks of the need 'to adjust for survival' (419), he is not merely voicing his own materialistic *credo*, but also reacting against a self-aggrandising rhetoric and complacency which, like Maire, he regards as debilitating. Further positive aspects of Owen's character appear in his camaraderie with Yolland and when he displays delight at Manus's success in gaining the hedge-school post on Inis Meadhon (423). Conscious of his responsibility for his brother's devastation at Maire's 'betrayal', he offers Manus sympathy, money and practical advice. It is that experience, combined with concern for Yolland's welfare and alarm at Lancey's threatened reprisals, that force Owen to reconsider the consequences of co-operation with the military. When he catches Hugh reciting the place-names he has helped translate, he snatches the Name-Book back, characterising his former activities as 'A mistake – my mistake – nothing to do with *us*' (444; my emphasis). The audience's last glimpse of Owen finds him setting off to meet Doalty in the hope of gleaning news about the Donnellys and Yolland's fate. His response to Doalty's defiant talk is guarded, ambiguous; there is no indication as to whether Owen's phrase, 'Against a trained army' (442), is an endorsement of Doalty's sentiments or an expression of scepticism about resistance's likely result.[135]

Through Owen's relationship with Yolland and Yolland's with Maire, the text examines the extent to which accommodations between the English and the Irish can be achieved. It illustrates how, at certain junctures in time, attempts to transcend 'history' and material political conflicts through cross-cultural personal relationships encounter intense, sometimes violent opposition. Signs of this feature long before the English officer's abduction and probable murder by the proto-militant republican Donnelly twins.[136] Yolland observes to Owen how 'Some people here resent us', citing in evidence an incident from the previous day when as he was passing 'a little girl ... spat at me' (413). Repeatedly he speaks of his desire to learn Irish, yet senses that however proficient he might become his knowledge could not guarantee acceptance: 'I'd always be an outsider ... I may learn the password, but the language of the tribe will always elude me ... The private core will always be ... hermetic' (416). For all its poignancy, humour and sexual charge, the love-scene between him and Maire is liable to engender ambivalence amongst audiences, not so much because of its consequences for Manus, but rather because of the immensity of the gulf separating the two. Unlike Horatio and Glorvina in Lady Morgan's *The Wild Irish Girl* (1806), or more recently Phil and Monica in Boyd's *The Flats* (1971), the lovers in *Translations* do not even share a common tongue, only pleasure in the gestures and sounds their Other makes (427).[137] From their respective exchanges with Manus and Owen, it is clear that Maire wants to quit her homeland as soon as possible while Yolland dreams of settling there.

While the portrayal of the English in *Translations* will have been shaped by Friel's experiences over the *whole* period of the Troubles, the play reflects, albeit obliquely, more recent shifts in British strategy. Concurrent with their hardline approach towards security and prisons discussed earlier, Westminster policy-makers in the mid- to late 1970s increasingly sought to foster 'community development and community cultural expression in Northern Ireland'[138] through agencies such as the ACNI, which provided a large proportion of the funding for *Translations*' first production.[139] Within the play, Lancey embodies the bullish stance often adopted by the British authorities. In acting on the assumption that subject peoples can be intimidated into submission, the captain repeats an error common in the imperial era and since. Like too many of the measures taken by British politicians and the Army in Northern Ireland in the 1970s, Lancey's prove counter-productive. The native response to the destruction of their cornfields, fences and haystacks and threats of evictions and clearances manifests itself swiftly, in the form of an arson attack on his camp and talk of guerrilla activity (440, 442). Whereas initially Lancey had been depicted as formal, officious and none-too-bright,[140] on his second appearance he is presented as rash and despotic. What particularly antagonises the audience is his crushing of Sarah, thrusting her back into the silence from which she had briefly escaped.

Ironically, the man Lancey is searching for, and for whose 'sake' the parish will be levelled, is one whose attitude to the Baile Beag community and Irish culture is entirely opposite to the captain's. '*A soldier by accident*' (404), but 'Already a committed Hibernophile' (407), the contradictory elements in Yolland's position and character are immediately established. His opening speeches are full of hesitancy, awkwardness, naivety, but equally sensitivity and insight. Unlike Lancey, he regards it as 'foolish … to be working here and not speak your language' (407) and realises that theirs is an intrusive presence. It is no accident that his defining verbal mannerism is 'Sorry-sorry?' which functions both as an apology and as a marker of his eagerness to understand and be understood. Clearly the play's title embraces him, since he is a translator, translated. Long before he develops a taste for poteen, his intoxication with Ireland's countryside (407), language and musicality (414), the vibrant cultural community (418), and, above all, its sheer otherness is displayed. His vision of Ireland as 'heavenly' (414), like his elevation of Maire[141] and Hugh,[142] arises paradoxically out of a need for groundedness. In flight from his father, England, modernity, a frenetic, work- and money-obsessed culture, he detects in pre-famine Ireland an 'experience … of a totally different order, a consciousness that wasn't striving nor agitated' (416). From their access to and observation of the individuals gathered around the hedge-school, and from what they have gleaned of subsequent history, the audience knows full well that Yolland's reading is, like all readings, partial.

Much of the play's dynamic, and no little amount of its irony, springs from its juxtaposition of different histories (Ireland's/England's, ancient/ recent), different time-perspectives (the characters' and the audience's). Whereas the young Englishman's key historical reference points relate to Britain's political, military and economic rivalry with revolutionary and Napoleonic France ('London', 'Bastille', 'Waterloo', 'Wellington', 'Bombay'), for the older generation of Irish who experienced it 'first-hand' and the younger generation now living with its consequences the main defining moments are the defeat of the 1798 Rising and its aftermath.[143] The Rising's significance only emerges in Hugh's penultimate major speech, which exemplifies why he, like Jimmy Jack, still drinks deep in 'mythologies of fantasy and hope and self-deception' (418). In sentiment and phrasing, Hugh's account of the march to Sligo is extremely Yollandesque.[144] He talks of finding 'definition', 'congruence', 'a miraculous matching', and depicts Ireland as a 'fresh', 'green' place in which 'rhythms of perception' were 'heightened', 'consciousness accelerated' (445). His and Jimmy Jack's failure to join the rebel cause is attributed to *desiderium nostrorum*, 'the need for our own'. Curiously, recognition of this need only occurred during their halt in 'Phelan's pub'; it seems not to have been a factor when Hugh first set off, 'heroic(ally)' abandoning his wife and infant child. Attachment to the parish, rather than a disastrous lack of co-ordination, becomes the reason for the Rising's failure, according to Hugh's dubious account of his own and Irish history. On the emotional turmoil he experienced after turning back and forsaking political commitment, he is extremely reticent; he speaks only of 'the *longest* twenty-three miles back I ever made' (446).[145] To view his closing translation from the *Aeneid* merely as a strategic retreat from painful personal memory would be to limit its significance, however. In a move paralleling that of many of Friel's literary contemporaries, Hugh turns to classical literature not to escape history but to find analogues for the present. Reciting Virgil, re-siting Carthage, the schoolmaster senses that the past does not simply mirror the present, it writes it *and* the future. He may well subscribe to the *Aeneid*'s deterministic reading of history, believing that the triumph of the English, 'a warrior nation ... sovereign over wide realms',[146] may have been decided by fate. He seems of the view that transience and decline are woven into the very text of existence. 'Always', the bi-syllable the lovers feverishly repeated to each other in their separate tongues (429, 430), he dismisses as 'a silly word' (446).

That 'confusion is not an ignoble condition' (446) is borne out by the play's closing cameo. Over the course of three acts, the audience watches as a flawed, inequitable, yet culturally vital order disintegrates before its eyes. Of the triad with which the play began, the downcast Manus has fled, and Sarah, who has lapsed once more into speechlessness, is absent. Only the 'inner émigré'[147] Jimmy Jack remains, his grip on reality more tenuous than ever as he prepares for his forthcoming marriage to Pallas Athena. The woman Sarah hoped to replace in Manus's affections now replaces her on stage. The once feisty, independent-minded

Maire is now utterly disorientated as a result of her want of Yolland, and twice admits to being off her head (436, 446). Like Jimmy Jack, she dreams of a magical future union, and defers indefinitely all thought of leaving Baile Beag since 'When he comes back, this is where he'll come to' (446).[148] Only Hugh, Manus's substitute, seems in command of his faculties, relatively speaking. Angry, but unbowed by his failure to secure the National School post, he is already starting 'to adjust for survival' (419) by accepting the painful necessity of using the imposed language and promising to teach it to Maire.[149] Although his rendering of the *Aeneid* confers an elegiac quality on the play's ending, it can also be viewed as an affirmative act in demonstrating literature's and indeed *Translations'* function, opening a dialogue with past cultures in order to make sense of present ones.

So acute are Hugh's observations throughout the play that it is tempting to confer on his pronouncements privileged status, particularly when after discovering the extent to which they draw directly on the writings one of the world's outstanding critics of recent times, George Steiner.[150] Quoting verbatim from Steiner's *After Babel*, Hugh describes Irish civilisation in the 1830s as 'imprisoned in a linguistic contour that no longer matches the landscape of ... fact' (418–19), yet his comments might equally be applied of Northern Irish political discourse, as well as to the political cultures in the Republic and mainland Britain in the late 1970s/ early 1980s. It is similarly difficult to dissent from his later assertion that 'it is not the literal past, the "facts" of history that shape us, but images of the past embodied in language', or from what one suspect to be Friel's own artistic credo, the conviction that 'we must never cease renewing those images; because once we do, we fossilise' (445). Yet in placing too much emphasis on Hugh's utterances and their authority, there is a risk of losing sight of the plurality of diverse perspectives the play contains.[151]

Translations was at first greeted with acclaim by audiences and critics throughout Ireland, Britain, Europe and America,[152] although in the period following the hunger strikes reservations began to be increasingly voiced. Some who regarded the play primarily as a political parable objected that in focusing on the Ireland–England axis Friel had ignored the sectarian dimension to the conflict,[153] and the parts played by religion and militant republicanism. Others, including John Andrews, whose book, *A Paper Landscape*, was one of Friel's most important sources, enjoyed the play immensely, but lamented its historical inaccuracies. Writing in *The Crane Bag*'s symposium on the play, Andrews points out that soldiers on survey duty went out without bayonets, and so Doalty could not have seen them 'Prodding every inch of the ground with their bayonets'

(434); that a 'junior army officer' like Lancey would have had no legal right to evict tenants from a landowner's property; that 'the real Lancey' would never called a parish 'a section'; that Yolland comes across as 'improbably and anachronistically classless' in falling for a local girl with blistered hands.[154] Finally, however, the historian is compelled to concede that the play subtly blends 'historical truth and – *some other kind of truth*' (my emphasis).[155] That is exactly the point. As Friel himself argues, in his riposte to Andrews' critique, while dramatists have a responsibility to acquaint themselves with the historical 'facts', they should not be expected 'to defer to them. Drama is first a fiction, with the authority of fiction. You don't go to *Macbeth* for history'.[156] The concern of the imaginative artist is, of course, not with the 'surface details of either past or present moments',[157] but with a larger narrative, composed of alternative lives, multivalent possibilities and truths.

The première of *Translations* in Derry's Guildhall marked the formal beginning of the Field Day project, which, through its productions and publications, would 'set the terms for critical debate in Irish Studies'[158] for a substantial part of the next two decades. Field Day was the brain-child of the Belfast-born actor, Stephen Rea, who in 1979 contacted Friel about the possibility of mounting a touring production of his new play. In order to secure funding from the ACNI they had to become 'an estab-lishment', and settled on 'Field Day' since it echoed their two names.[159] From the outset there was a political dimension to Friel–Rea's cultural collaboration, since their plan was to stage *Translations* in towns north and south of the border, and not initially in London, Dublin or Belfast. Interviewed by the *Sunday Independent* three weeks before the start of the first Long Kesh hunger strike, Friel made clear the scale of their ambi-tion, which was to use theatre as a forum for initiating an inclusive, comprehensive cultural dialogue on the island: 'For people like ourselves, living close to such a fluid situation, definitions of identity have to be developed and analysed more frequently. We've got to keep questioning until we find ... some kind generosity that can embrace the whole island'.[160] During the 12 months that followed that was no easy task.

II   The hunger strikes, the Anglo-Irish Agreement, and their aftermaths (January 1980–November 1986)

On 1 April 1980, the British government withdrew special category sta-tus for paramilitary prisoners in Northern Ireland. As a consequence, in late October, the republican leadership in Long Kesh decided to embark on a third phase of its campaign against 'criminalisation' with a hunger strike. Drawing partly no doubt on Richard Kearney's lucid, contemporaneous explication of republican 'theology',[161] Padraig O'Malley argues that this particular form of protest

> fuses elements of the legal code of ancient Ireland, of the self-denial that is the central characteristic of Irish Catholicism, and of the propensity for endurance and sacrifice that is the hallmark of militant Irish nationalism.[162]

Their aim in fasting was to force the prison authorities into several key concessions. They demanded the freedom to wear their own clothes and freedom from having to undertake prison work; the right to free association with fellow prisoners; the reinstatement of remission and the restoration of normal visiting hours, educational and recreational facilities.[163]

Seven men began the fast on 27 October 1980, and were joined 35 days later by three women prisoners in Armagh. Although the Northern Ireland Office attempted to engage the strikers in talks on 10 December, within days a further 30 prisoners began to fast. As one of the initial hunger-strikers approached death 52 days into his strike, Cardinal Tomás Ó Fiaich urged both Mrs Thatcher and the strikers to end the crisis. The next day, without consulting Bobby Sands, PIRA's OC at Long Kesh, the hunger-strikers' leader, Brendan Hughes, called off the protest, under the impression that the British had conceded to their demands. However, early in the New Year, 1981, it became clear that prisoners would not be permitted to wear their own clothes; rather they would be required to put on 'the new official issue civilian clothing'[164] provided by the authorities.

As a result, on 1 March 1981, the fifth anniversary of the withdrawal of special category status, a second hunger strike began when Bobby Sands,[165] the refused food. Like Pearse with whom he identified, Sands was fully conscious of the performative, sacrificial nature of his act: 'I am a political prisoner because I am a casualty of a perennial war that is being fought between the oppressed Irish people and an alien, unwanted regime that refuses to withdraw from our land'.[166] To maximise dramatic impact, the cast of ten taking part in the strike did not start their fast simultaneously; Francis Hughes, a neighbour of the Heaneys in Bellaghy, joined Sands after a fortnightly interval, and was followed a week later, on 22 March, by Raymond McCreesh and Patsy O'Hara.[167]

Crucial in the transformation of the 1981 hunger strike into an international story was the sudden death of the Independent Nationalist MP for Fermanagh/South Tyrone, Frank Maguire, on the fifth day of Sands' fast. As Maguire's constituency possessed a nationalist majority, it was clearly winnable again, provided the Catholic vote was not split between a constitutional nationalist and a republican candidate. At first the SDLP and the republicans backed the candidature of Noel Maguire, the MP's brother, for the vacant seat. However, following the intervention of Bernadette McAliskey (née Devlin) with her offer to stand as an Independent on the H-block issue, Sinn Féin recognised the propaganda potential in selecting an H-block candidate of their own. Although at the outset, Adams and other leading republicans had opposed Sands' decision to embark on a hunger strike,[168] they suddenly realised that fighting the by-election might be an excellent way of illustrating that paramilitary activity sprang from political motives, not from criminal ones. Within days of Bobby Sands' official nomination as a candidate for Fermanagh/ South Tyrone on 26 March, Noel Maguire came under intense pressure to withdraw from the contest, which he did 'fifteen minutes before the deadline'.[169] In the straight fight that ensued on 9 April between Sands and the UUP's Harry West, the hunger-striker secured victory by 1446 votes in an 86.9 per cent turnout.

Despite mounting criticism from the Irish Republic and within the international community,[170] the British Prime Minister and her Northern Ireland Secretary seemed unmoved by Sands' election or his declining state of health. Four days after Sands received the last rites, on 21 April, Margaret Thatcher declared at a press conference that her government was 'not prepared to consider special category status for certain groups of people serving sentences for crime'; the following week, Humphrey Atkins stated that 'If Mr Sands persists in his wish to commit suicide, that is his choice'.[171] As Sands approached his final days, Father Sean Rogan, a curate from Twinbrook, visited him, and urged him to bear in mind Pearse's decision in Easter 1916 to call an end to the killing, since 'he didn't want more deaths to result from what he was doing'. Sands, however, had replied angrily that it would be the British who would be responsible for deaths following his death.[172] In the words of another priest, Father Dennis Faul, Sands saw himself as 'Christ-like', messianic, 'and was determined to go ahead'.[173]

Within the northern nationalist community sympathy for the hunger-strikers grew in intensity, and expressed itself by means of demonstrations and occasional rioting, but also in prayers and religious iconography.[174] When, 66 days into his strike, on 5 May, Sands finally died, the news was conveyed throughout nationalist West Belfast by the banging of dustbin lids. At his funeral on 7 May an estimated 100 000 people turned out to pay their respects and demonstrate collective solidarity in the face of what they regarded as British intransigence.

One by one, between 12 May and 20 August 1981, nine other hunger-strikers died. Throughout the summer attempts were made by the SDLP, ministers and TDs from the Republic, the Red Cross and senior Catholic churchmen to broker a compromise that might end the crisis, but without success.[175] Following the hunger-strikers' deaths the surge in violence everyone had predicted did occur, though not on the scale that many had feared. In the period between Sands' death and that of Michael Devine, the tenth hunger striker, 52 people fell victim to the Troubles; on the day before Sands' funeral, a 14-year-old Protestant boy was killed in North Belfast and his father fatally injured when their milk lorry was attacked by a mob; on 13 and 22 May in separate incidents two young Catholic girls (aged 14 and 11) died in West Belfast after being struck by plastic bullets fired by the Army; two RUC officers were killed in IRA attacks on 6 and 14 May; and on 19 May a Saracen carrying five soldiers was blown to pieces by a 1000 lb IRA landmine in South Armagh. It was not until 3 October that the hunger strike campaign was formally ended after strikers' families announced their determination to intervene. Three days later, James Prior, recently appointed as Northern Ireland Secretary, granted many of the strikers' original demands, allowing prisoners to wear their own clothes, restoring remission, visits and the right to free association. The PIRA response was to launch a spate of attacks in London (10, 17 and 26 October), in which three people were killed and over 40 injured.

Bernard Mac Laverty *Cal*

Part of the initial stimulus for Bernard Mac Laverty's second novel, *Cal* (1983), came from a reflection of his wife's one night about the number of 'nineteen year-olds' in Northern Ireland 'who must have blighted their lives' through their involvement in paramilitary activity.[176] *Cal* relates the story of an unemployed young Catholic, living on an almost exclusively Protestant estate, where he and his father, Shamie McCluskey, are subjected to frequent acts of intimidation. Flashbacks reveal that Cal acted as an occasional driver on PIRA operations, but that now he wants to disengage himself wholly from them. He is haunted by memories of one particular incident in which he was an accessory to the murder of an off-duty police reservist, Robert Morton. A chance encounter with Morton's widow, Marcella, prompts his obsessive pursuit of her, a quest which is both religious and sexual in its motivation. He finds employment working for her and eventually moves into an outhouse in the grounds of her home. Even after their relationship deepens and is consummated, he cannot bring himself to name the act which binds him to her, and so is unable to achieve any measure of absolution.

The book's opening sentence depicts the title character in a liminal location, 'at the back gateway of the abattoir, his stomach rigid with the ache of want' (7).[177] Despite its predictability as a metaphor for Northern Ireland, the slaughterhouse helps quickly establish Cal's revulsion at and his 'friend', Crilly's, indifference to blood-letting. 'Ache' and 'want' turn out to be defining characteristics of Cal's condition, as each of his desperate needs feeds into another. References to stomachs and food recur in these early pages; 'Cal had had no breakfast' (7, para 1); the drinking of blood is prescribed 'for any anaemic with a strong stomach' (7, para 2); after his first cigarette of the day 'the muscles of his stomach relax' (8); 'he left his toast uneaten' (10); he serves his father 'black puddings ... He loathed them' (14); 'the tension in his stomach increased' (16); his father reproves him for abandoning the job in the abattoir because 'you hadn't a strong enough stomach' (18); Cal's stomach 'felt like a wash-board' (20). Given the period of the text's gestation and composition coincided with and immediately followed the 1980–81 hunger strikes, these may well be subliminal allusions to those traumatic events.[178] Certainly what is striking about the novel is its heady, claustrophobic intensity, and its engagement with many of the central concepts and tendencies of Catholic thought. Guilt, sacrifice, atonement figure prominently amongst its concerns, along with deep anxieties over sexuality.

From the outset, the narration privileges Cal's perspective and responses to events, giving access to his feelings of self-loathing, which are often voiced in schoolboy French. By stressing his vulnerability, and withholding from the reader the extent and nature of his involvement with 'the Movement' (10), the narrator encourages the reader to develop an empathy for Cal which the text subsequently problematises. Violence and its taint are in the first instance projected onto others, beginning with the ghoulish, anaemic Preacher. In contrast to the rosy-cheeked figures of medieval Catholic iconography who cup the blood of Christ, this tall, thin Protestant possesses the complexion and Adam's apple 'of a vulture'. An early indication that Crilly will emerge as the Preacher's satanic double comes when, with Cal, we hear the 'hiss' (7) that accompanies the sharpening of his knives. The burden of many of these and other signs, emblems and texts, which press in on Cal at every turn, is often only apparent at a second reading. To the majority of readers, the Preacher's tract ('The Wages of Sin is Death'), like his solitary mission, may appear simply archaic, a throwback to a sin-obsessed, Calvinist past. Talk of 'wages' may seem ironic given the scale of unemployment in Northern Ireland since the mid-1950s. Yet in fact Mac Laverty's text *exemplifies* the dire consequences of individual and collective wrongdoing – original sins – and thus inscribes the religious ideology it sets out to satirise.

Far more immediate in their import are the Union Jacks, Ulster flags and painted kerbstones which Cal encounters returning home from the abattoir. The text's emphasis on the intimidation (9, 27–9) and condescension (9) meted out on the McCluskeys by their Protestant neighbours implies that nationalist violence is generally *reactive*. The sequence leading to Cal's involvement with the Provisionals is carefully spelt out in the narrative. As a result of UVF threats to burn them out, Cal's father, Shamie, accepts from Crilly the loan of a gun (29); 'some weeks later', Crilly persuades the McCluskeys to store 'three cardboard boxes' in their roof space (30); then 'one night' Crilly asks Cal to drive him 'somewhere' to move 'something from one house to another' (30). These disclosures, which occur late in the first chapter, may well lead readers to modify their initial impressions of the McCluskeys, and also to question their representation thus far as innocent victims of sectarian prejudice. Before the chapter's close, however, sympathies are re-engaged, witnessing the disturbance the loyalists' warning causes father and son, the uneasiness of the relationship between them, and, above all, the massive impact of his mother's death on Cal during his childhood and his continuing adolescence.

The revelation of this loss, suffered when he was eight, offers *one* explanation for the introvertedness, aimlessness and troubled masculinity observed in Cal's behaviour up to this point. Early on, attention had been drawn to the 'female gestures' he developed as a result of the length of hair, and how that served as a way of 'screening him from the world' (10). His desire to forge an identity and find a language for himself lies behind his attachment to the Movement,[179] for whose 'sake' he had tried to learn Gaelic: 'but he never knew how to pronounce the written form of the words ... The words remained as printed symbols locked inside his head' (10). And yet despite his need to feel less peripheral, an enduring, though compromised sense of morality makes him resistant to republican ideology.

Like Kiely's, Mac Laverty's representation of republicans is profoundly negative, influenced perhaps by contemporary British perceptions of them as criminals utterly without conscience.[180] Thus, Crilly, like Corkman in *Proxopera*, is portrayed principally as a sadistic thug. Instances of his brutality and thieving during his school years are graphically described. In one of the most telling flashbacks, there partly to illustrate the willingness of Catholic authorities to collude in violence, Father

Durkin, the boys' Religious Knowledge teacher, exploits Crilly's reputation for getting things 'done'(18)[181] in a campaign to combat pornography; having identified the culprit, a boy with the improbable, Dickensian name of Smicker, Crilly headbutts him, knees him in the privates, and pockets the photographs (19), while Cal looks on.[182] Carrying out robberies and shootings for the Movement, like his job in the abattoir, gives Crilly license to indulge his appetite for power and inflicting pain, and in the process lining his wallet.[183] The presence in his home of traditional and contemporary republican texts and icons ('IRELAND UNFREE SHALL NEVER BE AT PEACE' / 'MADE IN LONG KESH CONCENTRATION CAMP') reinforces the impression that for Crilly politics and political thought are simple, unambiguous matters. Thus when his controller, Finbar Skeffington, engages Cal in debate and asserts that 'Not to act ... is to act', it is not surprising that 'Crilly looked confused' (65). Unconscious of the irony of his choice of folklore heroes, he had earlier defined his role in the Struggle by comparing himself to 'Dick Turpin' and 'oul' Robin Hood' (22).

A primary teacher, like *his* hero, Padraic Pearse, Skeffington is a Mephistophelean figure, who lends ideological legitimacy to Crilly's use of force. On each of his appearances, he deploys an arsenal of varied rhetorical devices, historical icons and contemporary analogies in order to justify republican killings and so draw Cal back into allegiance. During our first encounter with him, he tries to amuse Cal describing a recent 'sting' carried out by Belfast Provisionals. Tellingly, at the end of his anecdote, he speaks in praise of fiction, characterising it – rather than truth – as an essential weapon in the propaganda war: 'Stories like that are good for us. Even if they didn't happen we should make them up' (22). When Cal voices qualms about 'what's happening' and alludes specifically to the Morton case, Skeffington argues the suffering the Provisionals cause is, sadly, inevitable and minimal:

> 'People get hurt ... But compared with conventional war the numbers are small. I know that sounds callous but it's true. In Cyprus the dead hardly ran to three figures. That's cheap for freedom'. (23)

Repeatedly the narrative uses interjections by Cal to challenge the glib assertions and sophistry Skeffington is prone to, and thus contest what Mac Laverty regards as the specious rationale underpinning the Provisionals' strategy. Typical of their exchanges is one in which Cal questions the schoolteacher's use of a flip metaphor to describe the PIRA's efforts to eject the Brits from Ireland: 'How can you compare blowing somebody's brains out to a squeaking chair?' In reply, Skeffington simply shrugs his shoulders, and blithely invokes future 'history' in support of his view: 'That's the way it will look in a hundred years' time' (66). At Cal's retort that 'You have no feelings', he is outraged. Counter-attacking, Skeffington plays the Mother Ireland card as a way of demonstrating his sensitivity and patriotism. He recites lines from 'The Mother', a poem composed by Padraic Pearse just before his execution. Only a few months before Mac Laverty embarked on the first draft of *Cal*, Owen Carron at Bobby Sands' funeral had spoken of how the hunger-striker's mother epitomised a sacred tradition amongst 'Irish mothers who in every generation watched their children go out and die for freedom':[184]

> 'I do not grudge them: Lord, I do not grudge
> My two strong sons that I have seen go out
> To break their strength and die, they and a few,
> In bloody protest for a glorious thing ...
>
> And yet I have my joy:
> My sons were faithful and they fought'
> 'Unlike you, Cahal'. (66)

Cal's response is to dispute the validity of an interpretation of history which reads the current armed struggle as a simple continuation of the War of Independence, and of a literary aesthetics in time of war which omits 'the shit and the guts and the tears'. Skeffington dismisses the latter as 'not part of history', and, as if to confirm the charge that he regards the loss of individual human lives as of a little consequence within that grand narrative, he comments on how good it would be for recruitment 'If only they would let the Paras loose in Derry again' (67).[185] Impassioned, and determined to have the last word, he invokes Bloody Sunday as providing incontrovertible evidence that 1916 and 1972 form one single narrative in which the common factor is repressiveness and malevolence of the British:

> They had us cowering behind a wall . There was an old man lying in the open. In the rush one of his socks had come off and he was lying on its side. There was a big hole in the heel of his sock. Can you believe that? Will that be recorded in the history books? ... And we were all Irishmen living in our own country. *They* were the trespassers'. (67: original emphasis)

The teacher's scepticism over what 'the history books' will choose to preserve is indicative of militant republicans' deep suspicion of the intellectual establishment and *its* politics; he subscribes to the Althusserian view of academia as a branch of the ideological state apparatus. From this perspective the decision to bomb the library at the novel's close, on the grounds that it represents 'Government property' (145), has a rationale behind it. Readers, however, are clearly meant to regard it as an act of breathtaking stupidity, and indicative of the Provisionals' fascist, philistine tendencies.[186] Followed up immediately by Crilly's account of how he kneecapped a 16-year-old joy-rider (147), the library attack exemplifies the way in which Mac Laverty's narrative offers correctives to the compassion and sympathy which republicanism accrued in the world outside the text during the extended pain of the hunger strikes. Avoiding a direct engagement with that still raw, immediate hurt, the text recalls its analogue, Bloody Sunday, but then, 60 pages later, sets that in the scales opposite its 'Other', the Birmingham bombings (126–7).[187]

Skeffington is convinced, as Cal is,[188] the conflict could be swiftly ended by a 'British' withdrawal. Nowhere does either acknowledge that for the Protestant majority in Northern Ireland it is their country too, or that without some kind of political 'understanding' with unionists there will never be any prospect of resolution, or indeed progress towards the goal they crave. Significantly none of *Cal's* Protestant characters (Robert Morton, his parents, Cyril Dunlop, the Preacher) receives sympathetic treatment.[189] Yet their very *presence* in the text, as antagonists and as objects of Catholic animosity, alongside Carson, Craig and Paisley (73), is what makes complete and lasting unity 'an unattainable idea' (92), as Marcella is for Cal. To claim, as Kennedy-Andrews does, that *Cal* is not 'a political novel'[190] is to ignore the extent to which it is permeated by the competing, confused ideological perspectives of the early 1980s.[191]

Perhaps one of the text's least convincing aspects, as Mac Laverty has himself acknowledged, is its central romantic relationship and its presentation of Marcella. In an interview with Robert Allen, the author describes her as a 'thin, almost cardboard' figure, and attributes the weakness of her characterisation to the decision he made about the novel's focalisation, his wish to get 'inside this young guy's head'.[192] Even to Cal, Marcella is not a realised individual, but largely an emblem, an object capable of performing a range of desirable physical, psychological and moral functions. She serves as a locus for his feelings of guilt, but also of his dreams of atonement: 'He wanted to put his arms around her and to apologise to her' (107), 'He wanted to confess to her, to weep and be forgiven' (119). Socially and intellectually, she is his superior in class and education; she occupies a substantial property, and her cultural world consists of texts such as *Crime and Punishment* (107) and Grünewald's paintings (109). Marcella is a construct he assembles to replace two key absences, that of his mother and of his belief in the rightness of the struggle. Repeatedly she is depicted metonymically, voyeuristically perceived as a series of body parts.[193] In his confused, adolescent imagination, she simultaneously embodies sexual possibilities – she is an exotic, mantilla-clad, Mediterranean, experienced woman – and innocence. She rarely features in the text without her double, her small daughter, and reference being made to the intimate bond between the two; thus during the blackberry-picking scene, Cal observes enviously how 'they remained snugly together at the waist' (104).

One of the most perceptive critics of 'Troubles' fiction, Joe Cleary, has observed how many of 'these narratives represent a strange amalgam of romance and domestic fiction in which a political tale of the "national romance" kind and an antipolitical tale of escape into domestic privacy are often combined or overlapped'. Generally, he argues, the initial political thrust in these texts wanes, as attention shifts decisively towards 'the sexual union of the lovers' which 'can be achieved only by renouncing politics altogether'.[194] The extent to which this is applicable to *Cal* is debatable. In the pre-determined world its lovers are placed in,[195] romance has little prospect of enduring; like Maire and Yolland's, their relationship cannot escape 'history'; it haunts their love-making, unignorable like the spectral husband in Zola's *Thérèse Raquin*.[196] Explicit intertextual allusions to Rapunzel, Quasimodo and the Sleeping Beauty (115; 124; 124, 155), lines such as 'the kiss had broken the spell' (133), all lend credence to Kennedy-Andrews's categorisation of the text as part-'fairytale'.[197] Had he qualified the noun by adding the word 'Grimm', his allocation of *Cal* to the romance genre might have gained in credibility. Cal's rescripting of the Sleeping Beauty narrative, in which he imagines Marcella in 'a drugged coma' (124), is, as Haslam points out, deeply disturbing and illustrates 'incipiently necrophiliac'[198] traits in his psyche.

Cal is very much a text of its time, its characters habitualised[199] to cruelty and suffering, as a result not only of their recent past, but also of the sadistic and masochistic strains running through their culture. In the course of his upbringing, Cal, like most of the nationalist community at large, has become attuned to the merits of sacrifice and self-mortification, disseminated both by Catholic clerics and, more lately, by republican ideologues, none of whom appear capable of ever generating a positive vision. Given his early exposure to his mother's 'iron' belief and practices of self-denial (105), it is hardly surprising that Cal should be so receptive to the sermon on Matt Talbot (36), the reformed sinner who sought sal-vation by encasing his flesh in chains. For Cal, for much of the narrative, self-harm seems a way of constricting 'forbidden' sexual desire, hence his reflections on 'saints who slept on boards' (79), 'hair-shirts' (93, 102), the offering-up of pain (105), and his willingness to wear first damp (93) and later a dead man's clothes (101–2). That his last expressed desire should be for 'someone … to beat him within an inch of his life' (154) is entirely consonant with the ideologies that have shaped him; in his mind he deserves nothing less for the murder he committed, the decep-tions and betrayals he has perpetrated.

Critiquing PIRA ideological paradigms around the time of the first hunger strikes, Richard Kearney notes how the republican 'sacrificial victim must undergo his passion and crucifixion before arising to liber-ate his community from its bondage'.[200] For the lapsed, dejected Cal at the novel's close, there is not a remote chance of rising again or reinte-gration after his passion. Significantly his final moments with Marcella include one in which she displays for him 'Grünewald's picture of Christ crucified … the body with its taut ribcage … the flesh diseased with sores … the mouth open and gasping for breath' (153).

The short-term effect of the hunger strike crisis was first to consolidate, and then extend traditional republican, colonial readings of Northern Ireland within the alienated nationalist community. In another succinct, percep-tive statement on the crisis, McKittrick and McVea comment that 'the extended trauma of the months of confrontation seared deep into the psy-ches of large numbers of people … Community divisions had always been deep, but now they had a new rawness'.[201] The idea persisted that the entire problem sprang from imperial Britain's obduracy in hanging on in Ireland, and that once Westminster agreed to leave 'the dark places' would be 'Ablaze with love'[202] in the Six Counties. For eight months the republican prisoners and British authorities had been preoccupied with a struggle to break the other's will, and had thus utterly marginalised the unionist com-munity and its concerns. No real progress could or can ever be achieved without confronting the issue of cultural and religious division within Northern Ireland, without Protestants and Catholics resolving to accept and respect *their* differences and 'equally legitimate, political aspirations'.[203]

Most importantly, the prison campaign had a profound and enduring impact on the republican movement's long-term strategy. Their success in mobilising 30 492 votes for Sands in April and attracting international coverage for their cause encouraged their leaders to reflect on the benefits electoral support might yield. As a result when the Fermanagh/South Tyrone by-election was scheduled for 20 August, they selected Sands' former election agent, Provisional Sinn Féin's Owen Carron, to fight the seat as the 'Anti-H-Block Proxy Political Prisoner' candidate. On an 88.6 per cent turnout, and with the SDLP declining to enter the field, Carron won comfortably, securing 786 more votes than Sands. Buoyed by this second triumph, three days later Sinn Féin announced their intention to contest future elections in the province. Confirmation that the party had shifted from their traditional abstentionist stance came later that autumn when at its annual *ard fheis*, Danny Morrison asked delegates, 'Who here believes we can win the war through the ballot box? But will anyone here object if with a ballot paper in one hand and the Armalite in the other, we take power in Ireland?'[204]

The polarisation in Northern Ireland's communities which the hunger strikes had exacerbated deepened in mid-November 1981 when the PIRA murdered the Reverend Robert Bradford, the Ulster Unionist MP for South Belfast and a Methodist minister, and a fierce opponent of republicanism. Three gunmen, dressed as workmen, entered his political surgery in Finaghy, killed an attendant and then shot Bradford several times as he sat at his desk.[205] James Prior's appearance at the MP's funeral was met with a barrage of abuse from loyalists who jostled him and banged on the roof of his car; some in the crowd shouted out, 'Kill him, kill him'. In a further expression of their intense sense of outrage, loyalists staged a 'day of action' on 23 November. Memorial services were conducted in several towns and in Newtonards a 'Third Force' rally drew an audience of almost 15 000 men. Ian Paisley threatened to mount tax and rent strikes in the province if drastic measures were not taken to tighten security.

Republican paramilitary violence, accompanied by gradual electoral advances by Sinn Féin were recurring features during the years 1982–85. Among the deadliest attacks, or 'spectaculars' in Army parlance,[206] were those that took place on 20 July 1982, when 11 soldiers were killed by two PIRA bombs in Knightsbridge and Regents Park, and on 7 December 1982, when the Droppin Well disco in Ballykelly, Co. Derry, was targeted by the INLA; 17 people (11 of them soldiers) died in the blast, most of them crushed by masonry when the bar's roof collapsed. Exactly a week before Christmas the following year, a 30lb PIRA bomb outside Harrods in London killed six people, including two police officers and a journalist, and injured over 100 others. The bombing which filled the headlines worldwide, however, was that which took place at the Grand Hotel, Brighton, in the early morning of 12 October 1984, during the

Conservative Party Conference. Planted by Patrick Magee, the 25 lb device claimed five lives, including those of Sir Anthony Berry MP and Roberta Wakeham, wife of the Tory Chief Whip. Thirty people suffered injuries, amongst the most serious, Margaret Tebbit, wife of the Industry Secretary. Margaret Thatcher, its principal target, survived unscathed and unbowed. In a statement addressed directly to her after the bombing, the IRA admitted, 'Today we were unlucky, but remember we have only to be lucky once'.[207]

Between 1982 and 1985 Sinn Féin contested four elections in Northern Ireland and began to campaign with greater conviction in the Republic. Alarm at their results in Westminster and the Dáil provided much of the impetus for the Anglo-Irish Agreement of November 1985, which would transform British–Irish relations and the whole course of the Troubles. The first test of Sinn Féin's popularity after Carron's August 1981 success came in Northern Ireland Assembly elections of October 1982. In this they gained just over 64 000 votes and 10.1 per cent of the first prefer-ence votes; this contrasted with the SDLP's relatively disappointing per-formance of 118 891 votes and 18.8 per cent share. In the General Election of 9 June 1983, Sinn Féin's Gerry Adams unseated the long-serving, former SDLP leader, Gerry Fitt, in West Belfast, and SF's share of the vote rose to 13.4 per cent, in contrast to the SDLP's 17.9 per cent. Just over a year later in the European Parliament elections of 1984, John Hume achieved 22.1 per cent of first preference votes in contrast to SF's Danny Morrison's 13.3 per cent showing. In District Council elections in mid-May 1985, the SDLP polled 17.8 per cent and SF 11.8 per cent (and 59 seats).[208]

Hardly surprisingly, John Hume, the SDLP leader, was at the forefront of those wishing to see Sinn Féin's progress checked. In contrast to the lack of responsiveness he repeatedly met in London, where his dealings with Margaret Thatcher and successive Conservative Secretaries of State yielded very little, Hume enjoyed considerable success in Dublin, where he established an excellent working relationship with the leaders of both main parties, Fianna Fail's Charles Haughey and Fine Gael's Garret FitzGerald. His lobbying bore fruit with the decision in March 1983 to establish the New Ireland Forum, a body which aimed to bring together constitu-tional parties from north and south in order to discuss ways in which 'last-ing peace and stability could be achieved' and 'to report on possible new structures and processes'[209] which might enable these objectives to be fulfilled. Disappointingly, three important northern parties, the UUP, DUP and Alliance, declined invitations to contribute to the Forum, while SF excluded themselves because of their unwillingness to renounce vio-lence. Garret FitzGerald, in his inaugural address to the Forum on 30 May

1983, argued that the parties assembled truly represented 'the nationalist people of Ireland'. The 'unambiguous message' they collectively wished to send out to the 'men of violence' was that 'the future of the island will be built by the ballot box and by the ballot box alone'.[210] Amongst the most significant contributions to the Forum was one authored by Kevin Boyle and Tom Hadden. They spelt out clearly that any settlement would have to acknowledge 'the respective rights and identities of the two communities in Northern Ireland' and that the pre-requisite for such a settlement would have to 'a new relationship' between and 'joint action'[211] by Britain and Ireland.

Collectively participants in the Forum played an important role in the reconfiguring of Irish identity, and in the growth of a greater degree of political and cultural inclusiveness in the Republic. Nationalists were encouraged to recognise that 'the key to the problem' in the North 'was not Britain but the Protestant community ... Irish unity could only come about with Protestant consent. The real border, it was now said, was not geographical but in men's minds'.[212] When the Forum finally published its Report proposing a united Ireland, or a federal Ireland, or joint British–Irish authority as ways of solving the northern crisis, all three options were immediately denounced by the UUP and DUP, and dismissed by Margaret Thatcher in what became known as her 'Out, out, out' speech of 19 November 1984.[213] Given that her comments were delivered to journalists at the end of a two-day Anglo-Irish summit at Chequers, at which progress had been made, FitzGerald felt humiliated. At a closed meeting of his party back in Dublin, he described Thatcher's attitude and response as 'gratuitously offensive'.[214] Realising that she had placed possibilities for better relations and improved border security in jeopardy, Thatcher sought to make amends.[215] It was agreed to set up a committee containing many of the most talented British and Irish civil servants tasked with drawing up a new, far-reaching accord between the two governments, which would boost the constitutional nationalist position, lessen alienation in the North's minority community, enhance security and reduce violence. Rumours that a major Anglo-Irish announcement was in the offing prompted protests by loyalists on 2 and 14 November 1985, but the unionist parties were completely unprepared for the scale and nature of changes incorporated in the document that the British and Irish Prime Ministers sat down to sign at Hillsborough Castle on 15 November.

Unionists could not object to Article 1a) and b) of the Agreement, in which the two governments affirmed that any change in the province's constitutional status 'would only come about with the consent of a majority of the people of Northern Ireland'.[216] Article 2, however, established an Intergovernmental Conference, a forum in which for the first time Irish ministers and officials would have the opportunity to discuss political and legal matters, security issues, and questions of cross-border co-operation with their British counterparts; in order to service the Conference a permanent secretariat of British and Irish civil servants would be established at Maryfield, to the east of Belfast. To many unionists' dismay, Article 4 stated that the powers currently held by the Secretary of State would only be devolved 'on a basis which would secure widespread acceptance throughout the community';[217] so, if unionists wanted a return to devolved self-government it could only be achieved through power-sharing.

In a highly rhetorical address to the Commons three days after the signing, the UUP's Harold McCusker[218] spoke for the majority of unionists who, at the time, had difficulty in coping with their sense of betrayal. Instead of upholding British sovereignty, as she had so recently done in the Falklands War, and safeguarding the Union, the Prime Minister had made concessions to the very people who 'coveted their land':

> I never knew what desolation felt like until I read this agreement last Friday afternoon ... I shall carry to my grave with ignominy the sense of injustice that I have done to my constituents down the years – when, in their darkest hours, I exhorted them to put their trust in the British House of Commons.[219]

Before the mid-November signing Jim Molyneaux, McCusker's leader, had rather complacently assumed that no Anglo-Irish deal was possible without unionist politicians having their say-so.[220] Wrong-footed, outraged, the UUP and DUP now combined forces to mount a massive demonstration against the Agreement at Belfast City Hall on 23 November, attracting a crowd estimated variously at between 100 000 and 200 000 people.

The following week, after a two-day debate in the House of Commons, the Anglo-Irish Agreement received cross-party approval by a massive margin of 473 votes to 47.[221] Defeated at Westminster, unionist opponents of the Agreement quickly resorted to extra-parliamentary means to assert their will as they had so often before.[222] First, however, all 15 unionist MPs resigned their seats in order to force by-elections which they believed would demonstrate the strength of hostility in the Protestant community. In the event this strategy proved at best a partial success; they did secure 418 230 votes for their anti-Agreement stance, but lost one of their seats to the SDLP.[223] On the day that the Intergovernmental

Conference was scheduled to meet for the first time, 11 December 1985, serious clashes between loyalist protestors and the RUC at Stormont and at Maryfield left 38 officers injured.

Spring and summer 1986 again saw the RUC bearing the brunt of loyalist rage and frustration. On 3 March 1986, Jim Molyneaux and Ian Paisley called a 'day of action', but instead of the dignified, peaceful protest they may have been hoping for there were riots which resulted in 47 policemen requiring medical treatment and over 230 complaints about intimidation. Some of the worst disturbances that month occurred in Portadown, when on Easter Monday a banned Apprentice Boys' parade confronted a police cordon on the Catholic Garvaghy Road, a site of major conflict over the next decade and a half. In the course of the clashes which spilled into the following day, a 20-year-old Protestant, Keith White, was struck in the head by a plastic bullet while hurling missiles at the RUC; he died a fortnight later, without regaining consciousness.[224] Following the March day of action and the Portadown riots, attacks by loyalist gangs on police homes and their families became a regular occurrence. By late May, over 500 homes had been affected, and 150 families had been forced to flee. Unlike his deputy, Peter Robinson, Ian Paisley was forthright in his condemnation of such attacks which ceased soon after.[225]

The Secretary of State's decision to dissolve the Northern Ireland Assembly triggered further clashes in late June and July, unionist politicians seeing in the move further evidence of the British government's contempt towards them and their democratic mandate. Paisley, along with 18 DUP and three UUP members, refused to leave the building, and had to be forcibly ejected by the RUC. Already reviled by large sections of the British media, he was caught on camera shouting at the four officers who had borne him out, 'Don't come crying to me the next time your houses are attacked'.[226] Later that same day, he claimed that Northern Ireland was now 'on the verge of civil war' and urged unionists to mobilise to defend 'to the last drop of blood' their 'British and Ulster heritage'.[227]

As the climax of the marching season approached, Portadown again became the scene of clashes on 6 and 11 July, and, on 10 July, 4000 loyalists, led by Paisley and Robinson, occupied Hillsborough. Fearing worse loyalist violence, the RUC Chief Constable and Secretary of State Tom King succumbed to pressure and allowed the Portadown Orangemen to march down the Garvaghy Road on the Twelfth. This 'triumph' was swiftly followed by an upsurge in sectarian attacks on Catholic homes, churches and housing estates, along with increased assaults on the police. On 12, 14 and 20 July, three young Belfast Catholics were shot in random attacks by the UVF, leading Cahal Daly, Bishop of Down and Connor, to denounce the way 'the innocent on both sides are being used as pawns in a struggle for political leadership in both communities ... There are politicians, both clerical and lay, whose violent words have helped create a climate conducive to violent deeds'.[228]

Early November found Paisley again flirting with paramilitary activity. On the tenth, shortly before the first anniversary of the signing of the Anglo-Irish Agreement, he founded a new body called Ulster Resistance, whose purpose would be 'to take direct action as and when required'.[229] The following day, 2000 of its members, sporting red berets and military jackets, took part in a parade in Kilkeel, Co. Down. More impressively, over 200 000 unionists gathered for the anniversary rally at Belfast City Hall on 15 November, though the impact of the event was marred when loyalist youths went on a rampage in the city centre, looting and damaging over 70 shops. Two days of rioting ensued, in the course of which an innocent 29-year-old Protestant, Alan McCormick, was fatally injured in North Belfast by a police Land Rover, and a 68-year-old Catholic, Alice Kelly, died of heart failure, after a missile struck her home in Carrickfergus.[230]

As 1986 drew to a close, the militant republican movement was again in the throes of momentous change. Addressing a press conference soon after its signing, Gerry Adams recognised that the Anglo-Irish Agreement was motivated by a desire 'to isolate and defeat republicans'.[231] However, as Richard English points out, while Sinn Féin retained a total antipathy towards partition and the British presence to which now, in effect, Dublin assented, they welcomed the concessions their struggle had extracted from the British.[232] In order to help advance Sinn Féin's republican agenda in the Republic, on 14 October the IRA's General Army Convention formally resolved to break with abstentionism and permit elected SF members to take their seats in the Dáil. These proposals were again discussed at the Sinn Féin *ard fheis* held on 2 November, but met with fierce resistance from Ruairí Ó Brádaigh and Dáithi Ó Conaill. When it came to the vote the Adams–McGuinness anti-abstentionist line was supported by 429 delegates, and opposed by 161. One of those observing the debate, Michael Farrell, predicted that the IRA and Sinn Féin might well experience a great awakening as a result of their involvement in constitutional politics:

> When the movement was almost purely military, its leaders had little contact with the mass of the population ... Political campaigning inevitably brings them in contact with a much wider spectrum of

opinion. That may make them more sensitive to the effects of IRA actions on the public at large, and may lead to changes in the IRA's strategy.[233]

One other highly significant development dating from 1986 was the removal of John Stalker, Deputy Chief Constable of Greater Manchester, from an inquiry into an alleged 'shoot to kill' policy by the security forces. The Stalker case, like the cases he attempted to investigate, provides a useful reminder that the history of Northern Ireland, is, like any other history, not simply a sequence of verifiable 'facts', but something which will always retain 'cores of uncertainty'.[234] What had prompted Stalker's appointment was a growing controversy over the circumstances surrounding a series of shootings during the winter of 1982 carried out by a firearms squad which belonged either to the RUC's Special Support Unit (SSU) or to the Headquarters Mobile Support Unit (HMSU).[235]

The first of these so-called 'shoot to kill' incidents came in the aftermath of the murder of three RUC police officers. Sean Quinn, Alan McCloy and Paul Hamilton were killed when their car was blown to pieces by a PIRA landmine at Kinnego, near Lurgan. Shortly afterwards, an informer is said to have tipped off the RUC that two local PIRA men, Sean Burns and Eugene Toman, were responsible for the bombing. A fortnight later, on 11 November, Burns and Toman, along with a third PIRA man, were killed when their car was struck by over a hundred bullets fired by the SSU/HMSU unit. Toman was shot through the heart after stumbling from the vehicle. In their original account of events, the police claimed that the paramilitaries' car had crashed through a roadblock, though subsequently it emerged that the men, all of whom were unarmed, had been under surveillance for some time.

The explosives used to kill the three RUC men at Kinnego came from a cache hidden in a hayshed in Ballyneery, near Craigavon, which, it subsequently emerged, had been bugged by MI5 *prior to* the bombing. The shed, however, had also been placed under surveillance by the RUC. On 24 November, Michael Tighe, a 17-year-old Catholic with no connections to the paramilitaries, visited the hayshed with another man, whom Mark Urban identifies as 19-year-old Martin McCauley.[236] After watching them go inside, HMSU officers opened fire, killing Tighe in a hail of bullets and seriously injuring McCauley.

The third shooting, like the first, followed a republican paramilitary bombing, the devastating attack on the Droppin Well.[237] On 12 December, two unarmed INLA men, Seamus Grew and Roddy Carroll were stopped in their car near the border and shot dead. An HMSU officer killed Carroll first and then walked round the vehicle to the driver's door and shot Grew. Initially journalists were told that Grew and Carroll had driven through a roadblock, hitting a policeman. In fact the INLA men had been tailed by the RUC's E4A surveillance unit all day, and were ambushed when they crossed back into Northern Ireland from the Republic.

The Director of Public Prosecutions (DPP) directed that four officers involved in these six deaths should face trial. This took place on 29 March 1984, but all four were acquitted of murder. The presiding judge, Lord Justice Gibson, courted controversy not only by criticising the DPP's decision to prosecute, but also by praising the RUC officers for their 'determination in bringing the three deceased men to justice'.[238] The outcry over the judge's remarks was followed by an announcement in late May 1984 that John Stalker would conduct a full investigation into the 'shoot to kill' allegations. From the moment he arrived, Stalker encountered a lack of co-operation from the highest echelons of the RUC, many of whom were clearly anxious that 'sensitive material' from covert operations might find its way into the public domain. Key files and interviewees sought by the inquiry suddenly became unavailable and at one stage the Chief Constable, Sir John Hermon, even returned Stalker's letters unopened.[239] After two years' painstaking work, Stalker was suddenly recalled to Manchester in June 1986 to face disciplinary charges, which were later proven to be wholly groundless. Neither his nor his replacement's report were ever published, yet Stalker later concluded in his memoir that there had been 'an inclination, if not a policy, to shoot suspects dead without warning rather than arrest them',[240] and that all six deaths might have been unlawful killings. He was not alone in suspecting that his removal from the inquiry was a result of a conspiracy to prevent RUC officers from facing prosecution.[241] Stalker's claim that the RUC contained elements which were 'out of control'[242] would later be taken up as a central premise in Ken Loach's controversial film, *Hidden Agenda* (1990).

The whole murky affair placed considerable strain on post-Agreement Anglo-Irish relations, since it inevitably undermined belief in British justice and provoked, in Richard English's words, fundamental questions

about the state's use of lethal force and about its unpreparedness to investigate possible abuses in a thorough and open manner. The state, in Weberian manner, identified itself as holding a monopoly over legitimate force. But what if a democratic state used force in arbitrary and extra-legal ways, killing members of its population in dubious circumstances, and then refusing adequately to investigate those circumstances? Could the distinction between legal force and illegal paramilitarism remain crisp after such episodes?[243]

In the years that followed, rumours and allegations that members of the security forces had colluded with loyalist paramilitary killers would continue to act as a major source of contention.

III   Fiction, drama and poetry (1980–1986)

Since the mid-1960s – and indeed long before – poetry had been the preeminent literary genre in Northern Irish literature. Although poets like Hewitt, Montague and Simmons in poetry continued to produce important work and command considerable influence and respect, the dominant generation for much of the 1970s was that of Heaney, Longley, and Mahon, all of whom were in their late-20s when the crisis in the province took hold. Their achievements and that of Friel, the North's outstanding dramatist, served as a source of inspiration and verification for a new wave of writers, almost all of them belonging to post-war generations, which began to make its mark in the late 1970s and early 1980s. What is particularly significant in the period immediately following the hunger strikes is the sudden blossoming in fiction that occurred, the quickening in the cultural debate in reaction to Field Day's arrival, and the increasing impact of women writers on Northern Ireland's evolving literature.[244] Amongst the texts contributing to this significant reconfiguration in Northern Irish fiction were Ruth Hooley's pioneering anthology, *The Female Line* (1985), Linda Anderson's *Cuckoo* (1986), Frances Molloy's *No Mate for the Magpie* (1985), Mary Beckett's *Give Them Stones* (1987), and three texts by Una Woods, Anne Devlin (b.1951) and Deirdre Madden (b.1960) considered here.

Fiction: Una Woods, *The Dark Hole Days*; Anne Devlin, 'Naming the Names'; Deirdre Madden, *Hidden Symptoms*

In terms of narrative structure Una Woods's *The Dark Hole Days* (1984)[245] is more intricate than any of the previous fictional texts examined, deploying alternating first-person narrators for the most part, except for a protracted section just before its climax in which third-person narration is used. By means of parallel diary entries, images of the lives and interior landscapes of the two main characters are gradually, but partially disclosed. For, despite the intimacy of its narrative form, the novella retains a reticence, an unease at the self-exposure writing involves, a fear of 'giving too much away' (37) which both the characters and their author share.[246] It is only in the final pages that the reader discovers the appalling way their lives intersect.

Unnamed until pages 33 and 49, its protagonists, Colette and Joe, are jobless, vulnerable, working-class teenagers, like Mac Laverty's Cal. Like him, they dream of assuming control of the present and future, yet experience feelings of guilt at needing individuation. In domestic circumstances, in education, in maturity, and in the routes they pursue to escape constraints, they differ greatly. Colette belongs to a large Catholic family, is academically able and has aspirations to become a writer. Her journal is largely preoccupied with internal family problems and the ambivalence she feels towards her relationship with her boyfriend, Matt. From Belfast's Protestant community, Joe is fatherless.[247] An only child, he is desperate to detach himself from his emotionally dependent mother, and reach the state of 'manhood'. By acquiring a distinct function in the community as one of its 'protectors' (45), Joe hopes to rid himself of the burden and stigma of being unemployed.[248] Throughout, his diary is a much more adolescent affair than Colette's, filled as it is with coded allusions to paramilitary activity, anxieties about his controller's sexually predatory 'girlfriend', Vera, and fantasies about a nameless girl who works at the dole office.

Colette's initial entries portray the strain of life in mid-1970s Belfast, where there is little respite from uncertainty and fear. The opening sentence voices a widespread conviction that 'it's all about to blow up again', and is followed by a dismissive reference to 'initiatives', a term redolent of political failure. The intrusiveness of the crisis is registered in her brief account of her night out with Matt and homecoming; walking back from the cinema, she notes how 'we were a bit nervous'. Although she associates home with security ('Mam doesn't rest till the door's closed and we're all safe'), she also presents it as claustrophobic. Privacy for the couple is out of the question given the presence of her younger siblings 'milling around', wanting 'to see everything' (1). Symptomatic of the tensions circulating in the family and the city are the 'rings round' the eyes of her brothers and sisters, and the political discussion in which her father, Pete and Chuck are engaged, during which the latter attributes blame for the continuing divisions and violence to the politicians and the media.

Despite Joe's leaden attempts to mask how he passed *his* evening, it is obvious from the outset that he has become involved with loyalist paramilitaries, not least by the way he denotes time, ('0130 hours', '1300 hours'). Associating with them bolsters his sense of identity and self-worth, enables him to become 'part of something' and thus enter 'history' (2). In contrast to the nationalist family and acquaintances who *talk* about the political vacuum (1, 16), the young men with whom Joe mixes are committed to filling it, by taking 'action'. Joe's language betrays the extent to which he has already assimilated the rhetoric of the militants, who seek to project an image of themselves as a defenderist force, there to 'protect'[249] the unionist community. (It subsequently transpires that members of Joe's cell engage in arbitrary assassination attacks on Catholics like Colette's father). Mention of his father's early death (4) partly explains his need for male company and approval, but also evokes a degree of sympathy for him.

An aspect of northern Protestant culture to which the text frequently returns is its negativity towards women.[250] This is particularly reflected in Joe's attitude towards his mother, whom he generally views with a mixture of disbelief, condescension and contempt. Realising after a conversation with Gerry his ignorance of current political developments, Joe asks his mother what has been happening. However, when she tries to tell him about the latest initiative, he reacts rudely: 'Is that all, I said, and came up here. As Sam says, they haven't a clue'. Seconds later, in what at first seems a gesture of atonement, he decides to fill the coal bucket for her, having remembered that 'the hero's always good to women, so long as they don't get in the way of the work' (15).

One of the difficulties besetting Woods is how to sustain equal interest in both protagonists. As a result of his early subscription to and in the 'grand narrative', Joe remains a fairly static character until the novel's traumatic end. As a member of a secret, illegal, organisation, he is understandably reluctant to commit anything substantial to paper apart from the crass names where they rendezvous, like Hanky-Panky Alley (12) and Starker's Strip (19). Naïvely he imagines that he is important to the cell, one of the 'chosen' (25), and although he constantly expects summonses from his controller, Sam, these rarely materialise. Consequently, one of the week's highlights is his brief encounter with a clerk at the dole office where he 'signs on'. He convinces himself that she 'respects me', 'can see my dignity' (14), and that one day his feelings might be reciprocated. According to Sam, however, sexual relationships are a distraction from the 'bigger good' (11); so, when a fellow loyalist, Gerry, spots a girl he fancies, Sam piously intervenes, telling him that 'there'll be plenty of time for all that' (6), after the war is won.[251] Nevertheless, Joe persists in his partly-romantic, partly-sexual fantasies about the dole-clerk, which come to a head during his excursion to Bangor. In contrast to the very 'real' Gerty Mac Dowell who Leopold Bloom glimpsed on Sandymount beach, Joe's woman is a complete illusion, born of holiday advertising and Hollywood clichés. The episode again exposes the character's shallowness and immaturity, yet also the 'intense 'loneliness' that marks his life:

> She was facing outward, paddling in the water up to her ankles, hoisting up her skirt, even though there was no need to ... She turned towards him, shyly at first and then ran, spraying water from each foot in turn, and they were laughing and holding each other in a wilderness where only they mattered. (48)

Colette emerges as a far more engaging and developed individual, because of her propensity to question her own responses, and the culture and values that surround her. Early on, looking down on the 'wilderness' (3) of the estate, Colette sees something inchoate, yet infinitely various.[252] 'In every house there's a story' (3), she speculates, and dreams of being the mediator of those stories. For her, as for her author, writing becomes a way of envisaging and embracing other 'possibilities' (22), selves and places. Emblematic of this desire is the new suit she covets, which she imagines wearing for 'strolling in the country' (5), and the later trip to Birmingham where she hopes to gain a clearer perspective on herself, Matt, her troubled 'home'. She aims in her writing 'to capture a quality of ordinary life' (11), and indeed presents a far fuller picture of her immediate community and the differentiation within it than her opposite number, Joe. An attentive observer and listener, she chronicles the crisis's debilitating effect on her siblings, how Barney's schoolwork deteriorates, how Madge and Pete eat and drink to excess as a form of 'escape' (16, 20). Another casualty to whom she draws attention is their neighbour's daughter, Laura Munroe. 'Led back' (25) to Belfast by her family after two years free of care in Australia, she suffers a breakdown, and is found shivering by the roadside on the way to Aldegrove. Sitting in a café later that same day, Colette and her mother reflect on 'the sickness' afflicting the city: 'I had a feeling of being one with the people of this place, of this time, maimed by it all and not able to do anything about it' (27). Frequently, she notes in her diary the political debates that take place in her home, such as Chuck's contention that Northern Ireland should be re-partitioned because of the intransigence in both traditions: 'until everybody realises you can't change people's minds we'll get nowhere' (18). Whereas her father endorses the idea of political experimentation ('anything new is worth trying at this stage'), her mother asserts that economics is central to the problem. If unemployment were addressed, 'there's many who'd leave it at that' (18).

As the young woman's experience as a diarist extends, and her search for personal meaning intensifies, the complexity of her language grows. Increasingly she deploys metaphors as a way of articulating the unsettling joy she is experiencing, brought about by the prospect of leaving Belfast. Sensing her brother Pete's resentment at her imminent escape, she compares him to a 'black hole in the sand' filled by the tide, and 'bound to overflow' (32). Like the act of writing, the visit to Birmingham generates ambivalent feelings, and exposes an at times painful, disabling indeterminacy within her. It offers the 19-year-old a major opportunity to test herself by displacing herself, yet while the thought of 'branching out, just lifting up' (13) excites her, she is anxious about making a wrong decision in committing herself to Matt. Witnessing how 'at home' her mother appears to be 'with herself' (5), Colette wonders whether she should 'want more' than a settled relationship. Although she thinks she loves Matt, like many women elsewhere during the 1970s and 1980s, she recognises her need for a space to be herself, and fears having her identity subsumed by marriage. Unconsciously paraphrasing Joyce, who was similarly embarking on a critical departure, she asks 'Can there be many who understand me?' (20)[253]

To convey the estrangement Colette feels in being away in Birmingham, a switch to third person narrative occurs, though the focalisation remains solely from her perspective. To protect herself in this unfamiliar situation and surroundings, she retreats deep inside herself, adopts a role: 'she stepped inside the person who was waiting on the platform' (33). It is only in this section that her Christian name is revealed, and Matt metamorphoses into the more formal Matthew. Amongst the many things that disconcert her in Birmingham is the way her hosts, Matt's brother, Christopher, and his partner, Lin, exhibit so openly their physical obsession with each other: 'It upset Colette who thought, we don't do things like that in Belfast' (37).[254] Alone in the bedroom she will shortly share with Matthew, her mood fluctuates between 'anticipation of the stranger who would enter the room' and unease at 'being taken for what she maybe wasn't' (38) – his sexual property? Conscious that Matt regards the utterly domesticised, uncomplicated relationship Christopher and Lin apparently enjoy as model of what theirs might be, Colette rebels: 'If you want that with me you'll never have it' (41). Although subsequently she relaxes when they all eat out together, the Birmingham visit ends in a row, with Matt storming off to the pub alone. Instead of bringing them together, the trip emphasises how apart they are. To underline this fact, the images used to depict their return crossing are predominantly sombre; the sea is 'a huge blob of rippling ink', a 'dark blue desert', something cut and yet 'intact' (43). After Colette announces that they are 'nowhere', Matt clings on to her, 'as if afraid she might be sucked into black force of air and water' (43). Briefly, she wishes she could again lie with and 'in the warm *shape*' (44; my emphasis), but what lasts longer is her guilt at having failed to ask anyone about a job for her brother Pete.

Unsettled by the time away, Colette is unable to become reassimilated into her Belfast estate. Her deflation, along with a new feeling of alienation, are conveyed in an accumulation of gloomy images ('shade', 'dulled', 'drab', 'squatted', 'lowering', 'descending' (51)). When she first depicted herself 'looking down' on her home area, the verb referred only to a physical standpoint (3); on her return, however, it expresses a class position. She resents the 'commonness' and 'loudness' of children's voices, and their accents, and the press of other presences in her own home. Where once 'in every house' she sensed 'a story' (3), now she sees only a pervasive pettiness:

> And from house to house unimportant people lived unimportant lives, and around the city unimportant people were killing equally unimportant people … They were like little sparrows chirping around and pecking at each other to get at a few paltry crumbs, unable to see the open sky above them. (51)

As if to illustrate her point, a clash breaks out in her home over a game of darts, after the drunken, depressed Pete fails to get his darts to reach the board. When her father – largely an fairly anonymous authority figure up until now – manfully restrains Pete from hitting his brother, Denny, Colette notices, as if for the first time, a solidity and 'a strength in him which she admired' (53).

No sooner has she declares her fixed intention to go to England or Scotland, places not 'swamped with tears over country, territory, crown, religion, flags' (52), than she and her family are overwhelmed by tragedy, her father's murder. Her last diary entry records her father's funeral at which the rain 'never let up and I could find no break in the clouds'. What little autonomy she had seems forever lost. Instead of writing it herself, her future has been written over: 'We're stamped as victims now. We'll always be the victims of the troubles, and I thought I was before'. Her concluding metaphor directs the reader's attention back to the text's title; her native city and native province are a pit, 'The pit of mourning' (58).

At the text's close, Joe also faces into the darkness, and the prospect of 'one dark hole day' (60) succeeding another. In his remaining entries, it comes to light that he was a member of a loyalist murder squad which kidnapped and killed Colette's father. At the critical moment when their innocent, random target was being bundled into the car, Joe threw down his gun and fled (56). Fearing retribution because of his act of betrayal, he goes underground literally, hiding under the floorboards at his home. Into this confined space Joe takes with him his memory and an imaginary 'black and white snapshot' of the murdered man. Joe believes 'They would live together' (56), as surely as his mother does with her ghostly partner, his father. Necessity compels him into reconfiguring his relationship with his mother, as 'Only she could bring the food' and prise up 'the floorboards to hand it down' (57). In a darkly ironic turnaround, *he* is utterly dependent on *her*, and it is the thought of her, rather than the dole-clerk, that evokes 'a warm tingle of excitement'. At the same time in his imagination, she acquires a religious aura, comes to personify the chance of a saving grace: 'Already he saw her face looking down on him ... She would be like an angel with the light all around her' (57).[255] Yet, to the reader his angle of vision resembles that of a helpless baby staring up at its half-divine provider. And this is central to Una Woods's slant on Northern Ireland's tragedy, in which sectarian hatreds preclude possibilities for individuation, maturation, open skies. And it is with constraint that the novella ends. After dreaming a hereafter for himself in which he finally walks free, he comes up against 'a dead end', 'the realization' that there may be 'no exit'.[256] Set alone and apart, his postscript is bleak and arresting: 'All thoughts stop with Sam' (64).

A story of murder, sexuality, class, politics, deceptions and self-deceptions, 'Passages', the opening story of Anne Devlin's collection, *The Way Paver* (1986), provides a useful starting-point from which to approach 'Naming the Names', one of the most skilfully-constructed and disturbing pieces in the history of Northern Irish fiction. Like *The Dark Hole Days* and *Hidden Symptoms*, Devlin's stories are highly self-reflexive, and constantly foreground issues of narrative. As an analyst, the frame-narrator in 'Passages' spends his days interpreting intimacies, eavesdropping on others' lives and dreams, exploring what Finnula in 'Naming the Names' refers to as 'the dark corners of all rooms'.[257] In an observation which bears on the later text, he points out how tellers often implicate listeners in their guilts and transgressions, leaving part of their burden with them: 'dreams are very confessional; they offer a power relationship to the hearer in that they ask for absolution. They are a freeing device for the speaker, but the sin has to rest with someone' (4). 'Naming the Names' is in effect a confession, one delivered without prospect of absolution. In this, as in so many Northern Irish literary texts of the Troubles period, religious faith and any suggestion of spiritual solace are absent. It is only towards the story's close that the reader becomes conscious of the terrible crime for which the speaker is responsible and the context in which she delivers her account.

Eschewing a realist mode, Devlin employs 'a discontinuous structure', 'a jagged chronology'.[258] By means of 'jumps, anticipations and flashbacks',[259] Finnula McQuillen, a parentless young woman from Catholic West Belfast, proffers her account of her fatal relationship with 'history'. Brought up primarily at her grandmother's, she is made homeless during the burnings-out of August 1969. What prompts her involvement with the IRA, however, is the introduction of internment in August 1971, an event which coincides with the end of an affair with a British journalist, Jack McHenry. Acting on behalf of the IRA, she secures the confidence of a Protestant judge's son who by chance visits the bookshop where she works. Their relationship develops to such an extent that she falls in love with him. Yet, despite this, she finally lures him to his death in the park, which was once her 'playplace' (105) as a child.[260] Finn's mind and body become sites of a collision between individualist, transgressive impulses (manifest first in her 'screwing around like there was no tomorrow' (113), later by her intense relationships with a British media-man and a history student from a privileged unionist background) and familial-cultural-political loyalties, the latter quickened by sectarian violence and British government policy in Northern Ireland.

'Naming the Names' opens puzzlingly with an unidentified narrator reciting an unexplained litany of names: 'Abyssinia, Alma, Bosnia, Balaclava, Belgrade, Bombay' (95). Subsequently it transpires that these are West Belfast street names, which featured in a skipping-song Finn associates with her lost, unhappy childhood, but also her reeling off of this ABC is a way of blocking her interrogators' attempts to make her name her IRA contacts. Named after sites where imperial powers fought one another or struggled to suppress native resistance, the streets bear the imprint of a riven past, but also signs of recent conflict.[261] Unable to define herself, the names constitute for her a network of absence, a web of remembered relationships, which sustain, but also confine her. Ironically, in trying to map her home territory, she is compelled into using alien, imposed signs, thereby compounding her feelings of displacement and exile.

The story's second and third sentences add to the reader's disorientation: 'It was late summer – August, like the summer of the fire. He hadn't rung for three weeks' (95). While at first appearing to conform to conventional narrative strategy by providing the time of year, in fact the lines impede understanding, since they prompt a series of questions. Which year? What fire? Who hadn't rung? Why the delay? No sooner is one time reference established – late summer, August – before its shadow appears, 'the summer of the fire'. An initial impression that this might be the beginning of a story of summer love is strengthened by the introduction in the fourth paragraph of the four tramps, with their '*ménage à quatre*', in which Tom and Harry love Isabella, but no one loves Eileen.[262]

The third paragraph locates the narrator on the Catholic Falls Road, in a setting that bears several signs of instability, acts of substitution. The claim printed above the 'reconverted cinema' where she works is false, she informs us. The bookshop's success came as a result of the local library being fire-bombed. Finn's working day is spent immersed in texts, encircled by narratives, many of which are on the move. Juxtaposed with the 'vast collection of historical manuscripts, myths and legends, political pamphlets' (95) is lighter, more popular fare, the crime novels, westerns, romances, readers purchase and bring in to swap. On first reading the irony of Finn's peripheral involvement in 'an exchange service' is not apparent, only later it emerges that she is fulfilling just such a role for the IRA.

Attention is drawn once more towards the mysterious, unnamed male who preoccupies Finn's thoughts by placing her question, 'I wonder if he'll ring today', in the middle of a verbal exchange between Finn's named colleague (Chrissie), and the named, child customer (Sharleen), who wants 'three murders for my granny' (96). It is not until the second section (97–8) that information is provided about this man, and then by means of a catalogue of written texts ('Senior: *Orangeism in Britain and Ireland*; Sibbett: *Orangeism in Ireland and Throughout the Empire*'), which both complement *and* clash with the names in Finn's opening 'spoken' list. Five lines into the section there is a curious comment whose significance can only be grasped when the story is re-read and Finn's role in the IRA known: 'I looked at the name and address again *to make sure*' (97; my emphasis). The young man who arrives at the bookshop to inspect the goods is 'not what I expected' (97). Significantly, her description of him starts by stressing his physical attractiveness, but then moves on to his status as an outsider, as Other.[263] Making his first-ever visit to the Falls Road, he is searching for material for a thesis that he is working on, a study of late-nineteenth-century Irish history, 'Britocentric' in its focus. Given his connection with two centres of power, Upper Middle Class Belfast and Oxford, it is appropriate that their next meeting should take place in a café 'near the City Hall'. There, further transactions occur between them, exchanges of information concerning their prior commitments which *appear* to stake out the borders of their relationship: he lives in Oxford with Susan, a fellow student, she tells him 'about my boyfriend Jack'.[264] Framing these acts of partial disclosure are two more ambiguous comments. When Finn says 'And so it started', is she only alluding to their liaison, or to the train of events leading to his murder? Similarly, in stating that 'there didn't seem to be any danger' (97), to what is she referring? Could it simply mean danger of her becoming emotionally involved? As the very reason for gaining his confidence is in order to set up the assassination of his father, it is ironic that she should dismiss the notion of danger.

Although readers imagine they are gaining growing access to and intimacy with Finn and her feelings, huge gaps remain. The ultimate fate of the judge's son is not revealed until page 107, and then by Miss Macken, Finn's employer; it is she who refers to the discovery of a dumped body and a theory that the young historian is a victim of a callous act of entrapment. Before then, he comes across as a somewhat self-satisfied, patronising, calculating young man. He appears to have no qualms about stringing along one woman when already engaged to another, and only informs Finn of his forthcoming marriage *after* she has committed herself sexually to him and confessed her love (105). From their exchanges about Irish history, it appears that he subscribes to a decidedly Arnoldian reading of English/Irish, Protestant/Catholic cultural differences. Thus, he categorises unionist hostility to Home Rule as '*rational*', given northern Protestant industries' economic dependence on British markets. Yet when Finn tenders an alternative history, in the form of her grandmother's anecdotes, 'He laughed and said my grandmother had a great *imagination*' (98; my emphasis). Later, on his first visit to her home, he is quick to pass judgement on the 'strange' things he finds, such as the relics, the images of the Sacred Heart and the web which stretches from her books to the curtains:

> 'Yes, I like spiders,' I said, 'my granny used to say that a spider's web was a good omen. It means we're safe from the soldiers!'
> 'It just means that you never open the curtains!' he said laughing.
> (103)

Finn's assertion that her grandmother actually met Countess Markievicz[265] in her prison cell prompts him first to shake his head and then to tap Finn's nose, saying, 'Sometimes I think … you live in a dream' (105).

Yet Finn is not the elfin Celt he imagines. What she really inhabits is a web, a network of older loyalties and allegiances, which proves more durable than sexual love. At its centre is an absence, that of her late grandmother. It was she had who brought up and sheltered Finn, because her parents' house was overcrowded, and it is her narratives about Black and Tan atrocities and republican subterfuge that have shaped her political outlook. Her involvement with the IRA was a direct result, however, of her own experiences on the night of 14–15 August 1969, and subsequent actions taken by the state authorities, including the introduction of internment (114). She spells out to her interviewers in some detail what she had witnessed in August 1969, the despicable way the police colluded with the loyalist mob in the burning-out of Catholic homes (111–12). Two years later, in the summer of 1971, she met by chance the neighbour who had rescued her grandmother from Conway Street that night. Her assent to the abduction of the judge's son is, as she says herself, 'historical' (117) therefore, a way of repaying a debt to that man and responding to the violence inflicted on her and her grandmother's long-suffering community.

At one telling moment in Finn's account, however, her grandmother metamorphoses into something sinister. During a respite in her interrogation, Finn recalls how, towards the end of her affair with Jack, and while in a liminal state of consciousness, she underwent a nightmarish experience:

> an old woman whom I didn't recognise came towards me with her hands outstretched. I was horrified ... I tried to get Jack to see her but he couldn't. She just kept coming towards me ... She grasped my hand and kept pulling me from the bed. She had very strong hands like a man's ... She would not let me go and I could not get my hands free. (115)

Terrified, she had pleaded with Jack to stay with her, to cover the mirrors, and above all not to let go of her hand. When the apparition returns, she recognises it as her grandmother who seizes her again. Misunderstanding Finn's cry, 'Let go of me!' (116), Jack releases her, leaving her in the grip of the hag. This shape-shifting, composite figure is almost certainly Cathleen ni Houlihan/the Shan van Vocht/Mother Ireland, who resents her exogamous relationship and is determined to pull her back into line.[266] What the vision seems to signify is the hold history, memory, culture and place maintain on the northern nationalist psyche, how icons and myths from the eighteenth, nineteenth and early twentieth centuries persist in the 'dark corners' (119) of the unconscious.

The final paragraphs depict Finn facing a closed door, focusing on a corner of her cell where a spider busies itself with a new web. Locked on to this image, she thinks of the 'dark pattern' which wove her and which she wove. The spider's purposeful activity serves as a temporary distraction from abstraction ('An endless vista of *solitude*', 'An endless *confinement*', a 'gnawing *hunger* inside for *something*' (my emphasis)), her own arrested state. Whereas the 'angles of his world' (118) are in the process of becoming, hers continue to be erased. The street-names she names, which once defined 'her' space, now denote places 'Gone and going'; they are signs whose connection with their referents hangs by a thread. Her interrogators, however, have no interest in her indictment of redevelopers in West Belfast, only in persuading her to implicate others in the student's murder. Resisting their insistence to name names, she attempts to confront her own guilt. Albeit in a circuitous way, with a trail of ambiguous metaphors ('gradual and deliberate processes', 'fatal visions', 'the web's dark pattern') and metonyms (finger, hand, face, arm), she does arrive at her 'part' in an act she cannot name, which produced a victim she cannot name, on a date and in a location she cannot name.

'Naming the Names' reflects an extremely important consequence of the 1980–81 hunger strikes, which problematised perceptions and representations of 'terrorists'. As Edna Longley would later observe, 'A "terrorist" is no psychopathic aberration, but produced by the codes, curriculum and pathology of a whole community'.[267] To some extent, this is exemplified in Devlin's characterisation of Finn, whose fatalism, whose ideas of victimhood and sacrifice have been absorbed from her originary culture. (It is worth recalling how Fionuala, Finn's 'original' in Celtic mythology, fell victim to a jealous stepmother, and was condemned to a 600-year-long exile in the form of a swan.)[268] However, the narrative also makes clear that *external* forces played a major role in initiating nationalist violence, which Finn depicts as reactive, a response to state and loyalist aggression. While a case can be made for seeing Finn as a casualty of the times, as a vulnerable young woman exploited by each of the principal males (Jack, the judge's son, and her IRA contact), her complicity in a major crime cannot be ignored. She is an accessory to abduction, which ended in murder.[269] She appears to grieve only for herself, 'He was my last link with life' (106), and at no point expresses remorse for what she has done. An unnerving, unknowable character, she differs greatly from the other fictional paramilitaries discussed thus far, and indeed from Jude, the IRA hit-woman in Neil Jordan's 1992 film, *The Crying Game*.[270]

Like Woods' and Devlin's stories, Deirdre Madden's fiction reveals a preoccupation with myths of individuation. The young principals in her novels are presented struggling to find some sense of focus or direction, as they try to extricate themselves from the formerly enabling, but now excessively intense embrace of familial ties. Typically they are conscious of themselves as plural texts, complex compositions of 'inherited traits' and 'vestiges' from earlier generations, 'and yet still new people with their own particularities' (*Hidden Symptoms*, 18–19). The premature loss of one – or both – parents is not uncommon, and so the stress of dealing with absence features prominently in characters' attempts to reimagine their lives. In her first novel, *Hidden Symptoms*,[271] Robert's memories of his father – he died when the boy was eight – are so faint that 'he even wondered at times if he had imagined him' (38), while Theresa's father exists only as a random set of 'fuzzy' photographs (68).[272] 'Handcuffed to history',[273] to 'a subjectivity' which they are 'unwilling or unable to transcend',[274] Madden's characters engage in deeply troubled negotiations not only with the previous generation, but also their own over issues of allegiance in familial, cultural, religious and political spheres. Like the divided creatures imagined by Aristophanes in *The Symposium*, they long for a wholeness, unity and healing that will never be achieved.[275]

Matters of psychological, spiritual and cultural health are, thus, very much to the fore in *Hidden Symptoms*. Though the title and the author's origins might lead one to expect some kind of political diagnosis, the novel's focus is primarily on the personal consequences of sectarian killing rather than its underlying political causes.[276] Peopled by bewildered, bereft and broken individuals, from the outset it seems haunted by a profound sense of the impermanence and fragility of things:

> When Theresa was small she thought the saddest things she had ever seen was a Bavarian barometer with a little weather man and a little weather woman. It was so sad that always when Hans was out Heidi was in and vice versa: never together, always alone, so near, so far, so lonely. (9)

The deceptive simplicity of these opening lines – with its child-like vocabulary, lexical and structural repetitions, and insistent pathos – is typical of Madden, and illustrates how from the outset of her career she has been preoccupied with doubleness and duplicities in language, form and content. The barometer, like the narrative that contains it, is a measure of the climate of the time, and operates on several levels.[277] Most obviously it functions as a metaphor for the principal characters' psychological and spiritual condition. The enforced separation of Hans and Heidi prefigures a world of disconnections, anticipating the severed lines within Theresa Cassidy's life following the early death of her father and recent brutal murder of her twin brother, Francis. Equally the oppositional relationship of these figures looks forward to the class and cultural disjunctions in the identity of the novel's other main focaliser, Robert McConville, whose determination to re-make and re-position himself within the Belfast bourgeoisie divides him from meaningful contact with his sister, Rosie.[278] Yet the barometer also acts as an objective correlative for Northern Ireland, a miniature state riven by polarities, founded on exclusion and absence. Unwittingly in attempting to inter-vene, to 'correct' the anomalous, divisive situation, the young Theresa – like the idealistic civil rights activists of the late 1960s/early 1970s? – breaks the mechanism beyond repair.

Much of *Hidden Symptoms* is taken up with similarly allusive, yet resonant textual encounters, as it traces Theresa's attempts to reconfigure her life over a two year period. Like subsequent female leads, such as Catherine in *The Birds of the Innocent Wood* and Helen in *One by One*, Theresa is a fictionist, for whom imagining becomes a means of confronting the 'absolute loneliness' (33) of bereavement, seizing back 'the passionate transitory' (Kavanagh, 'The Hospital'). In a trope common in nationalist texts, she turns to ancestry as a source of verification, yet only to discover what little access it yields, and what little consolation it engenders. One point of origin she returns to 'again and again' is the framed photograph of her parents' wedding which 'hung over the china cabinet in the parlour' (67). Instead of bridging the space between their time and hers, such reminders of a remote and stable bourgeois age merely compound her sense of alienation.[279] The arrested narrative then transfers its attention to a snapshot of her father from his bachelor days, in which he looks 'so young and happy, as unaware of death as he was of the eye of the camera' (68). Her attachment to this particular memento has intensified as a result of her brother's killing, quickened in the bitter knowledge that 'History' and the newspapers had no time for either of them. When she tries to supplement this visual prompt or silent form by drawing on her mother's memories of their early married life, the results prove equally unsatisfy-ing. Though as a bereaved daughter she longs for details which might enable her to gain a fuller, more coherent picture of a pre-Troubles time when the family existed as a unity, another part of her remains sceptical about the reconstructions of the past her mother supplies. Given that, like her author, Theresa has studied formalist and post-structuralist ideas, it is hardly surprising that she should express an ambivalence about the currency of words, and the value and valency of narrative:

> She accepted her mother's evocation of Clifden as she accepted Dostoyevsky's evocation of St Petersburg. Each place was conceived

in the memory, language and discourse of others, then took life in her imagination, the illusory streets and squares and people rose before her. It would be futile to look for these towns, not because they had changed, but because in the form in which she saw them they had never truly existed (70).[280]

Insistently, and sometimes none too subtly, the novel worries at the intersections of aesthetics, religion and political violence, from a range of perspectives.[281] Its principal focalisers, Theresa and Robert, are writers, representatives of the newly intellectually-enfranchised Catholic middle class. At their somewhat contrived first encounter,[282] in a city-centre café, he approaches her just as she happens to have finished reading an article celebrating the North's 'literary renaissance'. Unaware that the stranger is its author, she lambasts what she regards as its pretentious claims that, like Dublin before it, Belfast has become a 'cultural omphalos' (12). Soon after, despite her trashing of Robert's work, she is invited to a dinner party at his flat which is enlivened by the arrival of a drunken, nameless interloper, a 'struggling playwright'. His brief to harangue the company on drama's superiority to other genres – 'Plays is the only useful art ... you get things done with plays' (26) – provides an opportunity for Theresa to refute the view that art's role is to help initiate political or social action, and to demonstrate her intellectual acuity.[283] Art should serve only its own purposes, she argues, though what those purposes might be is left undefined, or rather seen as beyond definition. When asked what she writes about, she replies that her subject is 'subjectivity – and inarticulation – about life pushing you into a state where everything is melting until you're left with the absolute and you can find neither the words nor the images to express it' (28). The state she describes refers not only to her own psychic condition following her brother's murder but also to that of Northern Ireland after 1969, where acts of barbarity reached levels of such intensity that any utterance, private or public, must have seemed diminished, inadequate. Shortly after this scene, Robert is presented recalling television footage of a bombing, in which 'the casual camera showed bits of human flesh hanging from barbed wire ... Firemen shovelled what was left of people into heavy plastic bags, and you could see all that remained: big burnt black lumps like charred logs' (30). This appalling memory and Robert's guilty reactions are clearly deployed to underline the novel's, and Madden's recurring concern over the appropriation and translation of violence into visual and verbal forms especially by the media, and how the repetition and dissemination of such images may have the effect of 'naturalising' atrocity.

The text's aesthetic deliberations take on a religious dimension when they are resumed later in a critical series of exchanges between Theresa and Francis placed in the novel's central section, whose subject matter and setting are reminiscent of George Eliot's *Middlemarch*.[284] Set in Rome, exactly two years prior to the narrative present, these defining moments accentuate points of affinity and difference in their ways of reading and reckoning the world as they confront a number of 'classic' works of Christian art. As in a later novel, whose migrant narrator claims to have 'found out more about my own country, simply by not being in it',[285] Europe, or specifically Italy, is deployed to offer a measure of (illusory) relief from the 'blackness'[286] of home. The significance of the encounter is signalled by a switch to the present tense and a change in voice, which finds the narrator affirming the 'authenticity' of the fiction by locating the characters in a precise spot in the 'real' world:

> As one walks across St Peter's Square in Rome, the four rows of Doric pillars which form Bernini's Colonnade merge and shift so that they seem to increase then decrease in number and their colour changes from golden-grey to deepest black. There are, however, two small stones in the vast, cobbled square ... and, when one stands upon these stones, all four rows fall into order, so that one sees only a row of pillars. (52–3)

As elsewhere, the narrative voice is highly conscious of the illusory effects art and artists can achieve, and admits alternative readings of the same phenomena. A construct in and of the world, the colonnade can paradoxically appear indeterminate and unfixed, yet beautifully plural in its transitions and colours. From a certain angle, or angles rather, however, it looks to confirm a sense of universal symmetry, order and definition. Though the latter standpoint – an orthodox Christian view of the world – might appear privileged because it is heralded by that authoritative 'however' and because it is placed second in a sequence of two, the phrase '*fall* into order' (my emphasis) suggests the regimentation that accompanies such a view, while the word 'only' implies limitations. In Francis's eyes, the spectacular quality of Bernini's art and the scale of St Peter's verify his belief in the awesome immanence of God, whose gaze is exacting and unrelenting:

> I see God in everything, but God also sees everything in me. There are eyes everywhere ... God looks straight out at me through the eye of every human being, asking me to look straight back at Him. But I know I can't because I'm not good enough, and I can feel the eyes

catch on me like hooks. Everywhere I look, I see only eyes, God's eyes, God telling me what He did for me and wanting to know what I'm doing for Him'. (53)

Theresa – like the vast majority of readers, one suspects – recoils from this vision of continual surveillance, suggestive as it is of existence under Big Brother.[287] For Francis clearly, existence is a ceaseless process of reading and evaluating, of being read and evaluated, and the 'worst thing in the world'[288] would be if there were no Author and no texts. Although initially Theresa gives no verbal endorsement to his conception of the deity, subsequently the narrator informs us that his utterances inspire in her 'a terrible passion for this God of whom he had spoken' (54–5), and with it an awareness of the insufficiency of Art as an expression of the absolute. Yet it is important to note that her apprehension of God at this point in the text is not a direct one, but mediated '*through Francis's words* and not through the lapis lazuli, the alabaster or the white Carrara marble' (55: my emphasis). Alongside the urge to cling more closely to her brother and merge her perceptions with his ('she tightened her grip on Francis's arm') runs a counter-impulse. Something in Theresa reacts with hostility to the sheer aesthetic excess of the Vatican's stone metaphors; she 'idly' imagines herself in the role of an iconoclast, taking a hammer to Michaelangelo's *Pietà*.[289] The moment is symptomatic of Theresa's latent, often suppressed aggression,[290] reminding the reader not only of incidents in her childhood when she had broken apart the family barometer and the souvenir snowstorm (54), but also of a larger network of instances in the text where violent images break surface.[291]

Shortly afterwards Francis modifies his Socratean stance on the problematic nature of religious Art as can be seen from his response to Bernini's famous statue of Saint Theresa of Avila.[292] Having previously maintained that the sublime beauty of a work such as the *Pietà* could actually be detrimental to the growth of faith – 'it obstructed what it ostensibly stood for, which is infinitely more beautiful' – he finds himself overwhelmed by the Bernini: 'It's *absolutely* beautiful. That's what it is to be lost in the eye which never closes or looks away' (55: my emphasis). Theresa, however, is appalled by the force of his desire for total unity with God which her stone namesake inspires, a desire which seems to write *her* flesh-and-blood actuality out of his story;[293] for her, it amounts to an immolation of the Self. This representation of him 'looking unflinchingly at the gilded arrow in the hand of the angel' (56) possesses an evident proleptic irony, anticipating as it does the unbeautiful death that awaits him.

The impact of that death and unresolved question of what it might 'mean' haunt the text and its characters, and serve as a focus for its mutually dependent personal, political and metaphysical concerns. Confronting the sealed coffin, imagining the suffering it contains and conceals, plunges Madden's fictional protagonists into a crisis of faith and identity, an experience horribly familiar to many individuals and families in the 'real world' of Northern Ireland beyond the text: what kind of God could have permitted this savagery to happen, and what purpose could have been served? Although previously Theresa 'had never in her life doubted His existence for a single moment' (43), now the possibility is broached that God Himself might be a fiction:

> If there was no God, death was the end and the people who had killed Francis really had destroyed him absolutely ... Each alternative was dreadful: a God with a divine plan, part of which was that Francis should be tortured and shot; or no God and no plan, so that all this was chaos and there could never be any justification or explanation. (52)

At the close of the funeral rites, she resolves to persist with belief in order to protect herself from falling into the 'deep, dark pit' (49) of despair; her faith is now a thing marked by resentment, marred by incomprehension, made on the premise that if God did not exist and there were no afterlife her loss would be absolute. It is only as the second anniversary of his killing approaches, however, in the narrative 'present', that the depth and ambiguous nature of her feelings are more explicitly intimated. The text's voice shifts uncertainly between focalisation through Theresa ('If only...') to an authoritative third person narrator who appears to attribute to Theresa desires of which she may have been previously unconscious. Conceivably guilt at having survived may have caused these repressed emotions to surface, or indeed generated 'false memories':

> If only he had been *a husband or a lover, anything but a brother*. His death had *pitched* her into love as much as grief; rather, it let her see how deeply and *hopelessly* she had been *steeped* in love, in *utter passion* for him since the day of their birth ... She swung from feelings of *betrayal and revulsion* at the idea of similarly loving anyone else to desperate loneliness from the knowledge that she could not do so. She thought that love should not make her feel so *trapped*, but it did, and she felt it beyond her power to change this. (82; my emphasis)

Following on from this, a few pages later, the narrator proffers one final touching epiphany from Francis and Theresa's holiday in Europe, when their hands accidentally meet in the water of a Lugano fountain. 'Now' in Theresa's imagination, we are informed, the 'small, blue, painted, *tainted* bowl' (my emphasis) serves uncertainly as an objective correlative 'for the distant Heaven where Francis was' (87). It is perhaps significant that in re-presenting it, she excises all reference to physical contact, though the word 'tainted' could be seen as alluding to that momentary – forbidden? – touch. But what leads her to imagine a 'tainted' heaven, one asks oneself? 'Tainted' by what or whom?

Barthes's concept of the writerly (*scriptible*) text[294] is useful to invoke in defining how Madden's fiction works. Though the incident at Lugano may simply function as a minor effect intended to heighten the reader's consciousness of the intensity of Theresa and Francis's communion and the pathos of its loss, one senses other elusive meanings in play.[295] A characteristic feature of Madden's early texts is their 'veilings', which, in the words of one critic, leave the reader, 'in a kind of disquieting miasma of non-knowledge that demanded-to-be-known'.[296] The arcane events and indeterminate relationships of her later novel, *The Birds of the Innocent Wood*, begin to form a pattern and 'make sense' once one concedes the possibility that incest may have occurred in each of its three generations. Yet one should not ignore that book's encoded warning about the act of reading, and in particular the act of reading Madden. Looking on in disbelief as one of her fellow characters inexplicably disappears, Jane struggles but fails to grasp the sense of what she has witnessed: '*You didn't imagine this ... You know what this is, but do you know what it means*'.[297]

It is in her detailing of the succession of conflicting emotions her grieving characters pass through that Madden's writing is often at its most convincing and powerful. Though at times Theresa gains consolation in the thought of a 'place of total and unqualified love' (72) which Francis inhabits; at others, she is stricken by the finality of loss, 'She would never see him again in this world, never never never never never' (73). One of her mother's strategies for coping with bereavement, a not uncommon one in the North over the past 30 years, is to confer on her son the status of martyr, thereby lifting him free from the particular historical moment and causes which framed his death in order to re-locate him within a longer, larger narrative of religious and political persecution.[298] When Theresa indicates the problematical nature of such a reading, pointing out that martyrdom necessitates an act of volition ('they just killed Francis because of his religion, he had no choice'), Mrs Cassidy's telling response is 'How do you know?'(42), another curt reminder, if one were needed, of the partial nature of texts.[299]

Gerry Smyth's brief critique of *Hidden Symptoms* privileges its meta-physics, even going so far as to describe the novel as 'a plea on behalf of the religious life'.[300] What his analysis does not take into account is the inextricability of religious affiliations and political identity in the North; Francis is not targeted because of his theological position, but because he belongs to the monolithic 'rebel' community of his murderers' imagin-ations. Like the Patricia Craig review cited earlier,[301] Smyth underesti-mates *Hidden Symptoms'* political elements, and the way it tries to reflect a range of nationalist/Catholic attitudes. On the first two occasions readers enter a domestic interior in the novel they encounter Theresa and Mrs Cassidy switching channels to avoid news coverage of an RUC man's funeral, and Rosie's husband, Tom, gloating over the killing ('Good sauce for the bastard'(p.16)). It is no accident that the most of the major scenes take place in July, the month in which the marching sea-son and civil disturbances reach their zenith.[302] The argument between Theresa and her mother over Francis's martyrdom takes place on 1 July, 'the Feast of the Holy Blood', but is immediately followed by a clash between Theresa and Robert over the significance of the 12th July for Catholics. When the liberal Robert opines that the bunting and process-ing is a harmless 'bit of folk culture', he lets himself in for the first of many lambastings at Theresa's hands: 'Harmless? You seem to forget, Robert … that the Orange Order is, first and foremost, an anti-Catholic organisation. They hate Catholics and hate is never harmless' (46). His endeavour to distance himself from his originary affiliations – and the crudely simplistic Catholic/Protestant binary – gets similar short shrift:

> 'Just tell me this: if you were found in the morning with a bullet in your head, what do you think the papers would call you? An agnos-tic? … Of course you don't believe: but there's a big difference between faith and tribal loyalty, and if you think you can escape tribal loyalty in Belfast today you're betraying your people and fool-ing yourself'. (46)

Both characters, it could be argued, fail to remain consistent to the stances they voice here. Robert never confronts his brother-in-law over his support for militant republicanism (16, 75, 76), or reproves his nephew for his sectarian jokes. Though a regular attender at Mass, there is little sign in Theresa's life of tribal solidarity. She ends as she began, torn between allegiance to her broken family and the need to 'rekindle the dying fire' (141) of her individuality. The novel's closure discovers her, like Walcott's Shabine, longing for 'the window I can look from that frames my life',[303] and an end to 'shadows cast upon glass' (141), to life as a mirror-image.[304]

Drama: Graham Reid, *The Billy Plays*; Frank McGuinness, *Observe the Sons of Ulster Marching Towards the Somme*

The early and mid-1980s witnessed the production of a number of plays on television and in the theatre giving voice to Protestant working-class experience, which, like that of Northern Irish women, had suffered from serious under-representation until this juncture. One of the dramatists seeking to redress this imbalance was Graham Reid (b.1945). Between 1982 and 1984, he wrote three plays for BBC television, *Too Late to Talk to Billy* (1982), *A Matter of Choice for Billy* (May 1983), and *A Coming to Terms for Billy* (1984),[305] revolving around Billy Martin, an 18-year-old Protestant from West Belfast. All three plays are domestic in their concerns, and focus on Billy's dysfunctional family background and difficult passage towards maturation. Targeted at a mainstream audience, they represent working-class Belfast Protestants grappling with the very same issues affecting individuals, families and different generations everywhere.[306]

In Reid's plays it is family history that persists and haunts the protagonists. The first, and perhaps most moving of the three, *Too Late to Talk to Billy*,[307] opens on a family in crisis. A wife and mother is dying slowly of cancer. Her husband's failure to visit her in hospital provokes intense resentment particularly in their eldest child, Billy.[308] Through flashbacks, the cause of his father Norman's apparent callousness is revealed. Several years earlier, while unemployment forced Norman to look for work in England, the children's mother had begun an affair with an insurance salesman, Stevie. Thirteen-year-old Ann, one of Billy's three sisters, graphically describes the scene she witnessed on her father's return, when after laying into her lover, 'He punched my ma one, right on the mouth ... she said she loved Stevie ... I thought he was going to cry ... or kill her' (30). As a result of his wife's betrayal and his own humiliation, Norman descends into frequent bouts of drunkenness, during which he takes out his frustrations on the children, beating his son and three daughters. Amid this maelstrom of male aggression and hurt, there is one still centre, the eldest daughter, 17-year-old Lorna. Adopting the role of mother-substitute, Lorna sacrifices career prospects and personal life in an effort to retain a semblance of family cohesion.

One of the play's most shocking exchanges (scene 33) occurs when Norman returns home under the influence of drink and guilt. His admission that he 'couldn't get away' (42) to see his wife provokes a succession of sarcastic retorts from Billy. In one of these, he compares Norman to an actor who is too much in demand: 'I'll have to write to your agent and see if we can book you for the funeral' (42). Able to command neither his son's attention nor respect, he resorts first to verbal assault:

NORMAN: ... I wish the whole bloody lot of you had cancer. I wish you
          were all bloody dying. I go out to work every day. Your
          mother never knew what it was like to have a broken pay.
BILLY: No, but she knew what it was like to have a broken jaw,
          and a broken nose.
NORMAN: I'm warning you, I'm bloody warning you.
BILLY: Why didn't you let her run off with her insurance man?
          ... He was a better bloody man than you. At least he
          appreciated her ... She despised you but loved him. (44)

Norman's response is to seize Billy by the throat and strike him repeatedly, '*bellowing as he does so*'. As the stage directions make clear, these are the actions of a man in pain. The scene dissolves into a flashback of the even more bloody episode Ann recalled earlier. Viewers are forced to look on as Norman '*keeps smashing Stevie's face into the wall ... and smashes his fist into JANET's face*' (44), before returning to the current, one-sided fight. Its resolution comes when Billy is literally thrown out into the street, and banned from his own home. It is only after their mother's death and their father's departure for England that a kind of peace settles on the family, symbolised by Billy's placing of their parents' wedding photograph on the mantelshelf (57).

The second and third parts in the trilogy continue with the successful formula of *Too Late to Talk to Billy* – conflicts in the private sphere, believable characters with whom the audience can empathise, outstanding performances (particularly those of James Ellis, Brid Brennan and Kenneth Branagh) and direction.[309] Already peripheral in the first play,[310] the Northern Irish political crisis becomes even more marginal in the sequels. Of far greater import is *sexual* politics, how reconfigurations in women's attitudes and expectations impact on the weak, but generally aggressive male characters. In contrast to the acquiescent, conservative Lorna, both of Billy's girlfriends, June (in *Too Late*) and Pauline (in *A Matter of Choice*), are determined to leave Belfast in pursuance of better life and career possibilities; June heads off to university in York, and Pauline comes within a whisker of taking a job in Toronto. Lorna and Pauline force Billy into confronting his fear of commitment and recognising how much he resembles his father. At one point, he confesses, 'I'm afraid of making the wrong choices and messing things up, the way my da did' (87). Only after Lorna's repeated urgings and with her 'permission' ('We have to break sometime' (104)), can Billy move away and settle down with Pauline. Despite Uncle Andy's references to her as 'a scheming wee Fenian' (107), Pauline's cultural identity barely registers as an issue between the couple or amongst the other younger generation characters.[311]

The fulcrum of tension in *A Coming to Terms for Billy* is immediately established in its opening cameo, which finds his father on board the Liverpool ferry, re-entering Belfast Lough. Tempered by change, more temperate as a result of his acquisition of an English wife, Norman arrives with plans to relocate his family in England. This reignites Billy's hostility towards his father, which extends towards his substitute-mother, Mavis. In yet another gesture of confused, adolescent defiance, he misses a meal Pauline has prepared to welcome Norman and Mavis to the flat they share.

While the climactic confrontation in *A Coming to Terms* calls to mind that of the first play, important shifts have taken place in terms of the generational and gender politics. Complex, unresolved sexual tensions again form an important element of the scene's subtext. On this occasion, it is Billy who arrives home drunk. As an opening gambit, he addresses Mavis and Norman as 'Mummy and Daddy', a sequence which emphasises his anger at his mother's replacement. He then accuses them of being 'kidnappers', and refers to them sarcastically as 'honeymooners'. In a rare allusion to sectarianism, he goes on to mention how, unlike them, he and Pauline 'can't get married … Northern Ireland … different religions. But we enjoy sex … don't we love?'[312] By taunting his father, Billy aims, consciously or subconsciously, to resurrect the father he is familiar with. He hopes to expose the old brutishness to the new wife, and thereby create a rift. Harking back to his expulsion in the trilogy's opening, he goads his father, 'You'll not throw me out on the street this time oul man' (158). As a result of Mavis's physical and verbal intervention,[313] Billy directs his offensive towards her. Knowing full well that she cannot have children – Norman told him so in scene 25 (150) – he jibes that perhaps if a 'little miracle' occurs, she will 'not have to kidnap my sisters'. In a further demonstration of the new sexual politics, it is Mavis who acts: *'Before NORMAN can move she is across the floor and has slapped BILLY's face, hard'* (159). Unlike the blows struck in *Too Late to Talk to Billy*, this has a psychologically beneficial effect, initiating the resolution of the play's central dilemma, the question as to where Ann and Maureen would best belong.

It takes a 'foreign', assertive female presence to release the alpha males in the Martin family from their paralysing fixity; ironically the mocking nickname Billy coined for Mavis, 'Save Us', proves entirely appropriate. After a brief intervening scene, Billy emerges from his bedroom to apologise to Mavis. Her observation on the similarities between father and son helps them both to laugh and *'visibly relax'* with each other: 'You two ... honestly ... if he was about twenty-five years younger, or you twenty-five years older, you could pose as twins' (162). This might lead one to conclude that underneath Billy's aggression and animosity burns a fierce, hurt love, comparable to that Biff displays to *his* father close to the end of Miller's *Death of a Salesman*. Unlike the latter, Reid's play veers decisively towards reconciliation and a restoration of father's and son's 'masculinity'. Immediately after the *tête-à-tête* with Mavis, Billy is depicted waiting in a bar for his 'da' (163), where they successfully join forces (166) against two UDA 'hard men'. Significantly, the cause of the fight is domestic, not political, a reminder of how Reid chooses in the *Billy* plays to present a unionist community prone to occasional intrafamilial, intra-communal bust-ups. His Belfast exists clearly at a far remove from that depicted in the fiction of Woods, Devlin and Madden.

Avoiding too reassuring an ending, the final frames of *A Coming to Terms* leave the audience with a qualified picture of family solidarity. Ann, Maureen, Norman, Mavis, Pauline and Andy are grouped together outside the Martins' house, while '*BILLY and LORNA remain inside*' (171) behind the window. In a reversal of the gesture with which *Too Late to Talk* ended, which signals his reluctant acceptance of the new order, Billy returns his parents' wedding photograph to a drawer. Part of what Billy has gained in the course of the trilogy is a recognition that exogamy, relationships outside the tribe, can open up possibilities for growth.[314] It is interesting to note how positively such unions are depicted in the *Billy* plays, in marked contrast to *Translations* and 'Naming the Names' where their endorsement cannot be said to be ringing.

The soundtrack accompanying these concluding images issues an ominous note, however. Although simply a background noise at first, the music performed by the loyalist band reaches a crescendo at the end of scene 39. As Lance Pettitt points out, the choice of 'Derry Walls' is indicative of mounting political and cultural assertiveness in the unionist community.[315] Indeed the whole trilogy might be usefully viewed as an early manifestation of this phenomenon, a reaction against the ascendancy of 'nationalist' discourse in the aftermath of the hunger strikes and the New Ireland Forum debates. In the sphere of Northern Irish literature and literary politics from the mid-1980s onwards considerable efforts were made to raise the profile of writing from and about the Protestant tradition, at times with the aim of countering the influence of Field Day and its alleged nationalist emphasis.[316] Although created by a writer from outside that tradition, the next text to be discussed illustrates perfectly the major reconfigurations taking place in culture on both sides of the border, and what Nicholas Grene has characterised as 'a new sort of imaginative reaching out in Irish drama'.[317]

Frank McGuinness originates from the historic kingdom of Ulster,[318] rather than the province of Northern Ireland, yet any examination of Northern Irish literature which omitted reference to his work would be the poorer for doing so. Given that the discovery of his own sexual orientation in his formative teenage years coincided with Derry's sudden translation into a war zone, it is hardly surprising that his masterpiece, *Observe the Sons of Ulster Marching Towards the Somme* (1985), should delve into the intersections of politics and sexuality. It marks a significant shift in cultural discourse emanating from the Irish Republic, since it breaks with the consensus maintained by Irish political, historical and literary texts that the principal, defining event of 1916 was the Easter Rising. Instead, like Michael Longley in 'Wounds', McGuinness memorialises those caught up in a different sacrifice from that year, that of over 2060 men from the 36th Ulster Division who perished at the Battle of the Somme.[319] In enlisting, the majority set out to demonstrate their loyalty to Britain and unwillingness to see their Protestant identity subsumed within a unitary state. The play's imperative is partly a revisionist one. In seeking to promote a more sympathetic understanding of Northern Protestants' traditions and to highlight the origins of their continuing resistance to a united Ireland, it is consonant with the reconfigurations already taking place in contemporary Irish politics, which gathered momentum during the period of the New Ireland Forum and culminated in the Anglo-Irish Agreement.[320]

Yet, as Anthony Roche points out, McGuinness's concern is equally to encourage a greater 'questioning of the norms and stereotypes of sexual identity'.[321] Sexual issues were increasingly moving to the fore in Ireland, north and south, during the 1980s; in the Republic there were referendums held on abortion in 1983 and divorce in 1986, both of which resulted in victories for 'conservative' forces opposed to changes in the law. What most affected McGuinness during the period in which *Observe the Sons* was composed, however, was the beginning of the AIDS pandemic; its presence was first diagnosed in Ireland in 1982 and it claimed its first victims in the mid-1980s. In a recent interview, the dramatist states that 'the subject of AIDS is very strikingly there' in his play, albeit in 'coded' form.[322]

Structured in four parts, *Observe the Sons* centres around eight soldiers, representatives from all six counties of Northern Ireland. Its frame narrator, and the sole survivor of the massacre, is Kenneth Pyper, whom we later learn is a sculptor, born into privilege in Armagh.[323] Now an old man, he delivers the play's prologue to the accompaniment of a '*Low drumbeat*', an aural reminder of recurrence. 'Again. As always, again', are his opening words, followed by a salvo of questions and statements targeted at an unknown audience, a composite group which appears to include God and McGuinness, as well as those in the circles and stalls. Trapped on stage, subject to the will of agents above and below, he denounces their plan to make an 'example' of him, to force him into the role of narrator and historical witness: 'I am angry at your demand that I continue to probe. Were you not there in all your dark glory? Have you no conception of the horror? Did it not touch you at all?' (9). He then extends his attack to the playwright and anyone else presuming to aestheticise horror or draw moral consolation from it: 'Invention gives that slaughter shape ... You have no right to excuse that suffering, parading it for the benefit of others' (9). The effect of such lines is, however, profoundly moral, since they remind the audience of their compromised position inside and outside the theatre as voyeurs of violence. By deferring any specific references to 1916 and the Somme, McGuinness establishes from the outset the text's intention to operate in multiple time.

In a movement which mirrors his own uneven passage in the play from self-dramatising, self-hating, self-obsession, Pyper's eyes gradually lift from his own lot ('Darkness, for eternity')[324] to those whose steadfastness 'taught me ... to believe' (10). In a significant shift between paragraphs 2 and 4, emphasis on 'horror' and 'slaughter' gives way to the concept of 'sacrifice', death with meaning. Before *our* eyes, the Romantic rebel, shaking his fist at the Almighty, metamorphoses into the orthodox Ulster Protestant. A kind of possession seizes him, converting him briefly into a mouthpiece for traditional loyalist, revivalist rhetoric: 'There would be, and there will be no surrender. The sons of Ulster will rise and lay their enemy low ... It is we, the Protestant people, who have always stood alone. We have stood alone and triumphed, for we are God's chosen'. On returning from the Somme, he informs us, he invested his energies in managing 'my father's estates', organising 'the workings of the province' (10), in preservation, not creation.[325] Much as he tries to resist the pull of memory, the appeal of his companions-in-arms and his sense of obligation to them prove too strong. Fragmentary, lyrical images begin to collect, connect and gather momentum: 'the sky was *pink*, extraordinarily *pink*. There were men from Coleraine, talking about *salmon* fishing' (11; my emphasis). Increasingly in this section Pyper interweaves the parochial and the transcendent, the secular and

sacred. The first name he recalls, that of David, is one rich in biblical resonances, associated with divine favour, military prowess, intense male
friendship.[326] The miraculous, transformative function David will perform
in his life is anticipated by Pyper's comment that after David spoke, 'I
looked and I could see again' and the reference to his 'turning from earth
into air' (11).

Ironically, immediately after this comment, first three, then four ghosts
materialise on stage. Images of severance, of sundered love dominate the
speech with which Pyper welcomes the initial group, which ends as it
begins, directly addressing David Craig, in short, elliptical sentences. He
enquires whether Moore is still searching for Millen, recalls how, after
McIlwaine was cut in two, Anderson fell on him 'as if his body could
hold McIlwaine together', and how this moment forced him to recognise their common lineage ('his blood was the same colour as my blood').
In a mood that oscillates between defiance and grief, he calls on his
comrades to act as his and Ulster's guardian spirits, for both his body
and the province's resembles a dark, abandoned temple (12).[327]

In Part One's final monologues, Pyper poses and answers the question
as to why 'we let ourselves be led to extermination' (12). His conclusion
is that an ethos of sacrifice, mixed with self-hatred and masochism, lies
at and corrodes the core of the Ulster Protestant psyche, and that only
an external *human* agency, his friends' saving grace, can restore its broken
state. As a second group of spirits rise to meet him, those of the Coleraine
and the Belfast men, he invites them to take their partners in the *danse
macabre* which is the play itself, the Somme, and the Ulster of 1985.

The audience's foreknowledge of the battle's outcome and the fate of
Pyper's companions has the effect of suffusing the characters' exchanges
in irony. The very first action performed and very first word uttered in
Part Two illustrate this. Aptly, given the play's historical subject – and
sexual subtext – 'Initiation' begins with blood. Accidentally cutting his
thumb while peeling an apple, Young Pyper exclaims. 'Damnation' (13).
What in its immediate context appears merely an expression of annoy-
ance becomes applicable to the psychological and, perhaps, the theological condition the soldiers occupy. The apple Pyper will shortly bite
into similarly accrues additional, plural meanings as the text moves
backwards and forwards in time, many of them linked to the idea of Ulster
as Eden raised at the close of Part One.[328] It is frequently Pyper, the artist,
who initiates this semantic play, which is then taken up by other characters.
Although he responds discouragingly to Pyper's coded, but hardly subtle
sexual invitation ('I can't tempt you?'),[329] Craig is soon drawn into
metaphorical sparring. Albeit with a cliché ('One bad apple spoils the

barrel'), he contests Pyper's sensualist reading of apples as fleshly, as 'Beautiful. Hard. White' (15). His remark also signals, of course, continuing disquiet over his room-mate's bizarre, attention-seeking behaviour. A supplementary comment, made seconds later ('Well, you're a rare buckcat'), reveals that he finds Pyper intriguing as well as disturbing. In conceding that 'We could end up dying for each other' (16), Craig unconsciously enters the indeterminate space Pyper has opened up, an ambiguous no-man's-land in which grand official narratives, religious and patriotic imperatives come under fire.

   The arrival of a further six volunteers, in pairs and singly, sees no let-up in Pyper's subversive role-playing. When Millen and Moore enter, the one joshing the other about his supposed sexual exploits, Pyper immediately makes them ill-at-ease. First he pretends to be an officer, then claims *his* name is David Craig. To impress his fellow soldiers, and assert his superiority in class, education and sexual experience, he fabricates stories about his time in France. The most hilarious of these follows on from Millen's, Moore's and Craig's pooled accounts of their UVF gun-running activities (26), and Millen's anecdote about a 16-year-old Fenian 'pup' whom he and fellow paramilitaries had 'disciplined' for the crime of daubing an Orange hall with an Irish tricolour:

MILLEN:	Shaved every hair off his head.
MOORE:	Cut the backside out of his trousers.
MILLEN:	Painted his arse green, white and gold.
MOORE:	That cured him of his tricolours. (27)

Although Pyper '*roars with laughter*' at this, soon after he replies with a tale in which sectarian mythology is openly in his sights. He relates to an increasingly avid, gullible audience a ludicrous yarn about his exogamous marriage to a French Papist whore, whom he married 'out of curiosity', and 'to make an honest Protestant of her' (29). He goes on to report how on their wedding night, after discovering she had three legs, he sawed the middle one off, out of his sense of 'duty as a Protestant' (30). Only when he explains how he ate his dead wife's body to hide his crime does Moore cotton on. What Pyper's narrative has helped expose is the ignorance and fear woven into the fabric of identity, but also the unhealthy association of sexuality and violence in his and their subconscious. Shortly afterwards, in a private exchange with Craig, he admits to finding women and men equally beautiful, and problematises the idea of 'difference' (31) in gender.[330]

   The testosterone-filled tensions in the barracks spill over into physical violence as 'Initiation' reaches its close. No sooner have two Belfastmen appeared on stage, than one of them, McIlwaine, hurls himself on the group's youngest soldier, Crawford, *'snarling and snapping'* (35). His nose and instinct tell him that Crawford is a 'Taig' (34).[331] In retaliation, Pyper plays a trick on McIlwaine's sidekick, punching him in the groin. The rationale he offers for this assault is to teach his companions of the need to fight 'dirty' if they are to survive the war. Yet in his penultimate major speech in Part Two, he voices a hope that 'I might survive from what I learn here' by bonding with 'Other Sons of Ulster' (36). In one last perverse gesture, expressing commitment and contrition, Pyper slits the palm of his left hand with his penknife. In so doing he is inscribing himself as a member of 'God's brotherhood', since a bloody hand was the symbol of the Ulster Division.

Moving on from the conventional dramatic form of the preceding section, Part Three of *Observe the Sons* disperses the stage action into four different locations, in which four alternating pairs of characters deal with the trauma brought on by a five month tour of duty in France. Each pair contains a casualty, and a would-be healer who attempts to revive their 'fallen' comrade's psychological state and restore their spirits. By so thoroughly exposing his characters' vulnerability, McGuinness subverts stereotypical representations of the Ulster Protestant male as unfeeling, dour and philistine. For Christopher Roulston, formerly an evangelical preacher, the crisis is spiritual. War has left his self-belief and faith in God in ruins. Ironically, the task of weaning him from dependency on external, supernatural agency falls to the cradle-Catholic, Martin Crawford. Elsewhere, the dyer, Willie Moore, is depicted paralysed with fear as he starts crossing the rope-bridge at Carrick-a-Rede.[332] Addressing him from the other side of the chasm, Millen, his former commander, encourages him to take the steps necessary to recover his sundered integrity: 'His heart's over there ... Walk over to him' (42). Of the two Belfast shipyard workers, it is McIlwaine who is failing to cope with the strain, convinced that their hopes of survival are doomed: 'We're on the *Titanic*. We're all going down' (50). What reinvigorates him, however, is his beating of the Lambeg drum, along with Anderson's ferocious tirade against Fenians everywhere. In a clever variation of the pattern established in the other pairings, the end of Part Three sees a reversal of roles, when McIlwaine holds up Anderson as the latter sinks into despair.

The most intense, intimate relationship, however, is that between Pyper and Craig, through whom McGuinness explores the problematic nature of art and the artist. The opening setting of 'Pairing' is Boa Island, in the Fermanagh lakes, Craig's home region. By emphasising the beauty and sacredness of this location, the text affirms the centrality of place within the Ulster Protestant imagination. For Craig, returning to and bathing in the Erne is a baptismal experience (39). Having breathed fresh life into his friend on the battlefield,[333] he hopes to inspire Pyper and reanimate his creative gifts by showing him the island's ancient carvings. For Pyper these are ambiguous figures. Male *and* female, stone *and* flesh, they occupy time, yet are beyond time. He projects onto them his own fragmented personal narrative, interpreting the carvings both as 'Domestic gods. Ancestral gods' *and* 'Living gods', like Craig. To Pyper, Craig is the instrument through which the Protestant gods have bestowed grace and forgiveness, and restored pattern and form in his life.[334] His history to date he characterises as one of futile rebellion. Yet despite his renunciation of his Protestant ancestors and their seemingly philistine culture ('their thick darkness' (47)), they retained their hold on him. Fleeing to France before the war, he sought to escape Ulster's politics ('Carson's dance'), 'to create, not destroy' (56).[335] Horror at the 'contamination' he carried inside himself – their biological and cultural imprint? – made him unable to create or procreate. Convinced that the only means of ridding himself of the burden of being 'their' creature was to destroy himself, he enlisted:

> I would take up arms at the call of my Protestant fathers. I would kill in their name and I would die in their name. To win their respect would be my sole act of revenge, revenge for the bad joke they had played on me in making me sufficiently different to believe I was unique, when my true uniqueness lay only in how alike them I really was. (57)

More important dramatically than these partial disclosures is the responsiveness they arouse. Craig's language moves up several gears. Earlier he had conveyed to Millen his belief that the future lay with engines (22); now, on Boa Island, he identifies himself with a past or passing way of life: 'Sometimes I look at myself and I see a horse. There are hounds about me, and I'm following them to the death'.[336] Part of his strategy for 'survival' is to merge his distinctness in a new, shared identity: 'I saw you. And from what I saw I knew I'm not like you. I am you' (57). Interestingly, these confidences end with an exchange of names (58), a litany which faintly resembles that of another doomed pairing, Yolland and Maire in *Translations*.

From the outset of the final section, 'Bonding', the extent to which relationships between the eight have been transformed is apparent. Separated in different locations in Part Three, they find themselves sharing once more a single space on stage, a trench on the Somme, on the eve of battle. No longer obsessed with calling the tune, Pyper is now a calming and cohesive influence, accepted and integrated within the group. The role of Cassandra has passed to Millen, the former UVF officer and gun-runner (62, 66, 71). To counter his predictions of imminent catastrophe, and repress their own dread, the others engage in banter, swap narratives, sing hymns, improvise rituals. What emerges as a common denominator in each of these solidarity-building strategies is a deep antipathy to Irish republicanism and Catholic culture. And so, when McIlwaine speculates what the Germans might be saying, Pyper claims that they are speaking in Gaelic:

MCILWAINE: Germans don't speak Gaelic.
PYPER: They all learn it for badness, McIlwaine. (64)

This triggers McIlwaine's scathingly irreverent account of the recent Easter Rising, in which 'this boy Pearse' allegedly 'took over a post office because he was short of a few stamps'. McIlwaine characterises their southern enemies as unmanly ('this boy', 'He starts to cry', 'Disgrace to their sex'), ignorant ('The Irish couldn't spell republic, let alone proclaim it'), and prone to fantasy ('He … got carried away and thought it was Christmas'). The final violence he inflicts on nationalism's 'sacred narrative'[337] is to have Pearse's mother shooting 'the cheeky pup' herself out of embarrassment at his misbehaviour.[338] Unashamedly he admits having no interest in historical accuracy, particularly if that clashes with his preconceptions as an Ulster Protestant: 'To hell with the truth as long as it rhymes' (65).

Soon afterwards, McIlwaine turns to an earlier, 'safer' period in 'history' as a means of boosting morale, when he and Anderson hit on the idea of re-enacting the Battle of Scarva. This foray into metadrama backfires on them, when King Billy (Pyper) trips and falls, and the haughty King James (Moore) survives. A sour note intrudes when Anderson voices his suspicion that Pyper deliberately skewed the battle's result, but then a wistful melancholy takes over. Taking their cue from Craig, who has been dreaming of Enniskillen, each man begins thinking of home and their natal waters, the Erne, Bann, Foyle and Lagan.[339] Too eagerly, Pyper tries to capitalise on this mood, denying the distinctness of individual attachments to place in an endeavour to forge a collective vision: 'We're not in France. We're home. We're on our own territory' (73). With the actuality of battle only minutes away, Craig has no time for his artist-friend's aestheticising manoeuvres. Moving centre-stage, it is he who speaks now with authority and an eerie foreknowledge of what is to come:

There's nothing imaginary about this, Kenneth … We're going out to die … Whoever comes back alive, if any of us do, will have died as well ... The Protestant gods told me. In a dream ... Get yourselves ready. Make your peace with god and man (74).

McGuinness's skills as a dramatist are fully displayed in these scenes, in which the audience repeatedly witness moving examples of change, unexpected instances of heightened awareness. For a while a rift appears to opens up between the lovers. Craig consciously wounds Pyper, accusing him of slumming it in the lower ranks: 'You're not of us, man' (76). Seconds later, he relents, however. His plea, 'Kenneth, don't die. One of us has to go on', leads one to conclude that by trying to break their bond he had hoped to lessen his friend's pain in survival. At this moment of sundering, another 'ghostly recurrence'[340] occurs. In a gesture of obvious affection, which recalls the episode in Part Two when Pyper gave Craig one of his shirts, Anderson presents Pyper with an Orange sash.[341] It is a symbol of acceptance and recognition that the aristocratic, unpredictable, homosexual Pyper is 'one of our own' (77). Anderson's action leads in turn to one of the most moving moments in the entire play, a silently performed ritual in which each soldier exchanges his sash with another character, Craig with Moore, Crawford with Anderson, Millen with McIlwaine, Roulston with Pyper. Following this latter act of reconciliation between former enemies, Roulston urges Pyper to speak and mediate on their behalf, as in effect he does throughout the play. For the audience there is a poignant irony in Pyper's imperatives and subjunctives, knowing as they do not only that his pleas will be ignored, but also that terrible carnage will be visited on their community and land in years to come: 'Save us. Save our country. Destroy our enemies at home and on this field of battle. Let this day at the Somme be as glorious in the memory of Ulster as that day at the Boyne, when you scattered our enemies' (79–80). Young Pyper's speech ends with a moving assertion of love for 'home' and 'Ulster', which, taken up and amplified by his fellow Ulstermen, translates itself ominously into '*a battle cry, reaching frenzy*' (80).

Observe the Sons' concluding lines take the form of a litany, in which, for want of Craig, the two Pypers merge as one, the younger repeating the elder's words from Part One:

YOUNGER PYPER:	The house has grown cold, the province has grown lonely.
ELDER PYPER:	Ulster...
YOUNGER PYPER:	The temple of the Lord is ransacked.
ELDER PYPER:	Ulster.

YOUNGER PYPER: Dance in this deserted temple of the Lord.
ELDER PYPER: Dance (80).[342]

That Ulster has become 'cold', 'lonely', 'ransacked', 'deserted', the locus for a terrible emptiness, the text acknowledges. Nevertheless, through the medium of the actors, the playwright, insists on the need to 'dance', on art as 'the love-act and its pledge'.[343] His drama serves as a timely reminder of how unionist imaginations in the present are haunted by the sacrifices of past generations, and how cultural growth and maturation are possible only when those who make up the people on the island come to terms with the heterogeneity within their ranks.

Poetry: Paul Muldoon, *Why Brownlee Left, Quoof*

Along with a surge in women's fiction and dramatic explorations of Protestant identity, the 1980s witnessed a leap forward in the literary careers of a younger generation of Northern Irish poets, which included Tom Paulin (b.1949), Medbh McGuckian (b.1950), and, a little later, Ciaran Carson (b.1948).[344] Paulin's profile rose following the publication of his second and third poetry collections, *The Strange Museum* (1980) and *The Liberty Tree* (1983), and a controversial book of critical essays, *Ireland and the English Crisis* (1984), but also as a result of his role as a director of Field Day. McGuckian's *The Flower Master* (1982) and *Venus in the Rain* (1984) rapidly established her reputation as a major voice in Northern Irish poetry and as the province's leading woman poet. Carson had initially come to prominence in the mid-1970s; he received ACNI funding for his poetry in 1974, wrote his famous critique of Heaney's *North* the following year, and published *The New Estate* in 1976. However, it would not be until the publication of *The Irish for No* (1987) and *Belfast Confetti* (1989) that the scale of his poetic achievement became widely recognised.[345]

At the forefront of this cluster of talent was Paul Muldoon, whose two collections from this period, *Why Brownlee Left* (1980) and *Quoof* (1983), were enthusiastically received by the reviewers and secured an increasing audience of admirers.[346] The dominant, recurring motif in *Why Brownlee Left* is that of journeying and departures, in content, language and form.[347] At its midway point is a group of poems recording the collapse of his first marriage in 1977. 'Holy Thursday' depicts a couple's last supper together, and their near-complete separation. Although notionally addressed to his ex-partner, the male narrator conveys only a sense of her absence. Unable or unwilling again to confront the 'something or other' or 'whatever' that caused the rift, he welcomes the distraction of watching one of the waiters taking his late-night meal. The rituals he observes are almost priestly; the man 'swabs his plate with bread/ And drains what's left of his wine', then neatly reimposes order on the table, 'and bows to his own absence' (31). 'Holy Thursday' is itself just such a gesture. In another, more bookish poem of parting, 'Making the Move', the speaker wryly identifies with Ulysses. The odyssey on which he has embarked, however, is only along the coastline of his book-shelf. A brief reflection on Pascal and 'the void to his left side' leads him to consider 'this wider gulf / Between myself and my good wife' (32). At the close, he accentuates his own unheroic, unHomeric stature, by adopting as his emblem a bow bought during his early teenage years. By drawing attention to its 'boyish', 'Unseasoned and unsupple' features, he may well be passing judgement on himself and his own lack of maturity.[348]

The majority of the poems in *Why Brownlee Left* preoccupy themselves with the intersections of family and locality, national and international narratives. In this latest stage in his poetic odyssey, Muldoon refuses to allow the contemporary political moment to dictate his route, preferring, like Hamlet, 'by indirections find directions out'.[349] Nevertheless, despite Pyperesque attempts at levity as a means of resisting its incursions, history troubles much of the text from the outset. The book's first sonnet, 'October 1950', immediately assaults convention and decorum, by adopting a crude, confrontational stance: 'Whatever it is, it all comes down to this;/ My father's cock / Between my mother's thighs' (9). Having swiftly established the biological mechanism behind his conception, the narrator speculates as to the arbitrary circumstances that led up to it, and so pushes the poem into more interesting metaphysical territory. With the admission in the closing line comes an acknowledgement of the unknowability and irretrievability of the past and of the origins of identity. Conceptually unable to grasp the chemistry behind the 'big bang' through which we came to be, all of us are left 'in the dark', without a point of source.

Self-orientation is the subject of 'The Geography Lesson' (10),[350] the poem which follows 'October 1950'. It harks back to a 'known world', a rural school in 1961, an unidyllic place and time before the Troubles. Rather than being a beacon of light, the school colludes in the social, economic and cultural marginalisation of its pupils.[351] The schoolroom is occupied largely by illiterates, whose fate is equated with that of 'internal exiles' in Stalinist Russia, those whom the regime regarded as political undesirables. Far from the seat of power, one of these, the ironically-named Mungo Park, stands out from the majority of his deprived class primarily through his ability to 'write his name' (10). In order to mark this singular achievement, he inscribes his name on every bench he moves to or is moved to. At the poem's midway-point, Park and his narrow horizons cease to engage the narrator, whose attention turns to Lefty Lynch, 'Who' allegedly 'knew it all'. The catalogue of 'facts' he has mastered, however, relates wholly to the natural world. Although initially confined to ladybirds, Lefty's world-view lifts off in stanza seven to encompass migrants like the cuckoo and the reason 'Why bananas were harvested while green'. Not unlike the poem's now maturer speaker, the bananas 'hanker after where they'd grown'.[352] In imagining the bananas' sighing from their peripheral location – in the ship's hold or beneath Lightbody's counter – Lefty anticipates the poet and his concern with displaced figures. Like the benighted inhabitants of 'A Disused Shed in Co Wexford', the bananas come to embody succeeding generations of casualties. Continuing with this self-reflexive reading of the text, it could be said that the poem's speaker has created something 'gold' from out of 'unremembering darkness', transmuted a memory of 'greenness' or immaturity into poetry. The closing pun may have been intended to set up a vague affinity between the speaker and his classmates. 'An unsteady hold' on language is, however, not what Muldoon possesses, as the neat rhymes and half-rhymes, clever imagery, and witty turns of phrase make clear.

Whereas in 'The Geography Lesson' *adult* figures of authority are absent, in 'Cuba' they are very much an invasive presence. This poem depicts the efforts of two different male authorities, a secular and a clerical father, to regulate and control female sexuality. Ludicrously in the opening lines a father berates his daughter for adding to the 'bother'[353] facing the world, by attending a dance at the time of the Cuba crisis, when America and the Soviet Union came close to the brink of nuclear war. He conflates American political and sexual power, characterising both in terms of 'touch and go', not inappropriately, perhaps, given later disclosures about John F. Kennedy's love-life. His suggestion that May should make her 'peace with God' results in her attending confession. There, a somewhat prurient priest tries to elicit details about the kind of physical contact she has had with the opposite sex:

> 'Did he touch your breast, for example?'
> 'He brushed against me, Father. Very gently'. (13)

If May's version of what happened is to be trusted, the boy's delicacy contrasts sharply with the priest's probing and the table-'pounding' of her father, which replicates that of Nikita Krushchev at the United Nations in October 1960.

Muldoon returns to school experience later in the volume, when in 'Anseo' (20–1), he delves into the pathology behind the present violence, in a narrative which reaffirms the Wordsworthian concept of the child as 'father to the man'.[354] The poem tracks Joseph Mary Plunkett Ward's transformation from humiliated victim to IRA commandant, from artist to revolutionary.[355] Interestingly, the opening stanza takes place in Collegelands, the primary school where Muldoon was a pupil and his mother a teacher. This is represented as a highly-regimented institution, in which the Catholic community's newest recruits learn obedience and fear. No explanation is proffered as to why young Ward should be first the butt of the Master's jokes, and then a regular candidate for caning.[356] The near-universal practice of using corporal punishment in British schools in the 1950s and 1960s to instil 'discipline' did, of course, create opportunities for adults of a sadistic bent to indulge their vice. The strategies the young Ward adopts for coping with this regular abuse – silence and subversion – anticipate those he will deploy in his adult career. Sent out into the fields to select the 'stick with which he would be beaten', the boy returns with a variety of weapons, 'an ash-plant, a salley-rod', and finally, and most significantly, 'a hazel-wand'. For the Celts, hazels were associated with 'the wisdom of the ages' and 'the accomplishments of poetry and science',[357] The instrument of correction Ward fashions functions as an *objective correlative* of the 'whittled down', 'polished', 'delicately wrought' work in which it figures. It points again to the highly self-reflexive nature of Muldoon's verse, his tendency to identify *traces* of himself and his art in very different characters and locations; in a contemporaneous interview, Muldoon comments, 'I'm very interested in structures that can be fixed like mirrors at angles to each other ... so that new images can emerge'.[358] Yet to claim, as Clair Wills does, too close an affinity between Muldoon and his characterisation is deeply mistaken; the ways in which poets 'disturb and disorder'[359] tend not to leave broken bodies on the streets. Equally to cite Ward's schoolboy's skill with a penknife as evidence that 'revolution is also creative in its way'[360] ignores the massive disjuncture between his creativity as a child and devastating capacity as an adult.

In the third and final stanza, the spheres of politics and poetry are brought into violent contiguity, when a famous phrase of Auden's[361] is re-worked and applied to Joe Ward's current field of activity. 'Making things happen' very much reflects how *Joe* views the IRA's campaign in the 1970s, although it is undoubtedly intended to be read as an appalling example of euphemism. Muldoon's aim in 'Anseo', like Heaney's in 'Freedman', is to expose the lineaments of oppression within his own natal culture and their subsequent 'whip-lash' effects, acknowledging that art can function as an effective form of social critique. Indeed, as one of his later personae, 'Louis', maintains, 'poetry *can* make things happen / not only can, but *must*' (original italics).[362]

Amongst the other poems in *Why Brownlee Left* which venture into political territory is 'The Boundary Commission'. This might be read as a rejection of demands that poets should make their religious allegiances or political loyalties explicit in their work. Although the concluding line conveys its narrator's refusal to take sides, the poem is not without political freight. The title itself harks back to a body created in the mid-1920s, tasked with making minor adjustments to the borders set out in the Anglo-Irish Treaty of 1921. In the event many of the changes the Commission proposed turned out to be advantageous to the northern unionists, but were accepted by the Free State, leaving the northern nationalist community feeling even more abandoned.[363] In Muldoon's text the divisions imposed by politicians, endorsed by their constituents, appear ludicrous because of their arbitrary nature. The poem begins interrogatively, questioning the sense of separating two halves of the same street into 'different states'. Having noted how 'cleanly' a light shower of rain halts in the middle of 'Golightly's lane', the narrator asks himself 'which side, if any, he should be on' (15). Yet perhaps where Muldoon most decisively deflects the call to 'engage' is in 'History', which opens enquiring, 'Where and when exactly did we first have sex?' (27). The remaining eight lines of the poem fail to solve the mystery, but point towards one possible time and location, 'that Thursday evening', Aquinas Hall, Belfast. However, as Edna Longley deftly shows,[364] this is a poem which punctures assumptions about the fixity and retrievability of history, whether personal or collective, nationalist or unionist, republican or loyalist. And lest we succumb to the illusion that the authorities on literature are inherently more trustworthy than other voices of authority, the speaker warns us that the momentous encounter may or may not have occurred in 'the room where MacNeice wrote "Snow"/ *Or* the room where *they say* he wrote "Snow"'(27; my emphasis).

Given that Muldoon's entire adult life had been lived out against the background of sustained onslaught, it is hardly surprising that at some point he should confront the violence in a more explicit manner. With its recurrent images of carnage and carnality, his fourth major collection, *Quoof* (1983), discloses an imagination flayed by the political events of the preceding years, in particular the prison protests which culminated in the 1981 hunger strikes. Allusions to the consumption of food and drink, to stomachs and entrails, digestion and defecation abound.[365] And so, when, in a brief introductory commentary to the book, Muldoon refers to a need 'to purge myself',[366] he provides a useful way into reading these poems whose language, form and content have absorbed and administered a shock to the system. Such is the 'toxicity'[367] circulating in the culture, and indeed in his own consciousness, Muldoon believes that only a dose of something astringent will palliate its effects.

One of the best places to view this fierce emetic in operation is the long comic-gothic narrative poem with which *Quoof* ends, 'The More a Man Has the More a Man Wants'.[368] Over the course of nearly 50 14-line stanzas or 'sonnets',[369] and with considerable difficulty, the reader trails in the wake of the poem's principal protagonist, Gallogly, and his pursuer and doppelganger, a native American from the Oglala tribe, an Indian called Jones.[370] Gallogly's name is a corruption of 'gallóglach', or in English 'gallowglass', originally a 'foreign warrior' or mercenary employed by medieval Irish chiefs; its second element (*oglach*) alludes also to *Oglaigh na h-Eireann*, a phrase used by the Provisionals to bolster their claim to be Ireland's defenders.

Although as fragmented, anarchic and elusive a figure as the narrative that contains him, it is necessary to try and delineate Gallogly's 'story' and the poem's 'action' if one is to gain any purchase on the text and the poet's intents. He is first encountered, squatting 'in his own pelt', like an animal, shortly after being abandoned by his unidentified mate.[371] He is next glimpsed on the run, dressed only in 'a candy-stripe / king-size sheet / a little something he picked up / off a clothes-line' (42). The improvised way with which he masks his nakedness invites comparison with the H-blocks' blanket-men, images of whom haunt the text. Despite such reminders of the deadly contest being fought out in Northern Ireland's streets and prisons, the narratorial voice consistently depicts Gallogly and his increasingly serious crimes in a light-hearted fashion. With the police on his tail, he commandeers a milk-van, after having given the milkman what the narrator euphemistically terms 'a *playful* / rabbit-punch' (42: my emphasis). Two sonnets later, no sympathy is offered to a husband whose wife has probably been raped and murdered. All these deeds are treated as 'much of a muchness',[372] just examples of Gallogly's breathtaking audacity.

> He's sporting your Donegal tweed suit and your
> Sunday shoes and politely raises your
> hat as he goes by.
> You stand there with your mouth open
> as he climbs into the still-warm
> driving seat of your Cortina …

> leaving you uncertain
> of your still-warm wife's damp tuft. (43)

By applying the very same phrase to a dead woman as to a car-seat ('still-warm'), and by depicting her solely by means of a metonym ('damp tuft'), the speaker reveals how deeply implicated he is himself in the misogynistic culture Gallogly embodies and which reifies women.

The ensuing stanza, which portrays a woman who has been tarred and feathered, substantiates these points. The paramilitaries have turned her body into a sign, a warning to other potential transgressors. Yet, by a grim irony, they have translated her into a figure whose appearance ('big-eyed, anorexic') replicates that of the starving prisoners in the H-blocks. Though republican campaigners, on the outside and inside, castigated the Long Kesh authorities for the brutalities and humiliations inflicted on inmates, the arbitrary justice meted out by local Provisionals can hardly be seen as enhancing the ethical reputation of their cause. What is particularly striking about the narrator's reaction to this scene is the absence of any moral judgement.[373] Unlike Heaney's persona in 'Punishment', Muldoon's has no qualms about acting as the 'artful voyeur'. He even slips in a few wry quips at the woman's expense, noting that she is dressed in a *'bomber* jacket', how 'Her lovely head has been chopped/ And changed' (43), and comparing her to a *grande dame* from France's *ancien régime*. Both Kendall and Wills, homing in on the religious location of this 'lesson for today', suggests that, as in 'Anseo', Muldoon is keen to establish a link between 'authoritarian religion'[374] and PIRA violence; by identifying one as cause, the other as effect, they ignore the way republican paramilitaries appropriate and distort Christian concepts, imagery and diction.

When Gallogly next surfaces, he is dumping the stolen Cortina in the River Callan, which forms part of the Armagh/Tyrone border. This is very much Muldoon's home territory. By informing us how this liminal area was *'planted* by Warwickshiremen' (my emphasis), the speaker highlights that critical historical moment in the early seventeenth century whose fruit is both political, textual and linguistic. This is exemplified in sonnet ten which begins with one of those 'cherished archaisms'[375] so common still in Ulster dialect: 'I'll *warrant* them's the very pair / o' boys' (44: my emphasis). The police have no clue as to the identities of the 'boys' they are pursuing, though one (Gallogly) has left a pile of 'half-chawed' damsons – or as he calls them 'damsels' – while the other (Jones) has sped off in an Avis van. Interpolated in the policemen's discussion is a line drawn appropriately enough from Shakespeare's tenth sonnet. Muldoon refrains from quoting the succeeding lines, despite, or rather because of their obvious applicability to current republican violence, including the self-harm occurring in the prisons:

> For thou art so possessed with murderous hate
> That 'gainst thyself thou stick'st not to conspire
> Seeking that beauteous roof to ruinate
> Which to repair should be thy chief desire.[376]

Gallogly meanwhile is holed out in a hayshed, a significant choice of location given the furore that surrounded the shooting in November 1982 of Michael Tighe.[377] Exhausted by hunger ('mad for a bite o' mate'), he is physically wasting away. The stolen tweed jacket and brogues 'Hang loose about him, like a giant's robe / Upon a dwarfish thief'.[378] In typical postmodernist fashion, the text sharply juxtaposes one cultural frame of reference with a very different other, the 'classic' (Shakespeare, Robert Louis Stevenson) with the popular (Hanna-Barbera cartoons). At the end of sonnet 12, Gallogly suddenly morphs into Yogi Bear, '*drawn* out of the woods' (45; my emphasis) by the smell of food. When he comes into the vision and sites of the UDR officer's wife, it is in the form of a series of refracted images, spied through a 'picture window', 'a glass of water', 'in the reflection of her face' (46). In presenting her response to the intruder, Muldoon deploys an incongruous mix of allusions and registers; after beginning with a resounding Churchillian phrase ('the integrity of their quarrel'),[379] he descends into the kind of clichés found in American gangster books ('let him have both barrels') and contemporaneous news-paper reports ('legally held shotgun', 'clear the air').

For a while it looks as if Gallogly is a goner. A 'bloody puddle' signifies his absence; he disappears 'up his own bum'; his body shrinks like that of a hunger-striker. That he still embodies violent potential is, however, clear from references to 'command wire', the Kalashnikov and the unstable explosive which has 'begun to weep' (47).[380] And like one of those crushed or shattered characters in children's cartoons, Gallogly has the capacity to spring instantly back into shape. He resumes his killing career in sonnet 19, murdering a UDR man, the husband of the woman who shot him. Once more the narrator laces his account of a crime with the stock diction of 'the hourly news bulletin';[381] the 'off-duty' officer is hit by a 'single high-velocity / shot', which leaves a huge 'exit wound' in his chest. What redeems his language from the formulaic are its unexpected touches, like the Christ-like invitation to the reader 'to put your fist' in the wound 'if you like', or the unusual simile applied to the stricken man, which sees him compared to 'an overturned paraffin lamp' (49).

Executing a sequence of defamiliarising 'swerves away'[382] from these arresting images, the speaker directs attention not only onto the perpet-rator of the violence, but also to a frequent literary presence in Muldoon's work, that of his precursor and fosterer, Seamus Heaney. Gallogly is pic-tured relaxing in a ditch or '*sheugh*', munching an apple. When combined with the *Sweeney*esque diet of watercress and garlic[383] consumed earlier, the very English-sounding Beauty of Bath causes digestive problems. The repetition and italicisation of '*Bath*' and '*Sheugh*' indicate Muldoon's arrival in the linguistic-cultural-political territory marked out in one of Heaney's best-known place-name poems from *Wintering Out*. Composed pre-Bloody Sunday, 'Broagh' imagined the North's plural linguistic heritage might act as a source of identity and site of reconciliation.[384] Writing at a very different historical juncture, and out of a different conception of what poetry can and should effect, Muldoon is deeply sceptical about lit-erature's capacity to heal or assuage, or confer rootedness on the deprived and dispossessed. Thus at the fictional 'core' of *his* protagonist's identity and cultural identity we find only indeterminacy and absence.[385] In con-trast to Heaney's poem, in which the 'final *gh*' excluded 'strangers', but offered a sound prospect for a coming-together of Ulster's divided com-munities, in Muldoon's the 'natives' are estranged, and like Montague's schoolchild 'slur and stumble'[386] in the unfamiliar tongue. Gallogly

> is finding that first 'sh'
> increasingly difficult to manage. (49)

Some critics have used these parodic allusions to Heaney's work, along with Muldoon's editorial decision to exclude virtually the whole of *North* from the *Faber Book of Contemporary Irish Poetry*, not simply to emphasise aesthetic, political and moral distinctions between the two, but in order to promote the one and diminish the other's achievement.[387] Those seeking a more nuanced reading of literary and personal negotiations between these equally major poets and their different merits should look no further than Neil Corcoran's 1998 essay on the subject.[388]

From the poem's midway point, sudden shifts in location and changes of cast accelerate. At one moment we are in a gallery in New York's Museum of Modern Art, watching Gallogly as he strains 'to get right under the skin' of the horse in Picasso's *Guernica*, the next we are on a train with Knut Hamsun coughing blood; we visit literary and hallucinogenic wonderlands with one Alice and then another, before our attention moves to the Staten Island Ferry where 'two men are dickering / over the price / of a shipment of Armalites' (54). For a while the whirligig halts, however, to provide unsettling glimpses of the 'action' back in Northern Ireland. There, shortly after strapping on his safety belt, a local politician is blown to bits by a car bomb:

> Once they collect his smithereens
> he doesn't quite add up. (53)

Yet again the *visually* acute narrator records a horrific event in what seems a dispassionate manner. He translates a victim into an aesthetic object, noting the resemblance between his severed calf and 'a severely / pruned-back shrub'.[389] As in earlier Troubles' poems like Heaney's 'Limbo' or Longley's 'The Civil Servant', the matter-of-fact description has the effect of transferring the emotional and moral onus onto the reader.

Finally, in sonnet 37, Gallogly's eagerness to inspect the massive hole left by a culvert bomb leads to his arrest and his incarceration in Armagh jail. There the killer turns voyeur. Let loose on the block, he spies on a young, thin female prisoner 'at stool', as, after a considerable effort, she produces a diminutive stub of shit. She uses this to decorate her cell with a sign of her national identity, her imagined point of origin:

> she has squiggled
> a shamrock, yes,
> but a shamrock after the school
> of Pollock. (60)

Clair Wills offers a convincing account of the significance of this and other allusions to modernist painting, linking the various art-works mentioned to Muldoon's obsessive concern in *Quoof* with the 'fragmentation of the represented body'.[390] Indeed the frame for the poem's climax comes from a painting or paintings by Edward Hopper[391] of a garage forecourt into which two paramilitary 'night hawks' ride. What they leave in their wake is a bucket of home-'brew' (63) whose lethal effects repeat those of sonnet 28. It is unclear from the final stanzas whether Gallogly or the Oglala Sioux or both kick the bucket; all that remains of one or both are smithereens, a 'head and torso', a 'frazzled ear', a 'hairy han' (64).[392] The only thing to survive the explosion is, according to one eye-witness, 'a lunimous stone', the 'pebble of quartz' with which Mangas Jones arrived at Aldegrove in sonnet two, and which Robert Frost might have glimpsed at the bottom of a well in 'For Once, Then, Something'.[393] As material and elusive as the poems it is found in, the pebble symbolises 'something', though what that something might be is left to individual readers. What Muldoon's poem certainly does register, like the gallful lyrics which precede it, is the near-complete desensitisation of a culture and people. Its narrator's deadpan delivery is symptomatic of this virulent condition, which at times seems to number compassion, art and meaning alongside its many individual casualties.

2
Towards an Ending: 1987–1995

I   From Enniskillen to the ceasefires (1987–1994)

Stewart Parker *Pentecost*

> If ever a time and place cried out for the solace and rigour and passionate rejoinder of great drama, it is here and now ... The politicians, visionless almost to a man, are withdrawing into their sectarian stockades. It falls to the artists to construct a model of wholeness by means of which the society can begin to hold up its head in the world.[1]

This declaration that art and artists might still play a potent, transformative role within the riven cultures of Northern Ireland appears in a lecture given by the playwright, Stewart Parker, two years before his death.[2] *Pentecost*, the third and final work in Parker's trilogy, *Three Plays for Ireland*, represents an attempt to offer a whole, inclusive vision, not least in its closing scene in which speech, music and light are combined to telling, dramatic effect. Its première took place in late September 1987 at Derry's

Guildhall under the auspices of the Field Day Theatre Company who had commissioned a piece from Parker back in 1984.[3] Its composition coincides with one of most turbulent phases in the Troubles' history, as the previous chapter made clear. The political turmoil generated by the Anglo-Irish Agreement, and its destabilising effect within the Protestant community in particular, no doubt influenced Parker's decision to set his play at another equally critical juncture in Northern Irish history, February–May 1974.[4] Its opening scene takes place in the period in which the power-sharing administration engendered by the Sunningdale Agreement was still alive and functioning, its closing scene four days before its existence was terminated as a result of the Ulster Workers' Strike.

From the outset Parker's concern with the interrelationship between private and public histories is apparent. The play's action is confined to 'a house eloquent with the history of this city' (165), a working-class terrace-dwelling dating from the beginning of the century.[5] The stage directions would lead one to conclude that the house, like the province and its inter-communal relationships, is stuck in a time-warp: '*The kitchen is cluttered, almost suffocated with the furnishings and bric-a-brac of the first half of the century*'.[6] Now run-down in appearance and musty in atmosphere, it reflects its Protestant owner's lifetime's pursuit of something better, '*tidiness, orderliness – godliness*' (147). Yet these initial indicators as to the late Lily Matthews's home and character turn out to be misleading, since beneath the façade of stasis and propriety lies a different structure, which the house's new, Catholic occupant progressively exposes. The researches of her Other and double, the antiques specialist, Marian, reveal a hidden history of pain, guilt and thwarted desire, making the audience reassess its early negative impressions of Lily and the chill, naysaying culture she seems to represent.[7]

The importance of the legacy of the Great War in the construction and fashioning of Ulster Protestant identity has already been explored. Like Michael Longley and Frank McGuinness before him, Parker depicts a culture in which suffering, victimhood and feats of endurance play no small part.[8] One of the first details revealed about Lily, the late resident of the house, is that she was married at 18 to a Passchendale survivor (156).[9] As a result of gathering and interpreting physical clues deposited around the house and gaining access to the diary which she had secreted in the cellar, Marian learns that Lily was herself a Great War casualty since the injuries her husband, Alfie, received in the battle left him sexually impotent (196).[10] Three years after the end of the war, 'history' again intervened in the couple's lives when Lily and Alfie's new home was broken into by republicans, during the violence that preceded Partition. After beating her husband unconscious, these 'cruel heathens' smashed up the interior and set the house ablaze, while Lily cowered in the pantry, pleading to 'Lord Jesus to deliver us' (157). Providentially, she was saved by the fire service.

Twelve years on, during the Depression, when they were in their early thirties, Alfie Matthews lost his job, forcing the couple to take in a lodger to help pay the bills (177). Subsequently, this outsider, an English serviceman, charmed his way into Lily's affections, while Alfie was away in England seeking work. At some time after what appears to have been a solitary sexual encounter, the airman disappeared into the sunset (195–6), leaving Lily pregnant.[11] Appalled by her fall into 'lust and fornication', and mindful of her husband's and her own good name, Lily abandoned the baby she gave birth to, leaving him in the porch of a Baptist chapel. Although initially in her exchange with Marian she endeavours to put a positive gloss on her action ('I entrusted him to the care of the Lord'), under interrogation she admits the terrible suffering this betrayal caused her, 'gnawing and tearing away at my own heart and lights, day in day out ... and nothing left but the shell of me' (196).

A ghost, an absence conjured intermittently in Marian's and the audience's imaginations,[12] Lily is central to the play's examination of the past's oppressive haunting of the present. As the drama unfolds, significant points of affinity and disparity between her narrative and that of the contemporary female characters emerge. This is particularly true in relation to Marian, the 33-year-old Catholic woman who acts as the medium through whom Lily materialises on stage.[13] Although the product of a different culture and period in which women are able to pursue careers and no longer feel obliged to remain in unfulfilling relationships, she is, like Lily, trapped. Formerly a successful, driven entrepreneur, who ran her own antiques business, Marian is clearly now undergoing some kind of spiritual and psychological crisis. In an attempt to reconfigure her life, she has sold her shop and flat, and impulsively offers to buy Lily's home, despite its location close to a sectarian frontline and within a redevelopment zone (154). Early in the exchanges with the spectre who occupies her, Marian acknowledges her own troubled state: 'the place where I'm least welcome is in my own skull ... I don't like me either' (157). The source of her problems, it emerges at the close of Act One, is her continuing inability to come to terms with the devastating loss of *her* child, Christopher, a victim of cot death, five years earlier.[14] Her discovery of an unused christening robe secreted amongst Lily's underthings brings to the surface the grief she sought to repress. At this moment of epiphany, Marian affirms her kinship not only with Lily, but also with her unhappily-married Protestant friend, Ruth: 'Maybe she lived in hope. Like you and me' (181). At first, however, Ruth asserts the particularity of her suffering, rejecting the idea of a sorority of sorrow. Up to this point the audience has become accustomed to regarding Ruth primarily as a victim of domestic violence, one who, like many women in such circumstances, is prepared to excuse the inexcusable, the abuse of a sadistic husband (162). The disclosure that she has endured *three* miscarriages[15] and so may never conceive again translates her into a much more tragic presence in the play, and enables us to recognise the aptness of her name:

> RUTH: What do you know about it, yours was alive, at least you had it at your breast ... oh Jesus if only I'd been able to keep just one of them ... we'd be all right, all different, if I can't have a child I won't live! (181)

For both women childlessness seems like a death sentence. Marian's fragmented, incomplete utterances, alternately declarative and interrogative, voiced in the conditional and the past, contrast with and echo Ruth's. Unlike Ruth's, however, they convey not only the despair of the character on stage, but also that abroad in their original audience at that time, in that place:

> MARIAN: Christopher would have been five in August. Starting school. If he hadn't gone. Left me. Given up the ghost in me. My own soul, left for dead. He was our future, you see. Future at a time like this ... what could it possibly mean – a future? In a place like this? (181)

In a gesture emblematic of the play's politics, and how consciousness of alterity does not preclude expressions of fellow feeling, Ruth '*goes to her, kneels by her, embraces her*'. The fading of the lights heightens the impact of this tableau, around which are assembled other unseen figures, 'uncompleted souls'.[16] Although associated directly with Lily, the small white robe signifies not just the child she lost.

Lack, the absence of any 'model of wholeness',[17] is equally a feature of the male characters in *Pentecost*; in their different ways, Lenny, Peter and David all exemplify symptoms of a crisis in masculinity which can only partly be attributed to the political and socio-economic situation.[18] It is no accident that the tune Lenny, Marian's former husband, plays on his trombone as the play gets under way is the Gershwin-Duke number, 'I Can't Get Started'.[19] Unemployed throughout his adult life, after dropping out of university and abandoning his father's chosen profession (163), Lenny has suddenly become a man of property. This has come about not through his own efforts, but as a result of his aunt's will, which dictated that on the death of its sitting tenant, Lily Matthews, Lenny would inherit her house. Marian relishes the irony of this as in earlier days he had left-wing sympathies: 'Property used to be theft in your book' (150). According to Lenny's account, their marriage only came alive during the five months following on from the birth of their son. Before then and after, constant sources of friction were her business success and the fact that much of his passion and energy he channelled into music.[20] In contrast to Marian who claims to have understood him only too well, he readily admits his failure to comprehend her and her needs (167).

The most striking example of his imaginative deficiency comes in his repeated assertion to Peter that Marian 'took' Christopher's death 'in her stride' (175, 176); it may be that subconsciously he wants to convince himself that this was so and thus exonerate himself. For much of this exchange, Lenny adopts a seemingly unfeeling tone in speaking about Christopher, referring to him twice as 'the sprog' and by means of metonyms ('bunched-up fingers and feet', 'a tiny silent shrivelled up rickle of bones and skin'). The exactness of his word-choice here conveys a degree of subtlety and sensitivity at odds with his usual wry, sardonic manner. Recalling the awful moment when he realised the baby was no longer breathing, the façade of indifference falls away: 'He was my son. She was my wife' (176). Since the child's death in August 1969,[21] Lenny, like Northern Ireland, has existed in a state of paralysis. After five bitter years, he imagines that 1974 might be the year when he will be able to make a clean break with a damaged past. As his friend Peter points out, however, he has talked 'a dozen times before' about attempting 'the great escape' (172,175), but never carried it through. In a subsequent, extravagant allusion to the Second World War – a defining period for his (and Parker's) generation – Lenny speculates that the province's Catholics may be facing imminent destruction: 'This right here is Nazi Belfast now, and it's us playing the Jews' (190).[22] To Marian and to later audiences, Lenny's use of such a historical analogy seems hysterical and wholly reprehensible. Long after the strike crisis, such rhetorical excesses continued to feature in northern political discourse.

Though more astute in certain respects than Lenny, Peter comes across as an equally flawed figure. Initially he seems a slightly ridiculous, fool-hardy character, as he staggers on stage carrying a heavy sack of muesli, which he anticipates will enable him to survive the strike. What has enticed him to return to the strife-riven province from his comfortable exile in England, is the opportunity to observe history in the making, the clash between disaffected loyalists and the Westminster authorities.

The prodigal son of a Methodist minister, his function in the play is partly to deliver hostile critiques of loyalist politics in particular and his originary community more generally, and so act as a contrastive voice to Ruth's and Lily's. Much about Ulster he despises. For him, as for the speaker in Mahon's 'Ecclesiastes',[23] Northern Ireland is a 'rainy, bleak, doom-laden' place, 'utterly devoid of human life' (171), occupied by people full of self-loathing. Several times he compares it to Swift's Lilliput, its people to 'angry munchkins' (171), who by now should have turned their attention to grown-up global issues (172). Whereas Ruth is enraged by Harold Wilson's broadcast in which he denounced the strikers' actions as 'undemocratic' and 'sectarian' (183), Peter endorses much of what the Prime Minister says.[24] The terrible injuries suffered in Northern Ireland are almost entirely 'self-inflicted', he argues. By supporting what he regards as the utterly disreputable alliance[25] behind the strike and alienating the Brits, the Protestant community is in effect committing 'a lingering tribal suicide' (184). To Ruth, such views, like his outrage at the police and Army's failure to halt the looting, beatings and hijackings, are indicative of his 'English' perspectives now. For her the Ulster Workers' Strike is an unambiguous sign of Protestant resurgence, evidence of *her* community's determination not to be 'coerced' or 'dictated to' (185) by the British government.

The vehemence with which these two voice their political positions exemplifies how deep and intense ideological divisions were within unionism in 1974, 1987 and today. The nature and trajectory of Peter and Ruth's relationship, and thus the scene's focus, alter radically after he enquires about her husband's stance on the strike. Having established that she has severed links with David, Peter begins flirting with her in a blatant manner, taking advantage of her emotional vulnerability, just as Alan Ferris had done with Lily 40 years before. After kissing her once, '*he guides her to the sofa, sits her down, lifts her legs ... so that she is lying with her knees bent*' (188). Just as his foreplay is beginning to progress, it is rudely intruded upon by the blare of Lenny's trombone. Fleetingly, Ruth resists the idea of making love in the front parlour, objecting that it was a 'special' (189) place for Lily. Indeed it was, as we discover on her next 'appearance', for it was there that she allowed herself to be seduced by the English airman, Peter's alter ego (196).[26]

At the close of Act Two the significance of the play's title at last becomes obvious, as traces of his New Testament 'source' surface with greater frequency within Parker's dramatic narrative.[27] Confined together, and fearful of the violence raging outside, the four occupants resemble Christ's followers huddling in the upstairs room in the wake of the crucifixion.

Specific allusions to the transformational effect of the Holy Spirit can be seen in Marian's claim that 'this home speaks for' (178) the working-class Protestant community, Lenny's accusation that he has heard Marian 'babbling in tongues in the middle of the night' (192) and her riposte, in which she says she is content to stay in the house 'with my tongues' (193).

The final scene actually takes place on the Pentecost Sunday, 1974, within days of the strike's end. Instead of tongues of fire, what dispels darkness on stage is a *'glimmering'* from celebratory loyalist bonfires and the *'blinding searchlight'* of an army helicopter, which illuminates the figure of Peter scrambling over the yard wall (198). Once he has caught his breath, he informs Marian how he has been set upon by drunken 'young bloods' rejoicing at the Executive's collapse. Little thinking of the painful associations his words might induce in Marian and Ruth, he repeatedly uses birth images in mocking the loyalists' assumption that a brave new era in Northern Ireland's history is about to begin. Rather, he suggests, the strikers and those who supported them are comparable to child-killers:

> They're beside themselves with the glorious deliverance of it … you'd think they'd given birth, actually created something for once, instead of battering it to death, yet again, the only kind of victory they ever credit … stamping the life out of anything that starts to creep forward. (199)

The manner in which speech tumbles from him in 'run-on sentences'[28] is reminiscent of Ruth in scene three mourning her childlessness. For Peter clearly the intimacy he enjoyed with her less than a week before counts for nothing. He responds to her concern over his injuries by thrusting into her face his bloody hand, a symbol of Ulster loyalist identity and resistance which makes him want to 'puke' (199). The animus he first felt for Ruth's politics has been reignited by the strikers' triumph and the beating just meted out on him. That this has been a traumatic experience is evident from his sudden breakdown and admission that he cannot understand why he keeps coming back to Belfast, 'what it is I think I'll find here, whatever it is *I think I'm missing'* (199; my emphasis). This revealing disclosure brings him into alignment with his abject companions, who also dream of achieving individuation and extricating themselves from the 'deep well of memory'.[29]

Peter immediately resumes a pose of flippancy on Lenny's return, telling his friend how during his visit to his parents his mother had attacked him with a broken bottle (200). Almost immediately afterwards, it is he who initiates the succession of monologues which dominate the play's ending.[30]

Back in 1969, just before the Ulster conflict had begun to intensify, he, Lenny and a Chemistry student, named Moog McManus, set off on a mission to transform mindsets in the province. Fired with 'a messianic impulse', and conceiving of themselves as 'a holy trinity' for the New Age, they planned to pour LSD into Belfast's water supply in order to purge the population of the contaminating effects of sectarianism. Unaware that loyalist paramilitaries had targeted the Silent Valley reservoir ahead of them,[31] the three kept running into police patrols in the Mournes and were forced to turn back.

Against the background of Lenny's gentle banjo-playing, Marian offers an account of Lily's experiences in the Blitz. Instead of remaining in the cellar as she promised Alfie she would, she lay down nightly on the sofa in the hope that a bomb would annihilate her and her shame, and silence 'the whole uncontainable babble' Alan Ferris had awakened in her head seven years before. Outwardly the war left her unscathed. Yet in Lily's confused and poisoned mind, according to Marian, survival was a sign of God's unwillingness to forgive her. Ignoring Christ's response to adultery in the New Testament,[32] Lily believed that she had been marked down for 'a life sentence' (202) for her sin. In the short interchange with Ruth and Peter that follows, Marian reveals the transformative effects of Lily's sorry, masochistic tale on her state of mind. Rather than preserving Lily's house as a monument to 'a *whole* way of life, a *whole* culture' (178) as she originally intended, she now resolves to renovate it (and herself) and let in 'air and light' (202).

Called upon to deliver his narrative, Lenny also takes checked desire as his theme. He describes how after a jazz gig in Kinsale the previous autumn, he went down to look at the ocean in the early hours of the morning. Accompanying him was a somewhat befuddled lady vocalist. As she stripped off and began to croon her way through the hymn, 'Just a Closer Walk with Thee', he became transfixed by the sight of a dozen or so nuns frolicking in the sea. Witnessing the woman beside him and women in the water behaving in completely unpredictable ways is an experience he finds both defamiliarising and deeply arousing: 'it doesn't take long to see that the nuns are experiencing their sex and the vocalist her spirit. And for a few crazy seconds I all but sprinted down to the nuns to churn my body into theirs' (203–4). Marian's outline of Lily's repressed history has enabled him to sense connections with his own. Twice in the closing scene (202, 204), he speculates wistfully on the kind of place Ireland might have been prior to the advent of Christianity, and whether there might have been a time when 'natural' instincts were allowed free play.

Ruth responds immediately by contesting the negativity of his reading of Christianity, yet in terms which concede that there is an element of truth in his assertions. Christianity is not '*only* denial', she maintains, it is '*meant to be* love and celebration' (204: my emphasis). It could be argued that in quoting at such length the New Testament account of the Pentecost story,[33] she is suppressing her own voice, and attempting to relocate herself *inside* the borders of orthodox Christianity, after her recent fall into transgression.[34] She and her erstwhile lover are soon vying with each other in reciting *Acts* from memory, until Peter breaks off in order to denounce once more his fellow countrymen and women:

> I mean they're never done calling on the name of the Lord in this wee province of ours, so it ought to be the most saved place on God's earth instead of the most absolutely godforsaken. (205)

Now roused, he proceeds to unleash his scorn for 'the holy family' who have given him shelter over the past fortnight. Marian he compares to the Virgin Mary, 'shielding us all', but especially 'faithful little Ruthie' from harm. What is most surprising, however, is the scathing way he speaks about his friend dismissing him as an impecunious, impotent clown, 'jiggling his limp thing like a dead man's thrapple' (206). Even after the enraged Lenny has hurled him across the room, Peter continues his tirade. Images of absence come once again to the fore as Peter pictures how the Son of Man might react if he were to materialise in Ulster:

> Can you see him? Here? Can you see him? ... watching at the elbow of the holy Catholic Nationalist zealot as he puts a pistol to a man's knee, to a man's brains, to a man's balls ... observing the votes being cast in support of that ... what would Jesus Holy Christ do with us all here, would you say? (206)

Overlooking the abuse he suffered moments ago, Lenny, somewhat implausibly, joins his Protestant friend in denouncing the pharisaism abroad in Ulster. His is an apocalyptic vision, in which a vengeful, pitiless Christ returns to torch churches and harrow their congregations.

Significantly it is the women characters whose voices dominate the play's close. Exasperated at having to listen to these privileged, self-righteous men pontificating about suffering which they have not directly experienced and for which they take no responsibility, Marian breaks her silence about the pain that has possessed her for the past five years. Instead of blaming churches and clerics for the carnage, they should look to their own failings, particularly their inability to recognise that 'There is some kind of christ, in every one of us'. (Anticipating the reaction of some of *Pentecost*'s critics, Lenny and Peter '*turn their faces against this language*'.)[35] For Marian 'christness' appears a commingling of love, hope, potential, but equally of fallibility, vulnerability and mortality. This illumination has come not through sudden divine intervention, but as a result of her 'dialogue' with Lily, which has enabled her at last to find meaning from loss. She explains how she had attributed Christopher's death to the malign nature of the place and its people, and even blamed the dead child for the 'raw scar' that seared her spirit. In so doing, she betrayed him.[36] Now she resolves to 'carry' him once more within her, his separateness absorbed into her being. The only way forward, she concludes, for both her and the province, lies in crediting the capacity for love 'in ourselves' (207) and others.

The stage directions indicate the impact Marian's words have had on Lenny; he is '*close to tears now*'. By touching her hand '*privately and unobtrusively*', he signals some apprehension of what she might have been through since their child and marriage died.[37] In her final speech, Marian proclaims the obligation they all owe to the innocent dead, 'those ghosts within us' (208), to charge the province with a positive energy. As if making good this commandment, the sky at the rear of the set grows brighter. Outside the house Lenny takes up his trombone to give a soulful rendition of 'Just a Closer Walk to Thee', accompanied by Peter on the banjo. Inside, meanwhile, Ruth reads aloud from *Acts* of the transfiguration generated at the first Pentecost, and in one final emblematic gesture opens the window to let in light and music.

Tom Paulin *Fivemiletown*

The epigraph to *Fivemiletown* (1987), taken from Tom Paulin's version of *Antigone*, describes how the sun illuminates Thebes, an ordered city with 'dead clear' gates which resemble an open book. What immediately strikes one about his collection, like those of his contemporaries, Paul Muldoon and Medbh McGuckian, is how nothing it contains is 'dead clear'; attempts to construct a coherent narrative within and between poems are possible, but leave many unanswered questions. Yet despite being 'full of gaps, loose ends, hits and misses', the poems in *Fivemiletown* may be usefully viewed as 'a framed group', as 'animated particles in complex relation with one another – quick, sudden, paired ... now bunched together or marking time'.[38] This is yet another text which operates at the intersections of personal and public histories. Repeatedly, like Stewart Parker in *Pentecost*, Paulin juxtaposes instances of momentous political change, drawn from British, Irish and European Protestant history, with clashes and collisions in the private sphere. The single period which has most indelibly left its mark on this particular collection, however, is that which followed the signing of the Anglo-Irish Agreement.

Initially, the incongruities and displacements the reader encounters are of a relatively innocuous kind. Vile taste, rather than violence, outrages the speaker in the opening poem, 'The Bungalow on the Unapproved Road'. On an overnight stay in Donegal he and his partner share a bed which leaves them 'wrecked' (1). The damage inflicted on their backs by a cheap, 'spongy' mattress is bad enough, but what really takes 'the biscuit' is the garish wallpaper chosen by their hosts. References on successive lines to the Bluestack Mountains and the River Glen ('a wet, chittering/smash of light') lead the reader to expect a sustained focus on the striking, revelatory quality of 'real' landscape, in contrast to the 'tequila' Costa Brava sunsets depicted on the wallpaper. Instead, in typical postmodernist fashion, the narrator's eye turns to man-made material, specifically, a black Vauxhall careering towards Donegal, cornering dangerously on its 'jammy springs'. The allusions to 'hooch' and the 'Oldsmobile' evoke images of smuggling in America's prohibition era, and thus draw us away from a solely Irish context. At the same time the idea of freight hidden in the trunk may well prompt consideration of other, more sinister types of 'unapproved' traffic passing back and forth on the Irish/British border.[39]

Linguistically, 'The Bungalow' is interesting not just because of its playing around with semantic linkages, clusters and contrasts ('spongy' / 'biscuit' / 'jammy', 'tequila' / 'hooch', 'Costa Brava' / 'Donegal', 'black vinyl' / 'black Vauxhall'). Paulin's self-conscious use of the word 'jeuked' demonstrates his preoccupation with Ulster dialect, in a vocabulary commonly deployed in Ireland, but excluded from 'the *OED*'.[40] In his important Field Day pamphlet, *A New Look at the Language Question* (1983), the poet emphasises dialect's aesthetic, political and cultural potential, its capacity to act as a source of beauty, intimacy and cohesion; he highlights the warmth of such language, and 'the bonds which it creates among speakers'.[41] Yet in the absence of a dictionary of Irish English, he argues, large numbers of dialect words are 'literally homeless', their condition analogous to that of Ulster's Protestant people.[42] The appearance of such words as 'slegging' (2), 'lunk' (6), 'geg' (7), 'creashy' (12), 'stramash' (15), 'scaldy' (19), 'scroggy' (25), 'scouther and skitter' (34) in *Fivemiletown* thus bears witness to Paulin's belief in the urgent need for redress and cultural reconfiguration on the island and commitment to the Field Day mission of forging imaginatively a 'fifth province'.[43]

The imprint of the political crisis is much in evidence in the early poems. In 'The Red Handshake', for example, it is treated with a dark and mordant wit. The poem's title seems to hint at the prevalence of freemasonry and its rituals within loyalist culture, particularly within such paramilitary groups as the 'Third Force'.[44] Whether any connection might exist between the recent presence of this Paisleyite body in the Antrim hills and the body the narrator imagines disinterring is left unsaid. Shrouded in black plastic, 'like a growbag', the corpse offers a dourly upbeat review of his own and the province's fate: 'Mind it can get no worse' (4). It is no accident that in the immediate wake of this poem comes 'André Chénier', which evokes simultaneously two revolutionary periods, days of 'quick terror', in which 'no one living looks quite human' (5). The ladder the poet scales in the opening line alludes to different moments of recognition; it directs our gaze towards the metaphorical heights Chénier achieved through his writings and, more prosaically, towards the guillotine where his life was cut short. For Paulin clearly, Chénier and Tsvetayeva, and later Akhmatova and Mayakovsky,[45] are exemplary figures because of their creative resilience in the face of extreme political violence and moral chaos.

'Waftage' confronts the reader with a very different territory and idiom. Its swaggering, macho narrator dwells primarily on private spaces, notably the bed and bath he once shared with a partner. In portraying his affair's sorry state, he adopts by and large a colloquial register and diction. Occasionally, however, the language undergoes a qualitative advance, such as when he compares his constricted condition to that of a pollack 'wedged in an ironstone wall' or cites the poet, James Fenton, on the '*subterfugue text*' (6: original emphasis). Whereas his lover occupies herself creatively in an elevated position ('in the *loft above* the stables'(my emphasis)), he feels trapped in the 'boxed-up, gummy warmth' of their 'open but empty' rooms. To kill time he escapes into Le Carré's crime and spy novels, conscious of the disparity between his situation and that of Fenton, who tackled Shakespeare's entire works as Saigon was about to fall. This reflection prompts several other instances of cultural 'flinching', when the provincial speaker's underlying feelings of inferiority come to the fore. Despite the deployment of a past tense ('I used think'), a strong possibility remains that he *still* regards himself and people in the province as 'boneheads'. Where his anxieties about difference seem at their most acute is within the domain of language itself, as can be seen in his account of the couple's final falling-out. 'For a geg' ('a laugh'), he buys his girl-friend a box of panties in the colours of the Union Jack. She is indignant, and expresses her anger forcefully ('slung', 'spat') and in a historically antagonistic tongue ('*Va-t'en!*'). Switching to English, she denounces his breath, taste and Ulster accent as 'simply foul'. Although it is plainly her decision to terminate their relationship, he tries to imply that it is his. That a huge social, cultural and linguistic divide separates them is underlined by the ostentatious way he addresses her at the close as 'Lady' and peppers his speech with 'non-standard' forms ('real cool', 'Dead on', 'chucked'). Sounding defiant, he merely exhibits his insecurity.[46]

For the narrator in the title poem, 'Fivemiletown', identity is a deeply burdensome matter. The opening stanza, which, aptly in the circumstances, lacks a finite verb, voices a yearning for release from the constraints of 'who and where we've come from' (15), and views sexual consummation as a means of escaping from thought and belief into oblivion, anonymity, naked honesty. Addressed to an unnamed 'you', the section that follows juxtaposes the exquisite pang of desire ('all of my life/was pitched in the risk/of seeing and touching you') with the prosaic realities which defer and quicken it. Yet, despite, or perhaps because of the intensity of his longing and the turmoil it generates, the speaker considers the option of turning back. The very world which he is attempting to evade – a world of objects, names, dates, events – presses upon him during his journey 'on the slow road to Enniskillen'. He cannot avoid passing comment on the fate of the significantly-named Imperial Hotel, reduced to a 'stramash'[47] days before 'our last Prime Minister' was humiliatingly 'whipped' from power in 1972 on the orders of the British government.[48]

On arriving at his destination in stanza four, the narrator is greeted with an absence of a different kind. Instead of awaiting his lover's return at the guest-house, the agreed site for their rendezvous, he wanders the town's main street, only to experience an intense sense of displacement; a measure of this is the way he refers to himself as 'this gaberdine stranger' and imagines that he is under surveillance. In an effort to shake off these feelings, he retreats into nature, relocating himself in a wooded spot, a '*margin* of larch and chestnut' (my emphasis). Here too he is ill-at-ease, observing a camouflaged military vehicle passing through the landscape, like him, an intruder who would 'never fit' (16).[49] As in 'Waftage', the deployment of French (*porte cochère*) serves to intensify the protagonist's cultural discomfiture. Already faint ('dwammy sick') anticipating the coming reunion, reprehensibly he toys with the idea of running away and putting on a show of indifference ('*See you*' (original emphasis)). Given the indecisiveness of its narrator, it is entirely appropriate that the poem should end without a resolution.

Later in the volume, however, there is a second visit to Fivemiletown. Back in the seventeenth century, the book's endnotes inform us, this small settlement in Co. Tyrone had borne a different name, imposed by its Planter founder, Sir William Stewart.[50] Somewhat surprisingly given his previous antipathy to post-structuralist theory, 'Mount Stewart' (38–9) finds Paulin operating in a decidedly Derridean vein.[51] From the very beginning the poem's speaker makes play with the instability of texts, the impermanent nature of signification. Sir William's hubris in trying to inscribe his name on the land in perpetuity at first excites feelings of incredulity, amusement and exasperation on the narrator's part. That 'local demotic' voices and forces have erased the imposed sounds and marks of an alien and military presence is a source of considerable satisfaction to him. Unexpectedly, he equates the knight's overt and very public act of expropriation with a secret, intimate, appropriative act of his own, performed on the same ground. There is, of course, a recent precedent for the deployment of such a contentious political-sexual analogy, Seamus Heaney's 'Act of Union'.[52] Far less 'imperial' than his predecessor, the male speaker in Paulin's poem nevertheless gazes with equal concentration on the genital 'terrain' he intends occupying, 'the grassy mouth of the plantation', the *'tout petit pli'* in flesh (38).[53] Though consensual, the sexual liaison that takes place there transgresses the loyalties of *'your* tribe', the narrator stresses (my emphasis). Engrossed in one another, he and his lover *'disappeared* from ourselves' (my emphasis), a choice of image which might imply abandonment of a different kind, a rejection of the identities and communities history had assigned to them. If, as Derrida claims, nothing outside the text exists, then resistance to such forms of inscription has little chance of success; however, if, as Corcoran points out,[54] *everything* is text, then the dominant discourses in the province which foster historical enmity and sectarian division can be contested.

In striving to incarnate an alternative text, the lovers function as agents of subversion, rather like Winston and Julia in Orwell's *Nineteen Eighty-Four*.[55] Having to conduct their relationship by stealth ('lying low', 'gone to ground') has given it an added charge: 'The *buzz* in our voices/brought blood to our cheeks' (my emphasis). Yet, however much the couple try to achieve their 'dream' of 'plenitude', they find themselves constantly bugged by presences from the past. One such 'presence' is Blessingbourne, a nineteenth-century mansion, which lies at the centre of a substantial demesne dating back to plantation times.[56] Beneath its sweet and 'whimsical' exterior,[57] sinister, atavistic forces are at work, according to the narrator. To him the house is a 'transmitter', one of many stations in a surveillance network monitoring their every move and utterance. That differences between the lovers in *language*, and thus culture and perspective, inflicted the greatest damage on their relationship is hinted at in the curt reference to how 'we … broke/only in speech' (39).

In comparing his partner's home-town to a womb, the speaker emphasises its constrictions, not its warmth or security. Indeed, a few lines later
he claims that her 'door' – the front of her house *and* body – is under
constant scrutiny, though by whom he could 'never figure'. That last
image conveys his frustration at the impenetrability of Fivemiletown,
a place with 'no centre'. A 'womb of fives', it withstands his interpretative
thrust, baffles him just as an earlier generation of its people thwarted
another outsider and pretender, and his attempts at possession. The
poem's closing lines appear to voice a longing for uncomplicated sexual
intimacies, free of the political freight and history relationships carry in
Northern Ireland. The sudden appearance of Transatlantic usages and
references at this juncture ('figure', 'rap', '6-motel', 'someplace') leads one
to conclude that the namelessness and anonymity the narrator craves
are associated in his mind with America. The irony is that that too is
a planted place and site of dispossession.

The two poems immediately following 'Mount Stewart' are preoccupied
by the increasingly disaffected mood within the Ulster Protestant community as a result of Westminster's accord with Dublin. In the first of these,
'Sure I'm a Cheat Aren't We All?', Paulin revisits a pivotal, defining
moment in his personal history which then functions as a vehicle for
broaching and interrogating a larger, shared narrative. Ironically, this
opens with an image of containment, an emphasis on how objects, like
people and their minds, are marked with identifying, classifying signs.
Saddled with a title proclaiming the universality of the *in*authentic, the
poem's extremely meticulous narrator informs us not just of the reference
number on a file-box he bought a dozen or so years back, but also of its
place of manufacture and maker, along with the specific place and date
of his purchase, 'March 24th 1972'. That particular day is imprinted on his
memory since on that Friday Northern Ireland lost its legislative independence, when the parliament at Stormont was prorogued. Passing the
morning in the 'gloomy belly' (40) of Oxford's Bodleian Library, like some
latter-day Jonah, he experiences sudden feelings of displacement. Unable
to source the cause of his unease, he resorts to filling out file-cards with the
names of weighty authors (Haeckel, Schopenhauer, Hardy), ominously-
titled tomes (*The Riddle of the Universe, The World as Will and Idea, The
Strings are False*). By comparing his actions to 'filling in ballot papers', he
reminds readers of his *different* origins, but also hints at the frequent
instances of corruption in Northern Irish elections. Surrounded by '*real*
scholars' (my emphasis), he feels, like Jude Fawley, an interloper. In order
to perpetuate that illusion, he employs a device used by the Caribbean
poet like Kamau Brathwaite,[58] piling one idea on another with a studied

scant regard to conventions about sentences and how they should be punctuated.

At the poem's mid-point attention shifts from the academic to the sexual domain, in which issues of politics and culture are equally 'present'. The confusing, confused triangular relationship to which he alludes could be seen as loosely mirroring that between the North, Britain and the Irish Republic. The unidentified addressee of the poem is accused of succumbing to a nationalist charmer, a priest who wears 'green shades' and taking young women on Riding trips.[59] The memory of how he was 'spurned' – like the unionist community in 1985? – colours the narrator's re-reading of the affair. Its authenticity is subverted first by his use of the phrase 'heavy pretence', dumped between 'made' and 'love', then by his dismissive description of one encounter as merely 'a drunken fuck'. What remains is insubstantial – a smell, 'a caked lie' (41) – a 'thing' devoid of pattern or stable meaning. The text itself trails off without resolution. Whatever went awry might be attributable to his own trapped state or to his sexual and social immaturity (his sappiness), the speaker concedes. In the course of the poem, as in the course of last 15 years, he has moved from a position of agency (from being the person who dropped cards in the box) to a contained condition, boxed in by history and lies.

Indeterminacy spills over into the next poem, 'An Ulster Unionist Walks the Streets of London', in which Paulin seeks to address 'the traumatized feelings of exclusion and betrayal ... many Unionists experienced'[60] following the signing of the Anglo-Irish Agreement. Staring up at the governor's mansion, one Friday, the poem's speaker is struck by an absence. No flag is flying. The words he then uses to voice his dismay at being locked 'outside' at this defining juncture, draw closely on those uttered by Harold McCusker at Westminster:

> I stood outside Hillsborough, not waving a Union ... not singing hymns, saying prayers or protesting, but *like a dog* and asked the government to put in my hands the document that sold my birthright. I stood in the cold *outside the gate* of Hillsborough Castle and waited for them to come out and give me the Agreement second hand. ... I felt desolate because as I stood in the cold outside Hillsborough Castle everything that I held dear turned to ashes in my mouth. (My emphasis)[61]

Paulin's narrator is similarly appalled by the actions of the governing powers. The loss of their own parliament at Hillsborough 13 years before meant that unionist politicians like him are denied a local forum in which to register their protest: 'there is no power/we can call our own' (42).

Instead he and they faced the indignity of having to travel to the metropolitan centre in order to denounce those responsible for their betrayal. Having been shuttled there from Belfast, the speaker compares his estranged condition with that of London Irish. It is unclear whether the nation he assigns them to is Britain or the Republic or indeed whether they are content with their 'child' status. Yet at least they appear to belong to a nation, and not to a province or outpost of the *imperium*. A visit to the House of Commons results in the narrator encountering something which resembles *his* language ('*We vouch*', '*We deem*' (original emphasis)),[62] though ultimately he rejects this 'Strangers' House' which has taken from him his sense of home. The aporia the politician inhabits is one he shares with his constituents; the people he and Paulin originate from do not constitute a nation, 'though they are in a state'.[63] The charge levelled by Peter McDonald that too often Paulin succumbs to a tendency to hold up Protestant culture 'to an outside audience for easy ridicule'[64] is certainly not supported by this poem, which treats the individual and collective predicament with great empathy.

The two literary texts discussed above exemplify how the Anglo-Irish Agreement continued to generate consternation, dismay and disarray within the unionist community long after its signing. The dissolution of the Northern Ireland Assembly in June 1986 meant that critics of the Agreement – unlike their counterparts in 1974 – lacked access to a platform from which to mount their opposition.[65] In what proved to be a fruitless attempt to persuade Mrs Thatcher to reverse government policy, the two principal unionist parties, the UUP and DUP, began amassing signatures on a petition to the Queen calling for a referendum on the Agreement. During the same month, January 1987, the UDA's political think-tank, the Ulster Political Research Group, published a document entitled *Common Sense* which argued that a devolved assembly be created in which nationalists should no longer be 'excluded from playing a full role in the affairs of Northern Ireland'.[66] The UUP and DUP were deeply hostile to such suggestions, the latter issuing a forthright statement in May rejecting any possibility of power-sharing. Later that year, however, the unionist leadership seemed to concede that flexibility in their dealings with the British government might yield better results than their obduracy had to date. Ending their 19-month long boycott of meetings with ministers, James Molyneaux and Ian Paisley agreed to meet the Northern Ireland Secretary, Tom King, in September, to open 'talks about talks'.

While the abandonment of abstentionism[67] was evidently intended to enhance Sinn Féin's chances of electoral success in the North and in the Republic, militant republicans continued to believe their campaign of violence had a decisive role to play in securing a British withdrawal from the island. In early March 1987, they murdered Peter Nesbitt, an RUC reservist, sent to investigate a bogus robbery, and then planted a bomb on the afternoon of his funeral which injured five police officers. Later that month the Provisionals shot dead Leslie Jarvis, a 61-year-old lecturer at Magilligan jail, while he was sitting in his car waiting for his night-class to begin at Magee College in Derry. Less than an hour after the shooting, a booby-trap device left on the car's back seat exploded, killing two policemen investigating the crime. In late April, a 500lb landmine claimed the lives of one of Northern Ireland's most senior judges, Maurice Gibson, and his wife, Lady Cecily, as they were returning from holiday to their home in Co. Down. A statement in *An Phoblacht* claimed that Gibson was a typical 'representative of the north's colonial judiciary; a unionist, bigoted and biased against nationalists, who constantly used the law to prop up British rule in the six counties'.[68]

Despite these and other 'successes', the PIRA suffered major setbacks in the course of the year. In May the SAS ambushed and killed eight members of the paramilitaries' East Tyrone unit, as they launched an attack on a police station in Loughgall, Co. Armagh. On 1 November, French customs officials intercepted the *Eksund*, a trawler the IRA had purchased, which was carrying over 150 tons of Libyan arms and explosives.[69] Exactly a week later, during a Remembrance Day service held at Enniskillen, an IRA bomb claimed the lives of 11 Protestants, six men and five women who were crushed to death when the wall of a community hall collapsed; 63 other people were injured in the blast. Amongst those who perished was a 20-year-old nurse, Marie Wilson. Her father, Gordon Wilson, who was also buried in the rubble, responded to his and his wife's loss with a dignity which earned him and his community huge respect. Speaking shortly after his daughter's death, he stated that he would 'pray tonight and every night'[70] for her killers:

> I bear no ill-will, I bear no grudge. She was a great wee lassie, she loved her profession. She was a pet and she's dead. She's in heaven and we'll meet again. Don't ask me, please, for a purpose. I don't have a purpose, I don't have an answer, but I know there has to be a plan.[71]

In a statement the following day, the Provisionals expressed deep regret for 'what occurred'.[72] Their intended targets were the security forces, they said, and went on to claim that the British Army counter-measures had triggered their radio-controlled device. Belatedly, after a lapse of 18 years, IRA sources confirmed that this account was 'nonsense'; the bomb had been pre-timed to explode *before* the service, but for some reason had gone off later.[73]

Revulsion at what came to be known as the Poppy Day Massacre was universal, and particularly intense in the constituency Sinn Féin most cared about, the Republic. There a minute's silence was held in honour of the victims. Over 50 000 people signed a book of condolence, which was significantly located in the Mansion House in Dublin where Sinn Féin held its annual *ard fheis*. The book was then delivered in person to Enniskillen by the Mayor of Dublin, Caremcita Hederman, 'who wept as she handed it over'.[74] In an article in *An Phoblacht* shortly after these events, Gerry Adams described the Provisionals' bombing of Enniskillen as 'a terrible mistake' which 'they must not repeat'.[75] The obloquy heaped on militant republicanism in the aftermath was undoubtedly one of the factors behind his momentous meeting with John Hume and Father Alec Reid at St Gerard's retreat house on 11 January 1988, which eventually led to the peace process.[76]

Peter McDonald 'Sunday at Great Tew'; Ciaran Carson *The Irish for No, Belfast Confetti*

Unlike the 60-year-old Gordon Wilson, the young poet, Peter McDonald described himself as 'utterly unreconciled' to the crime committed at Enniskillen. Born into a Protestant family in Belfast in 1962, McDonald was the only child in a family with strong Scottish connections and 'clerical blood'[77] in his veins. Educated at Methodist College and later University College, Oxford, his academic career has involved periods at the universities of Cambridge, Bristol and Oxford.

McDonald's poem, 'Sunday at Great Tew',[78] begins at 3.30 on the same November day as the bombing. Unusually for an Ulster elegy, it is located entirely in foreign fields, in England, in an Oxfordshire village. Yet throughout the poem is haunted by the political narrative in Northern Ireland, the 'shifting greys of a subtle fog', which, like the fog in Dickens's *Bleak House*, seems all-pervasive. In the poem two friends, who have been visiting a country pub, look back, literally and metaphorically, at the way they have come, witnessing how their steps on this particular cold Sunday have become translated into 'ghosts' footprints', 'slight marks' (58). Set against this process of sudden erasure is the illusory solidity of the England before him, with its 'sturdy, stone-built houses', its 'heavy and strong' manor house and its seeming immunity to change. However, the poem's speaker clearly recognises that this 'England' he sees is a construct, something the English and the cultures that they have marginalised have helped to create. Great Tew resembles 'a *replica* of some England'; it is like 'an idea on *show*', and later in section 6 a '*pretend* backwater with picture-postcard views' (60: my emphasis). McDonald is clearly writing back against the idealised England of Rupert Brooke's famous war poem, 'The Soldier' ('If I should die think only this of me'), an entirely apt manoeuvre given the location of the Enniskillen bombing. Subsequently he stresses how the manor house is '*concealed* behind thick trees and hedges', and might be owned by a millionaire 'who seldom *shows his face*' (my emphasis). Yet, as the poet is fully aware, the poem also practises a kind of concealment, in its determination to admit its political matter only in an oblique way.

Like Ireland, like the poem itself, England is a place which seems in thrall to its past, or rather an imagined version of its past: 'Every visit nowadays is an act of *remembrance*' (my emphasis). The weight this word bears – both because of its connection with World Wars and Enniskillen – contrasts with the seemingly lighter matter of the lines that follow. These recall previous, happier times when the pair swapped 'random gossip', whereas now their 'conversation' jumps from one silence to another' (58). On these earlier occasions, the narrator admits to feeling remote from 'far-off acts of war'. It is at this point that he reveals the name of the pub, the Falkland Arms, which enables him to establish a link between poetry and civil war in the seventeenth and late twentieth centuries. With section three, the narrator adopts a Northern Irish perspective, as he questions whether Lord Falkland, the manor house's owner, 'was a loyalist who found himself outmanoeuvred' and goes on to speak of John Milton as 'staunch', 'blind/ po-faced, pig-headed and holy, *almost* an Ulsterman' (my emphasis).

This last word heralds the bleak vision of section four. The local church, with its '*slabs* of memorial stone' (my emphasis), with its single poppy wreath which 'does its duty' of 'stiff homage', generates a strong sense of exclusion, along with its smell of damp:

> here too, we *must become* aliens, shut out
> from whatever we might be tempted to call our own.
>   (59; my emphasis)

There seems an inevitability or fatedness about the speaker's unbelonging. The desire to possess is viewed as a temptation. The poet feels as 'rootless' and papery' as the wreath he has described; unlike the handmade briars and clay-pipes on sale in section two, he is not 'the genuine article'. The centuries' accumulated violence as well as individual atrocities expose the inadequacy and impotence of verbal and visual signs, the fifth section asserts, with gathering momentum and anger, its 12 lines consisting of one sentence:

> There are no words to find for the dead, and no gestures,
> no sermons to be turned, no curses to lay now and for ever
> on one house, or the other, or on both. (60)

The reference to sermons and curses links back to the previous section where the church building failed to provide any shred of consolation. However, there is an irony, of course, in that this denunciation of language's failure is so forcefully expressed, and so decorously structured; it even includes a thinly-hidden allusion to Mercutio's curse from *Romeo and Juliet*, 'A plague on both your houses'.[79] The narrator's anger centres primarily on the British media, and its reductive, exploitative representation of the North: 'there is no need to watch television .../ and see the Irish slaughter one another like wogs' (60). The generous English, he implies, do not discriminate between unionists and nationalists, but lump them together as equally irrational, primitive types. Surprisingly, perhaps given the Provisionals' responsibility for the atrocity, the speaker's resentment is directed at the English 'Other', picturing an ITN team toasting their successful coverage of the bombing at the Killyhevlin Hotel that night.[80]

Like the grey, indifferent sky over their heads, the unmentioned killing has rendered the watchers 'incidental', rendered the men – along with any verbal or artistic intervention they care to make – as 'oblique marks set in the margin/swept out to the edges' of this post-imperial text. (There is a fear that the victims of this particular day will similarly be swept aside by history.) This focus on marginality continues in the eighth and concluding section, where McDonald gathers together a number of abandoned, uncertain signs or verbal parallels for his own sense of abandonment and exposure: 'a flower of *crumpled paper*', 'a *vacant* phone-box', 'an *empty* packet of Benson and Hedges', 'what looks like a bus-ticket', 'a *deserted* school' (61: my emphasis). They also serve as 'innocent' objective correlatives for the exploded lives, scattered bodies and personal belongings back in Enniskillen, which the text admits by not admitting. The poem closes with a banal series of formulaic actions, 'opening, closing doors, clicking in seat-belts, switching on/dipped headlights', and the visitors' claim that they have left 'absolutely nothing' behind them, no trace on Great Tew. Yet what remains is the poem itself, which re-energises the sense of loss, absence and bitterness with each re-reading.

The late 1980s witnessed not only the emergence of new generation of younger talents, like McDonald and John Hughes.[81] Two publications in three years, *The Irish for No* (1987) and *Belfast Confetti* (1989), caused a transformation in Ciaran Carson's reputation and saw him hailed as one of the most exciting poets of the period. Carson had previously published only one full collection in the mid-1970s, *The New Estate*, but was best known for his work as a Traditional Arts Officer at the ACNI,[82] as well as for his highly critical review of Seamus Heaney's *North*, 'Escaped from the Massacre?'[83] The concerns that piece raised about the dangers of aestheticising violence are carried over into *The Irish for No*'s intriguing opening poem, 'Dresden',[84] in which for the first time we encounter the distinctive, elongated blank verse lines which will feature in so much of Carson's later poetry.[85]

What also strikes one immediately about 'Dresden' is how markedly different it is in style from so many of the other 'war' poems of the period, particularly those of the Heaney-Longley-Mahon generation, and yet how conscious of their work.[86] While its ostensible subject is historical, the reminiscences of a character known as Horse Boyle, the gaps, hesitations, self-corrections, digressions and contradictions in the narrator's recollection of those stories make it very quickly apparent, however, that Carson is engaged by issues of form, language, narrative and textual authority. The less than illuminating disclosure that 'Horse Boyle was called Horse Boyle because of his brother Mule' places the reader on guard from the outset. It is not until line four when the narrator details the unprepossessing nature of Boyle's domestic circumstances – Horse shares a ramshackle caravan with his twin brother, in a remote spot outside of Carrick – that he begins to command attention. It is out of such impoverishment, economic, cultural and emotional, 'Dresden' obliquely implies, that so much of Ireland's current woes arise. For the narrator, however, the brothers' home-base is not devoid of attractions, albeit of an unconventional, postmodernist kind. Heaps of empty baked-bean cans form 'baroque pyramids', he tells us, alerting us to the eye he has for art. Made up of 'rusts/And ochres, hints of autumn' (11), worked upon by the elements and time, the tins have fused together – like the twins? – into an unstable sculpture.

'A great man for current affairs', according to his visitor, Horse also loves recalling anecdotes from the past, like that of young Flynn and his bungled arms-smuggling mission. Two key aspects of this tale remain puzzling; the narrator – as a result of inattention, or perhaps indifference to politics? – is uncertain whether this incident took place pre- or post-partition,[87] and whether the IRA man was arrested as a result of intelligence or by chance.[88] Seeing a policeman boarding the bus he was travelling on, young Flynn, the would-be bomber, is said to have surrendered straight away, and ended up going down for a seven-year sentence. What adds wryness to the story is that no one had in fact been tracking him, and the police officer had only got on the bus by chance, after his bike suffered a puncture. Horse then proceeds to delineate the wonders Flynn achieved in prison, and how, as for so many of his republican contemporaries, his education started in earnest there. Whereas Horse is in awe at the breadth of Flynn's linguistic knowledge – he refers to him acquiring 'the best of Irish' – readers of a more sceptical cast of mind might question the usefulness of learning the vocabulary for 'the third thwart in a boat' or the 'extinct names' (13) of insects and flowers. The young man's ability to gloss place-names stirs Horse to bitter reflections, first on the inhospitability of the local environment to any form of cultivation

> You'd be hard put to it to find a square foot in the whole bloody
>   parish
> That wasn't *thick* with flints and pebbles (13; my emphasis)

and then on his own fragmented education. Like that of his counterpart in Muldoon's 'Anseo', much of his schooling appears to have involved subjection to a sadistic Master. Deprivation partly explains, though does not justify the violence McGinty's exacts upon his charges, beating them strap 'stuffed/With threepenny bits'.[89] Horse's aside about his teacher 'nearly' becoming a priest leads one to speculate on how *Father* McGinty might have interpreted Christ's command to 'Suffer little children … to come unto me'.[90]

The poem's climax comes in stanzas eight to ten, which reveals how Horse emigrated to England, endured an arduous career in scrap in Manchester, before enlisting in the Royal Air Force during the Second World War.[91] The most devastating experience during the war for him was taking part in the fire-bombing of Dresden.[92] Beneath the 'rapid desultory thunderclaps', he could hear, or imagined he could hear 'a thousand tinkling echoes', as

> All across the map of Dresden, store-rooms full of china
>   shivered, teetered
> And collapsed, an avalanche of porcelain, slushing and
>   cascading: cherubs,
> Shepherdesses, figurines of Hope and Peace and Victory,
>   delicate bone fragments. (15)

The reference to '*the map of* Dresden' (my emphasis), rather than 'Dresden' stresses the importance of distance in the poem, how everything within it is represented and *re*-presented. For the air-crews, the city exists *only* as a diagram, a piece of made-up lines. The allusion to 'bone fragments' might lead one to expect some mention of the 35 000 Germans killed in the air-raid, yet both Horse and his proxy are silent on the human cost. Instead they focus exclusively on the ruin inflicted on the city's stocks of china, vividly recreating it for us as a visual and aural spectacle; by using words like 'avalanche' and 'cascading' they naturalise destruction, and so deflect attention from human agency. The 'writerly',[93] 'open' nature of Carson's poem compels its readers to supplement it with meanings and narratives of their own, considering the large moral questions raised by the mass targeting of non-combatants, and how in more recent, localised conflicts they continue to take the brunt of violence. In depicting the shattering of the cherubs, shepherdesses and abstract figurines – images betokening Christian and Enlightenment ideals – Carson hints at the fate of the grand narratives in the modern era. More particularly, the poet may well be casting a cold eye on Churchillian rhetoric,[94] which constantly encouraged Britain's war generation to concentrate on the goal of Victory. The poem deliberately avoids giving an answer as to whether the Dresden bombing was justifiable or not, but it does offer a glimpse of the rewards in terms of 'Hope' and 'Peace' that Horse and his like enjoyed in the post-war years.

As this 'Cold pastoral' moves to its conclusion, one last art-work is presented for our inspection, a statuette which figured importantly in Horse's childhood and adolescence. While the rest of his family were absorbed in their nightly devotions, his eyes would rise towards this *kitsch* figurine, which, as Neil Corcoran points out, functions as 'an erotic substitute'[95] or double for the Virgin Mary. The heart-broken, wifeless Horse is unable to forget how this china dairy-maid 'seemed to beckon to him, smiling/ Offering him, eternally, her pitcher of milk, her mouth of rose and cream' (15). Unlike the 'unravish'd bride' of Keats's imagining or Heaney's 'frail device'[96] which survive to embody universal truths, the object of Horse's reverence endures only as a fragment and a memory. He relates how on one unspecified day, trying 'to hold her yet again', he dropped her. In what proves to be the only action he performs in the poem, Horse takes down and shows the narrator a biscuit tin which contains all that is left of the ornament, 'a creamy hand', an 'outstretched/Pitcher of milk' (15–16). A container of spoilt, 'antique' remains, the tin is clearly analogous to the caravan which confines the Boyle twins in a loveless, womanless state.

What breaks the momentum and pathos Horse's narrative has managed to create is the 'scraping' and 'tittering' which heralds the return of his drunken brother. Mule's arrival clearly snaps 'the thread' connecting teller and listener, and serves as a cue for the frame narrator's departure. The closing obstacles he negotiates, 'the steeples of rust, the gate that was a broken bed' (16), exemplify the unconsoling, anti-Romantic nature of Carson's art, and the corroded, damaged spiritual and cultural environ-ment in which it makes its way and mark.

The preoccupation with texts, maps, translated places, artefacts and people exhibited in the opening poem is carried over into the rest of the volume and its successor. The central section of *The Irish for No* consists of a series of highly self-reflexive lyrics, charting Belfast life at the height of the Troubles. Conscious of the mediatory nature of their task, the nar-rating voices in these poems are unable *just to* record what they observe. Thus, the riot with which 'Belfast Confetti'[97] begins is figured simultan-eously in material and metaphorical terms. The sharp metal objects hurled by rioters at the security forces undergo a double translation, initially into water ('raining', 'fount'), then into the domain of print ('exclamation marks', 'broken type'). A detonating bomb similarly turns into an asterisk, gunfire into a hyphen. What makes the speaker's plight so disturbing is how *unheimlich* a familiar world has become, a maze from which he can-not escape. And yet long before the onset of the current violence, as the second stanza demonstrates, his native city had already been made strange. In the mid-nineteenth century whole swathes of west Belfast acquired exotic street-names commemorating Britain's imperial triumphs in the Crimean War. Now those same streets are being subjected to a new alien invasion, in the form of 'Saracens' protected by 'Kremlin-2 mesh', and police officers wearing Makrolon face-armour (31). The disorientations registered in the poem reach a new intensity in the closing lines as the nar-rator faces the prospect of his own translation from Troubles observer into potential Troubles victim. Both he and we as readers are all too aware how easily the 'fusillade of question-marks' could have become actual bullets, bringing his life to a full stop.

Subsequent poems bear witness to how other interrogations end. 'Campaign' portrays the horrific fate suffered by a barman at the hands of unidentified paramilitaries. After picking him up and grilling him for hours to establish his identity, they ascertain that he is not in fact 'involved'. His indifference to their cause presumably lies behind the decision to torture and murder him; having pulled out his fingernails, they then take the luckless man to a derelict patch 'near the *Horseshoe* Bend' (36; my emphasis) where they pump nine bullets into him. Stark, unsparing images convey the squalor, stench and waste which surround him at the point of death, a place strewn with 'burning tyres', 'Broken glass and

knotted Durex'.[98] A fragile, elegiac note is introduced in the closing
lines, when a first-person narrator materialises to provide a glimpse of the
barman in better times. By focusing on 'his almost-perfect fingers' and,
before that, his courtesy to 'strangers', the narrator encourages us to associate the man with beauty and grace. Ultimately, however, any impulse
to aestheticise and so find solace is firmly held in check. Contemplating
those fingers in retrospect the speaker cannot *not* recall how the nails
were torn from them by the knuckle-faced men that went on to kill him,
just as readers cannot help but identify those killers as 'scum'.

That the victim in 'Campaign' is represented by means of a metonym
is highly significant as it reiterates Carson's perception of the city and
province as a site of fragmentation and fragmented perception. In poems
such as 'Clearance', 'August 1969', 'Smithfield Market', 'Travellers', 'The
Exiles' Club', narrative voices keep returning to the way in which the
mapped, known city of their youth has been ripped apart by the bombers
and developers.[99] Unusually in 'Clearance' there are positive aspects to
the demolition process. Watching the Royal Avenue Hotel fall before the
'breaker's pendulum', the narrator experiences a double epiphany, as first
an elegant 1930s mural is exposed, then the presence of a greengrocer's
'I'd never noticed until now' (32), its produce vivid in colour, freshness and
smell. 'August 1969' begins with visual spectacles, the 'Niagara of flame'
engulfing Greeves's Textile Mill, nationalist jubilation at the arrival of
British troops, a confetti of charred receipts and bills floating over the city.
That the mill's destruction presages further, future devastation in Belfast is
implied by the telling line with which the first stanza ends: 'The weave is
set: a melt of bobbins, spindles, shuttles' (35). Turning from that prospect,
the speaker opts for simpler, happier, pre-Troubles times, and a different,
private Rubicon. The 'indelible' image with which the poem ends appears
to privilege the familial over the political. Yet the caption and date on the
photograph of his mother 'crossing the Liffey' during her Dublin honeymoon in September 1944 function as a reminder of how, like his own,
his parents' lives were shaped by war.

Possibly the most desolate pictures in the whole sequence are the ones
contained in 'Smithfield Market'. One of the oldest, most popular centres
for shopping in Belfast,[100] noted for its huge glass canopy and the diversity of its wares, Smithfield was fire-bombed by the UDA in 1974 and left
gutted. In Carson's poem the burnt-out shell becomes a simulacrum of
the city, a labyrinthine space filled with losses, absences, substitutions.[101]
The initial image of a 'fleeting', 'April cloud' (37) immediately establishes
the impermanence of things, natural and man-made. The poet refuses to
separate these domains. A cloud is thus characterised as 'pewter-edged',

while the market's structure is depicted by means of metaphors taken from nature ('inlets', 'branching'). Like the spectator surveying its progress through the building, it loses itself in recesses and dead-ends. Replacing the clothes, materials, metal and electrical goods, second-hand books and records, with which they were once piled high, the stalls now display 'mouldy fabric', 'Rusted heaps', 'electrical spare parts', scrap which could well be recycled in bombs. Instead of people, 'Maggots seethe' through the abandoned building. Amid the wreckage, the narrator catches sight of an old map of Belfast, a flawed text, incapable of showing 'exactly how it is',[102] yet incorporating a 'Something' powerful enough to stir memory and imagination into play.

In 'Turn Again', the epigraph to *Belfast Confetti*, Carson explores once more the deceptive potential of maps and the instability of texts generally.[103] This starts by citing a map which features a 'bridge that was never built', another 'that collapsed', along with 'streets that never existed', before proceeding to more recent representations of Belfast which deliberately suppress details of jails 'for security reasons' (11). In a characteristic manoeuvre in both volumes, the closing lines witness the introduction of a first-person narrator, one who is as troubled, but even more disorientated than his forebears. Questions such as where he lives, queries about directions, turn him in on himself: 'I remember where I used to live', 'I think again'. The lack of correspondence between the internalised map he carries inside his head and the city as it is now leaves him feeling vulnerable and confused. Such is his anxiety at being stalked by the past, or more particularly his double or earlier self, he habitually slips down side-streets 'to try to throw off my shadow', in the hope of altering 'history's outcome.

A recurring, but enabling presence in the collection is that of the poet's father, Liam Carson. The subject of one of its most skilfully-crafted and -executed poems, 'Ambition', he serves as an invaluable access-point to the various narratives that make up the family history, which repeatedly intersects with the history of the city and the province. Fittingly, given its title, the poem begins with an ascent. Having climbed to an elevated point above Belfast, its speaker tries to take in the panorama. What curtails any prospect of a Wordsworthian meditation on space and time, or indeed on the restorative power of water, is the smoke that restricts his vision and his unease at his father's absence. The son's relationship with his father is constantly defined through alternating images of separation and closeness; just before the older man 'wandered off somewhere'[104] – literally and metaphorically – the two had been smoking together, drifting back into their long-established roles in which the father narrates and the son listens. Ominously characterised as 'coffin nails', the cigarettes possess a multiple function in the text, not least as a means through which traces of the past filter back into the present. They prompt the father to recall his 'time inside'[105] as an internee, the perky aphorisms and practical mathematics that helped sustain him there; in the prison seven butt-ends constituted a cigarette, and, because of their scarcity, matches had to be split in four. Picking up on his father's repeated reference to the number seven,[106] the son recounts an apocryphal story about a beheaded saint who walked seven miles carrying his head, but later confided that it was *'the first step that was difficult'* (27: original emphasis). Already at this juncture several telling differences have emerged between the two; whereas the older man's anecdotes are derived from first-hand experience and delivered through the medium of speech, the son's tale originates in second-order experience, from a *written* text, which he re-transmits in *oral* form for his father's benefit.[107]

This narrative exchange leads directly into stanza two's reflections on the non-linear, non-progressive, uncertain nature of life's journey, how 'one step forward' frequently involves 'two steps back'. Time generates switchbacks, illusions, narrowings of perspective, the speaker maintains, proffering a sequence of apparently unconnected scenarios to illustrate the point. A sound link *is* made between the 'suburban tennis match' and the pigeons breaking out from a loft; the noise the latter creates is compared to 'applause'. While the immediate context for reference to 'the issue … not yet decided' is a sporting one, the phrase bears an obvious political resonance, particularly in the light of the indeterminacy of the situation in the mid-to late 1980s. Another metaphorical leap sets the narrator down in front of a 'breathed-on' window-pane, where, self-reflexively, he preoccupies himself by 'drawing faces' and 'practising my signature' (28). What draws attention to his artistic and intellectual credentials – and may well add to the readers' disorientation – is the allusion to 'sfumato', an early twentieth-century painting technique in which 'tones and colours shade gradually into one another'.[108]

How politics frames the lives of succeeding generations is emphasised from the third stanza onwards. At first it is as if we are watching a replay of the interrogation scenes featured in *The Irish for No* or from any period in the last 60-plus years of Northern Irish history: 'The one they're looking for is not you, but it might be you' (28). In the midst of the questioning, however, the speaker experiences another Proustian epiphany. The smell exuded from the soldiers' sodden uniforms evokes a sudden memory of his father and his postman's canvas sack. While the mention of canvas and tennis carries us 'two steps back' to the previous stanza, a succession of postal references conveys us 'one step forward' into stanza four, though not before registering the ironies stamped all over the Wimbledon commentator's remarks about angles, volleys, strategy, and how 'Someone is *fighting a losing battle*' (28: original emphasis). One 'loser' identified in the following stanza is the narrator's father. Several explanations are given as to why he never secured promotion, including a prank he committed at the Royal Mail sorting office in the 1930s and his refusal to attend a training course in England during the war. Despite the narrator's attempt to play down the first of these incidents as a minor matter ('His humour', 'the joke'), it seems obvious that he, like the authorities, recognises the political ramifications of his father's acts. The possibility that he might have been a victim of discrimination never occurs to the postman's wife, a somewhat marginal figure in this male-centred poem. In her 'version' (29) of his history, her husband's career failures were attributable to a lack of ambition and an over-conservative temperament. A voice from the present, and from a place preoccupied with contests of a very different order, intervenes to halt this retrospective. Not surprisingly, given the conditions he has lived with since the late 1960s, the narrator localises the tennis pundit's talk of '*perfect timing, perfect / Accuracy*' (original emphasis), and compares the 'tiny puff of chalk' raised when the ball strikes the line with an image of 'someone ... firing in slow motion' (29).

The tennis motif continues into the following stanza. This begins with the imprints left on a 'frosted tennis-court' by an escaping prisoner, and then depicts a province and a present beyond the wire-cages in which a 'tit-for-tat' exchange of cruelties is the norm. As the poem moves to its close, the speaker's father resumes his pivotal position. Partly in his own words, partly through the mediation of his son, he reveals how he endured seven weeks' humiliation as an internee, as a result of being mistaken – in two senses – for his brother. This disclosure casts the consoling maxims the old man repeatedly utters in a new light, as a reaction against the unfairness and hardships he has suffered in his life. The assertion that '*God never opens one door, but he shuts another*' (31: original emphasis) is not merely left unchallenged, but endorsed when the narrator informs us how the release of one brother coincided with a seven-year sentence being imposed on the other. The last seven lines reaffirm the likeness running through the Carson male line, the resemblances between uncle and nephew, brother and brother, father and son. The reference to his uncle's funeral and the 'smoker's cough' the nephew has inherited might explain why cigarettes are gruesomely termed 'coffin nails' in the opening stanza. 'Told to cut down' on his smoking, his father has evolved a ritual whereby he stubs the cigarettes out after taking 'three or four puffs', but then bizarrely relights them seven times. This and other signs remind the speaker how his father has already embarked on a gradual descent[109] towards the 'freezing furnace' (31). Appropriately, given the linguistic and educational gulf that divides them, son and father choose at the last to express their affection for each other by non-verbal means:

> he coughed, I coughed. He
> stopped and turned,
> Made two steps back towards me, and I took one step forward. (31)

Carson's choreography here as elsewhere illustrates how much he has absorbed from the cinematic as well as other arts.[110] A key aspect of his technique lies in the skilful use he makes of close-ups, as well as 'lowerings and liftings', 'interruptions and isolations', 'enlargements and reductions'[111] in poetic and narrative focus. Exposing the complexity and fragility of the historical and contemporary *urban* experience, 'the layered and dispersed temporalities of the city and its subjects',[112] Carson has hugely extended the scope of Northern Irish poetry.

Glenn Patterson, *Burning Your Own*

Carson's vision of the city as 'never finalised' as 'constantly redrawing itself, constantly rewriting itself'[113] is one that would increasingly be shared by the novelist, Glenn Patterson, whose debut novel, *Burning Your Own*, appeared in 1988. In this as in its follow-up, *Fat Lad* (1992), Patterson emphasises how twentieth-century urban landscapes, like their rural counterparts, are in a continual state of transition. Missing this point, a *Listener* review quoted on the back of the 1989 paperback edition, alludes to the '*stagnating* bigotry of Belfast' (my emphasis), before curiously proceeding to commend Patterson for 'leaving out the politics' from his portrayal of Belfast in 1969 and its 'ordinary people'.[114] Such observations reveal more about tastes on the British 'mainland' in the late 1980s than they do about a text deeply engaged with the extraordinary, complex, constantly evolving crisis in Northern Ireland between the late 1960s and 1980s.

Set on a predominantly Protestant housing-estate between the critical months of July and August 1969, *Burning Your Own* registers the psychological, cultural and political disorientations experienced by its central character and focaliser, ten-year-old Mal Martin. Shadowing him at every turn are the tensions, brutality and dysfunctionality he encounters in his immediate and extended family, and, equally importantly, the community and province. As early as the second paragraph the fractious state of his home life is established by the disclosure that 'There had been another argument at breakfast' (3). The principal bone of contention between his parents is economic, and arises out the fact that Mal's father has been unemployed following the collapse of his business in the previous year (102). Unable to fulfil the traditional role of breadwinner, he feels less of a man and is increasingly slipping into dependency on alcohol.[115] Almost immediately, however, the narrative encourages the reader to recognise parallels between the Martin household and the larger political context where 'old arguments were revived and repeated', prior to 'the inevitable descent into namecalling' (3) and brawling.[116] As their animosity intensifies during the first half of the novel, his parents become like the two sides of a vice in which Mal is literally and metaphorically gripped. His mother's hug 'gentle to begin with' is depicted becoming 'tighter and tighter' (24). Soon after, we observe how his father 'sought his son's shoulder once more and ... squeezed it. Hard' (38).[117] Immediately after his birth, it subsequently emerges, the boy's naming had itself been a cause of division; whereas his mother wanted to christen him Malachy, his father thwarted her wishes, registering him simply as 'Mal' on the grounds that her choice '*sounds* Catholic' (69; original emphasis).

Hardly surprisingly, Mal seeks authority figures outside the home. One of his principal mentors will turn out to be Francy (Francis) Hagan, a solitary Catholic teenager, a loathed and demonised figure in the eyes of local Protestants. Voluntarily Francy has placed himself on the margins of the town, setting up his own *alternative* republic amid the refuse and weeds on a local waste-ground.[118] A sign of his dominant influence is the fact that his are the words with which Mal's history begins: 'In the beginning ... was the dump' (3). This subversive reworking of the opening of St John's Gospel immediately establishes Francy's simultaneous role as visionary, historian, custodian and interpreter. Crucial in the reorientation of Mal's sense of place and identity, he offers an almost ecstatic image of the estate before the re-emergence of sectarianism in the mid-1960s. Fifteen years earlier, the idyllically-named Larkview estate was a place of diversity, he informs his disciple, attracting not just people throughout the province, but also drawing back 'home' those whom economic stagnation and decline had scattered:

> There were the lost ones as well; the ones who'd emigrated ... They felt the tug; felt it in Glasgow, Liverpool, Manchester, Birmingham, London; felt it in Toronto, Chicago, New York, Detroit, Wellington, Sydney, Perth ... They felt the tug, like they all do eventually, and were drawn back to Belfast, to a space less than Belfast. (17–18)

Francy's reading importantly directs attention to the part played by economic decline and thwarted expectations since the post-war period – the very concerns with which this study began. Another illustration of the teenager's extensive, in-depth knowledge of the local area comes towards the novel's close. He disabuses Mal of the erroneous belief, popular amongst Larkview's Protestant residents that Derrybeg's Catholic chapel had been destroyed by King Billy on his way to the Boyne.[119] In actual fact, according to Francy, it was burnt down by an anti-Home Rule mob as recently as 1886. Amongst those responsible was a contingent of young men who a decade earlier had attended a party to celebrate its construction: 'one of the Methodist ministers in the city brought a whole load of kids from his church to it' (216). The incident exemplifies not only how sectarian hostilities turn out to be frequently much more recent in origin, but also the prevalence in the North of totally inaccurate, distorted versions of history: 'They tell you one thing one day and something else altogether the next' (217). Such self-reflexive moments are not uncommon, nor surprising given the impact on Patterson of Salman Rushdie's *Midnight's Children*, a work preoccupied by narrativity, and how individual and collective identities are formed and forged.[120]

Another dissident who plays a prominent part in Mal's re-education is, Alex, his young Protestant girl-cousin, in whose home he recuperates following his physical and psychological collapse (107).[121] Coincidentally, like one of the principal female characters in Tsitsi Dangarembga's *Nervous Conditions* (1988),[122] Alex reacts with fury to the despotism of her bourgeois father, who constantly thwarts her burgeoning desire for self-determination (and sexual freedom): 'Always leave the bedroom door at least a foot ajar ... Otherwise the bad air will make you sluggish and irritable', 'No going out unless daddy drives us there and no driving anywhere at all, if he considers it unsuitable' (119, 120). At its earliest stages, one of the forms Alex's resistance takes is her creation of enigmatic, yet strangely articulate texts. Dismissed as 'dreadful' by an uncomprehending Mal, her painting expresses mounting frustration at her gendered, disempowered position[123] and restricted cultural co-ordinates. She covers the sheet of *pink* card with

> bright random swirls of unmixed yellows, reds and blues, and in the centre a tiny square of black, under which were written the words: *You are here.*
>
> 'It's a street map,' Cathy told him, by way of explanation.
>
> 'A world map,' Alex corrected her. (126)

Surrounding the tiny black space she occupies – her home, Belfast, the province, Europe, the World? – she is conscious of a force-field, discrete ('unmixed') and full of colour, energy and movement. Described as possessing 'a knife-edged sharpness', her painting embodies a violence which is psychosexual in origin. This is evident from the scene in which it shadows and then strikes Mal, while he is practising football in the garden, inducing a discharge of pent-up aggression against his uncle: 'His mind suddenly focused, Mal kicked the ball *ferociously* against the garage wall … in a *rage* of *disappointment* and *frustration*' (129; my emphasis).

In an appalling episode at the close of the same chapter, Alex's face itself becomes a textual sign, her cheek marked by the 'imprint' (136) of her father's wedding-ring. In response to her flip comment about having been 'out', he slaps her hard across the face, leaving 'an angry red welt' (134). During the family dinner in the restaurant that occurs that evening she refuses to eat, spending her time scoring shapes on the table-cloth. When asked by Mal what they signify, she answers 'Ireland', then adds – to his confusion – 'the old sow that eats her farrow' (149).[124] The image she evokes here of a culture gorging itself on its offspring produces, like her previous ones, an extreme reaction; Mal throws up. The exchange between Mal and Alex serves to underline Patterson's concern to foreground less 'visible' casualties of Northern Ireland's *ancien regime*, particularly its womenfolk and young people. The final glimpse Mal has of Alex in this section of the novel finds her in a 'plain and frumpy' (156) yellow dress, dropping a curtsey before him. Her action appears a mocking acknowledgement of his privileged status within the patriarchal order, but also echoes the gesture of obeisance the Catholic waitress was forced to perform following Alex's unjustified complaint about her (145–6).

'Nothing's ever settled, just let drop for a while. But it always comes back. Always, always, always' (136).[125] Alex's observation applies, of course, not only to her *agon* with her father. A key feature of the novel's middle section is its critique of the sectarianism endemic within Belfast, which revived in no small measure as a consequence of loyalist resentment at O'Neill's 'liberal' policies and hostility towards the civil rights movement.[126] Closing ranks against the latter, Simon employs his ineffectual brother-in-law, Mal's father, partly as a replacement for one of his Catholic workers, sacked for his involvement with People's Democracy: 'I *only took him on* in April when there was all that *flipping outcry* about discrimination' (142; my emphasis). Simon's comments betray his own dubious employment practice and standpoint that discrimination as an issue is a temporary distraction. Responding to his wife's description of the waitress as a 'slatternly wee girl', he asks 'Are you surprised? Name like Bernadette?', before proceeding to characterise all Catholics as lacking in deference 'where authority is concerned' (146–7).

The deteriorating atmosphere on the Larkview estate, observed by Mal on his return, reflects the growing polarisation in the province in the months after O'Neill's overthrow.[127] On discovering that the family of one of his friends has already departed for the nationalist enclave of Derrybeg, Mal notes that faced with this 'new order of things, the safest policy was not to pry too much' (167). What facilitates his re-entry into the estate's mostly Protestant teenage fraternity is his ownership of a new, expensive, *orange* football. At the outset the ball, like the province and community it symbolises, seems in reasonable shape: 'There were scores on a couple of the leather panels, but you had to look very close to see them and to all outward appearances the caser remained superbly orange' (170). News that an Orange parade has been stoned as it passed by the Unity Flats has an immediate impact on a late afternoon kick-around involving the local boys. After detailing how 'bottles, bricks, paving stones' and even 'shite' had been hurled down on the marchers, one boy, Andy, remarks 'That's what you get moving Catholics in where they've no right to be' (175–6). Shocked at hearing the term 'Catholics' rather than 'Rebels', Mal attributes Andy's usage at first to a slip of the tongue. Once the boys' Ulster Match of the Day gets under way, diversity gradually gets eliminated from the common ground. First, two Catholic cousins, the McMahons, are excluded from the game and then the aptly-named Pickles, the product of a mixed marriage, departs after being fouled (179–80). The decision not to allow the McMahons to join in is largely Mal's, and like his jibe about them – he calls them '*Derry*beggars' – signals an attempt to ingratiate himself with the majority. That 'scores' are increasingly a feature of the majority community becomes evident when the ostracised Mucker arrives at the close of the match, seemingly from out of the blue, and beats up Andy and his brother for grossly insulting him earlier (181–2).[128] What saves Mal from nothing worse than a tweaked ear is Francy's sudden reappearance, ordering Mucker to 'Leave the child alone' (182).

Their attempts to dissociate themselves from the resurgent sectarianism of July and August 1969 come at a terrible cost for Mucker and particularly Francy. In the wake of loyalist attacks on a housing development earmarked for nationalists,[129] a chapel and a priest's house (198), Mucker is framed[130] and arrested, and Francy's home is besieged by local vigilantes. Incandescent at the RUC's defeat in Derry and the deployment of the British troops as *protectors* of the nationalists (222), and to the accompaniment of automatic gunfire echoing 'in another part of the city', Larkview loyalists converge on the Hagans' home in *Brookeborough* Close. Their chants of 'Out, out, out' (230), like the reference to their 'torch-led procession', call to mind the moments in the New Testament when Christ is arrested and condemned to death. Sensing the threat Francy faces, and crossing 'some invisible barrier' (211), Mal 'threw his arms' around his friend and mentor 'and parting his lips kissed his open mouth'. Although the two go their different ways, it is clear that the kiss expresses love and solidarity, and is not an intimation of Judas-like betrayal. In a further biblical allusion, this time to the story of Veronica capturing Christ's image, the reader is told of how 'the imprint of his [Francy's] face still lingered on Mal's' (231).[131] A witness, soon after, to the Hagans' eviction, Mal cries out after the disappearing figures of father and son, 'Francy take me too!', and is immediately dubbed by his co-religionists a 'Fenian lover' (238).

The disclosure that he has had some kind of relationship with Francy widens further the schism between Mal and his parents. (Significantly it coincides with news reports of the massive escalation of violence in Belfast of Thursday, 14 August which which left six people dead, streets in flames, and hundreds of families homeless.)[132] Mrs Martin's anger at her son for associating with 'that filthy tramp' boils over into violence, and, in a scene which at first appears to replicate her brother's assault on Alex, she strikes him on the side of the head. Instead of submitting passively, Mal tells her to 'Fuck off', prompting a rain of blows 'about the bottom and legs' (239) which he absorbs, but which leaves her in tears. What intrudes upon his torpor is first a report that a Citizens' Defence Force has moved towards the woods to head off any possible incursion from Derrybeg, followed by a sighting of Francy in the vicinity of the dump (241). Tricking his father and knocking over his mother in the process, Mal rushes to the woods to observe what turns out to be his friend's final defiant performance. The paraffin he has been hoarding in cans and bottles Francy uses to feed three braziers and keep the Defence Force at bay while he conducts a mock sale of assets, a dictionary, a pram and an urn. The moods of sullenness, amusement and bafflement amongst his audience has by now hardened into hatred and disgust, especially after the urn is identified as belonging to the grave of the father of one of the vigilantes. Francy's antics with an Orange sash (246–7) and Irish tricolour are further calculated to affront the crowd. With his 'arsenal exhausted' and enemies surging forward, he retreats into the dump's centre, where he detonates the petrol supply amassed there, creating a fireball that forces everyone, 'save Mal' to drop to the ground. Consciously, despairingly it seems, Francy translates his body into a text as fragmented as the province, realising in three-dimensional, fiery form a *subjective* correlative of the image Alex had captured in her painting less than a month earlier. It is a far cry from the view of the earth seen from space by the Apollo 11 astronauts, 'whole and apparently tranquil' (203), or Mal's earlier vision of a unified city, 'linked, built up, each part depending on the others' (115).

During the first nine months of 1988, a series of meetings were held between Hume and Adams, and small delegations of the SDLP and SF, which on the surface appear to have yielded limited results. Repeatedly Hume, Mallon, Currie and Farren attempted to persuade the republicans that their campaign of violence was counter-productive, given that it exacerbated sectarian divisions within the North, alienated people in the Republic and made it more difficult for the British to leave. The Sinn Féin team's response was that the British still harboured colonialist and imperialist designs on Ireland, pointing to the substantial sums expended in maintaining their presence in the North and their willingness to sacrifice the lives of their soldiers for the union. Although talks broke up in September without agreement, a coming-together had occurred around the concept of 'national self-determination', and the need to involve 'the Irish people *as a whole*'[133] in the search for means and institutions which would bring about that goal.

Between January 1988 and December 1990, there was precious little evidence that the conflict might be moving towards an ending. In the first week of March 1988, three unarmed PIRA volunteers (Séan Savage, Daniel McCann and Mairéad Farrell) were shot dead in Gibraltar by the SAS in highly controversial circumstances.[134] Towards the close of the funeral ceremony for the three, held on 16 March at Belfast's Milltown Cemetery, a lone loyalist gunman, Michael Stone, fired indiscriminately at mourners and threw hand grenades, leaving three people dead and wounding over 60 others. After running out of ammunition Stone attempted to escape, but was caught by his pursuers and beaten unconscious; only the intervention of the RUC saved his life. One last bloody sequel to the Gibraltar killings took place three days later. A car driven by two British Army corporals in plain clothes inexplicably found itself caught up in the funeral cortège of one of Stone's victims. Panicking, the soldiers tried reversing at speed and even fired one of their weapons to try and scare off the crowd. Momentarily that happened. Yet soon the soldier's vehicle was again surrounded by stewards and mourners who assumed the occupants were loyalists intent on mounting a re-run of Michael Stone's attack. After pulling the men from the car, they began beating them. At this point a number of PIRA members at the scene took charge. Misreading an identification card held by one of the soldiers, the paramilitaries were convinced that Corporals Derek Wood and David Howes were SAS men working undercover, and after driving them to some nearby waste land, shot and stabbed them.[135] Almost the whole of the appalling sequence of events was captured on film by an army helicopter and broadcast on television.

During late spring and summer 1988 the Provisionals stepped up their attacks on British military targets. May saw them once more extending their operations into Europe, where they killed three young RAF officers stationed in Germany. In mid-June in Lisburn six soldiers who had just taken part in a charity fun-run were killed when a bomb planted under their van detonated. One soldier died and nine others were injured in the bombing of an Army barracks at Mill Hill in London on 1 August. The deadliest PIRA operation that year took place later that month. A bus filled with troops from the Light Infantry Regiment, travelling to their base in Omagh after a short spell of leave, was ambushed in Ballygawley, Co. Tyrone, on 20 August. A paramilitary team, lying in wait, triggered a roadside bomb, killing eight of the passengers – all aged between 18 and 21 – and injuring another 19. Ten days later, in what several newspapers described as revenge for the Ballygawley bombing, three members of the mid-Tyrone PIRA were ambushed by the SAS near Drumnakilly and shot dead.[136]

The intensification of violence following the Gibraltar killings prompted the British government in mid-October to introduce a broadcasting ban, similar to the one operating in the Republic, prohibiting representatives of paramilitary groups from using the airwaves 'to justify their criminal activities'.[137] Television companies and documentary makers wishing to incorporate statements from leading figures in Sinn Féin in their programmes resorted to using actors to overdub Adams' or McGuinness's words in order to comply with the new legislation. At around this same time representatives of the main constitutionalist parties (UUP, DUP, SDLP and Alliance) gathered in Duisburg, Germany, for two days in an attempt to kick-start political dialogue; no progress was made, however.

Loyalist paramilitaries, meanwhile, resumed their violent activities, boosted by a surge in recruitment prompted by the Anglo-Irish Agreement. They were responsible for 17 deaths in 1987, 20 in 1987, 23 in 1988 and 19 in 1989. Their highest profile victim was Pat Finucane, a Catholic defence counsel, who was shot dead in front of his family on 12 February 1989. Finucane was targeted by the UDA/UFF because he had regularly acted as a solicitor for republican clients, including Bobby Sands, and had several siblings who were linked to the IRA. Finucane's murder has been the subject of sustained controversy and successive inquiries, as a result of persistent allegations that the security forces had colluded with his killers.[138] In the course of making 'Licence to Murder', a BBC *Panorama* investigation into the murder in 2002, one of the murder gang was secretly taped admitting how police officers had urged loyalist paramilitaries to 'take out' the solicitor and how a UDA colleague, now known to have been working for Army intelligence, had taken him to Finucane's house on a reconnaissance visit. An inquiry conducted by the Metropolitan Police Commissioner, Sir John Stevens, which reported in April 2003, concluded that there was evidence that 'rogue elements' in the police and Army had assisted loyalists in this and other assassinations.[139] This issue of collusion would feature prominently in Gary Mitchell's play, *The Force of Change*.

While continuing to strike at British Army personnel and military sites in Britain and Europe during 1989 and 1990, the Provisionals extended their range of targets to include places of economic importance. A bomb planted at barracks used by the Royal Marines School of Music in Deal, in Kent, in September 1989, caused the deaths of 11 bandsmen and injuries to more than 30 others. Nine months later London became a major focus for attacks; first a Territorial Army base was hit, then the home of a leading Tory, Lord McAlpine, then the Carlton Club, a popular haunt of Conservative MPs. In late July they detonated a bomb at the Stock Exchange which created extensive damage, and followed this up at the end of the month with the murder of Ian Gow MP, a former minister and close friend of Margaret Thatcher, who died outside his Sussex home when a device attached to the front of his car detonated.

During this same period, however, significant movements began to occur on the 'sluggish'[140] political front, many of which enabled a momentum towards peace to build. A source of resentment among northern nationalists for many years had been the gross injustice they believed had been exacted on those prosecuted for the Guildford and Birmingham bombings in the mid-1970s.[141] Vindication came at last in October 1989 when the Court of Appeal overturned the convictions of the Guildford Four.[142] The righting of this wrong coincided with the early months of Peter Brooke's tenure as Northern Ireland Secretary. Brooke's solid pedigree made his appointment a welcome one to the Unionist parties.[143] The thaw in relations between them and the NIO accelerated to such an extent that the UUP decided to end their boycott of ministerial contacts in February 1990. It was not long before Brooke commanded respect from Sinn Féin.[144] An intensive reading of republican history prompted his prescient conclusion in November 1989 that the IRA could never be defeated by military means and that violence would only end when the paramilitaries recognised the benefits alternative strategies might bring:

> It would require a decision on the part of the terrorists that the game had ceased to be worth the candle ... There has to be a possibility that

at some stage debate might start within the terrorist community. Now, if that were to occur ... if in fact the terrorists were to decide the moment had come when they wished to withdraw from their activities, then I think the government would need to be imaginative in those circumstances.[145]

Coming so soon after the Deal bombing and, more recently, the IRA's murder of an RAF corporal and his six-month-old daughter in Germany, Brooke's comments provoked considerable flak in the House of Commons, and outraged unionist opinion. Yet it stirred interest amongst the Sinn Féin leadership and helped pave the way for the secret dialogue between the republicans and 'representatives' of the British authorities that began the following autumn.[146]

The circumstances in which Brooke made his next, even more crucial intervention seem at first sight distinctly unpromising. A fresh spate of sectarian tit-for-tat killings had broken out in October 1990, and the IRA again started coercing individuals into carrying bombs towards military targets, by holding their families hostage. In one such incident, which took place at a border checkpoint near Donegal, the proxy bomber, Patsy Gillespie, a 42-year-old father of three from Derry, was killed along with six members of the King's Regiment.[147] In a speech of 9 November 1990, delivered to his Westminster constituency, but forwarded to the PIRA in advance, Brooke declared that the British government had 'no selfish strategic or economic interest in Northern Ireland: our role is to help, enable and encourage. Britain's purpose ... is not to occupy, oppress or exploit, but to ensure democratic debate and free democratic choice'.[148] According to Mallie and McKittrick, Brooke's statement was in part instigated by John Hume, who for some time had been trying to convince Sinn Féin that their reading of Britain's continuing presence in Ireland as essentially a colonial one was deeply mistaken. His allusion to Britain's 'strategic' interest was pertinent given the ongoing turmoil in the Soviet Union throughout 1989 and 1990 and the disintegration of its empire. In their discussions with the SDLP, Sinn Féin had argued that the British desire to remain in Ireland was motivated by a need to protect Atlantic air and sea routes from the Soviet threat. Now that threat was no longer a factor.

Further illustration of how suddenly political landscapes closer to home were altering came on the very day Brooke's speech was made and later that same month. On 9 November Mary Robinson, a 46-year-old liberal feminist lawyer, was elected President of the Irish Republic, ushering in a period of radical change. Pluralist and internationalist in stance, the new Ireland of the 1990s distanced itself from its narrow nationalist past and, even more alarmingly for the isolated northern republicans, exhibited an increasing sympathy for the unionists and their plight.[149] On 12 December the Dáil debated a Workers' Party bill to amend clauses 2 and 3 of the Republic's constitution, which laid claim to the territory of Northern Ireland, though on this occasion the proposal was defeated. On 22 November Margaret Thatcher, militant republicanism's most resolute opponent, resigned as Prime Minister after failing to secure an outright victory in the Conservatives' leadership contest, to be replaced five days later by her Foreign Secretary, John Major.

John Major's opening years in office saw no let-up in the intensive, sustained campaign of republican and loyalist violence. In early February 1991 he and his new Cabinet were targets of a PIRA mortar attack on Downing Street; the bomb landed only 15 yards from the room where they were meeting. Between 26 March and 3 July 1991, Brooke hosted a round of talks involving all the North's constitutionalist parties, though little progress was made. Sinn Féin's exclusion from the table, on the grounds that they had yet to renounce violence, prompted Adams's initiative of 20 August 1991 in which he wrote to the British and Irish governments of his willingness to take part in 'open-ended discussions' and commitment to establishing 'a peace process capable of achieving the political conditions necessary for an end to violence'.[150] Meanwhile a loyalist paramilitary ceasefire, introduced for the duration of the party talks, ended in mid-July when a new cycle of killings was initiated; by the year's end the UVF had claimed 19 victims, the UDA/UFF 15. Following a surge in tit-for-tat sectarian killings in mid-November, extra soldiers were deployed in Belfast and there was even talk of reintroducing internment. Although for the second year running the PIRA called a three-day Christmas ceasefire, in the weeks leading to the festivities they created mayhem by planting massive bombs in Belfast and Craigavon and incendiary devices in Blackpool, Manchester and London.

The pattern of failed talks and sudden upsurges in violence continued into 1992. Two large bombs caused extensive damage to Bedford Street and High Street, Belfast, in early January, and close to Downing Street a small device left in a briefcase exploded. Much worse was to follow. On Friday 17 January, at around 5:30 in the evening, a 500lb PIRA landmine was detonated at Teebane Crossroads, Co. Tyrone, blowing to bits a van in which Protestant workmen were travelling. Eight of its occupants who had been engaged in carrying out repairs on an army base perished in the attack. Condemnation of those responsible was widespread. In the Republic books of condolence were opened, as after Enniskillen, and

Edward Daly, the Catholic Bishop of Derry, urged the media gathered to report the twentieth anniversary of Bloody Sunday to turn their focus on 'the current oppressors of the people in our city, the Provisional IRA'.[151] Unionists, already angry over the Teebane massacre itself, were appalled by Peter Brooke's appearance on RTE's *The Late Late Show* that same evening, when some time after expressing his profound condolences for the families of the dead, he foolishly agreed to perform a song for his host. Realising the inappropriateness of his actions, Brooke offered to resign. Although John Major rejected Brooke's gesture at this time, after the 9 April 1992 general election he appointed Sir Patrick Mayhew as Northern Ireland Secretary in his place. Retaliation for the Teebane killings came just over a fortnight later. UFF gunmen opened fire on Catholics in a betting shop on the Ormeau Road, Belfast, on 5 February, killing five and seriously wounding seven others.

The day after John Major's surprise victory at the polls, the Provisionals set off two bombs in London's commercial centre, killing three people, one a 15-year-old schoolgirl, and inflicting over £700 million pounds of damage. Talks between the Northern Ireland parties were restarted at Stormont at the end of April by Sir Patrick Mayhew. Some progress was made before discussions collapsed in November 1992; unionists now conceded that the solution to the crisis would have to include some form of power-sharing and an Irish dimension, while the SDLP recognised that joint authority over the North was a more realistic goal than Irish unity. In mid-December, Mayhew made an important speech in Coleraine, in which he argued that the nationalists' aspiration for a united Ireland was 'no less legitimate'[152] than the unionists' wish to remain within the United Kingdom. He went on to state that if the republican paramilitaries were to end their violence, then the British could be expected to show flexibility in their response. In preceding weeks, however, the Provisionals' bombing campaign had continued, causing injuries to innocent bystanders in Belfast (1 and 10 December), Manchester (3 December) and London (10 and 16 December).

A key turning-point in the peace process came in 1993. Like preceding years, it began inauspiciously. Between January and mid-March 19 people were killed by paramilitaries in Northern Ireland, eight by loyalists, 11 by republicans. On 20 March, Warrington, a town in Cheshire midway between Manchester and Liverpool, became a target of the PIRA, when two bombs left in litter bins in a shopping precinct exploded, claiming the lives of two children, Johnathan Ball (aged 3) and Tim Parry (aged 12). The degree of revulsion their murder generated in Britain and Ireland matched that which followed the Enniskillen bombing of 1987. In

O'Connell Street, Dublin, an estimated 20 000 people attended a peace rally organised by local housewife Susan McHugh. Amongst those on the platform endorsing the appeal for an end to the violence was Gordon Wilson, who subsequently carried this message in person to the PIRA, though without meeting a positive response, apart from an apology that innocent civilians had again perished.[153]

At this very juncture, however, separate, secret talks between leading members of Sinn Féin and Albert Reynolds's Dublin government, British government representatives and John Hume of the SDLP were gathering in momentum.[154] Hume had for some time been of the opinion that his militant republican opponents might call a halt to the killing in response to a joint British–Irish declaration of intent. As Hennessey points out, the prototype of the Downing Street Declaration of December 1993 was Hume's document of October 1991, *A Strategy for Peace and Justice in Ireland*.[155] Modified by Charles Haughey, it had been forwarded to London in January 1992, but quickly rejected by Major as excessively nationalist in its perspectives, and as 'little more than an invitation ... to sell out the majority in the North'.[156] A draft from June 1992 drawn up by Sinn Féin, but approved by Hume, called for an agreed timetable for British withdrawal from Ireland; an acceptance by both governments that a desirable outcome of negotiations would be a 'agreed independent structures for the island as a whole';[157] an expression of willingness by the British to act as persuaders, encouraging the unionist community to give their consent to the idea of a united Ireland. Sceptical that the British government would accept either a time-frame or the role of persuaders, Reynolds urged the republicans to revise this draft, but they proved unwilling to budge. In June 1993, he forwarded to Major a marginally altered version of the June 1992 draft declaration. Politically at home Major was going through a difficult time, facing rebellion from the right-wingers within his own party and so at times reliant on the Ulster Unionists during key votes. As a result, he delayed committing himself to a formal response. Frustrated at this hold-up, and against Reynolds' advice, in late September 1993 Hume announced to the media that he had forwarded a report to the Irish government on how the conflict might be resolved which had been jointly written with Adams. Both governments in London and Dublin were furious with Hume, believing that he had inflicted damage on the delicate process by exposing it to the glare of publicity.

Apprehension among unionists and loyalists over the emergence of what they viewed as a 'pan-nationalist front', as well as future British intentions, was already mounting in the autumn of 1993. What exacerbated tensions in the province and precipitated the worst violence since

October 1976 was the decision by Provisionals to bomb a fish-shop on the Shankill Road on 23 October. Their intended targets were the West Belfast UDA/UFF whose headquarters had been located in offices above the shop. Unbeknown to the republicans, weeks earlier the UDA had ceased using the building when they became conscious of being under surveillance by the security forces.[158] Although the original PIRA plan envisaged there being sufficient time for people in the shop below to be evacuated, in the event the timer connected to the bomb only allowed a maximum of 11 seconds.[159] Two children and four women were among the nine Protestants killed in the explosion, in which 57 other people suffered injuries.[160]

On the Shankill and within the unionist community more widely the bombing provoked an intensity of rage comparable to that generated by the IRA's attacks on the Four Step Inn and the Balmoral Furnishing shop in late 1971.[161] The UDA/UFF's response was to issue a chilling warning to 'John Hume, Gerry Adams and the nationalist electorate' of the 'heavy, heavy price' that would be exacted 'for today's atrocity'.[162] In the course of the following week, they fulfilled this threat. It was the UVF, however, which struck first, murdering a 72-year-old Catholic widower on 25 October. The next morning as they arrived at their depot two Catholic cleaning workers were killed and five injured in a machine-gun attack carried out by the UDA/UFF. Two Catholic brothers, aged 18 and 22, were shot in their home by the UVF on 29 October, while celebrating their sister's eleventh birthday; the authors of *Lost Lives* record how the girl 'told a local priest that when the gunmen brushed past her she had thought they were playing a Hallowe'en prank'.[163] The following evening, exactly a week after the Shankill bombing, as around 200 predominantly Catholic customers at the Rising Sun in Greysteel, Co. Londonderry, were waiting for a country-and-western group to begin playing, two masked men carrying automatic weapons appeared in the lounge. After shouting out 'Trick or treat?', the UDA/UFF gunmen began firing, shooting dead seven Catholics and one Protestant, and wounding a further 19. Thus, in the space of one week, 23 innocent people lost their lives.

Despite this carnage, or rather because of it, efforts to push the peace process gained momentum. A series of embarrassing leaks and disclosures meant that the omens were not good when John Major and Albert Reynolds met in Downing Street in mid-December 1993. Each suspected the other of double-dealing.[164] Yet after an hour spent trading recriminations in private, the two Prime Ministers emerged, 'very pale and very tense', but determined to agree a statement which might accelerate the removal of 'the causes of conflict', enable all parties 'to overcome the legacy of history', foster the 'healing' of 'divisions'.[165] The document they finally settled on, the Downing Street Declaration of 15 December 1993, incorporated *both* the Irish people's right to self-determination *and* the principle of consent without which there would be no prospect of Irish unification. Significant elements of the earlier Hume–Adams proposals, such as a timetable for British withdrawal and the idea of the British acting as 'persuaders', were omitted from the Declaration, though the British government did commit itself 'to encourage, facilitate and enable' dialogue on the 'new political framework'.[166] While keen to encourage republicans to abandon armed struggle in favour of constitutional politics, Major could not afford to alienate unionist opinion. Five times the issue of consent features in the Declaration; paragraph four, for example, refers to the British government's resolve 'to uphold the democratic wish of a greater number of the people of Northern Ireland', whether to remain within the Union or become part of 'a sovereign united Ireland'.[167] The year concluded more optimistically than many within the previous 25 years. Statements were issued by the UUP's James Molyneaux and by loyalist paramilitaries emphasising that they did not regard the Downing Street Declaration as a threat and the PIRA held a third successive three-day Christmas ceasefire. Although republicans had extreme reservations about the document, they acknowledged the fact that 'there could be no durable peace without unionist consent to new political structures'.[168]

During the first eight months of 1994 paramilitary killings continued, albeit at a slightly reduced level; for the second year running loyalists were responsible for more murders than the republicans.[169] In mid-January the Irish government lifted its ban on Sinn Féin speakers appearing on television and radio. At the end of that month President Clinton's decision to grant Gerry Adams a short-term visa to travel to the United States infuriated Major and the British government, though Reynolds and Hume believed that Adams's exposure to Irish America might alert him to the benefits of what came to be called 'the peace dividend', and the enhanced influence Sinn Féin might enjoy if the Provisionals' military campaign were ended. Brian Feeney suggests that the visit also provided Adams with an opportunity to convince American republicans of the wisdom of Sinn Féin's constitutionalist strategy.[170] Given that many of the American Irish 'were more militant than the IRA in Ireland',[171] there was a fear that some might fund dissident republican groups, whose activities might damage his party's political advance.

Prospects for peace seemed to worsen in the second week of March, on successive days, when republican paramilitaries launched mortar attacks on Heathrow Airport, though none of the mortars detonated. Early April witnessed yet another dramatic swing in policy when the PIRA announced a three-day ceasefire in the week after Easter. That came and went, and for much of the next three months the UVF, UDA, PIRA and INLA carried out single-target murder attacks; on a few, rare occasions their guns were turned on transgressors of their own community.[172] One of the worst incidents of the year occurred in mid-June when, in retaliation for the INLA's assassination of two of its Belfast members, the UVF targeted a bar near Downpatrick, Co. Down, where they shot dead six Catholics watching a World Cup football match between Ireland and Italy. Appallingly, seven weeks later UVF gunmen were also responsible for murdering in front of her children a mother of five, who was seven months pregnant at the time.[173]

Throughout spring and summer 1994, Sinn Féin's leadership had been engaging its core supporters in dialogue over their proposed strategy for operating in the radically altered, post-Declaration political climate. Despite the fact that a PIRA ceasefire had been mooted as a possibility at several junctures in the preceding years, their announcement on Wednesday, 31 August, that 'a complete cessation of military operations' would take effect 'as of midnight' was greeted with amazement and euphoria by large numbers of people in Ireland and Britain. A headline in the northern nationalist *Irish News* hailed the PIRA statement as marking the start of 'A New Era', while the *Guardian* spoke of 'The Promise of Peace', and 'an historic resolution of Northern Ireland's bloody Troubles'.[174] Nationalist Belfast and Derry witnessed instant scenes of jubilation, yet these only served to fuel suspicions within the unionist community that the Westminster government must have struck a deal with republicans.[175] What characterised the British government's response, however, was caution. John Major immediately asked for clarification from the republicans as to whether the cessation was permanent, and then over the next two and a half years continued to foreground the issue of decommissioning as a stumbling-block to Sinn Féin's inclusion in all-party talks. Nevertheless within days of the PIRA's announcement, British soldiers began patrolling in berets rather than helmets and started re-opening border roads.

Albert Reynolds and the Irish government, by contrast, had no qualms about making public their recognition of how far the republicans had moved. On Thursday, 6 September, after meeting Hume and Adams in his offices, the Taoiseach issued a statement affirming how all three of them were 'totally and absolutely committed to democratic and peaceful methods of resolving our political problems'.[176] Approximately six weeks later, on 13 October, there was further cause for optimism when loyalist paramilitaries declared their own ceasefire. The individual selected to make the announcement was Gusty Spence, convicted back in 1966 of involvement in the Malvern Street killings. In addition the loyalists issued an apology to the families of those innocent victims who had died at their hands over the past 25 years.[177] The loyalists' willingness to take these steps arose from a conviction that no secret agreement existed and that the Union was secure. In the coming months David Ervine and Billy Hutchinson of the Progressive Unionist Party (linked to the UVF) and Gary McMichael of the Ulster Democratic Party's (linked to the UDA) would receive and accept invitations to Dublin to put forward their views on what Northern Ireland's future might be. The year drew to a close with President Clinton sanctioning an increase of $10 million in America's support for the International Fund for Ireland and John Major's announcement of an investment package for the province worth £73 million. In the same speech on 14 December in Belfast he reiterated his demand that until 'significant progress' was made on the scrapping of IRA weapons Sinn Féin would not be invited to join in for- mal talks with other Northern Irish parties and his ministers. It would be Sinn Féin's continuing exclusion that prompted the PIRA's resumption of violence in February 1996.

II   Reconfigurations, and early poetic responses to the peace process and ceasefires

Medbh McGuckian, *Captain Lavender*; *Word of Mouth*; Eilish Martin, *slitting the tongues of jackdaws*; Gráinne Tobin, *Banjaxed*; Ruth Carr, *There is a House*; Sinead Morrissey, *There Was Fire in Vancouver*; Michael Longley, *The Ghost Orchid*; Frank Ormsby, *The Ghost Train*; Seamus Heaney, *The Spirit Level*

The poems in Medbh McGuckian's *Captain Lavender* were composed mainly in the course of 1993, during a particularly stressful period in her personal life and in the province. In both parts of the volume[178] the poet dwells on the subject of her father's final illness and death in October 1992, imaginatively trying to come to terms with their meanings. Despite the fact that he was in extremely poor health at the time, Hugh McCaughran, McGuckian's father, encouraged his daughter to take on the challenge of running creative writing workshops for loyalist and republican prisoners in the Maze (Long Kesh).[179] Given his own lifetime's commitment to education, it is not surprising that he should have urged her so.[180] Her experience working in the prison, like her experiences at home and in the hospital, had a transformative effect on her writing,[181] forcing her to

re-evaluate her position on the relationship between aesthetics and politics, and to confront in her poems 'two lifetime dilemmas at once – the
problem of death and the problem of violence'.[182] Paradoxically outside
the prison the political situation was more disturbing and more encouraging than it had been for some time; levels of violence were intensify-
ing, but there were also momentous advances in political dialogue,
between Hume and Adams, London and Dublin.[183] Thus, an intricate,
interwoven knot of concerns lies at the core of this, her fifth major volume, which diverges from its predecessors in its more explicit engagement with issues of political and cultural identity.

This is not to say that with *Captain Lavender* McGuckian's poetry ceases
to be any the less hermetic in nature. The legitimacy of the charge voiced
by the prisoners that in producing such gnomic, introspective work, the
poet might be 'misusing my gift and being selfish'[184] is one to which she
partly concedes, and has often been levelled at her by critics before and
since.[185] Her sensitivity to accusations of preciousness and evasion
undoubtedly lies behind the decisions to preface the collection with a
quotation from Picasso ('*I have not painted the war ... but I have no doubt
that the war is in ... these paintings I have done*')[186] and to deploy as a cover
illustration Jack B. Yeats's 'Communicating with the prisoners' (1924).[187]
Critics have cited a number of explanations as to why McGuckian has
such difficulty in communicating with a wider readership. The reason
for 'her poetry's opacity', according to Guinn Batten, arises from the frequency with which 'simultaneous and overlapping absences' haunt the
words. She goes on to assert that a McGuckian poem typically lacks 'a
clearly defined subject who speaks, a clearly defined referent, and a verifiable addressee to whom the words are delivered'.[188] In Cecile Gray's
view, the incomprehension many readers experience is caused by
McGuckian's complex use of metaphor, specifically her tendency to
'take the image and push it to its uttermost ... the image goes beyond
the initial experience and begins to weave itself out in more than one
direction at once'.[189]

In her own defence, McGuckian has argued that much of the 'problem'
is inherent in language itself, since it is such an intricate, inexact and
unstable medium. As a woman poet of Irish origin, her situation is further
complicated by the fact that she is obliged to work in a 'foreign' tongue,
the English language. Aligning herself with black writers struggling with
a colonial legacy, she claims that she feels spiritually 'tongue-tied'

> writing or speaking a language which you know was imposed histor-
> ically recently ... I use English awkwardly, as if I have no right to ... I

think when I write I solve the problem, I develop a specialised language
of my own ... which is not English, which subverts, deconstructs,
kills it, makes it the dream-language I have lost.[190]

In her quest to articulate this acute sense of estrangement and refine
her poetic utterances, she turns repeatedly to *translations* of Freud, Proust,
Tsvetayeva and Mandelstam.[191] By entering into dialogue with their
defamiliarising readings of the world and strangely-textured words, she
maintains the momentum of her own self-translation, personal and
artistic, and equally aligns herself to *European* tradition, rather than
'English' or 'British'. The downside of this and other aspects of her textual
practice, however, is that stretches of her work seem closed-off except to
aficionados.[192]

Certainly there is a refreshing clarity in one of the earliest poems in the
book, 'Porcelain Bells'.[193] Dedicated to her mother, but about her dead
father, it is an exquisitely controlled, meditative, elegiac sequence, rich
in Keatsian ambivalences, ambiguities and sensuous details.[194] Fragility,
beauty, music, the sacred conjoin in the title. In her response to bereavement, the poem's speaker moves continually and understandably between
a terrible sense of absence and the consolation that something survives.
At times, the father's vision is depicted as coterminous with hers, woven
'into all I see',[195] and indeed into the text itself. She senses the *instress* of the
father's being everywhere. Like an apostle after Pentecost,[196] she believes
that the *Logos* has passed onto a higher plane and beyond 'calvary' ('Lines
from a Thanksgiving'). A sacred duty has descended on her to speak *of*
and *for* him. Though to all appearances, he has stepped outside the year,
time and 'the motion of the earth', he remains immanent in all three:
'you would still be inside every leaf' (18).[197] At other points, however, the
elusiveness of her subject is at the forefront of her thoughts. His hands
that bear the signs of pain she compares to 'a book/or a two syllable
word I find ... unintelligible' (18); in life as in death, 'you refuse to be
understood' (19).

As the poem advances towards its self-reflexive resolution, an attempt
is made to transcend this sense of separation. In yet another Keatsian
moment, the speaker associates her father with the 'whole' cry and 'full,
upward' trajectory of a nightingale and affirms his continuing role as an
inspirer in her work. From his spent air ('driven out', 'used-up'), she
determines to make an enduring art: 'I will hold like a resurrection/to
my breath' (19).[198] Significantly in the closing lines first person singular
subject pronouns figure with increasing prominence, and the dominant
tense becomes the future rather than the present. Beautifully, in the

closing image father and daughter are united in a single movement, swooping and ascending like birds:

> I will dive you back to earth
> And pull it up with you. (19)

Many of the motifs and semantic clusters featured in 'Porcelain Bells' recur in succeeding poems. References, for example, to lips, mouths and speech emphasise how the collection in its totality might be viewed as an ongoing dialogue with self and soul. In 'The Appropriate Moment' the narrator's father along with the places she and he walk around dematerialise, as if already dissolving into represented forms; his voice develops 'a dry, old paper-feel to it', while the water in the lake changes into 'the colour of this page' (20). Once more the attributes of light are bestowed on him ('glint'), conferred as a result of a *female* gaze. Suffused with images of liminality, with objects undergoing translation, the poem, like the whole articulates the mutability, inseparability, shifting relations of things:

> I read the dark you by moonlight;
> you survive into the one flesh
> of my received dreams, shapelessly,
> a whisper above a lawn, a stretch of wall. (21)

Like Heaney, McGuckian depicts her parents as distinct individuals and yet at the same time representative of their family, generation, community. 'A thousand years of breeding' may have energised her father's tongue – the 'bright', and clearly phallic 'muscle of his mouth' – yet because of where and when he lived ('the mute province we call home') it is 'cramped' and confined.[199] Significantly, 'home' is conceived of as a silent, silenced space, a place we name, 'know', imagine, but whose meaning and identity we can never really access or possess.

The poet's agonising struggle to reconcile herself to death and loss is again apparent in 'The Finder has Become the Seeker', an intriguing, not entirely successful poem from the close of Part One. Here the speaker visits her father's grave to wrest something from his absence. From the outset, there is awkwardness in the manner with which she addresses him and uncertainty over the form in which he now 'exists':

> Sleep easy, supposed fatherhood,
> resembling a flowerbed. (41)

Whereas the imperatives, 'Sleep' and 'open', suggest that she is invoking a being capable of response, the use of the word 'fatherhood', rather than 'father', implies that he 'lives' only as an abstraction, a thing 'supposed'. What resembles a flowerbed might or might not be *just* a flowerbed.[200] She appears convinced of his retrievability ('I extract you') and presence ('here and now') in some guise, picturing him as a living plant and/or text, with 'newly opened leaves'. As a result of Shane Murphy's meticulous scholarship on McGuckian's 'sources' for this poem, it transpires that throughout the poem she is addressing not one, but *two* fathers, her literal father and a literary foster-father, the great Russian poet, Osip Mandelstam, from whose prose writings she has taken cuttings. Thus in the dual images of leaves and flowers Nature and Art come together, oxygenating the writer's bloodstream and so sustaining her creativity. From both the natural world and the world of letters, she breathes in a sense of 'what ought to be'.[201]

That father and daughter, like finder and seeker in the children's game, subsist in mutual dependency is reiterated through the metaphors of the second stanza. This represents the two operating independently, but in unison like a pair of lips, lungs or wings. A need to differentiate herself from him drives the third stanza, which is preoccupied with the father's separate state. Although its opening line depicts him as passive within the grave ('Night furs you, winter clothes you'), he is an object of the attention of potent entities. What elevates him into a figure of mythic proportion is the deployment of the adverb, 'Homerically', though in what sense he is 'studded' in his 'planting' remains uncertain.[202] Figuratively and grammatically he is restored to an active, subject position in line three ('You jangle the keys of the language').[203] Subsequent allusions ('sounds', 'thinking fingers', 'the acoustic earth') reveal that McGuckian's image is multiple in its associations, and includes the idea of *musical* keys, in particular the keys on a piano.[204] As a holder of keys, the father is an empowered figure, a custodian, capable of providing access to new, perhaps disconcerting meanings. Suggestive of a jarring plurality of sounds, jangling evokes the idea of a wake-up call, and so might be applicable to McGuckian's own poetic practice, striving as it does to liberate readers from the numbness induced by 'habitualisation'.[205] Like the father memorialised in Carson's 'Ambition', the father in this poem changes form to become a threshold through which a lost, other, 'outcast' Irish cultural past can be glimpsed.[206]

Affirmation provides the keynote through most of the final stanza, which once more imagines the father's body (mouth, tongue, fingers) as alive, articulate, at play. The closing, half-rhymed couplet contains an appeal to him to act as a guardian spirit or muse, overseeing the seeker's 'tightly conceived' odyssey into unknown, unknowable terrain.

The second section of *Captain Lavender* comprises of work which emerges directly out of the period in which McGuckian tutored prisoners in the Maze. In one of the most achieved of these, 'The Albert Chain', she forges links between her father's protracted sufferings and those of one of the inmates.[207] The opening pictures she creates are profoundly disturbing, like one of Bosch's or Beckett's dark epiphanies. At the extremity of a dead stem, beneath a tree 'riddled' – with disease or bullet-holes? – a piece of fruit hangs. She immediately compares its exposed state to that of 'an accomplished terrorist', a self-destroyed idealist like Judas. The area surrounding resembles a scorched forest, given its 'burning air', cinders, malformed growth. Into this infernal scene two victims of cruelty are placed, one, a wild cat, in the prime of its life, but with its skin half-flayed,[208] the other, a squirrel 'stoned to death' like the innocent martyr, Stephen. No internal evidence suggests that these two creatures might represent a single human being, 'the accomplished terrorist' of line one. In an interview with Rand Brandes, however, the poet explains that the animals' fate is intended as analogous to that endured by one particular prisoner, a man she believes was 'wrongly accused' and condemned to a 'living death'.[209]

The second verse is marked by a striking switch from third- to first-person narration. At the outset the speaker seems identifiable with the poet herself. References to 'going into war' and returning 'inside' plainly arise out of McGuckian's visits to the Maze, her encounters there prompting her to embark on a sustained phase of poetic and political self-questioning. Once within the confines of the prison and the self, the narrator's initial assertiveness fades. Absorbed into the tenebrous character of the place, she quickly loses her distinctness and comes to resemble 'a thin sunshine, a night within a night'. Lines five and seven see her morphing first into her dead father, then into the 'fallen' prisoner, 'swallowed ... up' like them in the earth and the rubble political violence has generated. Now a multiple persona, the three-in-one narrator journeys back to her/his/their very beginnings, only to be confronted by further signs of fragmentation: 'I was born in little pieces, like specks of dust'. At the stanza's impassioned, rhetorical close, poet, teacher and prisoner state what they have learnt from the balance-sheet presented by 'history'

> how every inch of soil has been paid for
> by the life of a man, the funerals of the poor. (68)

In the remaining stanzas the speaking 'I' appears to be a single individual once more, though acutely attuned to those other selves. Her attention is primarily focused on the prisoners and the psychological scarring they bear as a consequence of their involvement in paramilitary violence and the time lost in incarceration. In the opening lines of stanza three she describes how one inmate, possibly a sympathiser with 'the [Shankill?] butchers', breaks down before her under the weight of his own distress. His abasement sets him apart from the next character she introduces, a figure she invests with epic qualities and supernatural powers. 'Nailed to a dry rock', he is at first presented as a modern Prometheus. Much less grandly, she compares him next to an artillery piece, an improvised one at that, fashioned out of 'an iron/pipe'. Serving time for an offence he had not committed, he has become 'muzzled and muted' by the 'justice' system. Her inscription of him within 'the history of my country' is, like so many of her images, deliberately ambiguous. This might mean that, locked away, forgotten, one of many, he simply belongs to the past. Equally he is 'history' in another sense, however, one in a long line – or chain – of Irish victims of injustice.[210] Immediately after this, the narrator seems to question the efficacy of writing in such a location, at such a time, since the 'rhythm' he creates will prove 'incapable' of 'charming death away' (69).

At the beginning of the fourth stanza, however, the narrator endorses writing as means of establishing dialogue between conflicting parts of the psyche. In the case of the man above, 'one part of you' (the apprentice poet) is 'coming to the rescue/of the other' (the aggrieved prisoner). All she feels she can offer him is a small gesture, the poem itself in which his plight is partially disclosed. At this juncture the prisoner seems to melt back into the form of her dead father, an absent presence beyond her reach.[211] In one final act of identification, the speaker represents herself as imprisoned by her own

> unjust pursuit of justice
> that *turns* one sort of *poetry* into another. (69; my emphasis)

Meaning turns here on the ambivalent meaning of the verb, and on what the different kinds of poetry might be. McGuckian recognises that the artistic act is bound to be, on some level, appropriative, egoistical ('my own /... pursuit'), 'unjust' even, particularly in this place, and in these circumstances.[212] And yet, despite this, *poiesis* remains for her something sacred, a mysterious, priestly act, in which she becomes the medium through which 'everything that has been or will be' is embraced and made flesh.[213]

Until the new century, and the arrival of younger poets like Sinead Morrissey and Leontia Flynn on the literary scene, critical attention to women's poetry from Northern Ireland has rarely extended beyond Medbh McGuckian. Alongside the surge in the writing and publication of fiction by women in the mid- to late 1980s, there was also a significant increase in activity amongst the province's women poets. One manifestation of this phenomenon was the founding of the *Word of Mouth Poetry Collective* by Ruth Carr, Ann Zell and Sally Wheeler. Previously in 1986 the three had formed a group called *Writing Women* which met in Belfast's Linenhall Library to critique work in each of the literary genres. Its aim, like that of the later collective, was to combat the isolation of women writers, whose chances of getting together to help develop each other's creativity were often hampered by family and work commitments. After a while the founders felt that with its shifting membership and diverse focus *Writing Women* was not operating as effectively as it might. Consequently, Carr, Zell and Wheeler decided to create a new group, devoted to poetry alone, and with an invited membership of between nine and ten writers with whose work they were familiar.

Word of Mouth meets once a month in Belfast's Linenhall Library, and is partly modelled on Philip Hobsbaum's Belfast Group of the early 1960s. Indeed one of its members, Joan Newmann, was a member of the Group and through her press, Summer Palace, publishes work by individual poets in *Word of Mouth*. The collective operates simply by members reading aloud poems they have been working on, without any introduction and explanation. The other members of the group then comment on the work, subjecting it to close analysis. Only at the end of this process is the author invited to respond to the criticism. Introducing the 1996 *Word of Mouth* anthology,[214] Ruth Carr states that the driving force behind the collective was a desire 'to create an environment in which poetry would thrive, where it would be taken seriously' (1) and to combat the view that writing from community groups was inferior and less deserving of scrutiny than 'professional' work. Although her introduction stresses the importance of poetics rather than politics, there is clearly a political, though not a *party* political dimension to the collective's activities. Carr refers, for example, to how the *Word of Mouth* poets operate 'in a society which has not been known for receptivity to the work of women in any sphere', and speaks of the North as both 'a place of passionate history' and a 'stagnating moat'

(2).[215] Commenting on poetry's reception, she argues that work is assessed too often on the basis of which 'side' it has come from in the academia-versus-community divide, instead of being judged on its content or quality (3). Northern Irish women poets have struggled to get published, she argues, and have often been ignored by anthologists. Of the 27 poets in Frank Ormsby's *Poets from the North of Ireland* (1990), only one is a woman. Patrick Crotty's *Modern Irish Poetry* (1995) similarly features one solitary Northern Irish woman poet.

Not surprisingly, therefore, silences and silencing figure prominently in the work of the *Word of Mouth* poets considered here. Eilish Martin's first full collection *slitting the tongues of jackdaws* was published in 1999.[216] Like so many other Northern Irish literary texts, her poems are often self-reflexive, addressing the mysterious fact of their own creation. In 'Spade Work', she voices the not uncommon idea of writing as an act of retrieval, 'the shy recovery/of things deliberately/hidden' (57). Any Northern Irish poem about a spade these days is likely to prompt a comparison with Seamus Heaney's 'Digging', though Martin's description of the spade's steel 'having sunk its glitter/in the work' more specifically recalls the tinsmith's scoop in 'Mossbawn Sunlight'. What the allusion exemplifies is how enabling for women writers Heaney's cultivation of the rural terrain has been.[217] Yet Martin's poem should be valued as an achievement in its own right. In summoning a paternal spirit to verify *her* creative labour ('still in your deep holding,/keep close'), she proves herself an adept in words, images and sounds.

At first sight 'A Death in Autumn' seems like an exercise Martin has undertaken, an attempt to rewrite Heaney's 'Punishment'. From the outset her poem establishes a very different tone and perspective to the original, because of her choice of narrator. Intellectually aroused, but distanced, he speaks with the authority of an anthropologist:

> They probably caught her in a strange bed
> and it being Samhain (the evidence suggests) their outrage led
> to a ritual retribution. Naturally
> there were procedures. That would have been fully
> understood by every party concerned
> including the victim, whose role in these affairs was just as learned
> as that of prosecutor, judge and foreman of the jury.
> Although if truth be told, one masked actor usually played all three. (12)

Unlike the adulteress in 'Punishment', that of 'Death in Autumn' is given a voice, and makes clear the invasiveness of the ritual and the completeness of the reversal she experiences. She undergoes a translation, a transubstantiation, her flesh becoming like wine. At closure, the poem's focus is on the woman's unknowability, rather than a moral dilemma experienced by the narrator. There is also an interesting shift in the last lines, which admits the possibility that the woman may not have passively accepted her victimhood, but may have died defiant:

> I wonder (when all was said) did she put a brazen face on things,
> shrugging off the taught disgrace of the noose that rings
> her leathered neck with its unbroken promise
> or did she tongue the wind, its breath hard against her lips. (12)

'Behind Enemy Lines' equally addresses issues of language and power, and of who possesses them. Here Martin deploys ironic allusions to the predominantly male world of war and espionage, which is then subverted by images drawn from fairy-tales.

> We dropped words, one step behind
> our silences, expecting them to lead us
> back to safe houses. (52)

After the apparent playfulness of its early stanzas, the poem concludes on a more sombre note, in which the speaker senses the failure of words, their tendency to let one down. Words yield, betray silences, silences which are themselves vulnerable to malign forces. The wolves with which the lyric ends might be symbols of the destructive violence which stalks Northern Ireland, but equally could be elements in the literary culture which savage certain users of words. Martin's poetry works often by suggestion, by resisting neat resolutions, and refuses to be neatly pinned down.

Gráinne Tobin's work is, by contrast, marked by the immediacy of its language. Like that of many of her sister poets in *Word of Mouth*, her poems are predominantly lyrical, creating metaphorical spaces for experiences which are personal and general, familiar and defamiliarising. 'Abseiling', the opening poem of *Banjaxed* (2002),[218] details a mother's translation from 'buoyant force' into a stroke victim. There is a terrible gulf between the narrator's voluntary leap into the void and the mother's involuntary condition, which she tries to bridge in the poem. Even though she tries to establish likenesses, the reader is left with an awful sense of difference:

> Null air behind me and the face above
> Saying it's easy if I'd just lean back,
> gripping the rope one-handed, into the void ...

> The sinister stroke that cut old ties
> between mind and motion
> caught her unsteady,
> casting off into nothingness. (11)

The poem contains some nice word-play; the 'sinister stroke' refers both to the mother's medical condition, the severing in her mind and body and between mother and daughter. Beginning with 'Null', ending in 'nothingness', the poem braces itself for an imminent casting-off.

The speaker in 'Family History' revisits a painful episode from her past, the night when her family felt obliged to abandon their home. As in many other poems in the book which observe and empathise with others' suffering, the narrative voice comes across as that of an uncomfortable, destabilised survivor, someone marked by what she later calls 'the Ulsterisation of grief' ('Resistance'). As 'word was out/our house was next to burn', the young couple amass their varied, treasured possessions in the car, their 'children buckled in with lies and kisses', family photographs, and poignantly 'the cards/saying Welcome to Your New Baby' (22). The following day they return to discover the house intact and take up residence once more. Something irreversible 'had happened', however, to their concept of home:

> Since then are lives are portable,
> our houses stones.
> We keep the children's photographs apart.

The photographs function as signifiers of a shared collective past, but now have to be kept apart if that history is to be preserved. In this place, at this time, identity itself is too fragile, too easily destroyed.

Her editorial work on the *Honest Ulsterman* and *The Female Line: Northern Irish Women Writers*,[219] a pioneering anthology of the mid-1980s, has meant that Ruth Carr is the best known of the *Word of Mouth* poets. The early pieces in her first collection, *There is a House* (1999),[220] are predominantly domestic in focus, establishing lines of connection between her, her parents and her children, the 'absent strings'.[221] An electrician in the shipyard, Carr's father worked seven days a week in order to enable his children to attend good schools. This determination to give his children the best start possible meant that he was generally an absent figure in Carr's childhood. He makes a rare appearance in the collection's opening poem, 'Family Snap', where he is described as 'daddy in a disguise'; he is wearing a suit. A wry sad couplet marks the end of both the first stanza, 'Overtime pays for coats and shoes/Bread he wins and tales they lose' (11), and the last. Although the narrator refers to the photograph's 'uniting' of the 'three figures' in the family trinity, the image we are left with conveys a mutual unease and separation.

Hardly surprisingly, given the period at which she grew up and her father's intense commitment to work, the domestic sphere is invariably dominated by her mother. Not unlike many Northern Irish mothers of the time, her Christian Scientist mother always stressed during her upbringing the centrality of spiritual things, decrying the physical as inferior. A dressmaker, she fitted out her daughter 'in too big, too long/handmade frocks' ('Mother Love', 14) in order, Carr suggests, to mask her sexual development.[222] The poet frequently resorts to images of containment in her representation of domestic politics and the intensity of this primary relationship. The second poem in the collection, 'Boxed In', discloses 'a chamber/packed with *secrets*' (12; my emphasis). The word is consciously ambiguous, implying something unknown, exciting, mysterious, while at the same time suggesting exclusion. The lyric releases a sensual trace, the pressed flowers a fragile 'breath of summer left', a reminder of loss which the poet's words cannot remedy. The speakers in 'We Share the Same Skin' and 'Mother Love' address directly the difficulties a child encounters in constructing a sense of her own identity. 'To grow up/I built walls, defining/where you ended and I began' (24). In 'Mother Love' a girl tries to escape her swaddling, over-protective mother by retreating into a womb-like recess, the 'hot press/where *words* and looks could not come in' (my emphasis). What in childhood she viewed as invasive and associated with reproofs and threats, in adulthood becomes the very means by which she can achieve a belated individuation. However much she tries to erase the marks of her history, the imprint remains, 'the pattern a transfer on my skin' (14).

In the second half of *There is a House* the impact of a larger politics is more explicitly felt. 'Body Politic' and 'Community Relation' conjoin private experiences, such as the joy and anxiety that accompanies the arrival of a new baby, with less certain feelings surrounding public events. Dating from 1979, though not published for over a decade, 'Body Politic' moves beyond the 'partitioned room' of its setting, focusing instead on the 'remarkable note' struck by the new-born girl-child. Like that of the poet, the baby's is a resilient voice sounding out 'beyond blocked roads and minds' and 'every fixed thing' (46). Clearly a companion piece to 'Body Politic' is the more recent 'Community Relation', which progresses from questions about her future child's identity and to questions about the nature of that child's future.

Who can tell when the cord will be cut?
Wounds heal?
When recognition will blossom in a smile?
What the first new-coined words
of a common tongue might be?

To gather a child up to your shoulder,
cheek to your cheek,
is to hazard the perilous gift of love
into a no man's land. (48)

Like the longed-for ceasefire, the baby embodies a new possibility, a salving possibility, chances for a new articulation.[223] Carr's poem ends not quite able to free itself of the discourse and actuality of violence which has loomed across her adult life. The positive images of a new political currency and potential dialogue ('new-coined words' and 'a common tongue') are qualified by the tensions implied in the final lines. If love – or peace – is a gift, then it is a 'perilous' one, a 'hazard', and the 'no man's land' being entered can be a place of possibility, or a step towards further danger.

Set in a relatively peaceful contemporary Belfast, 'Mushroom' presents an everyday domestic moment illumined by a flash from what seemed to be history. As in Friel's *Dancing at Lughnasa* and Heaney's 'A Sofa in the Forties',[224] the radio in the poem acts as the agent through which the external world materialises in the home, unsettlingly. Like cruelties reported but not enacted on stage or film, the violence the speakers hears of is more horrific for being imagined. The lyric begins innocently enough, with a mother preparing a meal, observing with satisfaction her baby's eager appetite and a sign of her predictable development:

I am rinsing milk-white mushrooms
under the tap. Your mouth opens birdlike
to gulp all the world it can,

incautious and whole.
A sliver in all that pink –
the first tooth is through.

A radio programme commemorating the fiftieth anniversary of Hiroshima suddenly breaks in on this scene, compelling her to contrast the wholeness of her baby with the terrible damage inflicted on children's bodies by the atomic bomb:

> A girl's voice on the airwaves
> shocked by the hole
> where her sister's cheek should be (54)

Some images employed midway through the poem have the unfortunate effect of detracting from the immediacy of the catastrophe Carr evokes. The choice of verb in one line – 'Thousands of splinters mosaic her child form' – is too artful, needlessly aestheticising the tragedy: Given that a mosaic involves a *conscious* ordering of *exact* fragments, it seems an inappropriate metaphor to use here. The subsequent reference to 'the nuclear act embedded in flesh' is also unsatisfactory, I would suggest, requiring one to accept too much unlikeness in a single equation. Can a subconscious sexual or religious motive be ascribed to the decision to annihilate Hiroshima? How is the devastation and carnage there connected to St John's account of the incarnation of the Word? There is also too unbridgeable a gulf between the tens of thousands incinerated by the fire-storm that swept through the city and the programme's audience caught up in a metaphorical 'wave' of revulsion.

What characterises the final stanzas is a return to a directness of utterance, the individuality and impact of 'a girl's voice on the airwaves'. Its force is such that it 'fragments everything', so much so that her baby, who was the focus for the poem's beginning, never reappears. Looking beyond her domestic surroundings, the narrator confronts 'the blank white space that is a mushroom', can visualise only 'a mushroom field at dawn' (55). Within the space of nine three-line verses a massive distance has been travelled from milk-white innocence and a kitchen setting to the vast blankness of a Japanese landscape, turned to ash and dust by advanced human technology.

The collection closes with a number of elegies commemorating women whose deaths were untimely, a victim of the concentration camps ('Vera Matuskeva'), the novelist Frances Molloy who died from a stroke in 1991 ('Sister'), and a friend beaten to death by her husband ('Jennifer'). Referring to the latter in an interview,[225] the poet commented angrily on the need for decommissioning to start in the home. Only with an awareness of how the poem's subject met her end is the reader able to see through the profusion of lyrical, botanical images to the cruel narrative they evoke. The 'fuchsia *clipped* back', 'the hillside's / *trampled* grain', 'the blackberry's *bruising* blue' thus serve as correlatives for the woman, battered 'beyond recognition', left 'lying on the ground' (63: my emphasis).

In her overwhelmingly positive review of *There is a House*,[226] no less an authority than Medbh McGuckian commends its 'painstaking and hard-won insights', though misleadingly refers to it as 'Primarily "a woman's book"'. In my view there should be no gender partition when it comes to art and its audience. Although Carr's and the other poets' work arises often out of the personal and domestic domain, it responds powerfully to the larger cultural and historical contexts that framed its making.

Sinéad Morrissey's remarkable début collection, *There Was Fire in Vancouver*, appeared in the same year as the *Word of Mouth* anthology, and similarly contained many poems composed well before the ceasefires. Born in Portadown on 24 April 1972, educated at Belfast High School, Morrissey lived in the province until 1990 when she left to study English and German at Trinity College, Dublin. In a recent interview, she explains that since her parents were atheists, she felt culturally aligned to neither community, and thus gained 'a degree of impartiality'.[227] From its outset, this first book is concerned with 'double vision', the intersections of private and public spaces, as well as differences and distortions of perspective. The opening poem's initial descriptions of Belfast occupying 'a *shallow* bowl of light' or of the Black Hill constituting 'a *power failure /* touching the sky' (my emphasis) have obvious political resonances, though its main focus settles on another kind of failure. Whereas her visual and political experiences of Belfast emphasise accessibility and excess ('I've seen it all'), the narrator's personal relationship with her partner reveals an absence of both qualities. Socially, intellectually, geographically, the pair may have much in common, but in their perceptions of the place and the situation they seem miles apart: inside his head there is 'None of what I saw'. For him, it would appear, Belfast is somewhere amenable to scrutiny ('gone into') yet somehow devoid of presence ('gone'). In 'Double Vision's final stanza, the city's road signs and street-lamps are invested with power, and seem almost to be conspiring together to mock the exile's return: '*You're back*', they chorus (original emphasis), 'Glimmering with victory' (9).

Threats of erasure, images of dissolution recur in many of the Northern Ireland-based poems that follow. 'CND' starts with another double-take, the grinning face of a nine-year-old activist juxtaposed with the grim caption on a balloon, '*I want to grow up, not blow up!*'. The poem traces the girl's journey from 'innocence' to 'experience', evoking in stanza two her naïve pleasure at signing hate mail to the American President, collecting stickers, tasting beer. It is only when confronted with the macabre picture of two bomb victims ('two skeletons/Scared of the sky') that the

fear of 'being nothing too soon and too suddenly'[228] strikes her, silencing her *'for the day'* (my emphasis). This last phrase stresses the temporariness of the blow delivered to her political enthusiasms, and
encourages us to see the poem itself as a rejection of silence.

In contrast to 'CND', 'Ciara', 'Europa Hotel' and 'Belfast Storm' voice
sorrow and anger at devastation close to home. 'Ciara' is another poem
that arises from a childhood act of witness, and segues cleverly between
times and perspectives. Like the focaliser's, our initial response to the image
of a woman 'crying over potatoes' is incomprehension. Deftly, economically, Morrissey evokes the child's self-centred viewpoint, her disap-
pointments giving way to a glimpse of something larger, an intuition of
a connection between 'boiling' and 'catastrophe'. Towards the close,
a maturer voice intervenes to explain the potatoes' symbolic function, standing in for a son 'who had his knees blown somewhere else'. That image of
physical disintegration is repeatedly being re-run in his mother's 'shattered',
'fraying' mind, stranding her on the margins of life. Metaphors of repleteness serve as an ironic counterpoint to the 'mess' the poem makes present,
the 'frightening rain, *pouring out* / Of the Armagh sky' (12: my emphasis)
a sign of the fall-out[229] and psychological 'legacy' of the Troubles. The
reader's line of vision is directed upward again in 'Belfast Storm', which
fancifully attributes the atmospheric effects to the angels' rage and distress, as they look down on the city 'heads in hands and howling it out all
over us'.[230] A first person narrator suddenly materialises at the beginning of
line four, one who, after expressing surprise at the angels' reaction, sardon-
ically acknowledges a difference brought about by the 'peace dividend':

> I can't think what they haven't got used to by now
> The great gap in the street where his knees hit the wall
> Meant wheelchairs, rather than coffins. (17)

Such black, mordant humour is not untypical of Belfast people from
both communities, and surfaces again in another short poem across the
page from 'Belfast Storm'. Lighter in touch and tone than Ciaran Carson's
elegy for the bombed-out Smithfield Market, 'Europa Hotel' generates
empathy for a building targeted repeatedly by republican paramilitaries
during the poet's childhood and teenage years. She imagines the hotel
waking up to find its windows around its 'ankles' and smoke 'billowing'
from its head. The Europa will have to continue in this 'impaired' state for
the next fortnight, denied sight 'Of the green hills they shatter you for'
(16). This last line hints at the blinding absurdity of the militant republicans' bombing campaign, the mismatch between their idealised vision

of 'Ireland' ('the green hills') and the destruction they wreak on their homeland.

In a three-part sequence entitled 'Thoughts in a Black Taxi', Morrissey depicts her own return to Belfast and her problematic, liminal position as one who is neither/nor. Absorbed, watching loyalists preparing for the Twelfth, she thinks about questioning 'the bare-chested men swanking about' high up on the bonfire. In time she recalls how her curiosity might be received:

> One 'What are *You* called?' from them, and it would all go black.
> I'd have to run to stay whole. (19)

This prompts part two's recollections of earlier gaffes, such as demonstrating an unfamiliarity with loyalist paramilitary acronyms, or laughing at German visitors disparaging Ian Paisley while travelling in a black UVF-run taxi heading into East Belfast. Most tellingly, she remembers her father urging her to conceal her identity, lest she be taken for a Catholic: '*Never say Morrissey again*' (original emphasis). The closing stanzas take her back to her schooldays and the constant fear of being misidentified by nationalists. Going daily along the Grosvenor Road in Belfast High School uniform was 'like having *Protestant* slapped across your back':

> I always walked with my heart constricting,
> Half-expecting bottles, in sudden shards
> Of West Belfast sunshine,
> To dance about my head (20)

Ostensibly, a third of the way into this first collection, attention switches to other locations and situations, yet not surprisingly the North and Morrissey's upbringing there remain a constant background presence. 'Bosnia' recalls a specific incident in the mid-1990s, when an anti-war protestor set fire to and killed himself in the grounds of the Palace of Westminster. The poet's critique of Western indifference at atrocities committed in areas of little or minor strategic importance arises in part one suspects from her experience of media coverage of the North in the 1970s and 1980s. Her imagery stresses the temporariness of the impact the man's suicide makes, comparing it to a 'short circuit', to a firework and spark which quickly slips from view. Instead of persuading the British and European governments to intervene, his gesture affects only 'the wrong people', those who recognised that 'it meant giving a damn' (23). Fire reappears as the subject of the title poem, again as an object of spectacle. Paying no heed to the human cost, physical, psychological or financial, the watchers regard the conflagration as a theatrical performance, 'marvelled' at its visual effects, 'wondered' where it would next 'bestow its dance'. By conveying so strikingly the narrator's aestheticisation of violence, her translation of it into something sublime or epiphanic, Morrissey captures the morally dubious position of the artist and citizen in the twentieth and twentieth-first centuries, the dangers of becoming desensitised to catastrophe, natural and man-made.

The destabilising effects of family division and loss are central to a cluster of texts which maintains the book's preoccupation with the problematic nature of identity and art's restorative possibilities. 'Hazel Goodwin Morrissey Brown' records a final visit to the family home, which is the process of being disassembled. In an act which sets in motion the poem's creation, the narrator plucks from the débris an old photograph of her mother in her 'GDR-Worker phase', placing it alongside a recent business card. The fellow-traveller of yesteryear has morphed into an itinerant entrepreneur, promoting 'Nu Skin' in New Zealand. Cosmetic renewal gives way to reincarnation myth in stanza two, when the daughter in the poem 'discovers' – thanks to an antipodean psychic – that in a previous existence she had been her mother's mother. The neatly arranged rhymes of the final verse ('fight' / 'flight', 'space' / 'race', 'airport' / 'last resort') underline ideas of cycles of recurrence, her mother's journeying eastwards and southwards in pursuit of freedom presaging the poet's own. Later poems ('My Grandmother Through Glass', 'Losing a Diary') are unable to recapture the affirmation of this response to bereavement; departure generates an 'awful hush' (45) in the former, while the latter locates the author 'in open sea', neither 'moored' nor 'married'. Her craft cannot recreate 'the sad, fixed honesty of how it was' (46), she ruefully acknowledges.

As *There Was Fire in Vancouver* concludes, a series of short lyrics praising light radiates a late sense of benison. This *fiat lux* begins with 'September Light', which delights in the sun's alchemy, 'rareness making gold' (49). 'Twenty-One', a coming-of-age poem, picks up where that left off, thanking God for the gift of the world. This light display reaches its climax in 'The Juggler' and 'Restoration'. Like the young Heaney in his early eulogies to craftsmen, Morrissey stresses initially the quotidian, humble origins of the juggler's art. Instead of replicating the child's perspective we find in Heaney, she opts instead for the standpoint of a somewhat cynical, world-weary adult. 'God knows what/Anachronism he took up before', her narrator comments, dismissing the juggler's act as merely 'a side-show', a rather crass attempt to turn back time. A more nuanced reaction begins to emerge in stanza three, with an acknowledgement of the therapeutic effects the spectacle creates, providing – like the poet? – an escape from 'the *drain* / Of things modern' (my emphasis). From this point onwards the juggler, rather than the narrator, becomes *the* focal point ('we ring/Him with faces'), a figure imbued with insight, resolve, resilience:

> He knows
> How we anticipate failure
> And that what he owes
>
> His audience is a defiance
> Of breakdown. (56)

Accumulating references to 'magic', 'radiance', 'weightlessness' signal how much the speaker's perception has been transformed, while the repeated use of first person plurals indicates how he has whirled the audience into a collective entity. Ultimately, his role is perceived as comparable to that of an artist or priest, since he cajoles 'improbables …/ Into truth', and leaves us 'not so far out/From faith as we were' (56).

The concept of faith as something fixed or grounded contrasts, of course, with Matthew Arnold's vision in 'Dover Beach' (1867), which imagines it as a sea in retreat. Morrissey clearly has Arnold's poem in her sights in 'Restoration', the book's closing poem. In locating and dating its two parts, 'Achill, 1985' and 'Juist, 1991', the poet invites us to see the distinction between her world-view at 13 and *Weltanschauung* six years later. Desolation appears at first to be the dominant note in the first poem, whose narrator recalls watching, along with a single gull, a beached dolphin being ripped 'Of all its history', by an apparently indifferent 'Easter wind'. 'Abandoned', 'washed up', 'on the edge' of things, it might have seemed to mirror the teenager's own exposed condition, facing a sea 'wide and emptied of love'. Yet the memory of how 'its body / *Opened* in the *sun*' (my emphasis), and re-use of the verb 'Caught'[231] to reveal her captivation, seem anticipatory, making us re-read the experience as a moment of epiphany. The positioning of 'Juist, 1991' immediately after 'Achill, 1985', results in the collection ending as it began with double vision, a sense of here and there. Whereas Arnold's elegy opens in tranquillity, with a calm North Sea and white chalk cliffs glimmering in the moonlight, Morrissey's poem 'booms' at its outset and remarks on an absence of light on the beach and in the sky. The sea, however, is a revelation in light, of light; touched, 'the water explodes/In phosphorescence' (59). There, on Juist, here on the page, the sudden discharge of energy is illuminating, not life-destroying. The last lines seem possessed by an evangelical zeal, passing from uncertainty ('No one knows') into mystery, or rather *the* mystery of *creatio ex nihilo:*

> *Let there be light in this world*
> *Of nothing let it come from*
> *Nothing let it speak nothing*
> *Let it go everywhere* (60)

Like the sceptical audience watching the juggler, some readers may recoil from this apparent throwback to an earlier time and state; others might maintain that genesis is an entirely appropriate place for an emerging poet to set off from. Yet tensions remain despite the uplift in this resolution. Amid the assertions that light should simply 'be', a prohibition appears: 'let it speak nothing'. This seems to indicate a recognition of the limitations of, even a distrust of the very medium she employs.[232]

As is already apparent from the texts already discussed in this chapter, ghosts are a recurring presence in Northern Irish poems, novels and plays from the late 1980s to the mid-1990s, willed back in order to illuminate a lost past and bewildered present. They are certainly a major feature of Michael Longley's *The Ghost Orchid* (1995), a collection which celebrates the fragile and transitory, and marks Longley's return to the front ranks of Irish poetry. Like much of his earlier work, *The Ghost Orchid* exhibits a profound sense of the sacred. The book pays homage both to earlier text-makers – classical greats and less-known local artists – and to absent 'household gods'.

Significantly placed at the book's centre, 'Poseidon' opens a series of tender praise-poems to father figures. Looking up at a statue of the Greek Sea-God, a perspective which repeats the child's view of an adult, the poem's narrator focuses on 'the scrotum's omega', which immediately prompts a memory of another 'ω':

> When I helped Grandfather George into the bath
> The same view led me to my mother and me (31)

and engendered an early sense of origins and ends. Like Kavanagh, Hewitt, Montague or the Walcott of *Omeros*, whose poems similarly valorise the parochial and local, Longley exhibits not a whit of anxiety in comparing his protagonists with those from the classical canon. Soon after 'Poseidon' one encounters 'A Bed of Leaves', a beautiful translation of a scene from the

Odyssey, which subtly marries the Med and Mayo, and transports Longley
to other beds, others' uneasy dreams and underworlds. In his roles as
father, son, old warrior, diminished survivor, world-wanderer, the figure of
Odysseus is at times clearly contiguous with that of the poet's father, Major
Richard Longley, and on occasion with the poet himself. Whereas the former is represented, as before, as a man of action, as one who saw 'action'
which scarred him literally and metaphorically for life, the latter often presents himself as the confused spectator of his late father's and others' pain.

'The Kilt', for example, illustrates how the trauma of Richard Longley's
Great War experiences continue to haunt his son's imagination, compelling
analogies and contrasts between his own troubled times and a period 'so
long ago', yet perhaps not so 'unimaginably different',[233] when human
life and humane values were held equally cheap:

> I waken you out of your nightmare as I wakened
> My father when he was stabbing a tubby German
> Who wriggled and pleaded in the back bedroom. (35)

Although the final stanza serves as a rite of redress poem, it ends in 'nakedness', emphasising the continuing exposure, the denial of closure for past
and recent 'survivors' of war, forced to face repetitions and re-enactments
of their losses daily. Battlefields figure prominently also in 'Behind a Cloud'
and 'Campfires'. In the former appalling, almost surreal visions from his
father's youth are juxtaposed with moments of epiphany from the poet's
maturity. Its opening stanza recreates the father's progress 'over gassy
corpses', stumbling over bodies whose 'eyes were looking at the moon'.
This nightmarish scene is then vividly contrasted with a lyrical account
of the storm petrel's delicate, tripping movement 'Over the waves', and a
magic transformation made by a disappearing cloud which 'changed the
sea into a field full of haycocks' (36). Executed with acute skill and poise,
'Campfires' is a poem celebrating light, addressing itself both to the sublime ('a dazzling moon', 'a clearance high', 'the boundlessness of space')
and the down-to-earth, fragile beauty of 'crackling', sparkling man-made
fires on the eve of battle. The imminence of war is conveyed at the outset
through the allusions to 'no man's land' and 'the killing fields', and at the
close by the mention of chariots and horses. By setting such references
in contiguity, the text forges a continuity between diverse historical periods
and locations, Homeric Troy, northern and eastern France during the
First World War, Cambodia under the Khmer Rouge in the late 1970s.
The classical dimension of the poem is enhanced by the image of the

smiling shepherd, moved by the sight not of an Arcadian, but of a very Irish, local landscape, 'his luminous townland' (37). The tomorrow he anticipates bears no resemblance to that of the soldiers at ease around their fires or of their horses innocently munching their 'shiny oats and barley', unconscious of what awaits.

Longley's conflations of the Great War and the Trojan War, the Trojan War and the Troubles, reach their climax in the book's most affective, enduring pieces, the sonnet 'Ceasefire'. This was composed on 26 August 1994, five days before the IRA announced its ceasefire, and published in the *Irish Times* of 3 September 1994.[234] 'Ceasefire' opens with Achilles' painful recognition of the resemblance between Priam and his own father. Though he attempts to push him 'Gently away', Achilles soon finds himself joining in the old man's grief, their common 'sadness' filling 'the building'. Nothing can erase the killing or the memory of it, the poem acknowledges. Nevertheless, the ruthless warrior does make a gesture of atonement, tending to the body of the man he killed, laying it (anachronistically) out 'in uniform'. The phrase 'Wrapped like a present' (39) reminds us how in death Hector is diminished to the status of an object, albeit a still precious object. 'Ceasefire' stresses at its close that the barbarous cycle can only be ended by extraordinary acts of imagination, gestures of magnanimity, self-surrender, love;[235] otherwise as Longley and his classically-informed readers are fully aware, Achilles' son, Pyrrhus, will in the future go on to kill Priam, sons to kill fathers, fathers sons.

Frank Ormsby's *The Ghost Train* (1995) is another text marked by major reconfigurations in both the private and public spheres.[236] As thoughtfully structured as a Yeats collection, its final poem on the birth of his daughter, Helen – born a mere 19 days before the IRA ceasefire – directing the reader back to themes and images in the opening lyric, 'Helen Keller', a five-line poem which is simultaneously a prayer for his daughter and the province. Between these two Helens is a particularly effective sequence revisiting his father's death and lifetime enthusiasms, along with poems dealing obliquely with the history of Northern Ireland while referring to the end of the Soviet Union, and poems celebrating a new marriage and his wife's pregnancy, with its successful outcome.

Like that of other Northern Irish poets, Ormsby's work is frequently highly self-referential. *The Ghost Train* moves off with a poem about another writer, Helen Keller (1880–1968), who, though born healthy, became blind and deaf at 18 months, yet overcame this adversity. Ormsby's poem transmutes her into a symbol of creativity and resilience, beauty and gentleness, employing a sequence of gendered comparisons, which affirm the enduring, tactile power of art and the artist, by setting it against an obsolete militarism:

> Brighter than gold trumpets, swords of light,
> tougher than mailed fist or splendid spur
> and softer than pelts in young fur-traders' hands.
> White as the white wings lifting from the ark,
> those fingers moving in a soundless dark. (11)

With its consciously archaic references ('swords', the 'mailed fist or splendid spur'), its allusion to biblical narrative ('the ark'), its redeployment of the art/war opposition, its decasyllabic full-rhyming final couplet, the poem clearly possesses traditional elements. Yet at the same time it incorporates traces of the ideological re-readings that have occurred in Northern Irish culture with regard to politics and gender. It is significant that this collection from the mid-1990s should begin and end with poems celebrating female creativity and potential. Some feminist critics might demur at the way the ostensible subject of the poem, the female artist, is represented metonymically, by reference to her fingers, which in turn are compared to the fluttering wings of a virginal dove. Nevertheless those fingers are articulate, and challenge 'the soundless dark', a phrase which suggests a kind of primal chaos before the Word enters in, hence the appropriateness of the 'dove' allusion.[237] Another image worth brooding briefly upon is the reference to 'the sword of light'. This is a translation of the Irish phrase is *an claidheamh soluis*, a symbol which featured on the masthead of the Gaelic League newspaper. In privileging Keller's art and her individual struggle, Ormsby may well be rejecting the mythologised Ireland of his northern nationalist youth and its martial imagery, and an ideology that stresses cultural confrontation rather than fluidity.

    The poem with which the collection closes measures the tense progression of events that culminated in his daughter, Helen's birth and the ceasefire. Like its predecessor, it is a keenly affirmative poem, as one would expect in the circumstances, yet like Longley's 'Ceasefire', admits the possibility of continuing violence:

> The place knows nothing of you and is home.
> Indifferent skies look on while August warms
> the middle air. We wrap you in your name.
> Peace is the way you settle in our arms. (51)

For the couple, however, it seems that 'The place', Belfast, has been restored as a 'home'. Tiny 'fingers' enfold the parents, an act of embrace re-enacted later when they in turn 'wrap' the child in its name, and the poet writes the poem. And yet beneath the poem's assertion of the centrality of the domestic and intimate, there is a consciousness of what 'frames' the birth, a world 'Five floors below', where a train of events unfolds. Even the affirmative closing line, 'Peace is the way you settle in our arms', is haunted by the actualities of the political present, the issue of settlement and 'arms'.

One of *The Ghost Train*'s finest poems, 'Geography', takes the reader on a journey from the poet's originary terrain in Fermanagh to vast expanses of the Soviet Union, thence to the moon and back. While reminiscent of Heaney's, Muldoon's and Carson's earlier visions of the child's continually enlarging experience, Ormsby's poem is evidently deeply affected by the political transformations that occurred in Europe at the end of the 1980s, such as the fall of the Berlin wall and disintegration of the Warsaw Pact. These changes had a profound impact on Northern Irish and Anglo-Irish politics, not least on the republican movement and their strategy. The prospect of Europe's new geography had already made its mark on Northern Irish literature in the hopes voiced in *The Cure at Troy* for 'a great sea-change', 'a longed-for tidal wave'.[238] Ormsby's poem starts with memories of primary school, pre-Troubles innocence, a 'pre-Copernican doze', broken into, 'startled' by 'Signals' from a world 'beyond the big curtain where letters join/and the language is different. Multiply. Divide'. The 'curtain' here anticipates the Iron Curtain, which will figure in the poem's second half, but also the border separating Ireland, an equally potent symbol of long division. As the child-focaliser scrutinises the map to discover his home ground of Fermanagh, he finds it defamiliarised, coloured by his perception of a vast Otherness beyond it

> brown as the Matto Grosso, its two loughs slung
> between Baltic Cavan, steppe green Donegal (13)

The poem's injunction to 'Strike inland till you find it, your home place' contains an obvious echo of Heaney's 'Bogland'.[239] Yet for Ormsby, as for his fellow northern nationalist in 1969, there is the recognition that the *political* 'home place' may only be achieved imaginatively, '*inland*' (my emphasis), since the current constitutional arrangements are at odds with their aspirations.

Part Two opens with the narrator, like the Black Mountain transmitter, straining to pick out in the night sky a Russian astronaut as he orbits the globe. Sergei Krikalyov was a cosmonaut on the Mir Space Station, stranded in space for ten months following the failed attempt to overthrow

Mikhail Gorbachev in 1991, in the coup which triggered the collapse of the Soviet Union. Ormsby's poem takes on board the previous 70 years of both Soviet and Northern Irish history. Like the poem's speaker, Krikalyov grew up in a place that had once imagined itself 'fixed', 'known' and 'reliable', but has now been rendered 'Weightless, half-homeless' by his experiences of exile. With his ear 'cocked like a satellite dish', the narrator relays to us a fancied exchange between Krikalyov and Manus McClafferty, a radio buff 'somewhere in Donegal'. The exchange, like the poem and the events it alludes to, serves as an act of confirmation, which leaves Sergei and the reader 'restored/by the weight of a local accent', 'a dander in space'. If Heaney is a presiding presence in the first part of the poem, Patrick Kavanagh acts as an affirmative shadow at its close. As Krikalyov 'overtakes a tractor on Main Street Gweedore/and hurtles through Glenties', he passes into folklore and local parlance, transmuted into 'Crockallyove', 'Kirklove' and 'Crackallyev', as vivid a figure as the Duffys and the McCabes in Kavanagh's 'Epic'. Ultimately he becomes an objective correlative of the poet who too 're-shapes/his place on the planet, the geography of home' (14), and verifies himself by reconciling the local and the transnational.

One of high points of the post-ceasefire period for Northern Irish literature as a whole, and not just its recipient, was the presentation of the Nobel Prize for Literature to Seamus Heaney in December 1995, 'for works of lyrical beauty and ethical depth, which exalt everyday miracles and the living past'.[240] The following year a new collection, *The Spirit Level*, was published which suggested that home had at last been liberated from its inverted commas. Like *The Ghost Orchid* and *The Ghost Train*, Heaney's book is clearly responsive to the new climate, but remains haunted by constrained and constraining, defined and defining presences from the past.

A constant sense of change and returning runs through the volume, which delights in things 'almost beneath notice' ('Mint'), and celebrates the marvellous 'in the bits and pieces of Everyday'.[241] At first glance some poems may seem to be exercises in nostalgia, yet beneath their surfaces cultural and political narratives are invariably at play. Ever since the intensification of violence from 1969 onwards, the poet's 'first things'[242] have been backlit by fires, forelit by explosions, and alert readers have become accustomed to discerning 'the tick of two clocks' ('Mossbawn Sunlight'). *The Spirit Level* abounds in synchronic narratives, intertextual allusions, lyrics concealing and revealing parables with plural implications. Frequently an innocent, unremarkable object from a foretime – like a whitewash brush in 'Keeping Going', the paper boat in 'The Flight Path', the lorry in 'Two Lorries' – is imagined in its private, originary location.

Then as the text pushes forward or backwards in time and space and takes in other narratives, the initiatory image metamorphoses and accrues political colourings. In 'Mint', for example, the unpoetic, 'Unverdant' herb-clump dumped at the gable-end transforms itself by stanza two into an emblem for the latent energies, positive and negative, in the nationalist community in the period pre-civil rights. Here was something 'callow yet tenacious', which 'spelled promise', yet grew rife'. By comparing the mint to 'inmates liberated' in the last verse, and by talking of how 'we'd failed them', the narrator invites us to empathise with the 'disregarded', the newly-released 'we' had previously 'turned against' (6). Despite satisfaction at his own survival, the speaker cannot free himself from a sense of culpability to those sentenced in both a legal and textual sense in his community and family.

'A Sofa in the Forties', like Deane's *Reading in the Dark*, carries the reader back to the first decade of the writer's life. Heaney's poem starts re-enacting a children's game, but halfway through, like the imagined train, switches track. Through the medium of the wireless, external cultural forces invade the enclosed, barely self-sufficient world of the children, transporting them into 'history and ignorance'. Initially they fall subject to the allure of American culture, but whatever vistas of pleasure or possibility opened up by 'The Riders of the Range' become swiftly shut off by the regally, authoritative RP voice emanating from London. Heaney graphically sets at odds the light italics of the American refrain, '*Yippee-i-ay*', with the upper case/class-ridden enunciation of the BBC presenter announcing 'HERE IS THE NEWS'. Bernard O'Donoghue in his review of *The Spirit Level* describes the BBC presenter as a 'benign authority figure';[243] words such as 'absolute', 'gulf', 'reigned', and 'tyranically' suggest otherwise. In my view Heaney is reiterating the point about linguistic hegemony in Britain made by the Scots poet, Tom Leonard in 'Unrelated Incidents, 3': 'thi reason / a talk wia / BBC accent / iz coz yi / widny wahnt / mi ti talk ... wia / voice lik / wanna yoo'.[244] Heaney's 'absolute speaker' brings intimations of inferiority, delivers those heavy abstractions, 'history' and 'ignorance', which already afflicted the lives of an earlier generation in Northern Ireland, and will in turn affect *their* children in what will *not* be a post-war period. With the voice's appearance, a more sombre note pervades the poem, quelling the earlier *chooka-chook* sounds, checking the dumbshow.

The poem's close sees a shift towards political allegory, and compels a more subtle interpretation of what has gone before. What at first looked like another-threshold-of-growing-up poem, a little something for those who take their Heaney safely pastoralised, emerges having much more in common with 'Freedman' in *North* or 'From the Canton of Expectation'

from *The Haw Lantern*. All three poems voice anger at the northern
nationalist community's political, cultural and spiritual prostration, and
thus radically re-write earlier Mossbawns. The leather*ette* sofa and its
cargo, I suspect, come to represent the entrapped status of the minority
in Northern Ireland. Pre-1968, prior to the civil rights movement, their
political and church leaders, like their Unionist masters, encouraged
them to adjust themselves to 'the uncomfortableness' of the ride. The
belief was fostered that 'Constancy was its own reward already', and

> Our only job to sit, eyes straight ahead,
> And be transported and make engine noise. (8)

Within the innocuous phrase, 'Our only job', lies a reminder of the massive
unemployment in Northern Ireland throughout the 1940s, 1950s and
1960s, not to mention the 1990s. The 'tunnel coming up' represents not
simply adolescence, but the renewed outbreak of violence. The images
of 'distant trains', 'unlit carriages' and the passive participle, 'transported',
all establish a connection to the contemporaneous victims of Nazism.
Given the rash analogies between the victims of the Troubles and those
of the Holocaust attempted in the past by representatives from both traditions, Heaney is not unsurprisingly reticent about invoking the latter's
presence in his haunting representation of the 1940s.

Many of the book's poems address directly or obliquely the anticipated
end of violence. 'Mycenae Lookout' makes constant, at times strained
comparisons between the endgame at Troy and that acted out in the
North. Its narrator is a watchman, another artful, sidelined observer of
events and time, who, almost from the outset, admits that there can be
'No such thing/as innocent/bystanding (30). Though, like the author, he is
aware of the ambiguity of his position, his own 'half-calculating/bewil-
derment (31), at times the contradictions, like the images, do not add up.
His perception that the war is 'stalled in the inarticulate' (33) does not
square with the view proffered three lines earlier that too much verbiage
is a major source of the problem. There he heaps disdain on the ideologues whose repeated failure to confront inequities and move towards
accommodation created and maintained the vacuum which armed men
cruelly filled, leaving 'mothers' bearing 'their brunt in alley/bloodied cot
and bed' and a 'blood-bath' (35–6) in the homeland of O'Neill and the
house of Atreus. In its fifth and final movement, the potential of a future
presents itself. Here the two-timing narrator balances expectation against
foreknowledge, the smell of fresh water against the sight of 'A filled bath,
still unentered/and unstained', a waterwheel against 'the treadmill
of assault'. Even after a 'lifeline' materialises, the poet has difficulty

engineering the aesthetic resolution he has longed for for so long. Paradoxically, he can only envisage future restoration in terms from what he *imagines* as an untroubled past. In this foretime his fellow countrymen were 'finders, keepers, seers' (37), not killers, and the land articulate with plenty and the benison of water.

'After Liberation', part two of 'To a Dutch Potter in Ireland', resounds with the relief that greeted the cessation in violence in 1944, and the euphoria that briefly followed:

> To have lived it through and now be free to give
> Utterance, body and soul to wake and know
> Every time that it's gone and for good, the thing
> That nearly broke you. (4)

Although in retrospect the narrator's heady pre-Canary Wharf, pre-Manchester, pre-Killyhevlin optimism and talk of freedom may seem naïve and misplaced, at the point of time the poem was composed it must have seemed that the breaking of nations was over:

> Slow horses
> Plough the fallow, war rumbles away
> In the near distance. (4)

Like Thomas Hardy's war poem, Heaney's attempts to engage simultaneously with the current political situation and with what he trusts and believes can yield a means of transcending it – the aesthetic realm, the realm of dialogic and redress. An inevitable consequence of this belief is that his female 'subject', Sonja Landweer, comes across as rather an iconic figure. However, Heaney's narrator is frank about what he is doing, and at one stage playfully refers to the potter as a nymph and 'vestal of the goddess Silica' (2). Though she speaks only by report, it is evident that he, like Ormsby, values deeply all that the woman's renewing, reaffirming art embodies. Her work serves as a model for the poet's own and for Northern Irish art in general, fired as it has been in the heat of war.

Self-reflexivity and intertextuality remain central elements in the poet's work. They function as indicators of the writer's engagement in a continuing, collective debate about issues of value and identity. While they have the capacity to be enabling, intertextual allusions can equally prove disabling and distracting. Highly self-conscious, they work by drawing attention to themselves, and are sometimes used in *The Spirit Level* to signal the narrator's separation from a prior, less sophisticated self. References to Fragonard, Brueghel and Memling in 'The Swing', for example, serve as markers of the way 'we sailed/Beyond ourselves' (48), yet seem some-what artful when set beside the presence evoked at the poem's core, the figure of the mother. Much is implied, much left unsaid about this 'earth-bound' denizen, as she sits seeking temporary relief for her swollen feet, before having to dress again and redress 'the life she would not fail and was not/Meant for'. She is presented simultaneously through the eyes of a knowing adult-narrator and his uncomprehending child-self; whereas the former subjects her to a mock heroic treatment, comparing her to an empress and goddess, the latter has the grace 'to let her be' (49). The sudden shifts in register, swinging from 'high ('mitigation', 'ministrations') to 'low' ('rolled elastic stocking'), intensify one's sense of her hurt and humility. In addition they point up the contrasts between earlier and later generations in Northern Ireland, the older grounded 'stay at homes' (23), the younger granted permission to fly.

Amongst the many fine returns to be found in the collection is 'Tollund'. Composed in six rhyming, decasyllabic quatrains, it captures a very different scene and music to that of 'Tollund Man', 24 years back. Modernity has left its imprint on the once-mythic landscape, the traffic noise, a satellite dish, a 'resituated' standing-stone signs that 'Things had moved on' in this 'user-friendly' wilderness. Unlike his earnest predecessor, the spiritually and linguistically relaxed narrator of 'Tollund' depicts himself and his wife[245] as 'footloose', *happy* to be 'at home beyond the tribe'. Lifted by the ceasefire announced during their stay in Denmark, they feel ready

> to make a new beginning
> And make a go of it, alive and sinning,
> Ourselves again, free-willed again, not bad. (69)

Encoded within these lines is an allusion to Sinn Féin ('Ourselves'), harking back, I presume, to the nationalist party of that name which triumphed in the all-Ireland election of December 1918 and could legitimately claim to be the most important 'representative organisation of the Irish people in Ireland'.[246] That not just the nationalist cause, but *everyone* in Northern Ireland has been tainted by and implicated in the previous 25 years of bloody strife is implied in the poem's last two words. These express a modest desire for something better, and contrast with the more expansive aspirations embodied in the idea of 'a new beginning'. In the references to being 'alive and sinning' and a *restored* free-will one detects a longing to regain that sense of alternative possibilities fostered in the mid-1960s, when the younger generation to which the couple belonged enjoyed briefly their release from the stifling political and religious orthodoxies that had dominated their lives thus far.[247]

3
A Longer Road: 1995–2006

I Struggling towards closure (1995–2001)

In early 1996 the Provisional IRA ended its ceasefire. The origins of this huge setback in the peace process can be traced back to British reactions to the cessation of August 1994. In mid-January 1995 a ban on minister-ial contacts with parties linked to paramilitary organisations had been lifted. However, Sinn Féin cancelled its first scheduled meeting with offi-cials from the Northern Ireland Office on 9 February 1995 after discover-ing a bugging device in the room in which it was due to take place. Later that month the British and Irish governments issued *Frameworks for the Future*, outlining their initial proposals for a return to devolution. These envisaged the setting up of a single chamber assembly, elected by pro-portional representation, and an increasing degree of 'harmonisation' between institutions North and South in such areas as agriculture, trans-port, energy, health, trade and education. Any chances of *Frameworks for the Future* performing a role in a final settlement were dashed when on 10 March the UUP rejected the entire document. A few days earlier Sir Patrick Mayhew unveiled a three-point plan to enable Sinn Féin to enter talks which depended on IRA agreement to decommission its weapons 'progressively'. This proposal was also scorned by the unionist parties who regarded it as amounting to capitulation to the republican movement.

From comments made in Dublin in mid-April 1995, Gerry Adams's frustration at the continuing impasse is evident: 'If the British won't listen to reasoned and reasoned argument then let them listen to the sound of marching feet and angry voices'.[1] In early May a Sinn Féin delegation, headed by Martin McGuinness, met Michael Ancram, the Northern Ireland Minister, and again came under pressure to move on decommissioning. In mid-June, Mayhew reiterated the government's fixed stance on the issue, prompting McGuinness's retort that there was 'not a snowball's chance in hell of any weapons being decommissioned this side of a negotiated settlement'.[2] Summer found Major increasingly embroiled in a struggle to reassert his authority over his party, while in the province increasingly serious clashes took place between loyalists and the RUC in Belfast (5 July) and at Drumcree, near Portadown (9–10 July), where 10 000 Orangemen insisted on their right to march down the Garvaghy Road against the wishes of its nationalist residents. The sheer number of loyalist protesters forced the RUC into a compromise which allowed 500 Orangemen to walk down the Garvaghy Road, albeit without any accompanying bands. The sight of Ian Paisley and David Trimble, the Unionist MP for Upper Bann, hands locked and aloft, striding triumphantly through cheering crowds of unionists outraged the nationalist community and strengthened their demands that the RUC be abolished.

As so often in the past, intermittent rioting and sectarian attacks in Belfast and Derry kept the temperature high during the rest of July and August. British government ministers and unionist politicians frequently linked the PIRA's failure to budge on decommissioning to the issue of 'punishment beatings'[3] as evidence that republicans had not yet put violence and intimidation behind them. Indeed, immediately after his unexpected election as UUP leader on 8 September, David Trimble made this very point. The previous week, on the first anniversary of the ceasefire, Sinn Féin's president, Gerry Adams, spoke of his willingness to examine closely proposals on the destruction of arms. The very next day, however, an IRA spokesman denied that 'any decommissioning at all' would occur 'either through the back door or front door'.[4] Around October 1995, according to Feeney, 'Adams lost the support of the Army Council' and plans were laid by the Provisionals to transport a substantial bomb for an attack on London.[5] Talks between Michael Ancram and Sinn Féin held in late October and the first week of November came to nothing, prompting Adams to declare that the British were undermining the whole peace initiative. In late November, however, the British and Irish governments issued a joint statement affirming that all-party talks would begin before the end of February 1996 and an international commission, chaired by the distinguished American senator, George Mitchell, would look into the whole thorny issue of paramilitary arms. Two days later, on 30 November, President Clinton embarked on his historic visit to Northern Ireland, urging political parties of every persuasion to seize the opportunities opened up by the latest British–Irish communiqué. The euphoria generated by Clinton's visit dissipated in the weeks that ensued, which witnessed a sequence of killings carried out by a group calling itself Direct Action Against Drugs (DAAD), but which most people realised was merely a cover name used by the Provisionals.

On 10 January 1996 Sinn Féin submitted *Building a Permanent Peace* to the Mitchell commission saying that the destruction of weapons was possible *after* negotiations for a political agreement have been concluded. A fortnight later the commission report argued for *parallel* all-party talks and acts of decommissioning. It urged a commitment by all parties to pursue exclusively democratic means of resolution and called for a halt to punishment killings and beatings. Major rejected the first of these recommendations, reaffirming the government's view that decommissioning should *precede* entry to talks, and, to the fury of the nationalists and republicans already dismayed by the delay in starting negotiations, announcing that elections would be held in Northern Ireland. Major's 'bad faith' and unionist leaders' recalcitrance were cited by the Provisionals as the principal reasons for resuming military operations. An hour after announcing that the ceasefire was over, on the evening of Friday, 9 February, a bomb planted in an underground car park in London's Canary Wharf exploded, killing two people, injuring a hundred others, and causing over £100 million in damage to property. Condemnation came swiftly not only in Ireland and Britain, but also in the USA; Major pointed to the bombing as evidence of the 'urgent need to remove illegal arms from the equation'.[6] During the rest of the year the Provisional IRA continued to carry out sporadic attacks on mainland Britain, usually targeting London. In mid-June, they detonated a 3500 lb bomb in Manchester, devastating large parts of the city centre and wounding over 200 people.

The elections for the Northern Ireland Forum, held on 30 May 1996, which had been opposed by nationalist politicians, resulted in support for Sinn Féin rising steeply to 15.5 per cent, and only a small drop in the SDLP's share of the vote. The fact that both Hume and Adams personally received substantial numbers of votes was generally regarded as evidence that nationalists and republicans overwhelmingly endorsed the peace process. The PIRA's murder of Jerry McCabe, a Garda officer, in Limerick on 7 June, in the course of a post van robbery, along with Sinn Féin's subsequent reluctance to condemn the killing, led to further worsening of relations between the Irish government and Adams's party. As a result, the Fine Gael Taoiseach, John Bruton, aligned himself even more closely with Major's stance on arms and talks. Three days after McCabe's killing, the two Prime Ministers opened multi-party talks at Stormont, from which Sinn Féin were barred.

Drumcree proved to be the site of the year's most serious violence during the first weeks in July. Following an RUC ban on Orange marchers parading down the nationalist Garvaghy Road, loyalists engaged in violent clashes with police officers barring their way. Civil disorder spread to other towns in the province, where loyalists set up barricades. In parts of Belfast arson attacks and looting occurred. The Portadown UVF murdered Michael McGoldrick, a 31-year-old Catholic taxi-driver, and recent graduate in English and Politics at Queen's. John Major tried to resolve the crisis through talks with the UUP and DUP leaders, but both Trimble and Paisley were adamant that the RUC should be withdrawn from Drumcree and the marchers' wishes respected. Fearing loyalist violence and civil disobedience might escalate further and knowing that his force lacked the resources to cope, on 11 July the RUC Chief Constable backed down and allowed the march to proceed down the Garvaghy Road. To enable this to happen, he ordered his officers to clear nationalist residents from the street. This decision sparked riots in nationalist areas and provoked criticism from the SDLP and the Irish government, who accused the RUC of applying double standards in their treatment of the North's communities.

For a while there was a growing dread that Northern Ireland was on the brink of a Bosnia-like civil war. At several junctures in late summer and autumn 1996 it appeared that the loyalist ceasefires might not hold. On 22 July John Major invited representatives of the UDP and PUP to Downing Street for talks. Peter Taylor suggests his motives in so doing may well have been to demonstrate to the militant republicans that dialogue was possible once guns had been put aside.[7] During the last week of August and start of September internal frictions within their own community preoccupied loyalist paramilitaries, following the issuing of a joint UDA–UVF ultimatum to two hardliners, Billy Wright and Alex Kerr, who were told to quit the province or face the consequences. One incident said to have put the ceasefire in serious jeopardy was the PIRA's car-bomb attack on the British Army barracks near Lisburn on 7 October, in which 31 people were injured and one soldier died. Significantly the following week Mo Mowlam, the Labour opposition's Northern Ireland spokesperson, and David Trimble devoted time to visiting loyalist inmates in the Maze/Long Kesh in order to defuse tensions there.[8]

Deirdre Madden, *One by One in the Darkness*; Seamus Deane, *Reading in the Dark*

Traces of the political translations and cultural reconfigurations taking place immediately before, during and after the 1994 ceasefires can be easily descried in the fiction of the period. One interesting phenomenon is the appearance at this juncture of a number of comic and satirical treatments of the political and cultural climate,[9] in such novels as Colin Bateman's *Divorcing Jack* (1995), Michael Foley's *The Road to Notown* (1996) and Robert McLiam Wilson's *Eureka Street* (1996). A full-length examination of Northern Irish literary fiction in the 1990s might well involve detailed assessments of the work of Bernard Mac Laverty, David Park, Eoin McNamee, Ronan Bennett, Linda Anderson, Glenn Patterson and McLiam Wilson, all of whose writing merits close scrutiny. For the purposes of this study, however, I have had to confine myself to two texts, Deirdre Madden's *One by One on the Darkness* and Seamus Deane's *Reading in the Dark*, both of which movingly survey a substantial stretch of Northern Irish history and diagnose how the province came to its current pass.

Deirdre Madden's *One by One in the Darkness* was written between the summer of 1993 and July 1995. One of the earliest locations depicted in the novel is the Ladies at Heathrow, where we discover Cate Quinn examining in a mirror 'the tiny invisible scar at her hairline', the result of an accident when she was six. Clearly the scar figures as an originary emblem, lending the character 'a sense of who she was, in a way that looking at her own reflection could not' (2). Like Theresa in *Hidden Symptoms* and Catherine McKenna in Bernard Mac Laverty's *Grace Notes*, glimpsed staring at her own 'distorted face'[10] in a bus window on the way to the same airport, Cate is caught trying to establish some sense of who she might be, only to be confronted not with a defined self but with an image which 'other people see' (2).[11] A crucial element in her current state is the child she is carrying, which opens up possibilities for an alternative, affirmative narrative and embodies the latest manifestation of her desire for individuation.[12] Born *Kate* Quinn, she had attempted to fabricate a new, metropolitan identity for herself when she started working as a journalist in London by changing the spelling of her name because she felt that it was 'too Irish' (4).[13] However, like Theresa Cassidy's in *Hidden Symptoms*, her life has been overshadowed and profoundly destabilised by an event occurring two years previously, a brutal sectarian killing.

The text's opening thus immediately draws the reader into Madden's preoccupation with issues of authority and agency. In this novel, however, one finds a much more explicit engagement with the larger narrative of Northern Ireland and its impact on identity formation, alongside her recurring concern with the nature of family politics.[14] Like the representatives of previous generations, Cate and the other female protagonists encounter immense difficulty in flying by the nets which define and confine their identities. Growing up as Catholics and into women in Northern Ireland, they become accustomed to adding regularly to 'the already laden chains which they wore around their necks' (61).[15] Bonded by and to history and place, they illustrate a contention stated in an earlier novel, that 'If you are born here you can never belong elsewhere'.[16]

In order to convey the importance of intra- and extra-familial influences on the lives of the three Quinn sisters (Helen, Cate and Sally), Madden intercuts evocations of the sisters' present lives in Belfast, London and rural Antrim with recreations of their childhood in the 1960s and 1970s. Despite differences in personalities and experiences that emerge forcefully from puberty onwards, and changes effected by all their literal and psychic relocations, there remains an intensity in that originary relationship between the three sisters. This does not prevent them from reading each other negatively and decrying each other's choices of career (9). For outsiders, however, this closeness proves exasperating. One of the Cate's boyfriends remarks how tired he is of hearing about her family, and questions whether she ever thinks of anything else (148).

Blood is the factor that has intensified the blood-ties. Two years prior to the narrative present, the girls' father had been murdered by loyalist gunmen in a case of mistaken identity; their real target was his brother, a Sinn Féin member. As a result, like Theresa, each of the sisters is haunted by recurrent fears and a fear of recurrence, which 'like a wire ... connected them with each other and isolated them from everyone else' (9). One by one, the Quinn women have had to dwell on the changing signification of 'home', a word which no longer functions as a place of security and shelter, underwritten by larger texts of natural and liturgical order:

> The regular round of necessity was broken by celebrations and feasts ... The scope of their lives was tiny but it was profound, and to them, it was immense ... The idea of home was something they lived so completely that they would have been at a loss to define it. (74–5)

Earlier in the same passage, it is made clear that this sense of wholeness and homeliness has itself been achieved only by conscious, willed acts of exclusion: 'Yet for all this they knew that their lives ... were off centre in relation to the society beyond those few fields and houses' (75). The rural margins could not hope to hold off for ever the impact of the urban centres: 'Derry was little more than an hour away' (95). In Chapter Six, however, these two worlds are brought into violent conjunction, as the 'timeless' part-pagan Catholic past meets the turbulent Catholic present. In compensation for not being allowed to attend the first civil rights march in Derry on 5 October 1968, along with their father, Uncle Brian and their boy cousins, the girls' grandmother takes them on a walk to a local holy well (70–1). That afternoon while the women pray together and bless themselves with rags dipped in well-water to cure Sally's nose-bleeds,[17] the violent future begins. On the march their uncle is badly beaten, cut about the face by the RUC. In a prescient, proleptic moment soon after, as the family gather and debate the stand-off between the Stormont government and People's Democracy movement, Michael, another of the girls' uncles predicts, 'It'll end in a bloodbath' (79).

Too often critiques of its texts have overstated the homogeneity of the northern nationalist community, characterising its members as uniformly 'atavistic', 'traditionalist' and 'reactionary' in their thinking. Certainly the sense of siege within northern nationalist enclaves following the founding of Northern Ireland in the 1920s and again in the late 1960s and early 1970s, when violence erupted again, did generate a high degree of inter- and intra-generational solidarity, but Madden is at pains to present diversity in the reactions to the political crisis. Increasingly the Quinns in *One by One* read the same text differently. Charlie's civil response to the soldiers' intrusive questions (96–8) is contrasted with the angry reactions of his wife and brother. Though later he too becomes 'resentful towards the security forces' (99), in particular after the internment and torture of his brother and nephew, he never espouses militant republicanism. When, soon afterwards, the 19-year-old brother of one of Helen's school-friends is killed while planting a bomb, he refuses to applaud the IRA's graveside salute:

> Where did he think that was going to get any of us? Did he think he was going to free Ireland? ... Never forget what you saw today: and never let anybody try to tell you that it was anything other than a life wasted, and lives destroyed. (103, 105)

This moment marks an important transition in the text's presentation of Charlie's character and that of his community. Like Michael's, his prescience is deeply ironic. No longer the political naïf, he, rather than Brian, is alert to the terrible price that will be paid in the future should violence becomes *the* accepted means of redress. Madden makes explicit the political chasm separating Brian from his brothers in a heated exchange following the Bloody Friday massacre of July 1972, when IRA bombs killed nine people and maimed 130 in Belfast.[18] His attempts to justify and contextualise the atrocity confirm his Sinn Féin credentials, whereas Peter and Charlie's contempt for his argument and condemnation of all forms of violence suggest they align themselves with the more moderate stance of the SDLP (129–30). The significance of Bloody Friday, however, lies not only in the ideological divisions it exposes. The event has a profoundly emotional effect on Charlie, which in turn weighs upon his eldest daughter, Helen, as can be seen when she subsequently discovers her father weeping in the kitchen:

> She knew, now, all in a rush, what he was thinking; and there, in the darkness, it was as if she had already lost him, as if his loved body had already been violently destroyed. They clung to each other like people who had been saved from a shipwreck, or a burning building; but it was no use, the disaster had already happened. (130)

As for Theresa in *Hidden Symptoms*, Helen's access to the past comes in the form of memories, dreams and texts. One telling moment finds Helen alone in the kitchen, picking up and reflecting on a photograph of her father (26–7).[19] Studying this framed absence, she thinks of her own graduation picture of him back in Belfast, and of their shared pleasure at her accelerated rise within the legal profession. Setting down the photograph, she picks up next his copy of *The People's Missal*, bulging with memorial cards, and the other books that helped define his cultural identity: *Flora and Fauna of Northern Ireland*, *Field Guide to the Birds of Lough Neagh*, *Monuments of Pre-Christian Ireland*, *Celtic Heritage*. Significantly alongside these examples of unthreatening non-fiction, are Michael McLaverty's *Call My Brother Back* and Seamus Heaney's *North*, texts replete with images of victims, marked by a deeply troubled nationalism. As she reaches out for *North*, 'a figure standing at the kitchen window' breaks in on her rituals of remembrance; it is her Uncle Brian, whose presence now she deeply resents:

> She remembered sitting with him on the kitchen sofa at three o'clock in the morning during her father's wake ...
>   'It was my fault', he'd said abruptly ... 'It was me they wanted. I'm to blame'.

> 'You're never to say that again, Brian. It's not true and you know it'.
> ... He'd never repeated those words to her but since then the idea had
> always lain between them like a coiled snake ... She lost Brian too,
> that night: she did to some degree hold him responsible, and that he
> also blamed himself was of no real help to her. (28)

Shortly after this scene the reader visits yet another illuminating textual
site, Helen's pied à terre in Belfast. A newly-built house just off the
Ormeau Road, it reflects her need for somewhere which was 'psychically
a blank' (44), a place seemingly without a history.[20] While much of the
imagery used to describe the room where she occasionally entertains
('sterility', 'clinical neatness', 'chilly atmosphere') suggests an almost
ascetic rage for order, her unseen bedroom is an altogether more cluttered space, strewn with 'newspapers and political magazines which had
toppled over and blocked the way' (45). The significance of these textual
impedimenta is clarified later in the same chapter when the reader witnesses Helen's initially flinty encounter with a journalist, David McKenna,
at a party.

Her anger towards him stems from the media treatment of her father's
killing. The day after the funeral while shopping for groceries she had
been confronted with someone else's appropriation of her image and misrepresentation of her father:

> On the counter, on the front of one of the Northern Ireland news-
> papers, was a photograph of herself and Sally with their arms around
> each other weeping at the graveside ... Worst of all had been the
> British tabloids, where the death was reported coldly and without
> sympathy, much being made of Brian's Sinn Fein membership, and
> the murder having taken place in his house. The inference was that
> he had only got what was coming to him. (47)

As so often in Madden's fiction, texts are misread, and fail to do justice.
Having abused David at the party because of the press's callousness and
partiality with respect to her father's murder, she discovers the following
day that *his* father had suffered a similar fate; an electrician, he had been
murdered whilst working alongside a carpenter, who had been 'a big
shot' in the IRA. 'As far as the press were concerned, they were two terrorists, they got what they deserved' (49).[21] These acts of murder and the
acts of writing purporting to describe them have together inscribed
Helen and David's future for them, and determined them in their careers
and their pursuit of 'truth'.

In viewing the relationship between writing and suffering as frequently voyeuristic, often parasitical, and the narratives generated as invariably simplistic and crude, Helen articulates a widespread feeling. Journalism, she argues, 'isn't fitted to dealing with complexity, it isn't comfortable with paradox or contradiction, and that's the heart of the problem, if you ask me' (51). The chapter ends with Helen and David watching a television documentary marking the twenty-fifth anniversary of the start of the 'Troubles', her response to which reveals the acuity of her crisis of self-fashioning. Watching the images on the screen,

> she wondered how you ever got to the essence of things, of your time, your society, your self. It struck her as strange that out of her whole family, she, the only one whose life was supposedly dedicated to the administration of justice, was the only one who didn't believe in it as a spiritual fact, who perhaps didn't believe in it at all. (60)

These conclusions dramatically illustrate the extent of Helen's profound alienation following her bereavement, and the distance she has travelled since first expressing her enthusiasm for the law in school. There she had heeded the call of her sixth form tutor, the Derry-born Sister Philomena – 'Our educated Catholics have a role to play in this society. We need our Catholic teachers and doctors and nurses and lawyers' (158) – in the face of strong opposition from the headmistress, Sister Benedict, who, curiously for a nun, argued that self-sacrifice and idealism would change nothing in the North (158–9).

Neither imagination nor memory offers an escape or refuge. Our first extended glimpse of her marks her as a fictionist in the making, attempting to conjure sights and sounds from a lost and innocent time:

> In her rare moments of nostalgia she could sit there and half-close her eyes and imagine that it was twenty, twenty-five years ago, that if she were to go over to Uncle Brian's house now she would find it, too, as it was in the past; that if she listened at the kitchen door there long enough she would hear voices: Granny Kate and Uncle Peter, and the voices of children, one of whom was herself. But she could never make the illusion last as long as she desired. (21–2)

Having set up Uncle Brian and Aunt Lucy's kitchen as an imagined place of continuity, the narrator immediately subverts this reading. Whereas the rest of their house has remained unaltered over the years, the kitchen is 'the only room they had changed … About a year earlier they had had it completely modernised; the stove ripped out, fitted pine units installed, a vinyl floor covering laid over the red quarry tiles' (22).[22] Subsequently the reader learns that this was where the girls' father was shot dead two years previously, but it is only at the novel's closure that the 'missing' scene is finally revealed. Once more Helen is presented like a novelist, reconstructing 'somewhere between her dreams and her imagination' (178) the moment her father fell victim to sectarian assassins. Just as in Bernard Mac Laverty's *Cal*, the moment is captured as if on camera 'repeated constantly, like a loop of film but sharper than that, more vivid, and running at just a fraction of a second slower than normal time, which gave it the heavy feel of nightmare' (180).[23] However,

> this was no dream: she saw her father sitting at Lucy's kitchen table, drinking tea out of a blue mug. She could smell the smoke of his cigarette … He was talking through to Lucy … 'There's a car pulled up outside now, but it's not Brian by the sound of it.' And as soon as she spoke these words he heard her scream , as two men burst into the back scullery, and knocked her to the ground as they pushed past her; and then Helen's father saw them himself as they came into the kitchen, two men in parkas with the hoods pulled up, Halloween masks on their face. He saw the guns, too, and he knew what they were going to do to him. The sound of a chair scraping back on the tiles, 'Ah no, Christ Jesus no', and then they shot him at point-blank range, blowing half his head away. (180–1)

The precision and economy of detail – the blue mug, the cigarette smell, the exchanged commonplaces, the grating of the chair on the tiles – are particularly effective. There is a sharp irony in the encoded allusion to a previous Halloween celebration held in Brian's house. Then Charlie had laughed at the sight of three masked witches sitting in the back of his car, and told his daughters how terrifying they looked (72–3). At that stage, of course, the reader is unaware of most of the circumstances of Charlie's death; as a consequence, when Helen's imagined version is given at its close, it is encountered with the ghostly presence of the earlier scene. This marrying of dissonant moments and images is indicative of Madden's consummate skill as a novelist, her ability to establish poignantly ironic relationships between narratives within the narrative.

In this last novel, through the character of Cate, Madden appears to admit possibilities for a change. She is pictured imagining a memorial to the victims of the 'Troubles',

> a room, a perfectly square room. Three of its walls, unbroken by windows, would be covered by neat rows of names, over three thousand

of them; and the fourth wall would be nothing but window. The whole structure would be built where the horizon was low, and the sky huge. It would be a place which afforded dignity to memory, where you could bring your anger, as well as your grief. (149)

The antithesis of the 'solid stone house where the silence was uncanny' (1), the shrine, like the text itself, serves as a potential space for recuperation, a theatre for purgation. It is perhaps a fitting instance to end on, yet another illustration of the self-consciousness of Madden's art, which registers in its accounts the costs to individuals and their families of violence, including the violence of misrepresentation, of skewed reflections. Madden is a writer who merits and requires close reading, since her work is so deftly textured and has so much to say about the state of the 'moral economy'[24] on these islands.

Seamus Deane's *Reading in the Dark* (1996)[25] illustrates perfectly Seamus Heaney's contention that 'In emergent cultures the struggle of an individual consciousness towards affirmation and distinctness may be analogous, if not coterminous, with a collective straining towards self-definition'.[26] Though initially it might appear that Deane's focus is primarily a domestic, localised one, home and city serve as metonyms in a broader history of which the reader is constantly made aware. The novel's remit extends far beyond the dates heading each section of its six chapters (February 1945 to July 1971), since the text both looks back to the generations which witnessed and opposed the partition of the state of Northern Ireland and forward implicitly to what came after.

Taken from the popular Irish folk-song, 'She Moved through the Fair', *Reading in the Dark*'s epigraph prepares us for the crucial part silences and suppressions,[27] absences and ellipses will play in the content, structure and telling of the tale:

> *The people were saying no two were e'er wed*
> *But one had a sorrow that never was said.*

It will be the narrator's tireless pursuit of the unsaid that will shape his coming to consciousness, and isolate him forever from the two people he loves most.[28] In the process he discovers how impossible it has been for his parents and their families to extricate themselves from the nets of their own and the province's history, a history threaded through with intimate betrayals, critical confusions over and about identity, terrible injustice. He pieces together the story of how in 1922, some 13 years before his parents' marriage, his father's eldest brother, Eddie, was falsely accused of being a police informer and 'executed' by an IRA squad acting on the orders of his maternal grandfather (126). His researches later reveal the identity of the real informer, Tony McIlhenny, a man who had courted and then 'dropped' (187) his mother in order to marry her younger sister, Katie, in 1926. Despite the fact that he had abandoned her, the boy's mother helped engineer McIlhenny's escape to America after the IRA had received a tip-off that it was *he* who had been the 'tout'. Approximately four years after McIlhenny's flight, she had met Eddie's brother, Frank, the narrator's father, and married him. Years later, in 1952, when her father was on his deathbed, he confided to her details of his role in Eddie's death (126). The realisation that she will never be able to bring herself to inform Frank of his brother's innocence, of her father's responsibility for his killing, of her relationship with McIlhenny (187), has a corrosive effect on her and later on the narrator who had so passionately longed to unearth the mysteries of his family's past.

From the novel's outset, the reader is drawn into a double 'game',[29] conscious of the presence behind the child focaliser of a mature, sophisticated intelligence. The very first line speaks of 'a clear, plain silence' (5). Yet it quickly becomes apparent, that in this text silence – like Wilde's famous definition of truth[30] – is rarely pure and never simple. Features such as repetitions in vocabulary ('Stairs', 'stairs', 'staircase', 'steps', 'steps', 'steps', 'took you', 'took you'), use of the second person singular, the preponderance of simple sentence forms, along with the unnecessary meticulousness with which the number of steps and dimensions of the landing are specified, all serve initially to create the illusion of a child narrator. Contrastingly, the narrator's comment on the lino – its 'original pattern ... polished away to the point where it had *the look of a faint memory*' (5) – is indicative of an older, cultured sensibility, and initiates the novel's self-referential concerns, its preoccupation with unstable texts and the difficulties of their interpretation.[31]

A mere eight lines into the narrative the boy's perception of home as a space of settled co-ordinates and known gradations is suddenly and dramatically disrupted.[32] Interestingly the novel's first spoken words are an imperative, issued by an authority-figure whose sway over her son will never be fully regained. Ironically the mother's repeated cry, 'Don't move', only serves to mobilise the boy's curiosity over the identity of the figure she imagines on the stairs. What the 'something there between us' and who the 'somebody there' might be, she is unwilling to or possibly unable to name to her son or to herself. It is perhaps immaterial whether the shadow or 'sorrow' she senses is that of Eddie, or McIlhenny, or her father, or a 'compound ghost'[33] made up of all three; like her son, the reader cannot be sure. The importance of the encounter lies rather in its aftermath. The opening scene ends proleptically with images of separation and dissolution. Whereas the boy becomes all animation, transgressive energy, thwarted expectation – 'I was up at the window before she could say anything more, but there was nothing there' – the mother loses identity, translated in his eyes into 'a darkness' by the window, a 'redness locked' in the grating past. With the advantage of hindsight, the adult narrator *knows* that this is a momentous point in his relationship with his mother: 'I *could have* touched her', 'I loved her *then*' (5; my emphasis). His child-self he depicts as bewildered by his mother's crying and constrained in his actions. In a gesture of solidarity, he sits beside her and stares into the caged flames.[34]

Succeeding sections chart the frustrations the narrator meets with and advances he makes as a reader of unyielding texts. Increasingly he finds himself in a state of resistance, and under constant emotional and ideological fire both inside and outside the home. Immediately after the disturbing encounter with the ghost on the stairs he is troubled by a second 'disappearing act' (7), that of a circus magician, and questioning the reassuring, rational explanation of events offered by his sibling elders, Eilis and Liam. In another early, highly emblematic scene ('Feet'), which depicts the funeral of his younger sister, Una, a victim of meningitis, the eight-year-old fails to catch the meaning of any of the exchanges between his parents. From his constricted, partial vantage point under the kitchen table, however, he is able to record the choreography of pain and loss he can do nothing to relieve:

> My mother was standing at the kitchen press, a couple of feet away, her shoes tight together, looking very small … My father's boots moved towards her until they were very close … One of his boots was between her feet. There was her shoe, then his boot, then her shoe, then his boot … He was kissing her. She was still crying. Their feet shifted, and I thought she was going to fall. (15)

Shortly after this, his 'first death' (16), he presents himself again in an *aporia*, struggling with signs which are simultaneously familiar and estranging.[35] In describing his first experience of reading a novel, it is initially the supplementary material which engages him and which he in turn prioritorises. The presence of his mother's maiden name on the flyleaf prompts yet another epiphany, the realisation that she enjoyed a life 'before she was the mother I knew'. By emphasising the child-self's uncertainty faced with the apparent evidence of a previous existence – the letters of her name were 'faded, *but* ... very clear', 'seemed *as though* they represented someone she was', 'who *might not even have been* the same person' (19; my emphasis) – Deane subtly draws attention to his own text's larger fictional and metafictional concerns, its preoccupation with identities, inscriptions, representations, interpretations, contexts. It is not until the section's second paragraph that the novel with the 'green hardboard cover' is finally named and its contents 'released' by the narrator, thereby enabling the reader to recognise its function as an analogue for *Reading in the Dark*. The book is *The Shan Van Vocht*, a narrative set at another momentous point in Irish history, the time of the Great Rebellion of 1798,[36] in which 'fire', 'implied danger' and 'a love relationship' are forged in what the boy took to be an 'exquisite ... blend' (19). Locked within its title, 'a phonetic rendering of an Irish phrase meaning The Poor Old Woman', is a reminder of linguistic and cultural loss, but also an anticipation of the confused, oppressed state to which the narrator's mother will eventually succumb.[37] This encounter with fiction, 're-imagining all I had read, the various ways the plot might unravel, the novel opening into endless possibilities' (20), anticipates subsequent narrative acts, and his own role as an unraveller of the lines and lies in his family past.

Given its concentration on the boy's life between the ages of five and 17, the period of his schooldays, *Reading in the Dark* might almost have been subtitled 'A Portrait of the Artist as a Very Young Man'.[38] Joyce's fiction certainly comes to mind during the sermon delivered in the section entitled 'Grandfather' (22–6), which sows the idea that Deane's focaliser, like Stephen Dedalus, is a subject of and subject to two masters, 'the holy Roman catholic and apostolic church' and 'the imperial British state'.[39] Brother Regan functions as one of the novel's many ancillary narrators, who set before the boy 'a competing and bewildering array of aesthetic, religious and political imperatives',[40] and before the reader analogues for the Eddie-McIlhenny story. The occasion for the Brother's address to the primary school class attended by the narrator is Christmas 1948, a mere three months after Una's death. In order to maximise the impact of his words, Brother Regan stages his talk with care, illuminating 'his dark classroom' with the light from a single candle, placed before a statue of the Virgin Mary. He relates to the boys a story of a revenge killing carried out by Derry republicans in the early 1920s, who threw an RUC man, Billy Mahon, from the city's Craigavon Bridge as a reprisal for the shooting of one of their number.[41] Soon afterwards a man was arrested, charged and put on trial for the murder of the police officer, but was acquitted after a number of witnesses supplied him with a convincing alibi.

At this strategic juncture in his narrative, Brother Regan throws in a pointed remark about the sectarian nature of the Northern Ireland statelet, and how unusual it was for a Catholic to walk free: 'Innocence was no guarantee for a Catholic then. Nor is it now' (23). Ironically, immediately after this assertion, Regan informs the boys that the accused man was in fact *guilty*, as a local curate was to discover. After the man's admission that it has been 20 years since his last confession, the priest assumed that he had sought him out to reconcile himself to Mother Church.[42] Instead, it emerges that he wishes to confide rather than confess, since he knows that his action in committing the crime and lack of remorse for it have placed him beyond the reach of the sacraments. By reporting the man's claim that the RUC officer was drunk and simply 'looking for a Catholic to kill' (24), relating his account of how the man was forced to abandon his friend's body, Brother Regan quickens the boys' empathy for their own, and sense of themselves as members of a victimised minority within the province. Yet having conjured for them 'a world of wrong, insult, injury, unemployment … where the unjust hold power and the ignorant rule' (26), he urges them to adopt a response of spiritual resignation and political passivity, offering up their future suffering and their allegiance to a Higher Judge and Laws. That 'the whole situation' in Northern Ireland 'makes men evil' (25) is not a contentious statement. Yet for many young nationalists of Deane's generation it was reprehensible that the Catholic Church failed to take a lead in remedying that evil by practical, non-violent means.[43]

The eight-year-old narrator's reaction to the sermon is deeply confused. While correctly identifying the principal figure in Regan's homily as his own grandfather, he has difficulty in believing that the 'little', 'sick', sedentary individual he knows could once have been an impassioned man of action. Although he tries dismissing the story as 'just folklore', he recalls having heard scraps of it when he was much younger and, significantly, how he had imaginatively entered into this episode in the family narrative *as a victim*.[44] Within a month of hearing the sermon, the narrator has a direct, personal experience of police violence in his own home and at the station, after he, his father and brother are arrested for possession of a firearm and beaten, following a tip-off by an RUC informer (27–9).

A parallel episode during the latter stages of the boy's secondary school career provides another example of his exposure to ideological conditioning. Dated as taking place in November 1956, a month before the IRA recommenced hostilities, 'Political Education' presents an address to the boys at St Columb's delivered by an outside speaker, a British Army chaplain. The narrator gives at first an ambivalent response to this latest manifestation of adult authority. His younger self, the 16-year-old focaliser, appears over-awed at the sight of this 'smooth', 'tall', 'handsome' stranger and his 'exquisite' manners, whose clerical and military attire suggest that it may indeed be possible to be a servant of two masters. One senses also, however, the presence of an older, dissenting voice in the description of the man. By referring to his accent as 'smooth' in the second line of the section, the narrator forewarns us that his speech will be both mellifluous in sound and manipulative in content. Tellingly, the first sentence ends with the disclosure that the chaplain is acting on behalf of the Northern Ireland government, having been '*sent* by the Ministry of Education' (196; my emphasis). It is evident from his opening remarks that the kind of perspectives that move him are strategic, not aesthetic.[45] After briefly waxing lyrical over the outstanding beauty of the area, its 'bird-haunted mud flats' and 'dramatic landscape and seascape', his address shifts decisively in focus. In his eyes and those of secular powers he serves, the value of Derry lies solely in its geographical position, overlooking 'the eastern approaches to the North Atlantic', and so crucially placed in enabling NATO to combat 'the international communist threat'. In increasingly florid rhetoric, he details the terrible consequences for Northern Ireland should its people fail to band together against the Soviet menace; 'democracy and freedom' would come to an end, lands would be expropriated, prison camps would suddenly spring up to accommodate dissidents. Read in the context of Derry's history since 1600,[46] and nigh on 200 pages of the story that precedes it, the chaplain's speech is excessively ironic, particularly in its references to 'the solidarity of our Christian *family*' and in its characterisation of the city's deep political and religious divisions as 'internal disputes' of no more significance 'than *family* quarrels' (197; my emphasis).

The following day, the narrator and his classmates are subjected to a follow-up lesson in global and local politics from their history teacher, Father McAuley. He gives his wholehearted endorsement to the British padre's vision, arguing that 'old' denominational 'distinctions' in Northern Ireland needed to be set aside. (This is somewhat ironic since moments earlier he had explained to the boys that the chaplain was 'an Anglican, or what was called an Anglo-Catholic priest'.) Asked by the narrator whether Communism might prove a greater calamity than the Reformation, McAuley blithely replies that whereas 'the Reformation was history', Communism constituted 'a living threat' (199). When allusions are made to the discrimination suffered by the province's Catholics, the teacher rejects this as an 'irrelevance', a parochial matter when compared to the great game being fought out worldwide by the West. Although straight after class, McAuley's arguments are trashed by Irwin, one of the pupils, as merely 'British propaganda', the narrator finds himself, despite himself, temporarily seduced by the internationalist stance proffered by the chaplain.[47] Mimicking the latter in viewing the North's political inequities as a 'distraction', the narrator wonders whether the troubles in his own life to date, starting with his beating by the police, might *just* be the residue of 'a petty squabble' (200). Irwin's comments and McAuley's arguments prompt the narrator to think back to the young German prisoner-of-war befriended by his father at the end of the war. Whether his father's action sprang from Christian compassion, or from resistance to Allied readings of the enemy, or from his identification with someone who, like him in his youth, was alone and abandoned, or indeed from a combination of all three, is a mystery that the text never resolves.[48]

A great many of the situations and experiences represented in *Reading in the Dark*, like those above, are far from being unique to the boy, his family and Derry's Catholic working-class.[49] Indeed, the novel provides remarkable insights into the condition and psychology of the minority community throughout Northern Ireland in the period following partition, 'the years that incubated the troubles'.[50] That the authorities regard that community with considerable distrust and hostility is apparent from the measures they adopt; by means of informers, the judiciary and the RUC, they are able to monitor dissent, neutralise opposition and instil fear and suspicion. The most explicit indictment of the political system and the repressive apparatuses that support it is voiced by the narrator's mother in the section immediately after the chaplain's encomium to Ulster as a bastion of freedom.[51] The occasion for her outburst is a visit to the riven family home, in December 1957, carried out by the ubiquitous local policeman, Sergeant Burke. Close to retirement, the Catholic officer has come first to explain and apologise for his role in repeatedly causing pain to her and her family, and secondly to appeal for a complete cessation of conflict between them and the powers-that-be. Identifying points of contention which will shortly be taken up by the Campaign for Social Justice and the Civil Rights Association,[52] she gives a sequence of reasons 'in quick order' why that is not possible:

> Injustice. The police themselves. Dirty politics. It's grand to say let it stop to people who have been the victims of it. What were they supposed to do? Say they're sorry they ever protested and go back to

being unemployed, gerrymandered, beaten up by every policeman who took the notion, gaoled by magistrates and judges who were so vicious that it was they who should be gaoled ... for all the harm they did and all the lives they ruined? He had no answer to that. (203)

When reflecting on how 'Politics destroyed people's lives in this place', Burke is not expressing sympathy for the woman's plight, but rather cautioning her over what may lie ahead for her children if they were learn too much of 'all that *bother*' (204: my emphasis). Ironically, after asserting that 'People were better not knowing things', he adds to the woman's burden by disclosing further details of the 'big mistakes' (211) which have haunted her life since the 1920s. He informs her that her father was responsible not once, but twice for killing the wrong man,[53] and how 'their man', McIlhenny, had helped set up Eddie, before reverting to the role of a sleeper over the next four years.

One of the most terrible ironies in *Reading in the Dark* surrounds its concern with memory and history. Whereas for the author, the poet and novelist, memory functions as a potent cultural resource, for the narrator's mother it is a curse since it brings constantly to mind past transgressions, humiliations and failures. Like her father before her, after the murders in which he was involved, she finds it impossible to confess what she knows and what she has done and so believes herself to be beyond grace, in a state 'no penance could relieve' (24). When, late on in the story, her son asks what birthday gift would please her, her reply is deeply poignant, yet at the same time edged with reproof: 'Just for that day ... just for that one day ... to forget everything. Or at least not be reminded of it. Can you give that to me?'[54] The silence with which he answers her question prompts a more explicit comment about the disquiet he causes her: 'Why don't you go away? ... Then maybe I could look after your father properly for once, without your eyes on me'. In presenting his response, the narrator uses simple grammatical structures (consisting mostly of pronouns and verbs), an unadorned vocabulary. This austerity adds to the affective shock in the final sentence, which demonstrates the sensitivity and skill with which Deane choreographs the novel throughout: 'I told her I would. I'd go away, after university. That would be her birthday gift, that promise. She nodded. I moved away just as she put out her hand towards me' (224). Roles are reversed; it is she again who lapses back into silence, a condition that has characterised much of her life and which will become permanent following her stroke in October 1968 (230). The month and year coincide with shattering changes in her native city, which began after a small, determined section of its nationalist community rose up and marched against the 'dirty' system she herself had denounced to Burke.

The concluding sections, 'My Father' and 'After', give utterance to the sorrow and intensity of love the narrator felt for his estranged parents, and which undoubtedly haunted *Reading in the Dark*'s author as he fashioned 'their' narrative from the mid-1980s to mid-1990s.[55] These were, as we have seen, years which saw the sudden collapse of political, economic and ideological partitions which had been in place in Europe and large swathes of Asia since Deane's infancy. Closer to home, relations between Dublin and London governments had changed utterly, lending momentum to reconfigurations already underway in both parts of island. Plainly it is the imprint of the latter which marks *Reading in the Dark*, a text which, for all its poststructuralist and postmodernist features, is drawn back towards the parish, the 'small figure at the turn of the stair' (229).

Had it been composed a decade earlier, in, say, the mid-1970s, it is extremely unlikely that Deane's novel would have portrayed so frankly the extent to which the wounds and humiliations and betrayals suffered by the community were *self*-inflicted.[56] While some readers might identify partition as the 'big mistake' which 'so filled the small place they lived in' (211, 229), there are plenty of instances of nationalists in harming their own; it is the narrator himself whose keenness to access its secrets divides the family and maddens his mother; it is a *Catholic* policeman whose actions cause the narrator's family the greatest grief; it is Frank's own relatives who purloin his parents' property after their death and give nothing from the sale of their home to him and his impoverished siblings; it is the IRA who get things terribly wrong in 'executing' Eddie; it is the schoolteacher priests in the novel who collude with the state's authorities by repressing and beating and demeaning their charges.[57]

A moving episode at the novel's close, however, illustrates how, despite their own afflictions and the turmoil and violence swirling around them in the Troubles' early years, the narrator's parents retained a capacity for compassion. In the preamble to the scene in which they find themselves offering comfort to the grieving father of a dead soldier, the narrator catalogues a series of negative encounters the family had had with the British Army. He relates how they choked on CS gas, how their house was searched and seriously damaged by troops, how one brother was arrested and another beaten (230–1). One Wednesday, two days before one of the narrator's last visits home, a soldier had been killed on his parents' front doorstep, shot by a republican sniper during a street search. Shortly after arriving home on the Friday, the narrator responds to a knock on the door, and finds himself face-to-face with the soldier's father and, once more, the human cost of the Troubles. Short sentences convey the tension on both sides, particularly after the stranger has been invited in. Initially the family responds with silence to the Englishman, who understands how hostile 'people round here' feel towards the military. Like earlier victims in the novel – yet unlike the narrator and his mother[58] – the dead soldier is given a name, George. From a much less affluent background to his namesake in *Translations*, he was the son of a Yorkshire miner. Recognising the acuteness of his suffering, and perhaps that he belongs to the same class as them, the family treats the bereaved father with great courtesy. Despite his own shortness of breath, the narrator's father comforts the man by telling him that his son died instantly and looked 'peaceful' (232) in death, and the family join in offering their condolences. Immediately following the Englishman's departure, the mood of reconciliation is tellingly qualified in an afterword: '"Poor man" said my father. "I feel for him. Even if his son was one of *those*"' (232; my emphasis).

Deane maintains a sureness of touch right to the end. The sound of horse-hooves in the penultimate paragraph seems an echo from the beginning of the century when so much of the novel's main action occurred. Visually, aurally, physically there, the gypsy boy jogging on horseback at dawn through the debris-strewn streets appears only to disappear like a figure in a dream. A presence from the margins,[59] he evokes all the other lost, transient children peopling the text – the narrator, his father, Una, the orphans in Katie's story (61–71), the infant girl of McIlhenny's anecdote (209–11). Unable to return to sleep, the narrator sets off downstairs to make tea, hearing on the way down 'a sigh' that compels him to look back. Thus the novel concludes as it began in a liminal place, at a turn on the stairs and in history. The image of the spire reminds us briefly again of clerical power, of human aspiration,[60] before our gaze is redirected to the darkened altar below where the last and one of the text's principal victims 'so innocently lay' (233).

1997 and 1998 witnessed huge advances in resolving Northern Ireland's long and bitter crisis, though as so often before these were marred by a number of tragic and appalling events. A report into parades and marches published in late January 1997 recommended the creation of an independent Parades Commission, in order to try and prevent a recurrence of disturbances like those at Drumcree in 1995 and 1996. The Parades Commission's decisions were not always popular, but they played an invaluable role in reducing conflict. Though multi-party talks resumed in January 1997, they were dogged by intransigence and violence, according to their chairman, George Mitchell. On 12 February, 23-year-old Stephen Restorick, serving in the Royal Horse Artillery, became the last British soldier to die in Northern Ireland's Troubles, when he was shot by an IRA sniper in South Armagh. Amongst the other casualties early that year was a Catholic father of ten, John Slane, shot by the UDA/UFF probably in a case of mistaken identity; and David Templeton, a Presbyterian minister, who suffered a heart attack several weeks after becoming the victim of a punishment beating carried out by the UVF.[61] In one of the most brutal incidents of this period, a 25-year-old Catholic, Robert Hamill, was beaten to death in Portadown by a loyalist mob as he was walking home with relatives after a night out. It soon emerged that close to the spot where Hamill died an RUC patrol had been stationed in a Land Rover. Their failure to intervene, along with the fact that no one was ever convicted of the murder, provoked great anger in the nationalist community.

What reinvigorated the peace process was Labour's landslide victory in the Westminster General Election of 1 May, Tony Blair's premiership and Mo Mowlam's appointment as the new Northern Ireland Secretary. Evidence that the new Prime Minister viewed Northern Ireland as a priority can be seen from the meetings he hosted on successive days, soon after his arrival in Downing Street. On 7 May he held talks with David Trimble and on 8 May John Bruton, the Taoiseach. Visiting Derry a week after her appointment, Mo Mowlam stressed the need for a new PIRA ceasefire and the new government's keenness to include Sinn Féin in talks. The election results in Northern Ireland demonstrated the nationalist parties' continuing electoral advance. The UUP, as usual, had won the most seats (ten) and the highest percentage of the votes (32.7 per cent), while the DUP managed to secure only two seats and a 13.6 per cent share. The SDLP took three seats and 24.1 per cent of the votes, while Sinn Féin gained two seats and achieved a 16.1 per cent share. However, when added together the numbers of those voting for the SDLP and Sinn Féin were now nearly 320 000, in 1983 it had stood at 240 000.[62]

Late spring and early summer witnessed several vicious murders, all of which added to the urgency of reaching a settlement. Four days after Robert Hamill's murder, Sean Brown, a popular, highly-respected GAA official from Bellaghy, was kidnapped and killed by the Loyalist Volunteer Force (LVF).[63] On 1 June an off-duty policeman, Gregory Taylor, was kicked to death in Ballymoney by a loyalist mob, enraged apparently by recent decisions over the banning and re-routing of Orange marches.[64] Two weeks later, on 16 June in Lurgan, two other RUC officers were shot dead by the PIRA while on foot patrol. Evidence of the degree of disapproval and disgust such acts now provoked in the nationalist community is reflected in an *Andersonstown News* editorial of the time. Generally sympathetic to the republican cause, the newspaper described the Lurgan killings as not merely 'wrong' and 'brutal', but also 'counterproductive'.[65]

Blair's announcement in the House of Commons on 25 June that all-party discussions in Northern Ireland would be resumed in September was designed to lure the republican movement back into dialogue. He made it clear that Sinn Féin might find a place at the table, if a second ceasefire was forthcoming. Republicans were already feeling more positive about prospects for progress following the general election results in the Republic on 6 June. John Bruton's departure as Taoiseach was welcomed,[66] as was the formation of a new Fianna Fáil-dominated administration, led by Bertie Ahern. On 19 July the Provisionals announced their decision to restore the ceasefire, thus facilitating Sinn Féin's admission into preliminary talks. A huge rift opened up within the unionist political community over how to respond to the arrival of Sinn Féin's representatives at Stormont on 21 July. Whereas Paisley's DUP and Robert McCartney's UKUP immediately withdrew from the process, arguing that the republicans had in effect bombed their way into talks, Trimble and the UUP agonised over whether to follow suit or to remain in discussions which at some point would necessitate their coming face-to-face with Adams and McGuinness whom they deeply despised. Recent history, in the form of the Anglo-Irish Agreement, suggested that if the UUP walked away, the British and Irish governments might impose a 'solution' which might further erode the unionist position.[67]

Shortly before negotiations got under way during the second week in September 1997, the UUP's ruling executive authorised its leaders 'to take whatever decisions and what course of action it deems appropriate in response to the current situation'.[68] As a way of signalling the firmness of their commitment to the Union, representatives from the UUP and the loyalist UDP and PUP arrived together for the Stormont talks on 17 September. This show of unity, however, masked a deep unease over where the talks might lead. Within the republican movement there were also tensions over the ceasefire and the Sinn Féin leadership's decision to sign up to the Mitchell principles, which required 'total and absolute commitment to democratic and exclusively peaceful means of resolving political issues' and 'the total disarmament of all paramilitary organisations'.[69] These surfaced at an IRA Army Convention in Gweedore, Co. Donegal, in early October. At that meeting one leading Executive member, the IRA's Quartermaster General, denounced the current IRA strategy and demanded a return to armed struggle. Outvoted, he and a colleague subsequently resigned from the Executive and went on to create the Real IRA (RIRA).[70]

Meanwhile at the talks themselves progress was laboured. In order to lend momentum to the process, Tony Blair flew to Belfast on 13 October. During his visit to Castle Buildings, Stormont, he was introduced to delegates from all the participating parties, including Sinn Féin. Much was made of the fact that he shook hands with Adams and McGuinness, whom he was meeting for the first time. On the same trip he travelled to Derry to see Hume and to Craigavon to see Trimble. A walkabout in a shopping centre in east Belfast had to be swiftly curtailed, however, when Blair was confronted by an aggressive, intimidating loyalist crowd. Disquiet in UUP ranks, particularly over North–South institutions, intensified in the run-up to Christmas 1997, when four of Trimble's MPs wrote to him urging him to withdraw from the talks. Loyalist prisoners on 23 December issued a statement voicing their suspicion that the British government was offering too many concessions to the republicans.[71] Within days the province was in the throes of yet another bloody, destabilising phase brought on by the murder of the loyalist paramilitary leader, the LVF's Billy Wright, shot dead by INLA prisoners in the Maze. Wright's assassination was in revenge for his alleged role in a considerable number of sectarian killings as a member of both the UVF and the breakaway LVF. Twelve hours after his murder, the loyalist paramilitaries' retaliation began, when they killed a hotel doorman and former republican prisoner, Séamus Dillon. Four days later, on New Year's Eve, they murdered Eddie Treanor, a Catholic civil servant, and in January 1998 two more Catholics, Terry Enright, a cross-community social worker, and Fergal McCusker, a builder.[72] On the day following McCusker's death, Jim Guiney, a member of the UDA, was shot dead by the INLA. Loyalists responded by killing four more Catholics between 19 and 24 January.

Three days before all-party negotiations recommenced at Stormont, Mo Mowlam, in a courageous, but highly controversial move, went into the Maze Prison to persuade loyalist prisoners to resume their support for the peace process; she succeeded. On 12 January, the British and Irish governments jointly submitted a document entitled *Propositions on Heads of Agreement*, but although this gained a positive reception from the UUP and SDLP, it was subsequently rejected by Sinn Féin and by the IRA. In a step warmly welcomed by nationalists and relatives of the victims, Tony Blair announced plans on 29 January to set up a fresh inquiry into Bloody Sunday under Lord Saville. Within weeks, however, Sinn Féin found themselves temporarily expelled from discussions, as a result of two IRA murders carried out on 9 and 10 February.

Given how 'agonisingly close'[73] politicians were to agreeing a deal, the murder of two lifelong friends, one a Protestant, one a Catholic, in a quiet village in Co. Armagh on 3 March drew massive media attention.[74] Philip Allen and Damian Trainor were sitting in a pub with four other customers in Poyntzpass, discussing details of Allen's forthcoming wedding when two masked gunmen from the LVF burst in and shot them dead. Two other men, both Protestant farmers, suffered injuries in the attack. The *Guardian*'s correspondent, John Mullin, argued that the atrocity 'served only to galvanise the push for peace', and cited as evidence David Trimble's and Seamus Mallon's joint visit on 4 March to the bereaved families and the owners of the bar: 'Each spoke of redoubling efforts to find the political settlement which they hope will cut away the constituency for the terrorist'.[75] Unrepentant, the LVF issued a warning less than a week after the Poyntzpass killings that it intended targeting politicians, church leaders and businessmen, anyone in short responsible for 'colluding in a peace/surrender process designed to break the Union'.[76]

In late March, George Mitchell set a deadline of midnight 9 April, Maundy Thursday, for the participants to reach agreement. That particular date was selected because of Easter's 'historical significance in Ireland' and since it would facilitate possibilities for a referendum at the end of May and assembly elections in June.[77] In the early hours of 7 April, Mitchell submitted a draft settlement to the parties, which the UUP rejected as completely unacceptable. With the deadline fast approaching, this threw the process into crisis and necessitated both Blair and Ahern's presence at Stormont to address unionist objections to sections of the draft they had authored. Blair arrived that evening, and Ahern at seven the next morning to attend a meeting over breakfast with the British Prime Minister. At noon Ahern was due back in Dublin to attend his mother's funeral, but by late afternoon he had returned to Stormont; such was his commitment to the talks' success.[78] Blair and Ahern took the lead in negotiations throughout Thursday, 9 April, moving through draft documents 'word by word ... paragraph by paragraph'.[79] That evening Ian Paisley and around 150 of his supporters broke into the grounds at Stormont to denounce the negotiations and the UUP's alleged treachery. A news conference he gave soon after was interrupted by loyalists from the UDP and PUP, who repeatedly chanted 'Go home' and rather rashly predicted that 'Your day is over'.[80]

Shortly after eight in the morning British time, three o'clock in Washington on Friday, 10 April, President Clinton made a series of phone calls to each of the main party negotiators, a gesture which further reminded them of the critical importance of the project they were engaged in and of his own profound concern over its outcome.[81] The UUP continued to have major difficulties with the early release of prisoners and, above all, the issue of Sinn Féin's inclusion in the Executive if no decommissioning had taken place. A letter from Blair to Trimble that afternoon reassuring him that since 'decommissioning schemes' were 'coming into effect in June, decommissioning should begin straight away' convinced the UUP leader and his deputy John Taylor that they could in conscience sign up to the agreement. Their colleague and fellow negotiator, Jeffrey Donaldson, remained unconvinced that unionism's interests were being upheld and left Stormont.

At five p.m. George Mitchell summoned the parties to a plenary session at which for the first time television cameras were admitted. He announced that negotiations concluded successfully and outlined the principal features of what came to known as both the 'Good Friday Agreement' and the 'Belfast Agreement'. This proposed establishing a 108-member Assembly, elected through proportional representation. At its head would be an Executive Committee of 12 ministers, responsible for dealing with such matters as health, education, the environment, agriculture, finance and economic development. This new body would be tasked with setting up a joint North–South ministerial council, which would implement policies of benefit throughout Ireland and would send representatives to a new Council of the Isles, at which twice a year issues of common concern to Dublin, Belfast, Westminster, the Scottish parliament and Welsh Assembly could be addressed. The Agreement reiterated that a united Ireland could only come about 'with the consent of a majority of the people of Northern Ireland'.[82] The Irish government, 'in the context of this comprehensive political agreement',[83] undertook to introduce changes to the Republic's constitution, in other words modify articles 2 and 3 which laid claim to the territory of Northern Ireland. A section on 'Policing and Justice' announced the setting-up of an independent Commission 'to make recommendations for future policing arrangements in Northern Ireland',[84] arrangements that would require widespread support in both communities. A programme of accelerated prisoner release was to be introduced covering those prisoners affiliated to groups maintaining their ceasefire. On the thorny question of decommissioning, all participants agreed to co-operate with the de Chastelain Commission 'to achieve decommissioning of all paramilitary arms within two years'[85] of the Agreement being endorsed in referendums North and South.

Omens for the Agreement initially looked hugely positive. One of Ireland's most perceptive commentators, Fintan O'Toole, praised the 'careful, exquisitely delicate language' in the document which allowed people in the North to choose their nationality, and to identify themselves as 'both/and' rather than simply 'either/or'.[86] Trimble won key votes on 11 April when the UUP Executive backed the Agreement by 55 votes to 23, and on 18 April when the margin of victory at the UUP Council was 330 votes (540 in favour, 210 against). The results of the referendums held on 22 May seemed similarly encouraging. In Northern Ireland 71.1 per cent of voters supported the Agreement; an exit poll carried out on behalf of the *Sunday Times* suggested that 96 per cent of nationalists approved of the deal in contrast to 55 per cent of unionists. Over half of unionist 'No' voters cited plans for early prisoner release as the principal reason for their opposition, though 18 per cent spoke of their fear that the Agreement signalled a drift towards a united Ireland.[87] Elections to the Northern Ireland Assembly held on 25 June 1998 resulted, however, in pro-Agreement parties winning 80 seats and its opponents 28. Worryingly for future stability in the province, the unionist vote was split five ways, with UUP support falling to 21.3 per cent, the DUP's rising to 18 per cent, while the UKUP, PUP and UDP gained 4.5 per cent, 2.6 per cent and 1.1 per cent respectively.

An announcement by the Parades Commission that Orangemen would not be permitted to march down the Garvaghy Road in Portadown prompted yet another Drumcree crisis. Riots ensued from 5 July onwards. In one 24-hour period, there were almost 400 incidents reported throughout Northern Ireland, including 115 loyalist attacks on security forces and 19 injuries to police officers.[88] One of 96 petrol bomb attacks resulted in the deaths of three children from the same family in Ballymoney on 12 July, ten-year-old Robert Quinn, and his brothers Mark and Jason, aged nine and eight. All three boys lived with their Catholic mother, and the previous night had been out playing beside a loyalist bonfire.[89] Archbishop Robin Eames of the Church of Ireland echoed Mo Mowlam's condemnation of the attack and her call for an end to the Drumcree protests. Just over a month after the killing of the Quinn brothers by loyalists, dissident republicans were responsible for the worst single atrocity in Troubles history. On Saturday 15 August, at 3.10 in the afternoon, a 500lb bomb planted by the Real IRA exploded in Omagh's town centre, claiming the lives of 29 people and two unborn children, and injuring 360. In the days that followed, the Real IRA admitted responsibility, but claimed that they had been aiming 'at a commercial target', adding 'We offer apologies to the civilians'.[90] Tony Blair interrupted his family holiday to fly to the North and accompanied by Bertie Ahern visited the injured in Belfast's Royal Victoria Hospital. Gerry Adams and Martin McGuinness condemned the bombing, the latter describing it as 'indefensible'. The following Saturday,

22 August, thousands gathered in Omagh for a commemoration service for the dead, which was attended also by the Irish President, Mary MacAleese, the Taoiseach and the British Deputy Prime Minister, John Prescott. Two weeks later, Tony and Cherie Blair, Bill and Hillary Clinton visited the town to address relatives of the dead and injured. A commemorative plaque unveiled by the President voiced the hope that 'their memory' might 'serve to foster peace and reconciliation'.[91]

The Omagh bombing highlighted the need for progress on decommissioning and directly led to the first face-to-face meeting between Trimble and Adams, which took place in private on 10 September. The encounter was described as 'cordial and businesslike' by both men. Trimble emphasised the necessity for movement on the issue of IRA weapons if Sinn Fein were to join the Executive, while Adams politely reiterated that he was not in a position to deliver on this. As a result of the reduced paramilitary threat, British Army patrols in Belfast were brought to an end and hundreds troops were withdrawn from the province in September and November. In the days before the joint award of the 1998 Nobel Peace Prize to John Hume and David Trimble – an award that the latter suggested was 'premature'[92] – reports circulated that a recently held PIRA convention had decided that the conditions were not yet ready for decommissioning to commence.

Throughout the next year the republicans' unwillingness to destroy their weapons remained a major cause of contention, delaying the formation of the Executive. Although only six murders took place in the first half of 1999, the paramilitaries' continuing involvement in these and other crimes prevented the normalisation of civil life and reconciliation from proceeding. In late January, Eamon Collins, a former member of the PIRA and subsequently one of its most outspoken critics, was found stabbed and beaten to death, killed by unknown republicans. In mid-March Rosemary Nelson, a high-profile lawyer whose clients included Catholic residents in the Garvaghy Road, died in an explosion when loyalists booby-trapped her car. There were accusations in the minority community that elements in the RUC had colluded with the loyalists, adding to pressure on the government to respond to nationalist demands for police reform.[93] Following the murder of yet another drugs dealer by the Provisionals in May, Trimble called for Mowlam to be replaced as Northern Ireland Secretary for allegedly ignoring repeated violations of the ceasefire by republicans. In September, at Blair, Ahern's and Clinton's behest, George Mitchell arrived back in Belfast, his brief being to review progress since the Agreement and to find a way out of the decommissioning deadlock. Shortly after Mitchell began work, attention shifted to the impending publication of the findings of the Patten Commission into Policing. In order to create a police service 'capable of attracting and sustaining support across the community as a whole',[94] Patten called for the recruitment of equal numbers of Catholics and Protestants over the next ten years.[95] Changes in the culture, ethos and symbols of the police force, he believed, might encourage more members of the nationalist minority to join the service. To fulfil that aim and to underline 'the new start'[96] being made, he recommended that the force be given a new name, the Police Service of Northern Ireland, and new insignia 'entirely free from any association with the British or Irish states'.[97] Unionists were appalled at these latter recommendations, regarding them as constituting 'a gratuitous insult' to the RUC and whose 'officers ... have served the community, saved innumerable lives, thwarted terrorism and created the present opportunity for peace and stability'.[98] Resentment over Patten, along with concerns over collusion, are clearly key elements in Gary Mitchell's play discussed below.

George Mitchell's protracted labours finally seemed to bear fruit when at midnight on 1 December 1999 devolved government was finally restored in Northern Ireland. Despite 'years of stipulating that he would not go into government with Sinn Féin without prior or simultaneous decommissioning',[99] Trimble opted to do just that in the expectation that weapons would soon be 'put beyond use'. In order to persuade doubters in his party of the wisdom of this decision, he informed the UU Council that he and fellow UUP ministers would resign in February 2000, if no reciprocal gesture from the PIRA on arms was forthcoming.[100] It was known well in advance that as a result of the D'Hondt rules the new Executive would include two ministers nominated by Sinn Féin. Nevertheless, news that Martin McGuinness had gained the portfolio for education generated consternation amongst some unionists. Pupils in some Protestant schools staged walkouts in protest at his appointment; the fact that DUP members were in attendance at several such demonstrations led McGuinness and others to conclude that the students were being manipulated by 'anti-agreement forces'.[101]

Following a report in January 2000 from General de Chastelain's International Commission on Decommissioning that they had received 'no information from the IRA as to when decommissioning will start',[102] Sinn Féin and the PIRA faced renewed pressure from the British and Irish governments. Given the lack of progress, the Northern Ireland Secretary, Peter Mandelson, decided that it would be better to suspend the province's new institutions rather than allow them to collapse as a result of Trimble's resignation. Devolution had been in operation for merely 72 days.

On the morning of the day suspension was due to take effect, the Irish government announced that they had received notification from the PIRA of a 'major breakthrough' offer. Ahern's enthusiasm was not shared by the British, however, who welcomed the PIRA's statement, but felt that it did not go far enough. Mandelson went ahead with suspension on 11 February 2000, incurring bitter condemnation from both the SDLP and Sinn Féin; the Deputy First Minister, Seamus Mallon, accused the Secretary of State of prioritising 'the internal politics of the UUP'[103] instead of the province's needs.

On this occasion devolution was restored after a relatively brief period of suspension. What primarily made this possible was an undertaking from the Provisionals on 6 May that they would 'initiate a process' to put their arms 'completely and verifiably ... beyond use'.[104] They also agreed to allow regular inspections of their sealed arms dumps by two leading international statesman, the former Finnish President Martti Ahtisaari and the ANC's Cyril Ramaphosa. In return they stated that they expected the British and Irish governments to meet fully their commitments under the Good Friday Agreement. In a statement issued by Sinn Féin earlier on the same day, Adams again stressed the importance of 'a new policing service' to the minority. Before the Executive and Assembly resumed work on 29 May, David Trimble had to return yet again to the UU Council to ensure that they endorsed his re-entry into power-sharing with Sinn Féin. After surviving comfortably a leadership challenge in March, winning by 57 per cent to the Rev. Martin Smyth's 43 per cent, he must have hoped for stronger support from the Council. In the event only 53 per cent of its members approved the Executive's return, while 47 per cent voted against, providing more evidence of how unionist backing for the Good Friday Agreement, Trimble's strategy leadership was continuing to slip. A by-election in South Antrim in the autumn saw the second safest UUP seat in the province fall into DUP hands. Even though the UUP fielded an anti-Agreement candidate, many unionist voters clearly preferred the uncompromising line on power-sharing with republicans taken by Ian Paisley's party.

Drumcree yet again became a flashpoint for violence in the first two weeks of July 2000, after the Parades Commission banned the Orange Order from marching down the Garvaghy Road. After two nights of rioting when loyalists hurled bottles, stones and firecrackers at the police and army blocking their path, on 5 July engineers from the British Army erected a 20-foot high, 30-foot wide steel barrier across the Drumcree road in order to reduce injuries inflicted on the RUC. Loyalist protesters reacted by setting up roadblocks in various towns in the province, but large sections of the unionist community disapproved of the violence and the involvement of high profile paramilitary figures like the UDA's Johnny Adair at demonstrations. A simmering feud between the two main loyalist paramilitary organisations, the UVF and UDA, reached a new intensity when a 22-year-old UVF member was shot dead while celebrating the Twelfth beside a bonfire in Larne. The situation deteriorated rapidly in late August after the UVF killed two fellow loyalists, one a close associate of Adair's, and the UDA struck back by murdering a UVF man two days later. The Northern Ireland Secretary, Peter Mandelson, had attempted to defuse the crisis by deploying extra troops in Belfast and by arresting Johnny Adair, but the tit-for-tat killings continued for the rest of the year. During this same period loyalist paramilitaries carried out repeated pipe-bomb attacks on Catholic homes, but also, in one instance, the house of Johnston Brown, an RUC detective responsible for putting Adair in prison in the mid-1990s.[105]

However, it was not only the persistence of loyalist violence that undermined Northern Ireland's difficult transition towards 'normalisation'. Dissident republicans especially remained active. They were believed to be responsible for planting a device on London's Hammersmith Bridge, which caused minor damage. In late September and again in March 2001 the Real IRA attacked prominent buildings in the capital, MI6's headquarters and premises owned by the BBC. The car-bomb left outside Television Centre may well have been in reprisal for an edition of *Panorama* in October 2000 which identified four men who had allegedly played key roles in the Omagh bombing. Meanwhile the PIRA continued to co-operate with the Independent International Commission on Decommissioning (IICD), allowing another inspection of their arms dumps in late October. In December they re-stated their 'commitment to the resolution of the issue of arms',[106] provided that the British government fulfilled its obligations on policing and demilitarisation under the terms of the Good Friday Agreement.

Throughout the province in 2001, loyalist pipe-bombers maintained the frequency of their attacks on Catholic homes.[107] Although officially inter-paramilitary feuding involving the UDA and UVF had been halted in December 2000, the killings resumed in the New Year, which also saw members of the LVF and UVF targeting each other. In mid-June 2001 sectarian tensions flared around a girls' primary school in north Belfast, after loyalists claimed that Protestant families in the area had been experiencing intimidation. The RUC had to be brought in to protect the schoolchildren of Holy Cross when loyalists from the nearby Glenbryn estate threw stones at them and then later blockaded the school itself.

There were days when Catholic parents were compelled to take their children to Holy Cross via the grounds of another school, and other days when the school was forced to close. The end of the summer term meant that the focus of sectarian confrontation shifted elsewhere for a few months,[108] though at the start of September it reappeared at Holy Cross. Although the RUC and the British Army cleared loyalist demonstrators away from the front gates of the school, for several days children and parents ran a gauntlet of abuse, bottles and stones. On the evening of 4 September loyalist rioters launched major attacks on security forces in the area, hurling over 200 petrol bombs and 15 blast bombs, and injuring over 40 policemen and two soldiers. On the morning of 5 September a loyalist blast-bomb was thrown at children and parents and detonated injuring four RUC officers. From 7 September onwards, demonstrators resorted generally to less violent, but still intimidating methods of protest; on some days in late September and October, however, fireworks and balloons filled with urine were hurled at the girls and their parents.[109] Children continued to face hostility and abuse as they arrived and left school for most of the next three months, until 23 November, when, following talks with David Trimble and the new SDLP leader, Mark Durkan, residents from Glenbryn suspended their action.

That children at Holy Cross should have endured such sustained abuse is appalling, but sadly not surprising given the frequency with which paramilitary violence had been visited on young people in recent times. A report by Liam Kennedy of Queen's University Belfast, published in August 2001, showed that 'punishment beatings' by loyalists and republicans had increased in the two years since the Good Friday Agreement, as paramilitaries sought to tighten their grip over their patches of territory. Kennedy warned how parts of the province functioned now as 'Mafia-style mini-states, of orange or green complexion, operating vendetta-style justice and sustained economically by extortion and other forms of racketeering'.[110]

Reconfigurations in Northern Ireland's political map were evident following the June 2001 Westminster General Election, in which the UUP lost three of its nine seats, and for the first time Sinn Féin overtook the SDLP in votes cast. A report from the IICD that same month that they had not yet seen evidence that PIRA weapons had been destroyed triggered yet another political crisis. On 1 July Trimble resigned as First Minister over the decommissioning issue, initiating a six-week period in which efforts intensified to get the PIRA to make a move. In early August the British and Irish governments set before the North's parties an Implementation Plan designed to resolve those critical areas of dispute such as demilitarisation and policing reform which continued to undermine the stability of the province's new institutions. Although an offer from the Provisionals on 6 August to destroy their weapons was welcomed by the IICD and described as a 'historical breakthrough' by Gerry Adams, UUP members in the Assembly and Westminster concurred in the view that it did not go far enough and rejected both the Implementation Plan and the PIRA's offer. The decision by John Reid, the then Northern Ireland Secretary, to suspend the Assembly once again was strongly criticised by Sinn Féin. However, within days, republicans found themselves on the back foot, following the arrest in Colombia of three of their number, charged with aiding and abetting left-wing, drugs-funded guerrillas. The damage to Sinn Fén's standing was substantial, since the episode fuelled suspicions in Britain and America that the PIRA had no intention of abandoning their old ways.

What gave the greatest impetus to the process of decommissioning was the terrorist attacks of 11 September 2001 in New York, Washington and Pennsylvania. Just under a month after 9/11, the main unionist parties tabled a motion in the Assembly to exclude Sinn Féin from the Executive. When this failed the UUP announced that its three ministers would resign from the Executive in mid-October, thus jeopardising the continuation of devolved government. David Trimble made it clear, however, that he and his colleagues would return to office if the PIRA were to begin disposing of their weapons. Although Adams and McGuinness criticised British bad faith and obstructive unionist tactics for this latest crisis in the peace process, they urged the PIRA to make 'a ground-breaking move on the arms issue' in order to 'save the peace process from collapse and transform the situation'.[111] On 23 October 2001, the IICD announced that they had witnessed the PIRA's destruction of a quantity of weapons, ammunition and explosives. (Seven months later they were able to confirm a second similar event had taken place.) Such was the strength of anti-Agreement unionists now that it was only after a considerable struggle and political manoeuvring by other parties that Trimble was re-elected First Minister on 6 November 2001 with Mark Durkan as his Deputy.

Two days earlier, the Police Service of Northern Ireland (PSNI) came into being, along with the new Northern Ireland Policing Board. From now on, in line with the Patten recommendations, recruitment to the PSNI had to involve equal numbers of Protestants and Catholics. As a consequence a significant cause of nationalist alienation since the 1920s was all but removed from Northern Ireland's complex, multi-faceted political equation.

Gary Mitchell, *The Force of Change*

Born in North Belfast in 1965, Gary Mitchell shares similar working-class, unionist community roots as three other playwrights discussed earlier in this study, Thompson, Boyd and Parker. Mitchell left school at 15, and was for a long period unemployed before he began writing in 1991. Like his predecessors, he realises in his work individuals from a culture which has too often been caricatured, marginalised or vilified, yet whose conflicts and contradictions speak to audiences far removed from their point of origin. It is hardly surprising that readings of his work should have made much of his class and cultural roots, although at times he has voiced frustration at the limitations, inaccuracies and distortions this has entailed.[112] In a 2003 article, he points out how in Northern Ireland and the Republic his plays have been at times criticised, at times lauded, on the dubious grounds that 'it made Protestants look bad'.[113] During a run of one of his plays in San Francisco he was informed by an American friend that the reason for poor ticket sales was because republicans had spread the word in the local Irish community that he was a 'sectarian bigot who would not allow Catholics to perform, direct or produce any of his work';[114] fortunately he had an opportunity to expose the ludicrousness of such accusations, by pointing out that Catholics acting in and directing his work outnumbered non-Catholics by nine to one.

The Force of Change premièred at the Royal Court Theatre in London in April 2000. It is a deftly-constructed play, which is deeply watermarked by recent political concerns in Northern Ireland, engaging as it does in debates over the future and integrity of policing, which intensified prior to and following the publication of the Patten Report. Set in one of the North's most notorious police stations, Castlereagh, the play exposes corruption and collusion within the force, which the murders of Rosemary Nelson and Pat Finucane, the Stalker and Stevens inquiries had all thrown into sharp relief. Through its characterisations, it depicts a unionist community which has lost much of its self-belief and cohesion, as a result of three decades of successive batterings and shocks, such as the dissolution of Stormont in 1972, the signing of the Anglo-Irish Agreement in 1985 and Good Friday Agreement in 1998. Its brief lies beyond these specifics, however, since it reflects, like *Over the Bridge* and *Pentecost*, a wider state of cultural malaise and anxiety, manifest in politics and in the politics of gender.

The fact that the principal character in Mitchell's drama is a professional woman is highly significant and indicative of the shift in gender politics in the cultures outside and inside the theatre over the period covered in this study. The rise in women's groups in Northern Ireland from the mid-1970s onwards has already been noted, along with the increasing power and frequency of women's literary interventions. In the years immediately preceding the play's composition, the Northern Ireland Women's Coalition made its mark on the political scene following the inclusion of two of its members in multi-party talks on the province's future.[115] The career detective, Caroline Paterson, in Mitchell's 'taut thriller'[116] may also owe something to a fictional role model, Jane Tennison, from Lynda La Plante's *Prime Suspect* series, first aired in January 1992 and with sequels in 1993, 1994, 1995, 1997 and 2006.[117] The description Helen Mirren gives of Tennison, 'extremely direct, ambitious, talented, and very uncompromising',[118] could be equally applied to Caroline. Although it is easy to pinpoint differences in the characters' ages and domestic circumstances,[119] Mitchell, like La Plante before him, is keen to explore the internal dynamics operating between a successful policewoman and her male colleagues, and variations in their moral and ideological stances.

By enclosing the entire action within '*two interview rooms and a corridor*' (2), Mitchell amplifies the friction between the characters. These locations serve as performative spaces in a multiple sense, because of the amount of role-playing that takes place within them. Interrogators and their subjects, of course, take on changing personae in carrying out their respective tasks. Yet, in addition, frequently in the play, the audience are made conscious of major and minor deceptions being practised, the mismatch between the front characters display and their 'real' selves. This is particularly true of the first figure to appear on stage. Bill Byrne is a 57-year-old detective constable, who, it emerges later, has been repeatedly passed over for promotion (51) and is indebted to the UDA, literally so. In return for easing his financial problems, over the years he has supplied the loyalist paramilitaries with information, or, as he euphemistically puts it, 'little things' (59). This makes him a danger to his colleagues, in particular to one officer, 35-year-old Detective Sergeant Caroline Paterson. The play's action opens with Bill testing a tape recorder in Interview Room A prior to Caroline's interrogation of Stanley Brown, a member of the banned UDA. The thinly-veiled animosity between the constable and Caroline is immediately established by Bill's reference to his young, female superior as 'she' and the ironic banter when they meet soon after. In remarking that only five hours remain before Brown will have to be released, Bill is not simply informing the audience of the tight timetable Caroline is up against. He says it to increase the pressures on her to produce results. Encoded within her comments about his early arrival ('I didn't realise you were so keen. Is that something else you hide?')

is a scepticism about the very thought of Bill displaying keenness and commitment.

When Bill briefly absents himself, Caroline calls home, thereby allowing a glimpse of her private life. The way she skims through and then becomes engrossed in case files while discussing with her husband their parental duties suggest that her police career is a greater priority. She even lies to him about the Inspector having just appeared in the room in order to cut short their conversation. In fact the officer who has joined her is Mark Simpson, her equal in rank and the one fellow officer with whom she is at ease. His joking reference to the 'promotion' she has conferred on him serves as a lead-in to the disclosure that Caroline has applied for a higher position. What adds to her anxiety about the report the Inspector will shortly be sending is her consciousness of the negativity with which many of her male colleagues view her: 'people are gathering like ... vultures to see me fail', 'they want to stop me' (6, 7). Evidence that she is not merely being paranoid comes in the subsequent scene in Interview Room B, when David Davis, a 30-year-old Detective Constable, criticises her handling of the Brown case at the end of an exchange with Mark: 'She's fucking it up' (13).

Throughout the play's first Act, Mark's supportiveness is contrasted with Bill's resentment of her; the stage directions make clear that a major factor in Bill's antipathy is her gender.[120] In the next scene she and Bill share together, this becomes even more apparent. On his return with the tea, which he has deliberately delayed, Bill enquires whether 'lover boy' (i.e. Mark) has gone. She reacts to his inappropriate comment with a quip: 'Lover boy? I didn't know you guys had pet names for each other' (14). Repeatedly attempting to secure Caroline's attention as she reads through the files, he first questions her methods of interrogation and then informs her that he has made complaints to the Inspector about her 'style' and the frequency with which her husband rings her. Despite the fury she feels at this act of betrayal – it proves to be one of many such acts by Bill – she simply 'shakes her head in disbelief, takes a deep breath and composes herself' (16). This is not the time for a confrontation with a 'partner' officer; her main concern has to be extracting an admission from what she assumes is their common enemy, the criminal Stanley Brown.

References to aliases proliferate with Brown's arrival on stage, spotlighting the play's preoccupation with deception and duplicity. In the stage directions Brown is dubbed 'Muteman' (16), because of his preference to remain silent throughout interrogation. In the 'dialogue' that ensues Caroline several times tries to provoke him by nicknaming him 'Mr Shit' (17), 'Captain Caveman' (18), 'Mr Predictable' (19), and by drawing comparisons between him and his more glamorous 'doubles' on screen. Unconscious of how ironic her allusion is to the 'Undercover Cop', she ignores and thus fails to decode the significance of the sequence of glances that pass between Stanley and Bill (17–18). Having sent Bill away again to fetch some tea, Caroline persists with her sarcastic allusions to films with the aim of making Brown break his silence. The constant references to genre also have the effect of lulling the audience, laying expectations that the play will proceed along familiar lines: 'I bet you like a good weepy', 'you only like British movies', 'And you hate Irish ones', 'Do you like Horror movies?', 'What about Porno?' (19). Mention of the latter ushers in the disclosure of Stanley's most recent activities:

> Jackie Phillips liked Porno ... I know because I was in the process of investigating him when four men took him out of his house, set it on fire and then shot him in the knees. They probably saw it as part of their crusade against Pornography or part of their defence of the Protestant community in general. (19–20)

The speeches of Caroline that follow contain the nub of the play's indictment of contemporary loyalist paramilitarism, its leaders, personnel and practices, an indictment which anticipates and endorses much in Liam Kennedy's report.[121] The witness statements and subsequent retractions she reads out detail Brown's involvement in punishment beatings, intimidation and extortion. Three decades earlier, in the 1970s, the UDA performed a role with which she could have some sympathy; they existed 'to serve and protect the Unionist population of Northern Ireland'. The idealists who formed the 'great Protestant organisation' of those days have been replaced in recent times, she argues, by 'a bunch of half wit criminals like you'. Returning to her earlier image of him, she tells Brown to his face that he has nothing in common with King Billy or the Protestant heroes of yore: 'You're not the good guy on the white horse. In fact you're more like the shit the white horse drops behind as it walks' (22). Although Caroline manages to make him glare once (19) and stop smiling twice (22, 24), her derisive onslaught at first seems to have had minimal effect. She concedes as much, in deciding to take a break. Revealingly, immediately after she departs, Stanley accepts from Bill the cigarette he had earlier refused (25).

For almost the entire remainder of Act One, the scene switches to Interview Room B, where Mark and David perform an often hilarious double-act interviewing 'Rabbit' Montgomery. Their collaborative approach during Rabbit's interrogation contrasts sharply with the lack of partnership between Caroline and Bill. Rabbit, it had earlier emerged (9), is a car thief and joyrider. The police suspect that he may have started stealing cars for the UDA and hope to use him to bring Brown to book. As voluble and stupid as Brown is taciturn and malign, Rabbit is similarly able to withstand the police's gambits to get him to incriminate himself or anyone else. For the moment, he lives up to the slogan emblazoned across his knuckles, which Mark reads as 'Nof ear' (30). Before the audience tires of the humorous exchanges between the petty criminal and his playful interrogators, Mitchell effects a decisive change in mood and location. On our return to Interview Room A, the first voice we hear is Stanley's, demanding that Bill provides him with Caroline's name, address, phone number and car details. In terms of dramatic impact it almost rivals the scene in *One Flew Over the Cuckoo's Nest*, when the Indian Chief, who has convinced everyone that he is deaf and dumb, speaks for first time.

Act Two's opening is steeped in irony, since, unlike the audience, the two detectives (Caroline and Mark) sharing a snatched lunch are completely unaware of Bill's treachery and the vulnerable position in which he has placed Caroline and her family. Mitchell deploys a neat touch of gender role reversal in depicting the comforting, parental tone Caroline adopts in response to her worried husband's phone call, which concludes with a warning, 'I might have to work late though', and the promise, 'I'll make it up to you' (40). Although broached briefly at the start of each act, the Patersons' domestic order suddenly matters more now it is perceived as under threat.

The arrival of David Davis changes the dynamic in Interview Room A, bringing an end to the relaxed repartee between Mark and Caroline. When David tells them that he was looking for 'the Master', Caroline wrongly assumes he is alluding to her. In fact he is looking for Bill partly, one suspects, in order to get an update on how Caroline's interrogation of Brown is progressing. Like Bill, it later emerges, he is deeply hostile to the direction in which the force is heading, especially the new agenda requiring balance in religion and gender.[122] He deduces from Caroline's reference to her loss of appetite that all is not well, and adds to her unease when he reports that the Inspector has sent him to summon Bill (42–3). Mark tries to reassure her that in all likelihood the Inspector wants to give Bill a ticking-off. In characterising the old Royal Ulster Constabulary as a 'boy's own club' (44), he highlights its conservatism, a point he expands upon in his account of the discrimination a former Catholic colleague of his experienced from fellow officers. The parallels between this detective and Caroline are more apt than Mark at this point realises, as, like Caroline's, his success against the odds made him a target of people from his own community (45). As this section of dialogue draws to a close, there are more reminders of how the time for detaining Brown is running out. Mark's promise to pressurise Rabbit into divulging information she can use against their prime suspect demonstrates again his personal loyalty, a commodity in rare supply at this particular station.

When Bill at last materialises, he is evasive about his whereabouts and becomes prickly at Caroline's questions. After his admission that he has been seeing the Inspector, '*the three exchange looks*' (46), but neither Caroline nor Mark pursue the matter. What their boss wanted from Bill we never learn, but for Caroline it no doubt confirms her (justified) suspicions that he has again been stabbing her in the back. The strain of playing a double game is getting to Bill. When left alone on stage, he swears, paces up and down the interview room, and then intercepts Caroline in the corridor pleading to be given a chance to take the lead in the interrogation. She agrees to this ('Go ahead, Sherlock'), but refuses to permit him to talk to the UDA-man on his own. Ambiguities permeate the important, extended speeches from Bill which follow. The audience is left unsure over the extent to which they reflect his sincerely held views, and the extent to which they are part of his act. Outwardly he seems to be deploying 'a good cop' strategy, designed to secure a measure of co-operation from Brown. It may be that he hopes for some slight reciprocal gesture from the latter which may help him maintain his precarious position and the illusion of integrity. They certainly appear to yield insights into Bill's mindset, and how change has impacted on this long-serving, unreconstructed RUC officer. In his preamble on how organisations alter, Bill immediately raises the issue of gender. Thirty years ago he would never have believed that he would end up 'taking orders from a young girl' (48). He goes on to confide to Brown that the case against him is flimsy, and that the RUC's *real* targets are the upper echelons of the UDA. He draws a plausible, but false analogy between the extortionist and himself, in which they are both sorry victims of agencies and forces beyond their control. For him, as for those taking part in the Good Friday negotiations, policing is not an apolitical activity. Rather than issues of fairness or social justice or impartiality, what preoccupies Bill is how to preserve 'our' (i.e. Protestant) culture, identity and territory. The threat to these, according to his – and the anti-Agreement – analysis, is the peace process, which he regards as a nationalist-driven stratagem, devised in order to trundle Ulster into a united Ireland. The fact that these opinions are placed in the mouth of a tainted character might be seen as discrediting them. At the same time, however, it could be argued that by airing them in *The Force of Change* Mitchell demonstrates the valuable role theatre can perform in bringing widely-held, dissenting voices to the attention of audiences.[123]

That Bill is addressing a different audience on-stage is underlined by Mitchell's stage directions. Fittingly, Stanley makes no response when Bill professes that 'I'm just trying to be honest with you' (49). However, once he starts reminiscing about Vanguard, the 1970s, and the UDA's original brief as a defenderist force replacing the B Specials,[124] he achieves positive reactions from both Stanley who '*nods*' and Caroline whose eyes betray '*enthusiasm*' (50). Their endorsement lends momentum to Bill as he launches into a highly partial, heavily-edited version of Northern Irish history, in which he represents the RUC and loyalists as standing shoulder to shoulder 'Together' (50) in defence of 'the Protestant people of Ulster'[125] against their betrayers (the British government) and the aggressors (the militant republicans, and nationalists generally). Warming to his theme, Bill denounces what he looks upon as the emasculation of the force by Patten and calls for *covert* pan-unionist resistance to British policy. In a deliberately ambiguous turn of phrase, he speaks of a need 'to *get rid of* the people who are in the way' (50; my italics), that is, the current UDA and UDP leadership, if that process is to begin. In his next monologue, like a western, Cold War era military strategist, he depicts the dire consequences of a domino effect. Alluding to the recent ministerial appointment of Martin McGuinness, he warns Brown 'education today, security tomorrow' (51), in short, a nightmare scenario which could see the IRA running the police, Catholic judges 'enforcing the law' and Catholics deciding which marches can and cannot take place. Fusing patriotic and sectarian sentiment with strands of self-interest (Brown's) and personal grievance (his), Bill's appeal reaches a rhetorical climax worthy of the politicians he derides. Three times he uses the phrase 'People like you' in conjuring an image of Stanley as Ulster's redeemer and protector, a figure far removed from the extortionist who put a gun to Henry Walker's head (21) and the money-grubbers who, according to 'outsider' Bill, preside over the UDA's terminal decline (51).

Caroline's frustration at Stanley's unresponsiveness, even to his 'friend' Bill, impels her to change tack. Adopting an aggressive 'bad cop' persona, she threatens to 'set up' Stanley. However, just as she is working herself up, a telephone rings. Automatically she assumes it is her mobile and apologises, presumably to Bill. The sound triggers what turns out to be the play's *anagnorisis*, the moment when she recognises that her older colleague has been collaborating with Stanley all along. After Caroline discovers the mobile on his body, the loyalist breaks his long silence to 'explain' that he had picked up the phone in the corridor. She observes the anxious exchange of glances between the two men (53), and then decides to check the phone in case an incriminating message has been left. One has, from Bill's wife. Following this bombshell she leaves the room immediately, and orders David to bring Bill to Interview Room B. It is here that the drama's most significant role reversal is staged, with the interrogator under interrogation.[126]

Initially, in front of Caroline, Bill maintains a façade of defiance; he answers her cliché, 'This is the end of the line for you, Bill', with a well-worn one of his own, 'You can't prove a thing' (55). In this fraught situation, Mark and David are presented respectively as voices of calm and prudence, keen to establish the extent of Bill's culpability and dissuade Caroline from reporting him to their superiors.[127] A measure of her fury is her somewhat indiscreet assertion that the only reason why she has not gone to the Inspector straight away is 'I'm not sure how far up this goes' (56). What her instincts tell her are shown to be right. She *knows* from the outset that Stanley did not steal the phone, as Bill claims. Although reluctant at first to leave the men together 'to sort things out', she accedes to Mark's appeal to allow him and David ten minutes alone with Bill. Not surprisingly, her expression of confidence in Mark, 'You're the only one I do trust' (58), offends David. Yet while the comment betrays her tendency to be brusque and undiplomatic, later exchanges (67–9) confirm that her reservations about David are justified.

During the confession that follows, Bill withholds for some time the fact that he has passed on Caroline's details to the loyalist paramilitaries; when he does, his 'defence' is that it was a case of 'me or her' (61). In the early part of his narrative, however, his primary concern is to project an image of himself as a victim of external forces and factors. Convinced that he was about to gain promotion, he took out loans, amassed debts, made rash investments, and so placed his home, car and marriage[128] in jeopardy. At the outset, in return for dealing with his debtors, he explains, the UDA required only minor 'things' (59). Over time, however, their big guns become increasingly exacting and threatened his family.

These partial revelations spark significantly different reactions between Mark and David. Whereas David focuses on keeping Bill's duplicity under wraps, because of the harm the media would inflict on the RUC's reputation, his more senior colleague is intent on knowing the full extent of their brother officer's betrayals. Mark's initial reaction to the revelation that Bill has imperilled Caroline's life and family is to attack him physically. Quickly, however, and rather unconvincingly, he regains his composure, and orders David to arrange transport and a safe house for Caroline's husband and children (62). On her return, Mark informs

Caroline that the UDA have been gathering intelligence on her home and car, though not that Bill had been the source. In order to deflect her from her resolution to 'do' Brown and then Bill, he urges her to attend to domestic security and to postpone thoughts of Bill 'for the time being' (63). Whereas Mark tries to convince her that going to the Inspector will ruin her promotion prospects and draw attention to the large number of complaints made against her, David again stresses the dangers of the press getting hold of the story (65). Rather than wasting time on exposing misdeeds and 'irregular' practices from within their own ranks, David argues that all their energies should be expended on the 'real criminals' (66) like Brown.

Although a relatively minor participant in Act One, David gains increasing prominence in the latter part of Act Two. Thirty years old, a working-class Protestant, schooled at 'the university of street life' (69), he is another recalcitrant, unreconstructed character, and is used to reprise and play variations on Bill's earlier themes. In his eyes, 'fast-trackers' like Caroline pose a greater threat to the force than her foolish, venal 'partner'. To him she is a manifestation of all that has gone awry in the RUC. What was once a purposeful, coherent, *virile* organisation has been betrayed by those 'running the show' whom he describes as 'nothings', 'neutrals', time-servers, who have 'turned us away from our traditional enemies to block, fight and hurt the people of our own communities' (67). That David's function at this juncture is to illustrate further the persistence of sectarianism and sexism in the police force is evident from his derogatory references to the advancement of Catholics (67) and women (69). After living through three decades of reconfigurations in politics and gender politics, he is still able to dismiss all Catholics as whingers ('I mean they think every Protestant in the world is guilty of everything from the famine to Bloody Sunday') and women as incompetents ('tits don't get the job done, balls do' (70)).

After a considerable length of stage-time has been devoted to the ideological debate and moral dilemma engaging Caroline, Mark and David, attention shifts once more to the UDA suspects as the play moves to its resolution. Putting aside their differences, the three officers concur that the best way forward lies in breaking Rabbit in order to put away Brown, the very strategy David had proposed earlier (66). The proficient manner with which Caroline ties Rabbit in knots disproves David's contention that she cannot handle cases (70). Earlier he and Mark had failed to make headway with Rabbit. Within a relatively short space of time, however, she gets him to confess that the car he stole *was* for the UDA, for a paramilitary called Walter Thompson, and not for Stanley Brown. When pressured by

Mark to give them 'something' on Brown, Rabbit refuses to co-operate: 'What world do you live in. I'm saying nothing' (80). His impolitic assertion that Brown is far more frightening than Thompson, or an LVF family, or them, makes Mark flip. Forcing Rabbit's face down over the table, he threatens 'to break every bone is his body' if he does not come up with or rather make up something convincing on their chief suspect. Unwilling to condone Mark's use of violence, Caroline intervenes. In this, our last sighting of her in the play, she is presented as unwavering in her determination to stay within the rules and to do her job (81).

Significantly, in terms of its intervention in and representation of current gender politics, *The Force of Change* ends with exchanges between men. In the concluding scenes which disclose Stanley's fate, the dominant voice and personality are David's. In a manner which oscillates between the paternal ('Come with me') and fraternal ('You have to trust me mate'), he shepherds Bill back into Interview Room A, with the promise that 'I'll do all the talking' (75). Once there, David intimates to Stanley that he will shortly be released. Before this happens, however, he unleashes a verbal assault on the UDA man, arguing that much of the responsibility for the decline of the Protestant community and its reputation lies with criminals like him. Although the comparison he draws between Stanley and the hated republican Other is a telling one, the rhetorical excess he subsequently displays diminishes its effect:

> When I look into your eyes I see a reflection of every IRA man you claimed to be protecting us from. I see old men closing their shops and going home penniless because you took their profit and more. I see old ladies cowering in fear trying to forget what they witnesses in case you or your cronies come back to make them forget permanently. (76)

In the final scene, Bill joins David in lamenting the way the loyalist paramilitaries lost the plot, and degenerated into gangsterism. Instead of attacking the Provisionals, loyalists have ended up fighting one another: 'The IRA must be laughing their heads off at us. Loyalist feuds in Portadown. The LVF taking on the UVF and now this. UDA members threatening police officers' (82). David's very last words pick up on Stanley's recent justification for his activities, that it is a reaction to not feeling 'safe' (76). After warning Stanley of the fatal repercussions for him should anything happen to Caroline or family, he leaves him with the question: 'How safe do you feel now?' (83).

It is possible to discern in the dénouement of *The Force of Change* points of analogy to the Peace Process itself. Ultimately in order to fulfil her ambitions to attain power, Caroline is forced to temper her idealism and desire for justice. In words which resemble those of a cautious pro-Agreement politician, Mark urges her to settle for limited gains: 'You've got your family safe for the time being. I would suggest that we have to concentrate our efforts on ensuring that safety becomes permanent or as near permanent as possible' (67). In the theatre, as on the outside, the para-military is allowed to walk free, his capacity for violence intact. It is a resolution with which the audience and large numbers of people in both Northern Irish communities are extremely uncomfortable.

In the light of this, the illustration chosen for the programme cover for the original Royal Court production seems especially apt. The image of two hands handcuffed together – one clenched and white, the other open and stained – serves as a reminder of the dualisms in Northern Irish culture, the divisions *between* and *within* the communities. The hand on the left, which seems to be making a blocking or obstructive gesture, is obviously intended as an emblem of contemporary Ulster. It evokes the province's ancient symbol, a bloody, severed hand, and encourages us to recognise a continuity between past and present territorial conflicts.[129]

II   Roadblocks, roadmaps (2001–2006)

In the closing paragraph of *The Long Road to Peace in Northern Ireland* (2002), a collection of essays most of which were delivered at Liverpool University's Institute of Irish Studies, Marianne Elliott acknowledges 'the gravity of the problems remaining', but counsels those 'dispirited by the frequent crises ... to consider how far we have already come since June 1993'.[130] In that month, she notes, opinion polls suggested that a mere 6 per cent of the Northern Irish electorate believed that all-party talks would succeed. The months before and the years since Elliott wrote her largely positive, though measured assessment of the distance travelled and journey ahead have been marked by major obstacles and considerable acrimony, as will become apparent. For much of this time the people of the province have lived in a state of political limbo, consoled only by the fact that the scale of killings, maimings, bombings and burnings-out has massively declined since the appalling 1970s, 1980s and early 1990s.

When the Northern Ireland Executive and Assembly resumed work at the beginning of November 2001, it was against a background of spor-adic acts of sectarian and intracommunal violence, which in itself can be partly attributed to the political instability.[131] Although the Provisional IRA's reluctance to decommission its weaponry had been a central factor in the slow progress made since the Good Friday Agreement, equally troubling for the First Minister, David Trimble, and his Deputy, Mark Durkan, was the rise in loyalist paramilitary activity, which included attacks on Catholics and their properties as well as punishment beatings in their own community. In a Commons answer on 7 November 2001, Jane Kennedy, the Security Minister in the Northern Ireland Office, stated that of the 840-plus attacks since the beginning of the year 620 had been the work of loyalist paramilitaries and 223 of republicans.[132] The following week in order to assuage unionist anger at the 'loss' of the RUC, John Reid, the Secretary of State, announced that one million pounds had been be set aside to create a Garden of Remembrance and a museum to commemorate the work of the force. In the meantime, unionist support for the Agreement continued to ebb away in part in response to the DUP's constant challenging of Trimble's policies. At a meeting of the Ulster Unionist Council in December, the First Minister's policies were fiercely challenged by many anti-Agreement members of his own party, although in the end he did manage to defeat a number of motions calling for sanctions on Sinn Féin if decommissioning had not been completed by February 2002.

As 2001 came to a close, past crimes and injustices repeatedly resurfaced in the headlines and so added to the tensions. In early December a leaked report on the 1998 Omagh bombing, compiled by the Police Ombudsman, Nuala O'Loan, caused a great deal of controversy since it alleged that the RUC had paid insufficient heed to warnings received prior to the atrocity. On the same day, Gerry Adams urged the British government to set up an international public inquiry into the killing of Pat Finucane in 1989 and allegations that British security forces had colluded with the loyalist murder gang. A critical point was reached in the Bloody Sunday inquiry, when the High Court refused to accede to Lord Saville's request that soldiers directly implicated in the shootings be required to attend the hearings in Derry; lawyers acting for the soldiers argued that their lives might be put in danger if they were compelled to return to Derry to give evidence.

The people who had assembled in Derry in January 1972 had done so, one should recall, to protest against internment without trial, which had been imposed by Stormont with Edward Heath's backing in August 1971. Confidential British government documents relating to that year, hidden away under the 'thirty-year rule', entered the public domain in the January of 2002. One of these disclosed that British Army leaders in Northern Ireland had warned the Prime Minister that internment would only exacerbate the situation and boost recruitment to the IRA. On the thirtieth anniversary of the Bloody Sunday killings, 2000 people gathered in Derry to commemorate the event, and listened to a moving address from Edward Daly, the former Bishop of Derry. Rather than focus solely on their own grief, he called on the relatives to pray 'for victims every-where – here, in Afghanistan, the Middle East and New York ... all people who have suffered, of whatever race or religion or nation'. In encour-aging his listeners to make the connection between their suffering and that of thousands elsewhere, he was reflecting an approach which was becoming increasingly common in Irish culture in the late 1990s – one reflected in commemorations of the Famine and 1798 – and in the after-math of 9/11.

Over the preceding month, as the Bishop would have been all too aware, sectarian violence had escalated alarmingly, particularly in North Belfast. On 9 January Holy Cross Primary School once more became a flashpoint for conflict, a site of accusations and counter-accusations.[133] Over suc-cessive nights there were riots in Ardoyne, during which over 80 PSNI officers were injured and three soldiers; in one incident a British soldier was struck by an acid bomb hurled by a loyalist. Worse was to come, when on Saturday, 12 January, a 20-year-old postal worker, Daniel McColgan, was murdered by loyalist paramilitaries as he arrived for work at his depot in Rathcoole. Four days later a man's body was discovered at the base of Cavehill; it turned out to be that of 39-year-old Stephen McCullough who, hours earlier, had told several members of the security forces that he could shed light on the McColgan murder. Dismay and revulsion in both communities at this new spate of violence prompted trade unions in the province to organise peace rallies on Friday, 18 January, drawing in an estimated 25 000 people in seven different locations.

The case of three republicans arrested by Colombian authorities in 2001, accused of training FARC rebels, received extensive coverage in the early months of 2002. (A congressional meeting held in the United States in April heard reports that as many as 15 republican paramilitaries had visited Colombia since 1997.) For Ian Paisley's DUP this was further evi-dence of the Provisionals' continuing involvement in terrorist activities. They tabled a motion in the Assembly on 6 March calling for Sinn Féin members of the Executive to be expelled for 12 months. This was defeated, and dismissed by the First Minister as just another DUP 'stunt'. However, David Trimble was becoming increasingly anxious about the continuing decline in support for the Good Friday Agreement within his commu-nity, and the inroads being made by the DUP. Determined to re-assert his position as the unionists' champion, he vociferously opposed pro-posals for an amnesty for republican paramilitaries who were 'on the run'; this was an idea floated by the British government earlier in the year in order to induce additional movement from Sinn Féin and the Provisional IRA. In another attempt to regain ground with traditional UUP voters, he gave a highly contentious address to the Ulster Unionist Council (UUC) on 9 March in which he described the Irish Republic as a: 'pathetic sectarian, mono-ethnic, mono-cultural state'.[134] His speech included criticism of the work of the two SF ministers in the Executive and a suggestion that a referendum should be held to establish how many people in the North wanted to join a united Ireland. These comments provoked a great deal of anger in the Republic and among northern nationalists. Understandably Bertie Ahern took great offence at the gross, inaccurate description of contemporary Ireland, pointing out that it was in fact a pluralist, tolerant state free of 'Drumcrees or Garvaghy Roads'. The American President's adviser on Northern Ireland, Richard Haass, rounded on Trimble's lack of judgement, arguing that people in positions of authority should avoid talking 'in ways that sharpen sectarian conflict'.[135]

The unionist community's unease over and downright hostility towards power-sharing with Sinn Féin intensified following a break-in at Special Branch offices at Castlereagh which was discovered on Monday, 18 March. Although initially Ronnie Flanagan, the Chief Constable, was sceptical about paramilitary involvement, police officers subsequently accused the Provisionals of being behind the crime. In a gesture designed to exhibit their commitment to the peace process, the Provisionals invited General John de Chastelain to observe a second act of decommissioning, in which, in his words, a 'substantial' amount of weaponry was put beyond use. In an accompanying statement issued at the same time (8 April), they denied having anything to do with the Special Branch break-in. The growing atmosphere of distrust fuelled tensions during May and June, with rioting breaking out in North and East Belfast in which several people suffered gunshot wounds. David Ervine, leader of the Progressive Unionists, spoke of the 'substantial and serious crisis' now facing the peace process, and of rumours that the UVF was rearming. Although there were lulls in mid-June and in the run-up to the marching season, sectarian violence flared up again in North Belfast in the third week of July. Clashes on Sunday, 21 July, left a 19-year-old Protestant suffering from gunshot wounds, and in reprisal loyalist paramilitaries pumped five bullets into the back of Gerard Lawlor, a Catholic 19-year-old, as he walked home in the early hours of Monday morning. The UDA later described the killing as a 'measured military response'.[136]

Devolution in the province was plunged into deeper crisis during September and October 2002. Less than a fortnight after David Trimble threatened to abandon power-sharing in the New Year unless republicans provided evidence that they had renounced violence for good, the PSNI announced that they had uncovered a republican spy-ring operating at Stormont. Trimble's response to this development was to issue an ultimatum to the British government, calling on them to expel Sinn Féin from the Assembly. Rather than take this step, the Northern Ireland Secretary, John Reid, suspended devolution from midnight on Monday, 14 October, and resumed direct rule from London. (In December 2005 during a court case it emerged that Denis Donaldson, one of the three members of the alleged spy-ring, had in fact been a British agent for the previous two decades.) Addressing party leaders in the North four days later, Tony Blair argued that the political institutions there could never grow and mature if the IRA continued to be 'half in, half out'. In reply, Martin McGuinness stated that republican paramilitaries would never consent to the terms for decommissioning proposed by the unionist parties. There was therefore little surprise when on 30 October the Provisional IRA declared it had broken off contacts with John de Chastelain's monitoring body. The leaking in mid-December of a confidential Irish government document which stated that the Provisionals were 'still active' only served to confirm Trimble's suspicions about their duplicity and prompted him to walk out of multi-party talks.

In the course of the next four years, 2003–6, considerable advances were made over Provisional IRA decommissioning though this did not bring about the reintroduction of devolved government. The Provisionals' continuing involvement in criminal activity, along with Sinn Féin's reluctance to recognise the PSNI, remained massive obstacles to the two main unionist parties who refused to countenance partnership in such circumstances. An opinion poll conducted in February 2003 by Queen's University Belfast and the Rowntree Trust discovered that only a third of the unionist population said that they would endorse the Good Friday Agreement if there were a second referendum. An even lower figure of unionist support was established in a poll held by the *Belfast News Letter* in mid-May, though 76 per cent of respondents said that they would back the Agreement were the PIRA to disband. Through much of April and May 2003 Tony Blair and Bertie Ahern worked strenuously to secure a deal, but to no avail; what prevented the political impasse from being broken, according to Blair, was continuing 'uncertainty' over the PIRA's intentions.[137] In reply Sinn Féin's leader, Gerry Adams, insisted that resolution to the conflict was possible once all parties and the two governments met fully commitments they had made in the Agreement.

For huge numbers of people in Ireland and Britain in the early months of 2003 the imminent invasion of Iraq by American and British forces was the foremost issue of the moment. On 4 February 2003 a number of Irish writers, including Brian Friel and Tom Paulin from the North and Roddy Doyle and Brendan Kennelly from the Republic, co-wrote a protest letter to the *Irish Times* denouncing a war that would lead to thousands of innocent Iraqi citizens suffering terribly. In addition they voiced their suspicion that the 'actual motives' behind the invasion might be to secure access to the 'world's second largest oil reserve'.[138] Shortly after the online launch in late January of *100 Poets Against the War*, edited by the Canadian poet, Todd Swift, an anthology entitled *Irish Writers Against War* was published by Conor Kostick and Katherine Moore. Northern Irish writers represented in the collection included Brian Friel, who wrote the Preface, the poets Seamus Heaney, Medbh McGuckian, Sinead Morrissey, Robert Greacen and Ann Zell, and the novelists Sam McAughtry, Eugene McCabe and Bernard Mac Laverty. Friel begins the Preface condemning the 'strident' anti-American rhetoric of some opponents of the war, but then proceeds to deprecate the proposed invasion as 'not-thought-through' and 'wildly disproportionate',[139] a perception reiterated in Sinead Morrissey's contribution, 'The Wound-Man'. This speaks of post-9/11 America as a man who has been 'badly hit', yet 'Strong./ Loose in the world. And out of proportion'.[140]

David Trimble's endeavours to hold his party together and retain its backing for his policy suffered a serious blow in late June 2003 when three MPs, Jeffrey Donaldson, Martin Smyth and David Burnside, declared that they would no longer accept the party whip. Donaldson objected strongly to the International Monitoring Commission (IMC), set up by Tony Blair and Bertie Ahern to scrutinise the paramilitaries' activities, since it granted the Irish government an input in the province's internal affairs.[141] Paul Murphy, the Northern Ireland Secretary, countered this view by arguing that the IMC would provide a means of restoring confidence amongst the North's parties. Three days after David Trimble addressed the UUP party conference on the need for republicans to end paramilitary activities for good, John de Chastelain announced on 21 October that the Provisionals had carried out a third act of decommissioning, destroying a large quantity of weapons. For Trimble this was still insufficient and he again refused to re-enter government with Sinn Féin.

The results of the November 2003 Assembly elections saw the DUP emerge as the largest unionist party, with 30 members, three more than the UUP. Equally alarming from the Irish and British governments' perspective was the news that Sinn Féin had gained six of the SDLP's seats and so for the first time in Northern Ireland's history become the biggest nationalist party. Ian Paisley shortly afterwards declared that he too would never work alongside Sinn Féin until the Provisional IRA had been disbanded. The most important political event of the following year, 2004, were the intensive negotiations involving all the North's major parties and the British and Irish governments, which took place at Leeds Castle in Kent between 16 and 18 September. Tony Blair and Bertie Ahern were determined to try and find a historic compromise acceptable to both the DUP and Sinn Féin that might enable devolved government to be restored. There was general consent that 'significant progress'[142] was made on a range of topics, though demilitarisation once again proved to be a sticking-point. While the republican paramilitaries were willing to allow observers to witness further acts of decommissioning, they baulked at the unionists' insistence that the process should be photographed.

By the year's close hopes of a breakthrough had receded. Indeed they were to disappear completely following a raid on the Northern Bank in Belfast on 20 December in which 26.5 million pounds was stolen. Police in Northern Ireland and in the Republic were convinced the Provisional IRA had masterminded the robbery, a view later endorsed by the International Monitoring Commission. The Provisionals vehemently denied any involvement in the raid, and on 2 February 2005 announced that they had withdrawn an offer to destroy all their weapons.[143] The British government instantly condemned this move. A Downing Street spokesman went so far as to identify the IRA as 'the sole obstacle to moving forward'.[144] The unionist parties were even more scathing, with Ian Paisley suggesting that the IRA never had any intention of decommissioning their arms 'in a credible, transparent and verifiable way'.[145] Questioned later in the month about the raid, Gerry Adams criticised what he termed 'trial by the media' and stated categorically that 'Sinn Féin aren't bank robbers; Sinn Féin have not been involved in criminality'.[146]

Equally damaging to Sinn Féin was the disclosure that a number of IRA volunteers had taken part in the fatal stabbing of Robert McCartney, a 33-year-old Catholic from the Short Strand, following an altercation in a Belfast bar. Within days of the murder on 30 January 2005, McCartney's five sisters began a brave, intensive campaign to expose the killers and bring them to justice, knowing full well how reluctant many in their community would be to come forward with information about the crime. Allegations that the IRA were hindering the investigation, concealing evidence and intimidating potential witnesses were rife, and voiced by the McCartney sisters and by Sinn Féin's political opponents. In a statement issued in February the IRA stated that they had expelled three volunteers who had been involved in the crime, two of them 'high-ranking'[147] members. This move was dismissed as a cynical ploy by

Alasdair McDonnell, the SDLP deputy leader, who went on to claim that 12 IRA men had attacked McCartney, not three. Not surprisingly, for DUP and UUP spokesmen the McCartney case and the IRA's response exemplified once again the criminality within the republican movement and its lamentable recalcitrance over the issue of policing the North.[148]

The McCartney sisters' courage and determination to secure justice for their dead brother evoked sympathy and respect worldwide. They were guests of honour at the St Patrick's Day celebrations at the White House and in April received an invitation to meet the President of the European Parliament and address MEPs. Particularly difficult for Sinn Féin was the adverse reaction they encountered in the United States. For Senator Ted Kennedy to have cancelled a scheduled meeting with him was bad enough for Gerry Adams; worse was to come when Kennedy declared that the warmth of the reception the McCartneys had been given in Washington constituted a 'very powerful signal that it's time for the IRA to fully decommission', to 'end all criminal activity and cease to exist as a para-military organisation'.[149] In their Easter message that year, the Provisionals sought to distance themselves from the killing, by stressing that 'it was not carried out by the IRA, nor was it carried out on behalf of the IRA',[150] and by joining the chorus of those condemning it.

The Westminster General Election results in Northern Ireland on 5 May revealed how much the political map had altered since the June 2001 poll. Whereas in 2001 the DUP had five seats, in 2005 they returned nine members to Westminster becoming the largest party overall with a 33.7 per cent share of the vote. Their rise had been at the expense of the UUP, whose representation fell from six seats to one; their vote share slipped nine points from 26.7 per cent to 17.7 per cent. Amongst the UUP casualties was David Trimble himself, defeated in Upper Bann by David Simpson of the DUP. Despite the negative impact of the McCartney case, Sinn Féin gained one additional seat at the expense of the SDLP and increased their share from 21.7 per cent to 24.3 per cent. The SDLP remained with three seats, however, after capturing a DUP constituency in Belfast South. The results meant that any immediate return to devolved government would necessitate a situation inconceivable only a few years earlier, in which a DUP member would serve as First Minister in the Executive with a Sinn Féin member as his deputy.

When, on 25 September 2005, the IMC confirmed that the Provisional IRA had completed the process of decommissioning, the way seemed open for the Executive to resume office. Verification that 'the totality of the IRA's arsenal'[151] had been destroyed was provided by two independent witnesses, Father Alec Reid and the former Methodist president,

Harold Good, who had accompanied the IMC members at this momentous event. For the Irish and British Prime Ministers pleasure and relief at this 'landmark development'[152] were tempered by regret that it had not occurred shortly after the signing of the Good Friday Agreement and by the realisation that there were other obstacles in the road ahead. 'Many believed that this day would never come', said Bertie Ahern, giving voice to his satisfaction, but then added that 'many would say that this should have happened a long time ago'.[153] Tony Blair declared that '*an important step* in the transition from conflict to peace' (my emphasis)[154] had been accomplished. In Northern Ireland, reactions to the IMC statement ranged from the sombre (SDLP) to the scornful (DUP). Although welcoming the prospect of 'the gun ... at last being taken out of Irish politics', Mark Durkan, the SDLP leader, saw in the IRA's renunciation of violence a vindication of his own party's policies since its founding:

> Today's events ... demonstrate the utter futility of violence. Violence never won anything in the north. It costs. In lives lost, in economies ruined, in communities wrecked. That's something that so many victims of the troubles know too well. Today as we look forward, we must not leave them behind – isolated and forgotten.[155]

Reg Empey, leader of the UUP since June, acknowledged that the IRA's decision constituted a 'significant development', but maintained that for the republican movement to gain any credibility with unionists and create an environment in which power-sharing might work, they would need to dismantle their 'criminal empire'.[156] Having triumphed in the May elections by reiterating their 'unshakable' resistance to republicanism's advance,[157] the DUP were not in the mood for giving or forgiving. They claimed that John de Chastelain had been hoodwinked by the republicans, and that Alec Reid and Harold Good could not be deemed 'independent' witnesses as they had been 'approved' and 'accepted by the IRA'. Given that no photographs had been taken and 'no detailed inventory' provided of guns, ammunition and explosives destroyed, they argued that Tony Blair's promises that decommissioning would be 'transparent and verifiable'[158] had not been kept.

Early in December 2005 the case against three men accused three years earlier of running an IRA spy-ring in Stormont collapsed. One of those acquitted, Denis Donaldson, a senior figure in Sinn Féin, admitted that for the previous 20 years he had been receiving money from British intelligence and that 'Stormontgate' was 'a scam and a fiction'[159] dreamt up by the RUC/PSNI Special Branch. On 4 April 2006, two days before Tony Blair and Bertie Ahern met at Navan Fort, Co. Armagh, to announce their latest plan to re-establish devolved government in Northern Ireland, Donaldson's dead body was discovered at the remote Donegal cottage to which he had fled. The timing of the murder so close to the Navan Fort summit led to suspicions that mavericks within the intelligence services might have been involved, a theory dismissed by the Northern Ireland Secretary as 'fanciful'; he appears to have shared a more widespread view that this was an act of revenge, and quite probably the work of dissident republicans.[160] Conscious of the shadow the killing had cast over their meeting,[161] the two Prime Ministers nevertheless pressed on with the strategy they and their advisers had agreed which was to recall the Northern Ireland Assembly on 15 May and give the parties until 24 November 2006 to set up a new multi-party Executive. Failure to do so would result in the 108 members of the Assembly losing their salaries. Whereas both Sinn Féin and the DUP were broadly positive in response to news that the Assembly would reconvene, Ian Paisley remained sceptical about the likelihood of an Executive being formed: 'Currently there is no evidence that Sinn Féin/IRA will be any further advanced in giving up criminality in November'.[162]

On 4 October 2006 the IMC issued a report which concluded that the Provisional IRA was no longer a threat to peace and stability in Northern Ireland. It had transformed itself over the past three years and was 'now firmly set on a political strategy, eschewing terrorism and other forms of crime'.[163] Recruitment, weapons procurement and training had ceased, and individuals approaching the organisation had been 'redirected towards joining Sinn Féin'.[164] Exactly a week after the publication of the IMC report, Tony Blair and Bertie Ahern summoned Northern Ireland's political parties to St Andrews for three days of intensive discussions on the province's future governance. Few commentators expected a positive outcome to the talks, and, according to the *Observer*'s Ireland editor, a DUP walk-out on the evening of 12 October was only narrowly averted after Sinn Féin offered concessions on policing, education policy and local government reform.[165] On Friday 13 October, negotiations were concluded and the St Andrews Agreement unveiled by Tony Blair and Bertie Ahern. This envisaged a consultation process lasting until Friday, 10 November, during which the two main parties would encourage their supporters to accept power-sharing (DUP) and to endorse the authority and police in Northern Ireland (SF). On a date yet to be confirmed, though almost certainly 1 March 2007, elections to a new Assembly would be held along with referendums on the St Andrews Agreement north and south of the border. According to a senior British government official, quoted both by the *Observer* and Peter Hain, prospects for success were better now than at the time since the Good Friday Agreement was signed: 'This time everybody will be inside the tent, including Ian Paisley. If he is in government with Martin McGuinness, then it is well and truly over'.[166]

Whether 'it is well and truly over' will emerge over the coming months and years. This will plainly be an exacting time for Northern Ireland's largest two parties, which carry with them such a legacy of hatred and distrust.

III 'Falling Into Light': new generation poets

Sinead Morrissey, *Between Here and There, The State of the Prisons*; Nick Laird, *To a Fault*; Leontia Flynn, *These Days*; Alan Gillis, *Somebody, Somewhere*

Collections such as Ciaran Carson's *Breaking News* (2003), Tom Paulin's *The Invasion Handbook* (2003), Michael Longley's *Snow Water* (2004), Medbh McGuckian's *Book of the Angel* (2004), Derek Mahon's *Harbour Lights* (2005), Seamus Heaney's *District and Circle* (2006), Paul Muldoon's *Horse Latitudes* (2006) confirm that the power, originality and resilience of Northern Ireland's established poets remains undiminished in the new millennium. Two recent anthologies, Selima Guinness's *The New Irish Poets* (2004) and John Brown's *Magnetic North: The Emerging Poets* (2005),[167] provide evidence, however, that a new generation of writers has emerged, one which is beginning to re-shape the contours of Northern Irish litera- ture. Amongst the defining characteristics of the new poetry, according to Guinness, is a postmodernist distrust of grand narratives, an alertness to wider geopolitical concerns, and a preoccupation with domestic and family, rather than national history. For Brown, whose focus is exclu- sively on Northern poetry, the coming poetic generation displays a high degree of mobility and disparity in their work, a determination to cross borders, break silences, and proffer 'bifocal or comparative visions' (12) of changing private and public terrain. While not wishing to question the validity of these assertions in relation to a substantial number of these younger poets, I would suggest that many traits identified by Brown and Guinness are equally demonstrable in the writing of their literary fore- bears. Indeed, Brown himself points to continuities in content, form and style, and how poets from each generation developed different strategies in facing up to a common imperative, the need to address the appalling evil that destroyed so much of and in the province from the late-1960s onwards: 'Darkness remains both a felt, elemental or metaphysical presence ... the image of poetry as a "door into the dark is with us more than we care to acknowledge' (12). While altered political and social conditions since the ceasefires may have led to a diminution in the political pressures and expectations placed on poets, the imprint of the recent past, of 'ancestral', communal and family memory, is still clearly visible in their work.

Rather than survey a broad range of writers from the new generation, consideration will be given instead to work by four poets, Sinead Morrissey (b.1972), Alan Gillis (b.1973), Leontia Flynn (b.1974), and Nick Laird (b.1975). They all came of age at a turning-point in the province's history, the time when the peace process was gathering momentum, following a childhood and adolescence dominated by near-continuous political violence. Although its imprint clearly marks their poems, they should also be seen as beneficiaries of the relative normality that has existed since the 1994 and 1997 ceasefires, and the changes that have accompanied them. As the more detailed discussion of Morrissey's and Laird's poetry will show, geographical and cultural relocations have enriched their work and enabled them not just to look back on both their own and their parents' experiences, but also to look upwards and outwards to other cultures, places and times.[168]

The quality of Sinead Morrissey's second and third collections, *Between Here and There* (2002) and *The State of the Prisons* (2005), has enhanced her reputation as the most accomplished Northern Irish poet of her generation. An extended range and increased confidence are apparent in both volumes in which she explores not only disparate cultures and histories, but also, as John Brown puts it, the 'geography of the heart',[169] in all its intricacies, with all its uncertainties. *Between Here and There* begins surreally, with a voice slipping overboard in the Sea of Japan and making it to shore. The speaker imagines the voice's *'lonely sojourn'* (original emphasis) there, but also its return to her, 'burdened' with an awareness of the world's opulence and variousness, and the gifts that come with exile. Yet on turning the page, readers are transported to a very different location. The first three stanzas of 'In Belfast' provide a panorama of the city, an impression of its solidity and the weightiness of its grand structures. A place driven still by economic imperatives, its energies, as in the Victorian age, seem principally devoted to 'making money' (13). In part two the scene moves from wide-angle to close-up, a small corner, the private, imaginative space of a returnee who, like Odysseus, has spent ten years away. In alluding to 'history's *dent* and *fracture*' (my emphasis), the first-person narrator is reflecting both on a shared and a personal history. She is mindful of a 'delicate unravelling' in her own life, which renders the future indefinite and 'unspoken'. The poem ends acknowledging the complexities and ambiguities of the texts before her, a place which has woven itself into her consciousness. In spite of Belfast's less attractive attributes ('its downpour and its vapour') – which, as in Mahon's early poetry, appear both meteorological and spiritual – she associates the city also with tenacity, and concludes 'I am/as much at home here as I will ever be' (13).

Written with an equal measure of sorrow and anger, 'Tourism' offers a sardonic take on today's Belfast and those who participate in its 'marketing'. In this brave new city, commercial opportunism ('Our day has come') outweighs political aspirations and moral qualms.[170] The tourists are transported 'to the streets / they want to see most', and peddled the illusion that violence has ended: '*as though* it's all over and safe behind bus glass' (my emphasis). The Belfast the narrator portrays is a place shot through with gaps and holes, literal and metaphorical, like those left by the Titanic or at Stormont, 'our weak-kneed parliament' (14), revived and then inert again as a result of the politicians' ineptitude. The irony and indignation seem to run out in the last two stanzas, which voice what seems a genuine appeal for the European tourists to keep coming, to radicalise the locals, and to endow the province with 'new symbols' and a new identity.

Given the stage in her life *Between Here and There* 'covers' – the majority of its poems must have been composed when Morrissey was between the ages of 24 and 30 – illuminatory moments from periods of private crisis feature prominently. An early cluster of poems chronicle a failing relationship, albeit in an oblique manner. The speaker in 'Nettles' indicates unease at the prospect of following her partner into a region which she sees as tenebrous, exposed, and denying definition. In using his mouth to close her eyes, he might simply be making a tender gesture; alternatively, the phrase could imply a manoeuvre, physical or verbal, intended to prevent her from viewing their situation independently. The comparison of his mouth to 'a warm pool to rest in' (18) could also be read negatively, as signifying the temptations of languour and inaction. The middle stanza's opening words, 'But' and 'instead of', cast a shadow over recollections of their honeymooning, and prepare the ground for the nettles' invasion of their garden of love.[171] Strategically placed in lines 10 and 11 ('strangling', 'twining', 'growing over'), the present participles convey the nettles' destructive impact 'on the day's *attempted* harvest' (my emphasis). The weeds represent perhaps an accumulation of damaging experience whose imprint 'on my retina' appears permanent. Their 'presence' saps that of the addressee, an unrealised figure, who exists primarily as a metonym ('your mouth'), as part of what was 'we'. In contrast to the single, all-conquering image in 'Nettles', 'Street Theatre' deploys a variety of metaphors in depicting a breaking-apart. Aptly, given its title, relationship is figured as performance at pivotal moments in the poem. At the outset the pair appear in light opera, as white-faced '*Mikado* lovers'; by the close they are acting out a tragedy or, at best, a dark melodrama, 'back to back/in a frozen unnecessary duel'. What began in sweet abstraction concludes as a matter of 'coins' (19).

Morrissey's most explicit, chilling treatment of a relationship in crisis comes in 'Sea Stones', which starts with a sequence of jarring blows: 'It is exactly a year today since you slapped me in public'. What in retrospect adds to the humiliation and hurt the speaker suffered is his distorted reading of her reaction:

> You claimed I just ignored it,
> That I pretended to be hooked on the dumb-show of a sunset
> ... Too hooked to register
> the sting of your ring finger
> as it caught on my mouth (20)

Words like 'hooked', 'register', 'caught', 'ring finger' act as collective reminders of the distance travelled since the couple's engagement and marriage. An acute feeling of separation is realised in the last six lines, most vividly in the image of 'a fallen match', which links backwards and forwards to words such as 'struck' and 'lit'. This provides a bathetic, unglamorous conclusion to stanza three, which preoccupies itself with the genesis of their early love, signs like roses, butterflies, 'juvenile kisses', and the sea stones she once treasured. Tellingly, we find the personal pronouns, 'You' and 'I', stranded at either end of the closing stanza, and yet another instance of double vision.[172] Juxtaposing a near-shot and a long-shot, the narrator observes her partner turning away and the sun (and the radiance they once felt) disappearing over the horizon. And then there is one last shock, her perverse desire for him to slap her again, 'to keep the fire of your anger lit' (20).

Acts of containment and self-containment recur in Morrissey's latest collection, *The State of the Prisons*, in which her attention switches increasingly to wider political concerns. Continuing violence in her home province was what haunted much of her first book, *There Was Fire in Vancouver*; now in *The State of Prisons* we witness the scope of her vision ranging far beyond Ireland and its history to embrace the current international crisis. These larger pieces often take the form of monologues ('Flight', 'Migraine', 'The State of the Prisons') where she displays her remarkable skills as a creator of others' voices. The first of these evokes the brutal material and ideological constraints imposed upon '*one* Anne Bridlestone' (original emphasis), a fervent royalist living in England during Cromwell's reign. Like the contemporary speaker in 'Sea Stones', though for very different reasons, the woman in 'Flight' is unable to use her tongue. What compels the latter into 'swallowing silence' (10) is a metal device known as 'the branks', generally employed by vengeful husbands in the seventeenth century to deter wives from '*chiding and scolding*' (9; original emphasis). Her punishment is political, however, a consequence of her devotion to the fugitive prince's cause, and rejection of her husband's authority. 'Migraine' brings together two groups of silenced women from recent history. The poem revisits the terrible events of 23–26 October 2002, when 900 Russians were taken hostage in a Moscow theatre by a group of 40 Chechen terrorists, half of them women. It is voiced by one of the female survivors of the siege, which ended when 'special forces' (44) released a deadly gas in the theatre killing 129 of the hostages. Her fragmented speech, often consisting of phrases and compressed sentences, contrasts sharply with the elevated religious rhetoric employed by the victim in 'Flight'. In turning her face to the wall, she tries shutting out the women terrorists' passionate intensity, their

> lust for an ending that would splatter their message
> from the newsstands of Moscow to the gun slums of Washington. (44)

The book's most ambitious piece is its title poem, a portrait of the English penal reformer, John Howard (1726–90), whose dying reflections expose him as a 'justified sinner'.[173] Morrissey replicates convincingly the vocabulary and cadences of eighteenth-century public discourse, such as when Howard rejects the very idea of monuments ('Fame saddens heaven. Suffer no stone to be raised to me'). Although in this opening section he is keen to preserve his anonymity in death ('Erect a sundial over my head / Instead of an inscription'), at the close he instructs his admirers to 'Found a reform league' and 'Mark it with my name' (58). A likely reason for this change of heart is that in recalling a lifetime of service to prisoners, he recalls the disservice done to his son and heir, a boy who 'bothered me,/Mooning in my shadow like a criminal' (55). Incarcerated, neglected, racked and demented by syphilis, Howard's son and double resembles ironically many of the unfortunates whose sufferings the reformer sought to ease. Enlightenment Man, like Twenty-First Century Humanity, comes across as a doubled, riven figure, a product of his era and its contradictory ideology. A morally energetic, sometime liberal, Morrissey's Howard opposes hierarchies (57), is appalled by vice and corruption in the system (55), and, once comfortably off, gives generously to the poor (58). Yet part of him remains archly conservative, committed to 'Making order stronger' (58). Those destined for the gallows he wants saved for the Nation's 'mines and battlefields' (58); for those imprisoned for lesser offences he recommends ceaseless watching ('Let even their dreams be inspected'). His testament ends, however, with a belated measure of redress, leaving his son to receive '*whatever remains*', acknowledging that 'left undone' and 'so much harm' (58).

Fathers, actual and imaginary, feature repeatedly in Nick Laird's début collection, *To a Fault*, a book which exemplifies Edna Longley's contention that 'the speech or eloquent silence of the father' is one of the most important, recurring motifs in Northern Irish poetry.[174] That this should be so is unsurprising given how the experience of living through and with the Troubles intensified solidarity between the generations, as well as within communities. As other forms of political, social and moral authority collapsed, the father appears to have remained a still, defining point in the articulation of personal and artistic identity. Clearly within the poets the drive towards individuation and self-definition survives, though alongside the impetus to acquire other literary father- and mother-figures, such as MacNeice and Plath, Mandelstam or Tsvetayeva. At the same time the Northern Irish poets represent themselves often as deeply 'woven figures', as continuing and/or snapped-off threads in a complex familial and historical text.

Laird's book opens with a series of glimpses of his father, a figure who comes across as simultaneously present and remote. His first appearance is in 'Cuttings', a poem whose title is entirely appropriate given its setting (a barber's shop) and Laird's clipped, highly visual technique. Signs that the location is Northern Ireland are immediately apparent, when the sunlight highlights the *paisley* wallpaper. Deft and diplomatic with the customers, the barber avoids dangerous topics like 'the troubles or women or prison', confines the conversation to safer substitutes. The hairdresser's shop clearly functions as an emblematic space, a 'bandaged' place where diverse individuals temporarily find common ground. Into this unprepossessing frame, an initially unidentified male figure appears. The ambivalent feelings and 'contradictory awarenesses'[175] compressed in the phrase with which he is first defined are maintained in the concluding images, which present him negatively ('his eyes budded shut') and positively ('expectant and open'), his head filled with 'lather' and 'unusual thoughts'. The father remains for the reader – as for the speaker perhaps – an elusive, enigmatic figure; what fires his anger, we never discover. What Laird does present at the close is a man curious enough to reach for something beyond the quotidian and parochial, capable of engaging with the strange and the sublime.

To a Fault proves to be deeply engaged with the relationship between family and identity, conscious both of the need to belong and to break rank.[176] Something of this anxiety can be seen in 'The Layered', one of its lighter offerings. This finds the poet playing name-games, depicting, somewhat cryptically, three family members. First up is Matthew Thomas or, as the poem has it, 'Empty Laird', a man who in his last years lamented a dearth of opportunities, educational and political. His son is unflatteringly represented as 'a nit-picker ... a hair splitter', yet also as someone who feels terror at his own insubstantiality. Contrasted to these flawed males is the future Mrs Laird, a woman whose physical presence, repleteness and confidence impressed from the outset. The bizarre line with which the poem ends alludes to *Hamlet*, reinforcing the image of Laird Junior as a lack or absence which she, texts and text-making filled.[177]

Fecundity and criminality seem to be characteristics of the extended family portrayed in 'Pedigree'. Having established that the bloodline includes a shoplifter, a cattle-smuggler, a rustler-turned-killer, it is hardly surprising that the family blazon proposed by the narrator should be 'an enormous unruly blackthorn hedge', rather than a yielding willow. Trying to determine his own place in the family tree, the narrator – who shares a passing resemblance to the lawyer author – describes himself, understandably, as 'out on a limb'. When, mid-way through, the spotlight moves on to his more immediate forebears, an element of bathos enters in. The portrait of his father as a young man contains nothing of the dramatic, heroic, illicit or adventurous. Instead he is pictured fishing away his boyhood, longing for a Davy Crockett hat, polishing the medals of 'legendary uncles' all of whom had perished at the Somme.[178] Having disclosed the fact that neither of his parents left school with qualifications, the narrator lays emphasis on his mother's subsequent efforts to remedy that lack. His use of the adjective 'each' and the verb 'heave' to her nightly academic labour convey her determination, commitment and energy. In delivering his verdict on the relationships within his family – father–mother, brother–sister, but not father–son or mother–son – the speaker employs a strangely cheerless word: 'There is such a shelter in each other'. Home, thus, appears to be associated with protection and proximity, but not with emotional warmth or intimacy.

Directly after this, the narrator switches his attention to a very different location and entity, when its primary addressee is introduced and takes centre stage. He describes his lover padding from the bathroom, an embodiment of physical, linguistic and syntactical grace. In yet another self-reflexive touch, he identifies her as a kindred mark-maker in refer-ring to her 'singing ... footprints'. In the middle of his eulogy, a call from the past breaks in, suddenly compelling him to confront the gulf between his present and that past. He is made uneasy by the tone his partner adopts in speaking to his family from 'across the water'. Although the poem's closing statement seems to be an indictment of *her* for her inabil-ity to relate to them, one detects also feelings of guilt on his part, a fear perhaps that *he* no longer hears them properly, that *he* has forged a dis-tance from his point of origin.

Subsequently Laird extends his range beyond the family circle to pro-vide a number of highly evocative portraits of the province in the wake of the ceasefires. The aptly-titled 'Remaindermen' contemplates initially survivors of the Troubles years; praising their 'weathered' resistance and endurance ('their ability to thole'). Funerals regularly filled their days, which have been marred too by their loss of stock, their children's emi-gration. Contrasted with these solitary, pacific figures are the intransi-gent in the community, who the narrator characterises as preferring an 'ice-bound' world than one involving fluidity and compromise. In what proves to be one of many self-reflexive moments in *To A Fault*, the speaker notes how 'someone' charged with transcribing 'the last fifty years of *our* speech' (my emphasis) has yet to encounter the word 'sorry' or employ a question mark, an indication that truth might be plural. The poem ends with a wry, unconscious sign of the contrariness of the local towns-people who, in erecting a triumphal arch, inadvertently encouraged vis-itors to leave; those arriving were greeted with a 'Safe Home Brethren', while those departing were wished a 'Welcome'.

'The Signpost' maintains the collection's focus on the brutal semiotics of the North, and starts with the punishment beating of a loyalist para-military by two former drinking-companions, a not uncommon occurrence in the period under review. In its narrative, demotic style and sardonic humour it anticipates *Utterly Monkey* (2005), Laird's first novel, in which one of the leading characters, Geordie Wilson, is subjected to an identi-cal ordeal, having to wait for his attackers to bring a second gun to knee-cap him after the first one jams.[179] The damage to his legs, the speaker observes dryly, ruins all hopes of climbing Everest or playing football for Rangers, though not Glentoran (10). Splayed out after the shooting, his body is described as resembling a signpost, a pointed warning to others of the toll paid for transgression. The closing stanzas present the para-military/victim as bed-bound at the Royal Hospital, gazing out over the Belfast skyline. At a remove now from the men and guns which put him there, he observes two massive cranes, 'their *arms* low over the city / *as if*' (my emphasis) in a gesture of benediction.[180] As in 'Cuttings', the poem ends in an expression of wonder, how 'all that gathered weight' remains '*upright*' (my emphasis). The irony, of course, is that East Belfast is hardly or simply a place of benison, restraint and moral rectitude. Significantly, when he manages to locate 'his father's house'[181] – a metonym no doubt for the province – he notes that it is in a state of darkness.

One of the most accomplished of the early poems, 'The Length of a Wave' (6–7) illustrates how effectively Laird is able to switch from domestic, familial and local preoccupations to larger concerns, such as politics and the function of art. This sense of restless, continuing motion is signalled in the poem's opening line, which juxtaposes 'the mythic coast' and 'the kitchen stove', the phrase-structures and word-sounds echoing each other. The dominant presence in the early stanzas is again that of the narrator's father, this time as an increasingly disturbed, disturbing figure. Although initially depicted indulging merely in a little *schadenfreude*, the speaker then alludes to his tidal mood-swings ('dependent on the moon'), before informing us how twice he had smashed the light-switch. Outside the house, the father's voice resonates still, yet loses in power both as a result son's intellectual advances ('I could judge', 'by knowing') and more pressing concern, the desire for news from the poem's unidentified addressee, his lover back in England.

The poem's second movement monitors a sequence of alternative sound-effects, beginning with the waves rippling out from a bomb-blast. The bodies in the morgue 'awaiting recognition' might be those of the Omagh victims. Turning from that scene's horror, he attunes himself to noises closer to home, like the clatter made by a barley machine, a ball 'gonging' against a garage-door, the sound-swell created by speech, an 'adult' bird in flight, his sleeping beloved's 'tidal breathing', this last image transporting us lyrically into an unthreatening seascape, and far from the mortuary's stillness. In part three the auditory imagination switches to other frequencies associated with Northern Ireland. The reference to the Chinook's drone reminds one of how often images connected with surveillance figure in poems by Ciaran Carson, Medbh McGuckian and Ann Zell. In evoking the sound of a rifle shot – he compares it to a 'domestic slap' – he hints at how common violence has become outside *and* inside the domestic sphere. Initially 'the embassies of Home' with their 'quartered flags' appear as if wreathed in light, associated with sanctuary, stability, the assertion of individual identities. In the pivotal tenth line, however, they emerge as places where there is a struggle 'to stay intact'. What troubles the narrator's own sense of home is the verbal aggression exhibited by his father, whose final question encodes a demand for allegiance to family and origins. Although the young man's answer seems at first equivocal ('I'm still not sure'), the closing stanzas convey a commitment to originary locations, specifically Donegal and its liminal beauty. There he imagines watching 'light complicate the water', wading out into the 'stinging cold saltwater', which, like poetry, possesses transformative power. Its waves are credited as capable not only of restoring silver, but also, tellingly, of 'disinfecting wounds'.

Although it frequently alludes to continuing violence back home, *To A Fault* demonstrates the extent to which the decade since the ceasefires has freed up Northern Irish writers to engage with wider, global and historical concerns. The most striking illustration of this new breadth and confidence in Laird's collection is 'Imperial'. A parable about war and power-politics, which would have fitted well in the *Irish Writers Against War* anthology, it spans the centuries and bears its readers from ancient Mesopotamia to present-day Iraq. The poem, whose appearance in the *London Review of Books* coincided with the beginning of the US campaign to topple Saddam,[182] sets up a Saidian analogy between nineteenth-century, early twentieth-century and contemporary colonial adventurism.[183] Like Shelley's 'Ozymandias', the poem invites us to reflect on the transience of empire and the monumental follies political leaders continue to commit. At the same time, it should be added that Laird's perspective is itself ineluctably 'compromised' since it regards the east through Western eyes.

Its first two parts portray the working practices of the archaeologist, Sir Austin Henry Layard (1817–94), whose surname resembles the poet's own. By publishing the results of his successful excavations at Nineveh and Babylon, Layard achieved celebrity status in early Victorian Britain. In Laird's poem, however, the archaeologist comes across as a contradictory figure. The early stanzas depict him in hostile mood, 'scattering' anyone who threatens his occupation. Anticipating the colonial administrators who would follow in his wake, he has arrived at certain conclusions about those whose cultural legacy, not to mention rights and territories, he has helped to appropriate.[184] Fearful that 'his' relics might be pilfered, he has no qualms about carrying out 'summary punishments' from time to time *pour décourager les autres*. When it comes to artefacts, however, he is delicate in his labour, easing 'pieces out from the flesh of the earth / as a midwife might' (11), so that they can be delivered intact into 'pale' hands in the British Museum, and their new, surrogate owners.

Subsequent sections move into pastoral terrain, casting the archaeologist – and readers – in the role of observers of nature. Oxen plodding along beside the riverbanks become symbols of timelessness, like the old horse in Thomas Hardy's 'Breaking of Nations' poem.[185] What disturbs the tranquil, companionable mood, generated by images of cattle lying down or 'ambling .../... between milking and darkness', are the monstrosities Layard uncovers by the north-west walls of the palace in Nineveh. With the head of a lion and body of a man, one such carving is the exact physiological opposite of Yeats's 'rough beast' in 'The Second Coming'. Monuments to imperial might, these part-human, part-lion, part-avian figures were created to instil fear, to warn those contemplating opposition or transgression of the swift, vicious retribution they could expect. Having established the predatory nature of the indigenous imperialist régimes (ancient Assyrian, modern Ba'athist), the narrator's focus turns to the *external* agents out to topple them. The 'voice from the south', which over-confidently predicts 'Nineveh's imminent demise is *simultaneously* that of the biblical prophet, Jonah, and the current American President, George Bush.[186] Interestingly, the Old Testament original stresses the humiliations and deprivations the Ninevite king and people endure in order to ward off destruction,[187] which prompts Yahweh to deal with them compassionately.[188] Laird's poem foregrounds those who make a swift profit from crisis. The 'saved' he speaks of might be identified as locals who have managed to survive the onslaught or Republican-backing, Christian fundamentalist, American entrepreneurs and their companies, rewarded with reconstruction contracts by a grateful administration.

In part three, the cattle reoccupy centre stage, their passive demeanour contrasted with the frenetic comings and goings of the empowered – money-men, prophets, warriors, an unnamed 'white man on horseback' (Layard?), and 'the slip of a cowherd' – coward? – 'who keeps them'.[189] Docile, resigned, 'pool-eyed' watchers, they are themselves a recurrent object of the narrator's observations. The answer to his own question has the effect of humanising them, but also of registering them in the long history of cruelties inflicted by humans on their own kind and kine. 'They catalogue hurt' (12).

Imperialist discourse, then and now, privileges its own, and fails to differentiate between the natives. Underlining this point, the poem's closing section, like its first, begins naming another interloper. A successor to Layard, and beneficiary of his project, Gertrude Bell (1868–1926) served in the Arab Bureau during the Great War and subsequently as 'Oriental secretary to the British military high command in Iraq'.[190] First world intervention in the Middle East is characterised as a casual affair. After an agreeable afternoon's riding in the desert, Bell is seen trailing 'a walking stick behind her', marking out the frontiers for the 'new countries' the victorious western powers brought into being. Yet their attempts at inscribing their presence in the region face repeated resistance, which Laird renders mainly in nature imagery. By moving 'under the borders', the rivers subvert them. Pitted against the 'kingdom of here', its 'relics', 'oilfields' and 'satellites', is an older, elemental technology which erases man-made lines in the sand. Momentarily, at this critical juncture, the narrative shifts from third to first person, implicating its readers in the recurring history of intervention it decries: '*We* are *again* among these ruins and the dying' (my emphasis). This, like the allusion to 'oilfields' and the reworking of one of T.S. Eliot's most famous phrases,[191] brings us very much into the twenty-first century and current 'grief' in Iraq. In speaking of 'Satellites mistaken for portents', the poem hints at the part played by faulty intelligence in the justification for the coalition invasion. Broken into its component parts, prefix and root, the participle epitomises much that has gone before in the poem and in history.[192]

Like that of his predecessors, Laird's work reflects a recurring concern with texts, textuality and intertextuality. 'Poetry' sets the self-reflexive agenda. Here the art-form is primarily envisaged as observation, the recapturing of fragmentary images and spots in time. In the first of a sequence of analogies, the speaker compares his art to the view from the top deck of a bus, in which everyone and everything is envisioned 'through my own reflection'. There is something distinctly Kavanaghesque in the way Laird intercuts the secular and the religious, and finds transformative potential in the everyday. The poem closes with a form of release, with an image of two unwieldy oak doors flapping open 'to let us out'. Like the building from which they leave (a church?), the poem resembles an 'injured bird trying to take flight' (5).

'The Riddles of the Ardcumber Book' sees the poet donning a scholarly persona, as well as indulging in a little post-structuralist play. At the outset its speaker informs us that he has spent the previous 20 years of his life on a recently discovered theological text which incorporated in its margins a sequence of riddles composed 'in a rustic Latin'. The fact that it is the marginalia which has fired his passion is, of course, highly significant, especially given Laird's own cultural 'provenance'. Interspersed in the academic's discourse are tantalisingly short, enigmatic fragments from the Dark Ages. Thus, in the midst of a comprehensive dismissal of previous scholarship on the riddles as either scant or slipshod, he slips into the text in brackets and italics quotations from his fictional primary text. Despite dismissing others' speculations on the anonymous author's identity, he is prepared to offer his own, picturing him as 'a cowherd bedded in heather', or perhaps as a Gaelic laird, an escapee from the massacre, 'waiting out time / far from the burning and bloodshed'. That the riddler's word-games have had a salutary, even salvatory effect on the academic is suggested by his cryptic reference to falling. Like myth, and like art,

> the riddle springs from the need to vest life
> in the garb of the coldly fabulous. (33)

Having listed a delightfully disparate range of alternatives, the speaker asserts that the solution to the conundrum is not as one critic claims, 'God', but rather 'riddle', yet then immediately attacks the idea of there ever being a definitive answer. Poetry lies in the 'seeking', he concludes, and readers should shun those making dogmatic statements as to its meanings.

At times 'pitched closer to anger than wonder' ('An Appendix'), *To a Fault* is a book which delights and impresses. Poems like those discussed above will not look out of place in future anthologies, and reflect the continuing strength in depth of Northern Irish poetry. This is exemplified in two other début collections published in the past two years, Leontia Flynn's *These Days*, awarded the Forward Poetry Prize for the best collection of 2004, and Alan Gillis's *Somebody, Somewhere*, which received the 2005 Rupert and Eithne Strong Award for a best first collection and was shortlisted for the prestigious *Irish Times* Poetry Now Award. Leontia Flynn's work is often highly self-reflexive, and features personas who are wry, savvy and smart. Midway through *These Days*, for example, she introduces us to her dream mentor, who is forthright about what it takes to coin success in the poetry market. Abrasiveness sells well, he suggests: 'If you can fashion something with a file in it for the academics/to hone their malicious nails on – you're minted'.[193] The acute sense of displacement registered in Sinead Morrissey's 1990s poetry, composed while violence was still raging, is largely absent from Flynn's work, much of which appears to circle around family, domestic spaces, everyday objects, albeit 'under a ticking', intermittently 'bewildered sky'.[194] Significantly, 'Naming It', the opening piece in *These Days*, transports us from 'the gloomiest most baffled/misadventures'[195] into a sudden 'clearing' where the unfamiliar can be relished. Mercurial, lyrical, street-wise and wry, her poetry exemplifies a quality she praises in an ex-partner, the ability to 'take the clockwork out of things', to strike 'a new sound from a dud motor'.[196]

Equally impressive is Alan Gillis's first foray into verse. A high-point in *Somebody, Somewhere*, 'Progress' offers a wry, but moving reflection on not-so-distant times in Northern Ireland, and one worth quoting in full. Its initially somewhat uncertain, tentative narrator imagines the traumatic violence of the last four decades being suddenly, miraculously, put

into reverse.[197] As so often in Laird's and Flynn's poems, register and diction
veer between the informal/conversational ('it's great now', 'So I guess')
and formal/lyrical ('explosively healed', 'coalescing into the clarity'):

> They say that for years Belfast was backwards
> and it's great now to see some progress.
> So I guess we can look forward to taking boxes
> from the earth. I guess that ambulances
> will leave the dying back amidst the rubble
> to be explosively healed. Given time,
> one hundred thousand particles of glass
> will create impossible patterns in the air
> before coalescing into the clarity
> of a window. Through which, a reassembled head
> will look out and admire the shy young man
> taking his bomb from the building and driving home.[198]

The poem deploys a simple idea, one which so easily might have descended
into embarrassing and tasteless whimsy. Yet like Laird's, Morrissey's and
Flynn's, Gillis's control of his material is exemplary, compelling readers
to contemplate once more the devastation and horror which so recently
afflicted somewhere which is and is not 'home'.

NOTES

The notes to Volume 2 include short references to titles already cited in full in Volume 1.

Introduction

1. J. Hillis Miller, *Hawthorne and History: Defacing it* (1991), pp.152–3.
2. For an account of the rationale behind this two-volume study of Northern Irish literature and its selection of particular texts, see the Introduction to Volume 1.
3. Declan Kiberd, *Inventing Ireland* (1996), p.4.
4. Seamus Heaney, *The Cure at Troy* (1990), p.77.
5. Preface, *New Ireland Forum Report*, 2 May 1984, cain.ulst.ac.uk/issues/ politics/nifr.htm.
6. Speech by Peter Brooke, 9 November 1990, qtd in Thomas Hennessey, *The Northern Ireland Peace Process*, p.69.
7. In a note to the author, 27 November 2003, Nicola Nemec describes how she was 'born during a particularly unpleasant spell of the Troubles. The neighbour who ran my mum to the hospital that night still reminds me every time I see him that he risked his life getting me there on time'.
8. Interview with the author, 1 August 2002.
9. Edna Longley, *The Living Stream*, p.55.

1 Name upon Name: 1975–1986

1. McKittrick and McVea, p.114, note the fall in Army casualties in these years. Whereas over 250 soldiers were killed between 1971 and 1974, there were 29 deaths in 1975–76. These years saw a major reduction in numbers of civilians killed by troops, 20 in 1975–76 as compared with 170 in the previous four years.
2. Paul Durcan, 'In Memory: The Miami Showband: Massacred 31 July 1975', rptd in Ormsby's *A Rage for Order*, pp.202–3. The poem updates Bloom's confrontation with 'the Citizen' in *Ulysses*, Chapter 12.
3. *Lost Lives*, p.561.
4. Eoin McNamee's novel, *Resurrection Man* (1994), fictionalises elements of Murphy's killing career. See also *Lost Lives*, pp.921–4.
5. Ronan Bennett, in 'An Irish Answer', *Guardian: Weekend* , 16 July 1994, p.7, comments on the recurrence of charnel houses and abattoirs as locations and meat imagery in such texts as Kiely's *Proxopera* (1977), Mac Laverty's *Cal* (1982) and Madden's *Hidden Symptoms* (1986), all of which this chapter examines.
6. *Lost Lives*, p.612.
7. ibid., pp.611–12. For a discussion of Michael Longley's poem about this murder, see below, pp.23–4.

8. See McKittrick and McVea, p.123.
9. Bowyer Bell, p.475; *Lost Lives*, pp.663–4.
10. Qtd in Bishop and Mallie, pp.289–90.
11. 'The Peace Movement', letter to *Irish Times*, 3 November 1976.
12. Bishop and Mallie, pp.290–1; Moloney, p.363.
13. Statement by Corrigan and Williams, October 1976, qtd in Bishop and Mallie, p.290.
14. McKittrick and McVea, p.117.
15. Mason, qtd in McKittrick and McVea, p.119.
16. Mason, qtd in Moloney, p.149.
17. Bishop and Mallie, p.321.
18. See White, pp.190–6.
19. That positions had not changed since the collapse of power-sharing is apparent from Part III of the Convention Report, 'The Way Ahead: Continuing Political Activity'. Paragraph 153 states that

   the UUUC remains convinced that maximum stability will be obtained with a Prime Minister and executive, chosen on conventional Parliamentary lines. The SDLP and other groups favour a 'power-sharing' or 'coalition' system. This is the basic difference of view. In addition, the SDLP supports an institutional link between Northern Ireland and the Republic, in relation to security and other fields, whereas the UUUC regards such a link as undesirable window-dressing which prevents proper attention being given to greater co-operation from the Republic on security. (cain.ulst.ac.uk/convention/nicc75report/htm)

20. By the strike's third day, the RUC had received over a thousand complaints about intimidation.
21. *Lost Lives*, p.721.
22. Moloney and Pollok, pp.378–9, point out that the DUP doubled its representation of councillors. The UUP lost 35 seats, while the other two parties linked to the UUUC experienced meltdown.
23. McKittrick and McVea, p.121. See also Moloney, pp.151–2, English, pp.217–18.
24. *Republican News*, 18 October 1975, qtd in English, p.181.
25. Moloney, pp.150–1.
26. McKittrick and McVea, p.128. See also English, p.244.
27. Qtd in Jack Holland, p.129.
28. ibid., p.130.
29. These points appear in an Army intelligence assessment from November 1978, which fell into PIRA hands. McKittrick and McVea, p.131.
30. Moloney, p.157. Opposition to this proposal is discussed, pp.158–61
31. See below.
32. *Lost Lives*, p.744.
33. ibid., p.746.
34. McKittrick and McVea, p.129. Gerry Adams, in *Before the Dawn* (1996), pp.263–4, speaks of being 'depressed by the carnage and deeply affected by the deaths and injuries'. Immediately after this admission, he adds 'I could also feel two years of work go down the drain'.
35. Padraig O'Malley, *Biting at the Grave: The Irish Hunger Strikes* (1990), p.21.

36. See *Lost Lives*, pp.728, 730, 736, 771. On 12 December 1978, three prison officers' wives were injured when parcel bombs arrived in their homes (Bew and Gillespie, p.131).

37. Tom Hadden, 'The Blanket Brigade', *Fortnight* 153, 16 September 1977, rptd in *Troubled Times*, pp.41–2.

38. Bishop and Mallie, p.352.

39. Qtd in McKittrick and McVea, p.140.

40. *Lost Lives*, pp.799–802.

41. Holland, p.152. A White Paper produced by Humphrey Atkins, the new NI Secretary resulted in talks involving the DUP, SDLP and Alliance, but these broke down by the end of March 1980, and were boycotted by the UUP.

42. Qtd in Bew and Gillespie, p.136.

43. IRA statement, 2 October 1979, ibid., p.137.

44. The first of these, *Land without Stars* (1946), had been a tale of two brothers, one an IRA man, who is finally killed fleeing from the RUC.

45. Michael Kenneally, 'Q & A with Jennifer Johnson', *Irish Literary Supplement*, 3:2 (1984), 27.

46. Joseph McMinn, 'Contemporary Novels on The Troubles', *Études Irlandaises*, 3:5 (1980), 117.

47. Here Kiely recalls the IRA's murder of Judge Rory Conaghan on 16 September 1974, murdered in front of his eight-year-old daughter (see *Lost Lives*, p.475).

48. Laura Pelaschiar, *Writing the North: The Contemporary Novel in Northern Ireland* (1998), p.71; Elmer Kennedy-Andrews, *Fiction and the Northern Ireland Troubles: Deconstructing the North* (2003), p.74.

49. Benedict Kiely, *Proxopera* (1988), p.3. All quotations are from this edition.

50. Pelaschiar, p.74, defends the allusion on extremely dubious grounds. On pp.26–7 of *Proxopera*, we learn that the lake contains the body of a murdered publican, which hardly makes it comparable to a site where approximately 32 000 people died.

51. Kennedy-Andrews, *Fiction*, p.74, notes how the line resurfaces on pp.25, 27, 93 of *Proxopera*, along with variations: 'the world will never be the same again' (34), 'that pub would never be the same again' (68), 'that spring will never be the same again' (76).

52. ibid.

53. These suicides are cited again on pp.80, 81, 83.

54. Kiely, in an interview for the *Irish Literary Supplement*, 6:1 (Spring 1987), 10, describes the Omagh of his childhood as a place without bigotry, pointing out how two of the town's leading Protestants opposed the introduction of gerrymandering there.

55. Catullus, *Carmina*, v.

56. His first sexual conquest, Mary Cluskey, is named (37). Women are generally peripheral and anonymous in the text, with the exception of Minnie, his defiant, aged housekeeper.

57. See Chapter 3, note 36.

58. John Keats, 'Ode to a Nightingale', stanza II.

59. Pelaschiar, p.77.

60. References to 'cowboy country' (14) and Corkman 'blowing into his pistol' (22) similarly diminish the sense of threat. In the 1987 *ILS* interview, 11,

Kiely mentions how the initial idea for *Proxopera* came after reading a newspaper account of how a proxy bomber in Kesh turned round his car and drove at the gunmen, who took to their heels: 'This incident brought an element of the Keystone Cops into an abominable situation'.

61. The gunmen are compared with other archetypal figures, including Guy Fawkes, Lundy (35), and Cain (36).

62. He seems unconscious of the irony of what he says; Binchey, whom he is sending to kill and possibly to be killed, is one of *his* own.

63. The rapist, Peter Cook, wore a hooded mask during a series of eight vicious attacks over spring and summer 1975.

64. See above, p.1, note 1.

65. Kennedy-Andrews, *Fiction*, p.75.

66. Ironically, he believes that he is being watched throughout the journey.

67. To claim, as Pelaschiar does, p.77, that 'violence and death' are merely 'evoked', 'yet kept far from the pages of *Proxopera*' is to ignore the power and significance of these crimes.

68. The titles of the plays mentioned are all heavily ironic, '*The Coming of the Magi, The Plough and the Stars, The Shadow*, God help us, *of a Gunman*'(78).

69. See Vol.1, Chapter 4.

70. 'We feel in England that we have treated you rather unfairly. It seems history is to blame' (Joyce, *Ulysses*, p.17).

71. William Cullen Bryant (1794–1878). The ballad begins: 'Chained in the market-place he stood / A man of giant frame / Amid the gathering multitude / That shrank to hear his name'. The chief, the brother of the King of the Solima nation, eventually became mad when his captors refused to accept ransom for him.

72. T.D. Sullivan (1827–1914). The final verse of 'God Save Ireland' begins: 'Never till the latest day shall the memory pass away / of the gallant lives thus given for our land'.

73. Binchey's son has just been handcuffed and beaten by the IRA men.

74. Horslips, 'Time to Kill', *The Tain* (1973).

75. The schoolboy principal in Barry Hines's novel, *A Kestrel for a Knave* (1968).

76. It has become routine, for example, for children to pick up pebbles on their way home in case they run into any soldiers (19). Later, Joe and Kathleen encounter a shopkeeper who has been robbed so frequently that he closes up early to avoid being caught on his own premises (58).

77. Kennedy-Andrews, *Fiction*, p.228.

78. Christine St Peter, in *Changing Ireland: Strategies in Contemporary Women's Fiction* (2000), p.105, stresses the significance of failed masculinity in the text.

79. Her language echoes that of the equally disillusioned Pegeen Mike at the end of Synge's *Playboy*: 'There's a great gap between a gallous story and a dirty deed' (144).

80. Kennedy-Andrews, *Fiction*, p.228, argues that her role is to provide 'a powerful humanist lament at the tragic effects of political violence'.

81. Kathleen cites her parents' antipathy to northerners; they were 'never too keen on the North ... They looked on the border as a sort of necessary protection' (88).

82. Later, p.186, when his mother asks the name of Brendan's girl, Joe withholds it and denies his own intimacy with her.

83. Her parents belonged to different faiths and classes; her mother was a Protestant and teacher, her father, a Catholic and publican (54, 89).
84. Joe suspects from his first glimpse of her that 'she was ... staring at the inside of her head' (23); later she confides to him how she talks 'too much. To myself all the time' (90).
85. On Joe's first visit to her flat, she speaks of her fear 'of something awful happening' (55).
86. The mid-1970s witnessed a surge in the number of women's groups, North and South. Margaret Ward's article, 'Feminism in the North of Ireland', *HU* 83, Summer 1987, 59–70, highlights the wide range of social and political issues addressed by activists in the Coleraine Women's Group (founded 1974), the Northern Ireland Women's Group (f.1975), the Socialist Women's Group (f.1976) and the Belfast Women's Collective (f.1977).
87. See Pelaschiar, p.61.
88. 'I wrote a photographic rather than a real book. Nothing was, in effect, totally true ... Basically, what I should have confronted was not the little boy ... The character in the book I should have been looking at was Brendan ... It turned out to be quite a charming story about a little boy ... The British all say this is brilliant, and this is Derry city as it really is. That's not true' ('Q&A with Jennifer Johnson', 26).
89. The handling of this is unconvincing. Johnston employs a rhetoric which seems inappropriate for a twelve-year-old boy: 'What have I done? Deliberate destruction. I hated him. Only because ... for some nameless reason. Some reason I don't understand. Father I have sinned ... I have told the truth only to destroy. I too am destroyed. So forever is the destroyer destroyed' (p.184).
90. Frank Tuohy, 'Destroyers' Derry', *Times Literary Supplement*, 15 April 1977, 451.
91. Amongst notable examples of earlier elegies to individual victims are James Simmons's 'The Ballad of Gerry Kelly' (*Poems 1956–1986*, p.123) and Padraic Fiacc's 'The Ditch of Dawn' (*Ruined Pages*, p.143).
92. For discussions of these poems, see, for example, Jahan Ramazani, *Poetry of Mourning: The Modern Elegy from Hardy to Heaney* (1994), pp.344–9, Corcoran (1986), pp.136–8, Vendler (1999), pp.60–5, or Parker (1993) pp.159–64.
93. Ramazani, p.12.
94. Michael Longley, *The Echo Gate* (1979), pp.12–13.
95. See above, and footnote 46.
96. *Lost Lives*, pp.474–5. His killer stood trial in April 1977 and was given a life sentence.
97. 'The huge irony of textual death should be borne in mind: textual death is a production of absence, of nothingness, of something beyond the limits of the sayable or the writable' (Herron, 'Body in the Post', p.196).
98. Jim Gibson's wife was carrying a child at the time of the murder. See *Lost Lives*, p.406.
99. McDonald, p.136, comments that these 'nouns are meant to soothe, though they cannot (and do not) pretend to console'.
100. See above.
101. See above.
102. *Macbeth*, II, iii, 115.
103. For an extremely insightful reading of the 'Wreaths' sequence and its motifs of 'dispersal', see Herron, pp.197–9.

104. As Willy Maley has pointed out in 'Varieties of Nationalism, *Irish Studies Review*, 15 (Summer 1996, 34–7), nationalism embraces 'a complex range of discourses, often contradictory and confused' and should not be regarded as 'a flat homogeneous whole'. In a piece for *Magill* in December 1980, Friel affirms that 'There will be no solution until the British leave this island', then adds that 'even when they have gone, the residue of their presence will still be with us'.

105. Sean Connolly, in 'Dreaming History: Brian Friel's *Translations*', *Theatre Ireland*, 13 (1987), 43, argues that Friel gives a grossly distorted picture of the Survey which 'made a very substantial investment in the investigation of the Irish language, culture and antiquities'. Amongst those who praised its work in 'raising the level of national consciousness' was Thomas Davis, one of Young Ireland's foremost figures.

106. Jackson, p.84.

107. Friel, 'In interview with Paddy Agnew', p.86.

108. Brian Friel, *Excerpts from a Sporadic Diary*, 1 June 1979, in *The Writers: A Sense of Ireland*, ed. Andrew Carpenter and Peter Fallon (1980), p.59.

109. ibid., 22 May 1979.

110. '*Translations* and *A Paper Landscape*: Between Fiction and History', *The Crane Bag: The Forum Issue*, 7:2, 1983, 122.

111. Qtd in Terence Brown, *Ireland*, p.51. The author of a study of the hedge-schools in penal times, Father Corcoran, Professor of Education at UCD, was one of Gaelic's most influential advocates. However, as Roy Foster 'piquantly' notes in *Modern Ireland*, 'Father Corcoran ... did not himself speak Irish' (p.639).

112. Michael Tierney, 'The Revival of the Irish Language' (March 1927), qtd in Terence Brown, p.53.

113. ibid., p.189.

114. Flann O'Brien, *An Beal Bocht* (1941), rptd 1988, p.49.

115. Terence Brown, p.192. According to statistics cited in The *Irish Times*, 24 June 1968, in 1938 Irish was used to teach all school subjects in 30 per cent of the Free State's secondary schools. By 1968 this had dropped to 8 per cent, and 72 per cent of schools did not teach any subject through Irish.

116. For an account of this partial revival in Gaelic's fortunes, see Terence Brown, pp.230–1. On the state of the language since the 1970s, see Kiberd, pp.568–70.

117. Mairead nic Craith, *Plural Identities–Singular Narratives: The Case of Northern Ireland* (2002), p.151.

118. Adams, p.246. One of the most proficient Irish speakers in Long Kesh was Bobby Sands, according to Eamonn Mallie, qtd in O'Malley, p.45.

119. See Volume 1 Chapter 3, pp.158–62, 162–4.

120. Qtd in Terence Brown, p.193.

121. 'Interview with Paddy Agnew', pp.85, 87.

122. Edna Longley, *Poetry in the Wars*, p.191. Sean Connolly, p.43, similarly describes the portrayal of the hedge-school prior to the English soldiers' arrival as 'so unrealistic and idealised as to cast doubt, not only on his history, but also on his art'.

123. Pilkington, p.216.

124. Manus for Maire ('How will you like living on an island?'(424)); Sarah for Manus ('Manus ... Manus! (430)); Jimmy Jack for Athena (443).

125. 'There's ten below me to be raised and no man in the house' (394).
126. 'I brought the cow to the bull three times last week but no good ... The auld drunken schoolmaster and that lame son of his are still footering about in the hedge-school, wasting people's good time and money' (389).
127. Sean Connolly's claim, p.44, that Friel presents Baile Beag's community as 'passive victims' of 'cultural and military imperialism' is clearly inaccurate given Doalty's gesture, Manus's hostility, and Maire and Owen's positive responses to the English.
128. According to nic Craith, p.123, the impetus to learn English in the 1830s 'came as much from parents as from their teachers'. See also Kiberd, p.616.
129. To them, he is Roland (407). In medieval legend, Roland appears as a rash young man, whose fatal self-belief, during an ambush, resulted in his own death and that of his companions.
130. 'I read into O'Donovan's exemplary career ... the actions and perfidy of a quisling ... Thankfully that absurd and cruel reading of O'Donovan's character and career was short-lived. But it soured a full tasting of the man' ('*Translations* and *A Paper Landscape*', 123).
131. 'The status of *native* is a nervous condition introduced and maintained by the settler among colonized people with their consent' (Jean-Paul Sartre, Preface to Fanon's *The Wretched of the Earth*, p.20).
132. Moments before he had mistranslated Maire's sardonic enquiry, reassuring Yolland that 'she's dying to hear you' (407).
133. 'I hope we're not too – too crude an intrusion on your lives' (407); 'Some people here resent us' (413); 'It's an eviction of sorts ... Something is being eroded' (420); 'Would anybody object if I came?' (425).
134. J.H. Andrews, *A Paper Landscape*, p.135, emphasises O'Donovan's passion about the accuracy of names. He protested if asked to decide on a name without visiting the place.
135. Cairns and Richards, pp.148–9, claim that Owen makes 'a clear statement of intent to join with Doalty and the Donnelly twins in some form of armed resistance'.
136. That their activities are shrouded in silence is apparent from Doalty and Bridget's initial references to them (393). Their subsequent 'appearances' are invariably linked to criminal acts and an anti-English posture (398, 413, 436, 442).
137. MAIRE: Say anything at all. I love the sound of your speech.
    YOLLAND: Go on – go on – say anything at all. – I love the sound of your speech. (427)
138. Pilkington, p.209.
139. The ACNI contributed £40 000, the Arts Council of Ireland £10 000. (Morash, p.235).
140. He addresses the hedge-school assembly as if addressing children, and appears to believe that if spoken loudly enough English is intelligible to foreigners; somewhat improbably, he is unable to distinguish Latin from Irish (405).
141. Significantly her home is situated '*above* where we're camped' (413). In their love-scene, he admits to spending 'his days either thinking of you or *gazing up* at your house'(429).
142. To Yolland Hugh represents an alternative 'father'.

143. The year in which Friel was working on *Translations* saw the publication of a very successful fictional account of the 1798 Rising, Thomas Flanagan's *The Year of the French* (1979).

144. *Translations* is deeply engaged with the idea of cultural distinctiveness and the difficulties of 'crossing borders', yet its very language demonstrates the permeability of cultures. As Pilkington, p.213, points out, there is considerable irony in Hugh's scornful comments about the 'plebeian' nature of English and claims that 'Gaelic and classic culture make "a happier conjugation"; his actual formulation of this view is an etymological pedagogy that demonstrates exactly the opposite: that it is English, not Irish, that has extensive roots in Greek and Latin'.

145. Friel may be recalling here Montague's concluding stanza to 'A Severed Head', one of *Translations'* literary forebears: 'A high stony place ... / Not milk and honey – but *our own*: / From the Glen of the Hazels / To the Golden Stone may be / *The longest* journey / I have *ever* gone' (*RF*, p.40; my emphasis).

146. Virgil, *Aeneid*, trans.W.F. Jackson Knight (1968), p.27.

147. Heaney, *North*, p.73.

148. Murray, *Twentieth Century Irish Drama*, p.212, notes how in her last scene Maire makes no allusion to Manus's disappearance.

149. Kiberd, p.615, argues that here Friel demonstrates his grasp of 'the realities of politics' and 'the truth of Foucault's thesis that "discourse is the power which is to be seized".'

150. An Appendix in Richard Pine's study of Friel, *The Diviner*, pp.359–63, places quotations from *Translations* alongside their sources in Steiner's *In Bluebeard's Castle* (1971) and *After Babel: Aspects of Language and Translation* (1975).

151. Shaun Richards, in 'Placed Identities for Placeless Times: Brian Friel and Postcolonial Criticism', *Irish University Review* 27:1, Spring/Summer 1997, 55–68, challenges the critical consensus on Hugh's centrality.

152. For a full account of Northern Irish, Irish and English critical responses, see Richtarik, pp.51–63.

153. Edna Longley, in 'Including the North', *Text and Context*, Autumn 1988, 20, criticises the omission of Ulster Protestants from the depiction of Ireland's past. However, as Richtarik notes, p.52, the absence of a sectarian component to the conflict may have contributed to the play's success with northern audiences.

154. '*Translations* and *A Paper Landscape*', pp.120–1. Pilkington, p.218, avers that 'extensive historical references' in the programme notes for the Derry, London and Dublin productions fostered the impression that the play was 'grounded, unproblematically, in fact'.

155. ibid., p.122.

156. ibid., p.124.

157. Kiberd, p.630.

158. Marilynn Richtarik, 'The Field Day Theatre Company', in *Twentieth Century Irish Drama*, ed. Richards, p.191.

159. Friel, 'In Interview with Ciaran Carty', rptd in *Essays, Diaries, Interviews*, p.81.

160. ibid., pp.83–4.

161. Richard Kearney, 'The IRA's Strategy of Failure', *The Crane Bag*, 4:2, Winter 1980, 62–70.

162. O'Malley, p.25.
163. English, p.194.
164. Statement by the Maze Governor, 14 January 1981, qtd in English, p.195.
165. Bobby Sands (1954–81) had grown up on a mainly Protestant North Belfast estate. In his mid-teens, in the early 1970s, his family fled their home because of loyalist intimidation. After their move to West Belfast, Sands joined the IRA, was arrested in 1973 and given a three-year sentence. In 1977 he was again arrested and sentenced to 14 years after being stopped in a car that contained weapons. During his time in prison he became fluent in Irish and read voraciously, particularly the works of Connolly, Pearse, Fanon and Guevara. His ordeal and death turned him into a republican icon; a foil to the unyielding Mrs Thatcher. Marianne Elliott, in *Catholics of Ulster*, p.449, argues that he translated himself into a figure of Pearsean stature, 'the noble rebel, battling against insurmountable odds'.
166. *The Diary of Bobby Sands*, qtd in English, p.198. O'Malley, p.51, cites lines from one of Sands' poems in which he talks of having 'To walk the lonely road / Like that of Calvary / And take up the cross of Irishmen / Who've carried liberty'.
167. The other hunger-strikers were Joe O'Donnell (PIRA), Martin Hurson (PIRA), Kevin Lynch (INLA), Kieran Doherty (PIRA), Thomas McElwee (PIRA) and Michael Devine (INLA).
168. Holland, p.156, quotes a letter from Adams to Sands: 'Bobby, we are tactically, strategically, physically and morally opposed to a hunger strike'.
169. O'Malley, p.60.
170. Holland, p.157, cites protests in the United States and Australia.
171. Bew and Gillespie, pp.148–9. Mrs Thatcher took an identical line when she informed the Commons of the death of the member for Fermanagh/South Tyrone: 'He chose to take his own life. It was a choice his organisation did not allow to many of its victims' (qtd in McKittrick and McVea, p.144).
172. O'Malley, p.63.
173. ibid., p.64.
174. ibid., pp.149–50.
175. White, p.223. John Hume warned Margaret Thatcher of the grim consequences for constitutional nationalism in Ireland if the strike continued and that Irish-American money would again pour in to the IRA's coffers.
176. Bernard Mac Laverty, interviewed by the author, Glasgow, 18 October 1987.
177. All references are to the 1984 Penguin edition.
178. In a letter to the author of 10 May 2005, Bernard Mac Laverty states that he began writing *Cal* 'on Monday, 26 October 1981. I averaged somewhere between 500–1000 words per day until the first draft (about 48,000 words) was finished on Monday 28th December 1981'.
179. From p.37 it is clear that Cal's initiation into republican myth came at his mother's knee. He recalls her singing with gusto 'Roddy McCorley', 'The Croppy Boy' and 'Father Murphy'.
180. See above, pp.6–7.
181. Skeffington uses the same phrase about Crilly, p.40.
182. For a discussion of links between voyeurism and violence, and Mac Laverty's use of photographic imagery, see Richard Haslam's 'The Pose Arranged and Lingered Over', in *Contemporary Irish Fiction*, eds, Harte and Parker, pp.192–12.
183. He creams off part of the proceeds of the off-licence robbery on p.62.

184. O'Malley, p.119.
185. Father Benedict in *Lamb* voices an identical stance towards individual loss, as Haslam, p.202, observes.
186. The Provisionals fire-bombed the Linen Hall Library, Belfast on 31 December 1993, along with ten other sites. Minor damage was done to the library, which includes a substantial archive relating to republican tradition, which the bombers might well have destroyed.
187. See Volume 1 Chapter 4, pp.220–1. Reference to the bombings occurs in Marcella's diary, where she says it makes her 'deeply ashamed of my country'. Joe Cleary, p.252, believes the text reflects 'a complex sense of guilt' among nationalists 'about their own continued investment in the goal of reunification' because of the Provisionals' atrocities.
188. Cal tells Marcella that Ireland 'will only have a future when the British leave' (118).
189. Marcella states that her late husband was a serial adulterer and that her mother-in-law only employed Cal in order 'to prove to the world that she was not bigoted' (114). Dunlop's endorsement of Hitler's methods for dealing with opponents (110–11) invites comparison with Skeffington's.
190. Kennedy-Andrews, *Fiction*, p.91. When I first interviewed him in 1987, Mac Laverty spoke of his keenness to find a three-letter name for his protagonist, one that would match or counter existing names such as 'IRA, UDA, UVF'.
191. Appropriately the music cassette Cal chooses at the novel's start is by Muddy Waters (14, 16).
192. Bernard Mac Laverty, interviewed by Robert Allen, 'In Print', nd.
193. After the initial glimpse of a 'small and dark-haired' woman 'with very brown eyes' (12), his eyes focus on her hands (16), legs, heels, breast (71), elbow (72), right foot (73), the nape of her neck (91).
194. Cleary, 241.
195. Richard Kearney, reviewing *Cal* in the *Irish Literary Supplement* 2:2, 1983, 24, comments that 'The overriding sense of ineluctable doom ensures that the characters are deployed as quasi-mechanical props in the author's scenario. Even Oedipus, one feels, had more room for maneuver'.
196. A highly successful, three-part adaptation of Emile Zola's novel was broadcast by the BBC in 1979.
197. Kennedy-Andrews, *Fiction*, p.91. He rather overstates his case referring to the lovers occupying a 'chocolate-box scene of bucolic bliss', particularly since the 'the ugly realities of the outside world' (p.88) are always close at hand.
198. Haslam, p.199.
199. In her diary entry for November 1974, Marcella maintains that people in Northern Ireland have developed a degree of immunity as a result of repeated exposure 'to the most horrific events' (127).
200. Kearney, 'The IRA's Strategy of Failure', 62.
201. McKittrick and McVea, p.146.
202. Derek Mahon, 'Afterlives', *The Snow Party*, p.1.
203. *The Good Friday Agreement* (April 1998), clause 5, in *The Long Road to Peace*, ed. Marianne Elliott (2002), p.223.
204. Qtd in *Republican News*, 5 November 1981.
205. *Lost Lives*, pp.886–7. In reprisal for Bradford's murder, the UVF initiated a sequence of random killings of young Catholics on 15, 17 and 24 November.

206. Mark Urban, *Big Boys' Rules: The SAS and the Secret Struggle Against the IRA* (1992), p.86.
207. Qtd in McKittrick and McVea, p.162.
208. Statistics taken from Bew and Gillespie, pp.166, 172, 180–1, 186.
209. Preface, *New Ireland Forum Report*, 2 May 1984, cain.ulst.ac.uk/issues/politics/nifr.htm.
210. Qtd in Bardon, p.750.
211. Kevin Boyle and Tom Hadden, *Ireland: A Positive Proposal* (1985), p.101.
212. McKittrick and McVea, pp.164–5.
213. 'A united Ireland was one solution. That is out. A second solution was confederation of the two states. That is out. A third solution was joint sovereignty. That is out'. Mrs Thatcher, qtd in Bew and Gillespie, p.185.
214. Qtd in Bardon , p.755.
215. Holland, pp.188–9, emphasises the role of President Reagan in persuading Thatcher to adopt a more conciliatory stance.
216. *The Anglo Irish (Hillsborough) Agreement*, November 1985, in Elliott, *The Long Road to Peace*, p.195.
217. ibid., p.196.
218. For a later response to McCusker's speech, see Chapter 2.
219. Qtd in Bew and Gillespie, p.193.
220. McKittrick and McVea, p.164.
221. In the Dáil, approval for the Agreement was by narrow margin, 88 votes in favour to 75 against. The Labour Party Senator, Mary Robinson, had earlier resigned from the government on the grounds that the accord would be 'unacceptable to all sections of unionist opinion' (qtd in Bardon, p.757).
222. Although set at the time of the 1974 Ulster Worker's Strike, Stewart Parker's play, *Pentecost* (1987) contains several unionist characters whose disaffection and recalcitrance seem contemporaneous in origin.
223. Seamus Mallon, the SDLP's deputy leader, won Newry and Armagh. His party only chose to contest four marginal seats.
224. *Lost Lives*, p.1035.
225. Moloney and Pollak, p.397.
226. Bardon, p.765.
227. Moloney and Pollak, pp.398–9.
228. Qtd in *Lost Lives*, p.1043.
229. Qtd in Bardon, p.767.
230. *Lost Lives*, p.1054.
231. Speech of 18 November, ptd in *An Phoblacht/Republican News*, 21 November 1985.
232. English, p.242.
233. Qtd in Eamonn Mallie and David McKittrick, *The Fight for Peace* (1997), p.42.
234. Michael Frayn, *Copenhagen* (2000), p.94.
235. Urban, p.151.
236. ibid. *Lost Lives*, p.926, does not name Tighe's companion. Urban, on p.154, writes that McCauley had been named by an informer as an accomplice of Burns and Toman in the Kinnego bombing.
237. See above.
238. Urban, p.153. On 25 April 1987, Lord Gibson and his wife were killed close to the border by a massive Provisional IRA landmine.

239. Bardon, p.780.
240. John Stalker, *Stalker* (1988), p.253. After 1983, the SAS and the Army's 14th Intelligence Company took over the role of the RUC's Special Support Unit, killing 20 members of the Provisionals over the next four years.
241. According to Urban, p.158, Peter Taylor concludes in his 1991 documentary on the subject that Stalker's removal 'was unconnected to his criticisms of the RUC'.
242. Stalker, qtd in Holland, p.178.
243. English, p.238.
244. Patrick Magee, in *Gangsters or Guerillas?: Representations of Irish Republicans in 'Troubles Fiction'* (2001), pp.113–14, provides statistics illustrating the surge in the publication of fiction by women.
245. All references are to the Blackstaff edition of 1984.
246. See Colette's comments about feeling 'ashamed' of her writing (22).
247. At the novel's close, as a result of Joe's fellow paramilitaries' actions, Colette is left fatherless too.
248. Margaret Thatcher's Conservative party employed the slogan 'Labour isn't working' in its bid to gain power in 1979, yet under her administration unemployment exceeded three million by 1983, a rise of 141 per cent.
249. He uses the word and its variants four times in his opening entry.
250. This partiality emanates largely from her choice of narrator.
251. Joe's next diary entry (7–8) reveals that Sam's relationship with Vera is not wholly political. Later Gerry laughs at Joe's assertion that Sam is 'a one-woman man' (23).
252. On p.15, Joe is similarly depicted looking down from the hills at the city. All he sees, however, are lights and districts in need of 'defending'.
253. 'Is there one who understands me?' is the question Joyce posed to Nora Barnacle in September 1904 to ascertain whether she might be willing to leave with him for the continent. The question features also in *Finnegan's Wake* (1971), p.62, and is the title for an acclaimed RTE documentary on Joyce broadcast in 1982.
254. Later, on p.42, Christopher and Lin disappear to bed, abandoning their guests.
255. Unflatteringly, he had compared his mother earlier to 'a big hen', who 'Makes me feel I've just hatched out of an egg' (18).
256. St Peter, pp.101, 108.
257. Anne Devlin, *The Way Paver and Other Stories* (1986), p.119.
258. Ricoeur, qtd. in Onega and Landa, p.134.
259. ibid.
260. An Eden, it becomes a site of betrayal, like Gethsemane.
261. Many of the streets Finn names were attacked by loyalists during the riots of summer 1969.
262. It could be argued that apart from her grandmother no one loves Finn unconditionally.
263. She later notes how 'he pronounced Parnell with a silent "n", so that it sounded strange' (98).
264. Both withhold crucial facts. Her relationship with Jack had ended some time ago. It is only after his and Finn's relationship has intensified that he discloses the extent of his relationship with Susan.

265. Countess Markievicz (1868–1927) took part in the Easter Rising and was the first woman to be elected to the Westminster Parliament. The fact that the judge's son does not recognise her from her portrait suggests limitations in his familiarity with Irish history.

266. The twin themes of exogamy and betrayal feature also in Devlin's plays, *Ourselves Alone* (1986) and *After Easter* (1994).

267. Longley, *The Living Stream*, p.55.

268. T.W. Rolleston, *Myths and Legends of the Celtic Race*, p.140.

269. On p.109, she informs her interrogators that the judge was the real target.

270. At the beginning of the film, Jude acts as the bait in the IRA's kidnapping of a British soldier, Jody. She is depicted as an utterly ruthless operative, responsible later for a high-profile assassination attempt in London.

271. Deirdre Madden, *Hidden Symptoms* first appeared in *Atlantic Monthly* in 1986. Citations here are from the Faber 1988 edition.

272. Robert's mother has died only six years previously (38). Another of the novel's principal characters, Kathy, has been led to believe 'that her father died when she was a baby' (23), though it later emerges that this is not the case (96–7).

273. Salman Rushdie, *Midnight's Children* (1982), p.9.

274. John Wilson Foster, *Colonial Consequences* (1991), p.31.

275. Significantly twins figure in both her first two novels. A recurring feature in her fiction is her use of alternating narratives, whose doubling effects are intensified by repeated shifts backwards and forwards in time.

276. Madden tends to be oblique in her handling of political material in the text, yet at a number of points the pull of originary allegiances is strongly felt. See, for example, pp.16, 45–7, 75–6.

277. Coincidentally perhaps, the image features in Margaret Atwood's *Surfacing* (1997; first published 1972), p.18.

278. Such is his alienation from his working-class origins, that he feels compelled to shower after each visit to her home, to wash off the 'smell of poverty' (p.17).

279. At the novel's close, Robert comes to value his sister and her family, which he sees as 'a living souvenir of an age lost and gone' (114).

280. Clifden is the resort where her parents spent their honeymoon. Theresa's unsentimental attitude to her parents' past contrasts with that of Francie Brady, the protagonist of Patrick McCabe's novel, *The Butcher Boy*.

281. Gerry Smyth, in *The Novel and the Nation*, p.119, maintains that Francis is the 'most important figure' in *Hidden Symptoms* and presupposes that Francis's religious views are privileged in the text. For me, Theresa is its principal focus of interest, other characters serving to provide contrastive perspectives to hers. Madden's characterisations voice a variety of political and religious positions, none of which can be assumed to have authorial endorsement.

282. One of the last scenes reverses this situation when Theresa approaches Robert in the library at the very moment when he is reading a newspaper account of Francis's death and funeral (132–3).

283. During her spat with the playwright the focalisation shifts momentarily to Robert, who repeatedly in the novel attributes to her a phallic power: '(E)ach statement was a *goad* ... and *honed* to cruel *sharpness* before being *lunged* with heartless success at its *target*' (27: my emphasis). See also Robert's later

speculation that 'To embrace' Theresa 'would be like driving an iron spike in his chest' (65).

284. See George Eliot's *Middlemarch* (1974), Chapters 19–22. This phase of the novel finds the Casaubons honeymooning unhappily in Rome. Like Theresa, Dorothea senses a future of 'desolation' which she in part attributes to 'her own spiritual poverty' (224).

285. *Remembering Light and Stone* (1992), p.2.

286. ibid., p.32.

287. There is a certain irony in her reaction in that the urban population in Northern Ireland has been the subject of a massive surveillance operation for years, as part of the British government's efforts to maintain 'security'.

288. George Orwell, *Nineteen Eighty Four* (1983), p.244.

289. The word 'idly' masks within itself the word 'idol'.

290. See, for example, the scene when she arrives drunk at Robert's flat and informs him of Kathy's secret. It would appear to be motivated by her possessive feelings towards Kathy, her only close friend, but also by a desire to wound him (106).

291. On pp.30–1, Robert is caught speculating on his feelings if Kathy were to be killed in a bomb-blast, and discovers in the process that 'he did not love her'. Twenty pages later, Theresa pictures her mother 'having half her head blown away by a stray bullet', or with her body smashed into pieces after a bombing (50). Lest such fantasies should be simply dismissed as 'ghoulish', the text reminds the reader that 'for so many people' in Northern Ireland during the Troubles such sudden, catastrophes constituted everyday 'reality' (30).

292. 'The allegorist must acknowledge the dangers of the medium and the possibility that instead of leading to divine revelation, his own figurative discourse could replace the love of God with an inordinate enjoyment of its own metaphors' (Rufus Wood, *Metaphor and Belief in The Faerie Queene*, p.128).

293. Earlier that same day Francis had already called into question the quality of kinship ties. 'No matter how good family and friends are, they can't look at you absolutely in the eye always and forever; it's never perfect, never total. Other people never understand fully and never love fully' (p.54).

294. Barthes discusses the distinctions between 'writerly' and 'readerly' texts in *S/Z* (1970). A 'writerly' text is one which requires the reader to generate their own interpretations, to become producers rather than consumers of meaning.

295. Another mysterious incident which might be merely a case of mistaken identity or a hint at Theresa's repressed desire occurs when Robert tries to put the drunken Theresa to bed in his flat: 'When he put his arm around her waist to heave her into the bedroom, she hadn't even known who he was. Three times she had called him "Francis" ' (p.108).

296. Christine St Peter, letter to Michael Parker, 26 March 1999.

297. Madden, *The Birds of the Innocent Wood* (1988), p.125.

298. The memorial prayer in the Catholic Order of the Mass asks that God 'Look with favour on your Church's offering and see the Victim whose death has reconciled us to yourself', and explicitly links the sacrifice of Christ with that of subsequent 'martyrs and saints'. The depiction of the living Mrs Cassidy mourning over her dead son on p.43 anticipates the *Pietà* scene on p.55.

299. A further instance of this, and of the text's concern with repressions of all kinds, comes in the television documentary referred to on pp.72–3, which conceals more than it reveals.

300. Smyth, p.120. I am dubious as to whether Theresa's confused state of mind or the exposition of her faith (pp.137–8) would promote a surge of religious piety.
301. See note 273, above.
302. The novel's 'present' and past are primarily set in the period between late June/early July and September. Francis and Theresa's European trip takes place in July, his killing and the christening of Rosie's baby in September (122).
303. Derek Walcott, 'The Schooner Flight', *Collected Poems 1948–1984*, p.350.
304. It is possible to link this final image of Theresa to one of the first in the novel. Symbolically rummaging through the attic, she discovers an old and favourite doll, Rose, with '*Empire made* stamped on the nape' (2). With its seam running across its 'moulded head', the doll clearly is analogous to Theresa, as postcolonial and feminist critics would be quick to point out.
305. All references are to the 1987 Faber edition.
306. Lance Pettitt comments, in *Screening Ireland: Film and Television Representation* (2000), that 'the plays are strong on delineating the generalised socio-economic conditions that produce filial conflict, wife beating, male street violence and unemployment, but few links are made between character and the wider community or the political contexts of their environment' (235).
307. It was awarded the Samuel Beckett Prize in 1984.
308. In Bob Flynn's 'A Peace of their Mind', *The Guardian*, 7 June 1996, 4–5, Graham Reid states that his experience as a ward orderly at Musgrave Park Hospital was 'what drove me to writing'.
309. For an account of the huge, overwhelmingly positive response to the play, see Jonathan Bardon's *Beyond the Studio: A History of BBC Northern Ireland* (2000), pp.103–6.
310. Inexplicably that opened with an encounter between two low-level UDA paramilitaries.
311. See p.158. *A Coming to Terms for Billy*, scene 31, includes a good-humoured exchange between Pauline, Norman and Mavis about the Twelfth of July celebrations. All three view the Twelfth as a charming folk festival/heritage event (157).
312. Murray, in *Twentieth Century Irish Drama*, pp.202–3, argues that by eliding sectarian issues Reid's early plays 'disguise rather than illuminate the politics of the North'.
313. 'MAVIS: (*Getting in front of* NORMAN) Norman, will you please go to bed. I can take care of myself'. (158)
314. It is worth noting that the *Billy* plays were actually written in London.
315. Pettitt, p.236.
316. Amongst Field Day's foremost opponents was the critic Edna Longley, whose *Poetry in the Wars* contains important critiques of literary texts from both traditions. See also Volume 1, Chapter 4, pp.250–1, note 363.
317. Grene, *Politics*, p.244.
318. McGuinness was born in Buncrana, Co. Donegal, in 1950.
319. Interviewed for *The Independent*, 27 September 1989, McGuinness states that the play was partly inspired by seeing war memorials in Coleraine which listed the names of the dead.
320. See above.
321. Roche, p.271.
322. 'The Healing Touch', *Sunday Independent*, 21 April 2002. 'I don't feel terrorised by it but I do think that whatever form of sexuality you are involved

in you must remember that this awful disease is part of the landscape ... And lots of people I know did die from Aids ... I never wanted to write an "Aids play" ', but the reality of Aids is in the writing'.

323. Grene, *Politics*, p.246, identifies similarities between McGuinness's play and Arnold Wesker's *Chips with Everything* (1962), which focuses on nine men undertaking their National Service in the RAF. One of them, Pip Thompson, is, like Pyper, highly educated and from an aristocratic background.

324. The first word the Younger Pyper utters is 'Damnation' (13).

325. Grene, *Politics*, p.258, suggests that Pyper helped create the conditions which led to the present carnage in Northern Ireland, since his labours maintained an inequitable, illiberal, sectarian status quo.

326. *Samuel*, I, 18, describes the deep affection between David and King Saul's son, Jonathan: 'The soul of Jonathan was knit with the soul of David, and Jonathan loved him as his own soul' (v.1).

327. For Christ's image of the body as a temple, see, for example, *St John's Gospel*, 2, v.19–22.

328. Helen Lojek suggests that the apple serves as an invitation to 'the recruits and us to eat of the tree of knowledge and re-examine the tenets of inherited faith' (47–8). See 'Myth and Bonding in Frank McGuinness's *Observe the Sons of Ulster Marching Towards the Somme*', *Canadian Journal of Irish Studies*, 14, 1988, 45–53.

329. Moments earlier, holding up his cut thumb, he had asked Craig to 'Kiss it better' (14).

330. Roche, p.271, comments: 'The sexual difference according to Freud is a penis, which Pyper has already confounded by attaching it to a woman'.

331. It emerges on p.54 that Crawford's mother was a 'Fenian', and that he may have been baptised a Catholic.

332. Although the text does not identify the bridge as Carrick-a-Rede, its location not far from Coleraine on the Antrim coast makes it the likeliest location for this scene.

333. Moore speaks of how Craig 'blew his own breath into Pyper's mouth' (53).

334. We never discover the nature of the 'evil' (47) Pyper 'carved out' in Paris, or the identity of the woman (53, 56) for whose death he was responsible.

335. Lojek, p.48, convincingly suggests Pyper's hostility to Carson and his 'dance' is connected to Sir Edward's role in the prosecution of Oscar Wilde.

336. There may be a faint echo of Shakespeare's Antony: 'Sometime we see a cloud that's dragonish, / A vapour sometime like a bear or lion ... / Thou hast seen these signs:/ They are black vesper's pageants' (*Antony and Cleopatra*, IV, xiv, 2–8).

337. Grene, *Politics*, p.249.

338. Lojek, p.50, argues that the episode 'is not funny at all, but edged, providing another Yeatsian image of parent murdering child, with obvious implications about what Ireland is doing to its future'.

339. Pilkington, p.222, emphasises the importance of this 'passionate devotion to place' amongst the play's Protestant characters.

340. Roche, p.269. For a perceptive, recent analysis of the motifs of recurrence and ghostliness in the play, see Tom Herron's 'Dead Men Talking: *Observe the Sons of Ulster Marching Towards the Somme*', *Eire-Ireland*, 39: 1, Summer 2004.

341. In Part Two, it should be recalled, Anderson was punched in the groin by Pyper (35), partly to avenge McIlwaine's attach on Crawford, partly to empha-sise the need to 'fight dirty' in war.

342. The Younger Pyper's final line is an echo of Craig's on p.58.

343. Kavanagh, 'The Hospital', p.153.

344. Paulin was born in Leeds, brought up in Belfast, and after gaining degrees at Hull and Oxford, became a lecturer in English at Nottingham University. McGuckian and Carson were both born in Belfast and educated at Queen's. In the early 1980s McGuckian taught English at St Patrick's College, Belfast, while Carson worked alongside Michael Longley in the ACNI. Their later work is discussed in Chapter 2.

345. See below, Chapter 2.

346. *Why Brownlee Left* was awarded the Geoffrey Faber Memorial Prize, and was selected as one of the four Poetry Book Society Choices of 1980. *Quoof* in turn became a PBS Choice.

347. For an illuminating discussion of the volume, particularly its American influences, see Clair Wills, *Reading Paul Muldoon* (1998), pp.61–85.

348. Kendall, p.17, quotes Muldoon attributing the failure of his first marriage to his own 'incorrigible immaturity'. A bow features on the cover of the 1985 paperback edition of *Why Brownlee Left*.

349. *Hamlet*, II, I, 66. Wills, *Reading PM*, p.66, emphasises Muldoon's suspicion of those committed to a *single* direction or grand narrative.

350. 'I myself grew up, through geography lessons, to think of Northern Ireland as a linen-weaving, ship-building Utopia' (Muldoon, in Haffenden's *Viewpoints*, p. 138). Frank Ormsby's 'Geography', in *The Ghost Train* (1995) – discussed in the next chapter – is almost certainly indebted to this earlier foray of Muldoon's.

351. Kendall, p.9, quotes from Muldoon's 'Chez Moy: A Critical Autobiography' in which the poet states that his father, 'received no secondary education, and throughout his life could read and write only with difficulty'.

352. cf. the narrator in 'Bran', p.12, who 'weeps for the boy on that small farm', embracing his labrador, 'Who knows all there is of rapture'.

353. The use of this word inevitably links Muldoon's poem to Kavanagh's 'Epic', *Collected Poems*, p.136.

354. Wordsworth, 'My heart leaps up', *Poetical Works*, p.62.

355. Wills, *Reading PM*, p.82, points the irony in JMPW's naming. 'Joseph Mary Plunkett was a poet, and friend of Patrick Pearse, and one of the sig-natories of the 1916 Declaration of Independence, who was executed in the Easter Rising'. She goes on to inform us that Ward (Mhac an Bháird) means 'son of the poet'.

356. Wills suggests it is because he is 'the school rebel and persistent truant' (81). The Master's question does not necessarily imply that JMPW is absent, however.

357. Rolleston, p.256.

358. Haffenden, p.136.

359. Wills, *Reading PM*, p.83.

360. ibid.

361. Auden, 'In Memory of W.B. Yeats', *Selected Poems*, p.82.

362. Muldoon, '7 Middagh Street', *Meeting the British* (1987), p.59.

363. See Foster, *Modern Ireland*, pp.530–1.

364. Edna Longley, *The Living Stream*, pp.259–60.

365. A riffle through poems immediately preceding 'The More a Man Has' yields references to a 'dessert' ('A Trifle'), a pickled womb and broiled heart' (from 'Last Poems'), a woman making 'wine of almost everything' ('Kissing and Telling'), varieties of mushrooms and a woman's 'entrails' ('Blewits') 'gin and Angostura bitters' ('The Destroying Angel') and 'Doctor Maw' ('Aisling').

366. Muldoon, *Poetry Book Society Bulletin*, 1983, rptd in *Don't Ask Me What I Mean*, eds Clare Brown and Don Paterson (2004), p.193.

367. An image highlighted by Wills, *Reading PM*, p.96.

368. The title comes from a famous quotation by Benjamin Franklin: 'Money never made a man happy yet, nor will it. There is nothing in its nature to produce happiness. The more a man has, the more he wants. Instead of filling a vacuum, it makes one'.

369. McDonald, pp.165–9, is illuminating on Muldoon's use of this form.

370. Muldoon may well be alluding to Spielberg's Indiana Jones, the hero of *Raiders of the Lost Ark*, one of summer 1981's hit films.

371. This repeats the scenario in 'Aisling', p.39. Squatting images feature in Heaney's 'Tinder' (*Wintering Out*, p.44) and Mahon's 'Entropy' (*Lives*, p.31), which favours the ironic over the apocalyptic: 'We have pared life to the bone / And squat now / In the firelight reading / Gibbon and old comics'.

372. 'Aisling', p.39.

373. The sonnet does, however, include an ironic apostrophe to the 'Child of Prague', a statue said to possess miraculous powers of intervention.

374. Kendall, p.113; Wills, *Reading PM*, p.94. Earlier in her book, p.34, Wills refers to 'the narrow-minded repressions associated with organised Catholicism', as if these were the only features of the religion.

375. Heaney, 'Traditions', *Wintering Out*, p.31.

376. *Shakespeare's Sonnets*, ed. Stephen Booth (2000), p.12.

377. See above, pp.XXX–X.

378. *Macbeth*, V, ii, 20–22.

379. It comes from a speech by Winston Churchill, during the 1922 debate on the Irish Free State bill, qtd by A.T.Q. Stewart, in *The Narrow Ground* (1977) p. 14, and by John Hume, in 'The Irish Question: A British Problem' in *Foreign Affairs*, 58:2, Winter 1979/1980:

> 'The mode of thought of men, the whole outlook on affairs, the grouping of parties, all have encountered violent and tremendous changes in the deluge of the world, but as the deluge subsides and the waters fall, we see the dreary steeples of Fermanagh and Tyrone emerging once again. *The integrity of their quarrel* is one of the few institutions that have been unaltered in the cataclysm which has swept the world. Other cataclysms have since supervened, and are themselves now forgotten, but "their quarrel" endures, now in a more grisly form than ever.' (My emphasis)

380. There may be an echo here of Heaney's 'The Grauballe Man', whose body 'seems to weep / the black river of himself' (*North*, p.35).

381. Brown and Paterson, p.193.

382. Seamus Heaney, 'The Pre-Natal Mountain: Vision and Irony in Recent Irish Poetry', in *The Place of Writing* (1989), p.52.
383. In Seamus Heaney's, *Sweeney Astray* (1983), p.21, the exiled king is depicted feeding off 'nature's pantry' at Glen Bolcain. Here like Gallogly in sonnet 18, he feeds off 'green-topped watercress', 'sorrels', 'berries' and 'wild garlic'.
384. See Chapter 3.
385. Sonnet 37, p.58, lists Gallogly's various aliases, which conclude with 'English'.
386. Montague, 'A Severed Head', *RF*, p.39. Interestingly, the penultimate stanza of 'The More a Man Has' alludes to 'a gallowglass / … from a woodcut/by Derricke'.
387. The most blatant examples of this tendency can be seen in Edna Longley's *Poetry in the Wars*, in which at one point she dubs Muldoon as 'a Joyce' in contrast to 'Heaney's Corkery' (p.208). Even Kendall occasionally slips into this mode: 'While Heaney *withdraws* from atrocity into *the abstract decencies* of Art and Life, 'The More a Man Has' derives its horrific *power* from a *dispassionate* voyeurism which records the mundane, the magical and the obscene alike' (97; my emphasis).
388. Neil Corcoran, 'A Languorous Cutting Edge: Muldoon Versus Heaney?', *Princeton University Library Chronicle*, 59:3, Spring 1998, 559–80.
389. Muldoon's horticultural use of 'pruned' contrasts perhaps with Heaney's application of the word to describe the beheaded girl of 'Strange Fruit', who is described as 'prune-skinned', with 'prune-stones' for teeth (*North*, p.39).
390. Wills, *Reading PM*, p.96.
391. Edward Hopper (1882–1967), a New York artist whose work had a considerable influence on Pop Art and the New Realist school. The Hopper 'picture' Muldoon evokes may be a composite drawn from 'Gas' and 'Portrait of Orleans', though neither of these possesses the 'spooky glow' found in one of his most famous paintings, 'Night Hawks'.
392. Kendall, pp.115–17, is particularly helpful in unpicking Muldoon's allusions to Frost, Bishop and R.L. Stevenson.
393. Robert Frost, *Selected Poems*, p.131.

2   Towards an Ending 1987–1995

1. Stewart Parker, *Dramatis Personae*, John Malone Memorial Lecture, 1986, 19.
2. That Parker had always seen drama in these terms is evident from his early journalism. In 'The Tribe and Thompson', *Irish Times*,' 18 June 1970, 11, he commends Sam Thompson's exemplary contributions to Northern Irish culture: 'All through his work flows a swift deep current of love for his people and a conviction of their giant potential, thwarted though it has been down the years'.
3. Richtarik, p.238, states that Parker's commission coincided with a decision to devote the next series of Field Day pamphlets to 'the Protestant idea of liberty'.
4. In the period in which Parker's play was being written, a new loyalist paramilitary group, Ulster Resistance (UR), began to make the headlines. UR was formed in November 1986 by the DUP's Ian Paisley and Peter Robinson, with the aim of opposing the Anglo-Irish Agreement.

5. All page references relate to Stewart Parker's *Three Plays for Ireland* (1989).
6. In an early article, in *Gown*, 9 November 1962, p.4, Parker decries the 'stifling' quality of life in the province, an expressionless place where 'everybody has been dead for years'.
7. The play and its location are certainly intended to be read as partly allegorical. On one level, Lily's house represents a paralysed status quo thrown into turmoil as a result of nationalist advances.
8. At different points in the narrative three of the four living characters arrive on stage bearing wounds, Ruth (158), Marian (189) and Peter (198).
9. In 'An Ulster Volunteer', *Irish Times*, 6 March 1970, 11, Parker refers to the leg-wounds his grandfather acquired on Passchendale Ridge and at Hellfire Corner during the First World War.
10. His fate mirrors that of Clifford Chatterley in D.H. Lawrence's *Lady Chatterley's Lover* (1928).
11. Her brief sexual encounter on the front-parlour sofa is repeated by Peter and Ruth (189).
12. Parker's stage directions establish the fact that Lily is partly a construct Marian has generated; Marian, we are told, is *'aware that her mind is playing tricks on her'* (155).
13. Roche, p.223, rightly identifies the significance of Lily's unfinished knitting. This represents the dead woman's narrative, which Marion unravels and 'completes'.
14. At his death he was five months old. It is perhaps no coincidence that Faulkner's power-sharing administration survived for an identical length of time.
15. On p.163, Marian refers to Ruth's 'first miscarriage', brought on by David's violence.
16. Parker, Introduction to *Three Plays for Ireland*, p.9.
17. Parker, *Dramatis Personae*, 19.
18. During an early verbal tussle between them, Marian states that Ruth's husband's sadistic behaviour predated the Troubles and his police career (163).
19. Words and music by Ira Gershwin and Vernon Duke. Those familiar with the song would appreciate the irony of this choice, since the opening verse ends, 'I've got a place, a show house / But I can't get started with you'.
20. When Marian enters, her first act is to switch off Lenny's tape recorder which has provided him with a backing track.
21. This was the month in which Parker returned to Northern Ireland after five years of teaching in the USA.
22. In more recent times, disaffected nationalists and republicans have identified themselves with the Palestinians, unionists with the Israelis.
23. See Volume 1, Chapter 3, pp.165–6.
24. See Volume 1, Chapter 4, p.219. It is ironic that Ruth should object to Wilson's reference to 'spongers', given that she and Peter are currently both taking advantage of Marian's goodwill.
25. 'Shipyard Bible-thumpers, unemployed binmen, petty crooks and extortionists, pigbrain mobsters and thugs' (184).
26. Retrospectively, Lily imagines her lover as 'a dark angel' (197), a Tempter who carried her skyward.

27. Nicholas Kent, in *Fortnight* 278 (1989), ed. John Farleigh, reminds readers how each of *Pentecost*'s living characters are 33-years old, 'the age of Christ crucified'.
28. I am grateful to Paul Livesey for this information.
29. Julia Kristeva, in *Powers of Horror* (1982), writes that for the *abject* 'discourse will seem tenable only if it ceaselessly confronts that otherness, a burden both repellent and repelled, a deep well of memory that is unapproachable and intimate' (p.6).
30. Elmer Kennedy-Andrews, in 'The Will to Freedom: Politics and Play in the Theatre of Stewart Parker', in *Irish Writers and Politics*, eds Okifumu Komesu and Masaru Sekine, pp.267–8, criticises Parker's deployment of this 'battery of stories', arguing that the 'self-conscious break with naturalism' which they initiate diffuses the energy the play has amassed.
31. See Volume 1, Chapter 2, p.95.
32. *St. John's Gospel* 8, v. 3–11.
33. *Acts*, 2, v.1–21.
34. Marian's reference, on p.201, to the used condom she found behind the parlour sofa reminds the audience of how Ruth has recently strayed in committing adultery.
35. Murray, in *Twentieth-Century Irish Drama* p.220, refers to the 'strain on a contemporary audience' imposed by characters reading aloud from the New Testament.
36. She makes an implicit analogy between herself and the biblical Peter, but also the Peter in the play who, in despising his place of origin, betrays himself.
37. Roche, p.228, observes that this gesture replicates the one between Marian and Lily on p.197.
38. Tom Paulin, *Writing to the Moment: Selected Critical Essays* (1996), p.x. Paulin is describing the contents of his essay collection, rather than his poetry.
39. One recalls 'the movement of guns' in Paulin's 'Settlers', *A State of Justice* (1977), p.8.
40. Paulin, 'A New Look at the Language Question', rptd in *Ireland and the English Crisis*, p.191.
41. ibid., p.187.
42. ibid. p.186. Several paragraphs later, on p.188, he refers to homelessness as a defining element in the contemporary 'loyalist imagination'.
43. See Friel's 1984 comments on the 'fifth province', qtd in Richtarik, p.245.
44. See Chapter 1, p.47.
45. André-Marie Chénier (1762–94) was of part-French, part-Greek origin. Known primarily for his political journalism, his poetry was only published in 1819, long after his death on the guillotine. The work of Marina Tsvetayeva (1892–1941), Anna Akhmatova (1889–1966) and Vladimir Mayakovsky (1893–1930), which Paulin translates and adapts, was deeply marked by the political, moral and aesthetic convulsions generated by the Revolution and its aftermath.
46. In 'Involved Imaginings', an essay in Corcoran's *The Chosen Ground*, Bernard O'Donoghue identifies the 'chucked lover' in the poem as Margaret Thatcher (p.184). While allusions to submarines, torpedoes and yomping might lend some substance to this suggestion, the fact that the split

between the couple occurs in July, not November, makes it doubtful that the poem's 'hidden' subject is the Anglo-Irish Agreement.

47. 'A state of ruin' (*Shorter Oxford English Dictionary*, Fifth edition, p.3052). The word is first recorded in the early nineteenth century, and chiefly occurs in Scotland and Northern England.

48. Many unionists regarded the imposition of the Agreement as adding insult to earlier injury.

49. Although Paulin's narrator only encounters *one* armoured car rather than a convoy, the episode echoes that described in Heaney's 'The Toome Road', *Field Work*, p.15.

50. See 'Notes to Poems', *Fivemiletown*, p.67.

51. For an illumating analysis of the poem, see Neil Corcoran's 'Strange Letters: Reading and Writing in Recent Irish Poetry', in Paul Hyland and Neil Sammells's *Irish Writing: Exile and Subversion* (1991), pp.234–47.

52. *North*, pp.49–50.

53. In his eyes, the woman's breasts resemble the shape of 'the sloping fields'. Heaney's narrator is similarly fixated on the female body's 'gradual hills' and 'gash'.

54. Corcoran, 'Strange Letters', p.244.

55. Interviewed by John Haffenden in *Viewpoints*, Paulin twice refers to Orwell as a key early influence. See pp.158–9.

56. Discussing his second collection's title poem, Paulin says that he envisions the Irish past 'as a fixed museum' (*Viewpoints*, p.173).

57. The architectural guide he quotes, A.R. Rowan's *The Buildings of Ireland: North West Ulster* (1979), describes it as 'fancy', while the poem's narrator compares it to a cake.

58. Examples of this strategy can be found in the selection of Brathwaite's poems in Penguin Modern Poets 15 (1969) and in poems in his later collection, *Middle Passages* (1992).

59. The names of other locations to which he takes her are equally sexually charged: '*Horn*sea', 'Spurn' – sperm? – 'Head'.

60. Wills, *Improprieties*, p.146.

61. Harold McCusker, *Hansard*, 27 November 1985. The consternation of Paulin's unionist at what has occurred 'in our own province' echoes that of the republican school-teacher in Mac Laverty's *Cal*, speaking about Bloody Sunday: 'And we were all Irishmen living *in our own country*' (p.67: my emphasis).

62. These are 'cherished archaisms' used still in Northern Ireland, as Heaney notes in 'Traditions', *Wintering Out*, p.31.

63. Eamonn Hughes, 'Place in Tom Paulin's Poetry', in Graham and Kirkland, p.182.

64. McDonald, *Mistaken Identities*, p.104.

65. Thomas Hennessey, *The Northern Ireland Peace Process* (2001), p.49.

66. *Common Sense*, qtd in Hennessey, p.52. One of its authors, John McMichael, was murdered by the Provisional IRA in December 1987.

67. See Chapter 1, p.52.

68. Qtd in English, p.253.

69. Mallie and McKittrick, pp.46–7, state that the previous four, undetected shipments 'gave a new lease of life to the IRA and left it better armed than ever before in its history'.

70. Qtd in Bew and Gillespie, p.210.
71. Mallie and McKittrick, p.58.
72. English, p.255.
73. *Lost Lives*, p.1095; English, p.255.
74. *Lost Lives*, p.1096.
75. *An Phoblacht*, 19 November 1987.
76. Mallie and McKittrick, pp.79–82.
77. McDonald, interviewed in *Brangle*, 2, 1997, 39.
78. Peter McDonald, *Biting the Wax* (1989), pp.58–61.
79. *Romeo and Juliet*, III, i, 110.
80. In the *Brangle* interview, p.33, McDonald refers to the 'unintelligence and opportunism' of the media industry in the UK.
81. John Hughes, like McDonald, was born in Belfast in 1962. His first book, *Something in Particular* (1986), was followed up by *Negotiations with the Chill Wind* (1991).
82. Nicholas Carolan's review of *A Pocket Guide to Irish Traditional Music* (*HU*, 83, Summer 1987) makes no allusion to the fact that Carson writes poetry.
83. See Volume 1, Chapter 4, p.250.
84. The poem first appeared in *HU*, 79 (Autumn 1985), 3–6.
85. His first book's title poem presages his use of this form. In 'The New Estate' he speaks of 'the swaying lines / Of a new verse' (*Poets from the North of Ireland*, ed. Ormsby, p.185).
86. Herron, in 'The Body's in the Post', p.201, questions the categorisation of Carson's poetry as unproblematically postmodern. He suggests that it should read it as exemplifying 'a play of modern and postmodern, traditional and innovative, oral and semiotic' strains.
87. '... the RUC – or was it the RIC?' (12).
88. We are told first that the police 'Got wind of it', later that the arresting officer only got on the bus after an accident, and 'didn't know young Flynn from Adam' (12).
89. Carson is clearly interrogating Heaney's poetic legacy once more. Flynn's journey into place-names inevitably invites comparison with Heaney's in *Wintering Out*. One of McGinty's lines, '*Tell me, an educated man like you*' (original emphasis) echoes that of the victim in 'Casualty': ' Now you're supposed to be an educated man' (*Field Work*, p.23). In 'The Ministry of Fear' (*North*, p.64), Heaney refers to days when 'the leather strap / Went epileptic' in his much more privileged school.
90. *St Matthew's Gospel*, 19, v.14.
91. Corcoran, in 'One Step Forward', from *The Chosen Ground*, p.221, rightly points out that 'Horse is a mule too'. More problematic, given the scale of carnage, is the comparison he goes on to make between what Horse does 'for England to beautiful, strategically insignificant Dresden' and 'what poor farcical Flynn would do to England for his idea of Ireland'.
92. Allied estimates are that 35 000 civilians died in the Dresden raid of 13 February 1945, though German estimates are considerably higher. Sir Arthur 'Bomber' Harris, the man behind Britain's saturation bombing policy, died in 1984, not long presumably before the poem was composed.
93. See above p.252, n294.

94. In Churchill's first speech as Prime Minister, on 13 May 1940, he stated that the aim of British policy could be summed up in one word, victory: 'victory at all costs, victory in spite of all terror, victory, however long and hard the road may be; for without victory, there is no survival ... no survival for the British Empire ... no survival for the urge and impulse of the ages, that mankind will move forward towards its goal' (www.winstonchurchill.org/i4a/pages/index.cfm).

95. Corcoran, 'One Step Forward', p.220.

96. Keats, 'Ode on a Grecian Urn'; Heaney, 'The Harvest Bow', *Field Work*, p.58.

97. The term 'Belfast confetti' is said to date from the 1920s and originally referred to nuts, bolts and pieces of scrap metal used to bombard Catholic workers in the shipyards. Since the onset of the later Troubles it has been used more loosely to refer to any material thrown by rioters or packed into nail-bombs.

98. Herron, in 'The Body's in the Post', pp.202–3, argues that Carson's dystopic representation of the waste-ground in 'Campaign' is central to his critique of nationalists and unionist ideology. Both traditions have in different ways iconised the field (Latin, *campus*), imagining it as a place redolent with 'integrity, wholeness' and 'tenure'.

99. cf. Anne Devlin's 'Naming the Names', p.118.

100. Patricia Craig's *The Belfast Anthology* (1999), pp.413–19, includes ten entries devoted to Smithfield.

101. Twelve years later, in the year before *The Irish for No* was published, a much smaller replacement building was erected on the Smithfield site.

102. Carson, 'A Sense of Place', www.bbc.co.uk/northern ireland/schools/11_16/poetry/senseofplace3/

103. Shane Murphy, in 'Sonnets, Centos and Long Lines' (*Contemporary Irish Poetry*, ed. Campbell, p.204), comments how in Carson's work the map functions 'as an *aide-memoire*, facilitating an ultimately doomed project of reclamation, retrieval and remembrance'.

104. 'Hamlet', the final poem in *Belfast's Confetti*, p.108, closes with an image of 'a cry, a summons ... / Like some son looking for his father, or the father for his son'.

105. The reference to prison is anticipated five lines earlier, when the son speaks of the 'cold *sharp shock*' (my emphasis) of icy spring-water. The phrase was applied in the early 1980s by Conservative ministers to the more punitive policy they intended adopting to deal with juvenile offenders.

106. The poem acquires a folk-tale ambience as a result of these repetitions.

107. 'The speech or eloquent silence of the father is an important motif in Northern Irish poetry' (Edna Longley, *The Living Stream*, p.65).

108. *Shorter Oxford English Dictionary*, Fifth edition, p.2780.

109. This is a reversal of the upward movement of stanza one.

110. Herron, in 'The Body's in the Post', p.202, commends the 'photographic clarity' of Carson's work.

111. Walter Benjamin, 'The Work of Art in the Age of Mechanical Reproduction', in *Illuminations*, trans. Harry Zohn (1992), p.230.

112. David Lloyd, *Ireland after History* (1999), p.50.

113. Glenn Patterson, *Celebration*, Granada Television, first broadcast 12 September 1993.

114. Glenn Patterson, *Burning Your Own* (1989). All quotations are from this edition.

115. John Goodby, in 'Bhabha, the Post/Colonial and Glenn Patterson's *Burning Your Own'*, *Irish Studies Review* 7:1 (April 1999), 65, 68, highlights 'a more general crisis of maleness' amongst the characters.
116. Statements with dual meanings recur throughout the novel. The important bonfire scene finds the teenagers engaged – like the province's unionist establishment – 'in a desperate attempt to sweep' the fire together again. But no sooner did they succeed in shoring up one spot, than another was undermined and subsided' (92). Towards the close, the patch where the bonfire stood is compared to 'a scab on top of a scab, re-opened yearly so that the grass would never heal' (203).
117. This motif, associated with familial repressiveness and violence, resurfaces on pp.118–19.
118. Kennedy-Andrews, *Fiction*, p.103, argues that Patterson's characterisation of Francy burdens him 'unconvincingly with all kinds of symbolic significance'. Certainly under his influence Mal experiences some amazing epiphanies for a ten-year-old.
119. This is first mentioned on p.45.
120. Patterson's indebtedness to Rushdie is acknowledged in *Peripheral Visions: Images of Nationhood in Contemporary British Fiction*, ed. Ian A. Bell (1996), p.151. Francy himself exists in mythic form in the imaginations of local loyalists. They tell stories about his trained rats, fed supposedly on 'miscarriages he stole from the hospital' (10).
121. Curiously Alex's role in the text has been largely ignored. No mention of her is made in Klaus-Gunnar Schneider's 'Irishness and Postcoloniality in Glenn Patterson's *Burning Your Own'*, *Irish Studies Review*, 6:1 (April 1998), 55–62, to which Goodby's article is a riposte. She is also omitted from Kennedy-Andrews' discussion in *Fiction*, pp.102–6.
122. Tsitsi Dangarembga's *Nervous Conditions* (1988) is mainly focalised through the eyes of a young girl, Tamba, sent to live with the family of her older girl-cousin, Nyasha. The increasingly tyrannical manner with which her uncle responds to Nyasha's sexual maturation resembles Uncle Simon's in *Burning Your Own*. Their confrontations leave Nyasha psychologically drained, and she becomes anorexic.
123. She does a 'cutesie' kind of Shirley Temple dance a few pages earlier, on p.121.
124. Alex is, of course, quoting another famous dissident, Stephen Dedalus, in James Joyce's *A Portrait of the Artist as a Young Man*, p.220.
125. Kirkland, p.49, writes of Belfast as 'a city haunted by myth … a city condemned to endlessly reconstitute its past'.
126. On p.113, Simon opines that 'your man Paisley was right: the Civil Rights is nothing but a bunch of IRA men and Communists'.
127. The prevalence of sectarianism on the estate is stressed in many earlier scenes. At the close of Chapter Seven, pp.85–92, local families gather round the Twelfth bonfire on which, in preference this year to the Pope, an effigy of '*Gerry Fitt, Agent of Rome*' is burnt.
128. Andy, p.177, had claimed that Mucker was sexually as well as politically impotent.
129. On p.131, it is revealed that Simon has a contract to build these houses. It would appear from hints on pp.187–9 and 198–9, that Mal's father is one of those who burnt them down.

130. See Francy's comments, pp.207, 215.
131. Not for the first time, Mal sees Francy and Alex as akin to one another (231). Goodby, p.69, is particularly informative on Francy's role in Mal's sexual initiation.
132. See Volume 1, Chapter 2, pp. 101–3.
133. Hume, qtd in Mallie and McKittrick, p.85 (my emphasis).
134. See *Lost Lives*, pp.1112–15.
135. ibid., p.1121–2.
136. *Lost Lives*, p.1143, notes that one of three, Gerard Harte (aged 29), had been questioned by the police about the Ballygawley bus attack. He is known to have been a friend of Mairéad Farrell.
137. Douglas Hurd, British Home Secretary, qtd in Bew and Gillespie, p.220.
138. *Lost Lives*, pp.1159–62.
139. See 'A Question of Truth?' (13 September 2004) and 'Finucane killer uncovered' (14 September 2004) on news.bbc.co.uk. The self-confessed murderer was sentenced to 22 years in prison on 16 September 2004. See also Taylor, *Loyalists*, pp.205–9.
140. Mallie and McKittrick, p.97.
141. See Volume 1, Chapter 4, pp.220–1.
142. On 14 March 1991, the Birmingham Six were similarly freed by the Court of Appeal.
143. Mallie and McKittrick, pp.97–8.
144. Martin McGuinness commended Brooke as the first Northern Ireland Secretary to show 'some understanding of Irish history' (qtd in McKittrick and McVea, p.276).
145. ibid., p.99.
146. ibid., pp.104–7. As Hennessey points out, p.70, the British representatives were members of the security services.
147. In a similar attack in Killeen, near Newry, a 21-year-old Royal Irish Ranger died; the proxy bomber survived with a broken leg.
148. Hennessey, *Peace Process*, p.69.
149. Mallie and McKittrick, pp.142–4.
150. Qtd in English, p.270.
151. Qtd in *Lost Lives*, p.1270.
152. Qtd in English, p.270.
153. For Gordon Wilson's account of this meeting, see Mallie and McKittrick, pp.168–9.
154. Hennessey, *Peace Process*, p.70, states that between February and November 1993 messages passed between SF and the British at the rate of one a week.
155. ibid., p.75.
156. John Major, qtd in Hennessey, p.75.
157. This phrase recurs in Draft 2 (June 1992), Draft 8 (March 1993), Draft 10 (May 1993). See Mallie and McKittrick, pp.411–20.
158. *Lost Lives*, p.1329.
159. ibid.
160. One of the two bombers, Thomas Begley, aged 23, died in the blast; his accomplice was severely injured.
161. See Volume 1, Chapter 3, pp.138–9.

162. Qtd in *Lost Lives*, p.1329.
163. ibid., p.1334.
164. See McKittrick and McVea, pp.194–5.
165. 'The Downing Street Declaration', in Elliott's *The Long Road to Peace*, p.207.
166. ibid.
167. ibid. Bew and Gillespie, p.285, state that the UUP leader, James Molyneaux, had a hand in drafting the final text.
168. Statement by republican H-block prisoners, qtd in English, p.273.
169. Loyalists killed 38 people, republicans 27.
170. TUAS was the acronym used in referring to the new strategy. Though originally taken to stand for a Totally Unarmed Strategy, 'it later transpired that the letters referred to Tactical Use of Armed Struggle' (English, p.283).
171. Feeney, p.405.
172. The UVF killed one of their own on 12 April for his alleged involvement in the murder of Margaret Wright, a 31-year-old Protestant woman, mistakenly identified as a Catholic. Two weeks later the IRA shot a man whom they alleged had been dealing drugs.
173. *Lost Lives*, pp.1373–4.
174. Qtd in English, p.286.
175. A *Belfast Telegraph* poll in early September found that 56 per cent of respondents believed the ceasefire formed part of a secret deal.
176. Qtd in Bew and Gillespie, p.295.
177. Taylor, *Loyalists*, p.233.
178. The comment on the dust-cover of the first edition states that much of Part One was 'prompted by the author's father death' (*Captain Lavender*, 1994). In fact the father's presence pervades the whole book.
179. 'My father had died between the time I was invited and the time I decided; he had joked about it being "the safest place in the country" … So I felt him with me' (*A Dialogue with Medbh McGuckian, Winter 1996–1997*, by Rand Brandes, *Studies in the Literary Imagination*, Fall 1997), 37–47. http://www.findarticles.com/p/articles/mi_qa3822/is_199710/ai_n8772942/
180. Hugh McCaughran was a primary school teacher from Ballycastle, and later became Vice-Principal of Holy Family School in Belfast.
181. 'I feel now that it was a step that moved my life on. That I have a different perspective and insight and a certain kind of trust in things that before frightened me. That it added a vital pinch of salt to my knowledge. That it exposed my poems to a new side of what other people suffered and I had been insulated from' (*Dialogue*, p.6).
182. ibid., p.9. Earlier in the interview, p.6, McGuckian refers to the 'living death' of the prisoners.
183. Edna Longley, *Poetry and Posterity*, p.310.
184. *Dialogue*, p.4.
185. Shane Murphy cites three less than positive reactions to McGuckian's poetry in the opening paragraph of ' "You took away my Biography": The Poetry of Medbh McGuckian', *Irish University Review*, 28:1 (Spring/Summer 1998), 110.
186. Clair Wills, *Improprieties*, p.50, argues that McGuckian's concern with gender inevitably makes her work 'political' since in Ireland especially 'women (the female body, sexuality and reproduction', are at the centre of public policy and legislation'.

187. Edna Longley, introducing her McGuckian selection in *The Bloodaxe Book of 20th Century Poetry*, p.329, suggests that her choice of epigraph may be a response to her exclusion from Ormsby's *A Rage for Order* (1992).

188. Guinn Batten, ' "The More with Which We Are Concerned": The Muse of the Minus in the Poetry of McGuckian and Kinsella', in *Gender and Sexuality in Modern Ireland*, ed. Anthony Bradley and Maryann Gialanella Valiulis (1997), p.226.

189. Cecile Gray, 'Medbh McGuckian: Imagery Wrought to Its Uttermost', in *Learning the Trade: Essays on W.B. Yeats and Contemporary Poetry*, ed. Deborah Fleming (1993), p.171.

190. McGuckian, letter to Stacia L. Bensyl, 8 February 1989, qtd in Murphy, 'Biography', p.120. She makes an identical point in conversation with Nuala Ni Dhomnaill, in 'Comhrá', *The Southern Review*, 31:5 (July 1995), 605–6.

191. I must acknowledge Shane Murphy's help in enabling me to begin negotiating McGuckian's poetry. In *Sympathetic Ink: IntertextualRelations in Northern Irish Poetry* (2006), Murphy stresses how McGuckian almost always gives her borrowed lines a new twist. On p. 48, he identifies 27 borrowings from the C.K. Scott Moncrieff and Terence Kilmartin translation of Marcel Proust's *Swann's Way* in *Captain Lavender*'s opening poem. In her recent study, *Consorting with Angels: Essays on Modern Women Poets* (2005), pp. 175–86, Deryn Rees-Jones demonstrates how from the outset of her career, McGuckian incorporated in her texts material from canonical male writers.

192. No poetic slouch himself, Sean O'Brien, in *The Deregulated Muse*, p.257, refers to the 'feelings of disorientation and irritation' McGuckian's work has generated particularly in 'some male readers'.

193. Batten, p.229, identifies several poems from *On Ballycastle Beach* (1988) and *Marconi's Cottage* (1991) which concern themselves with 'the breakage of porcelain, perhaps uterine, vessels'. If, as she suggests, these texts are in part attempts to come to terms with the loss of a child as a result of a miscarriage, this might further explain the intensity with which the poet deals with her father's loss.

194. In a sense the poem is a belated kiss to both parents. See 'Comhrá', pp.584–5.

195. In 'Mourning and Its Relation to Manic Depressive States', from *Love, Guilt and Reparation* (1984), p.362, Melanie Klein states that 'the characteristic feature of normal mourning is the individual's setting up of the lost loved object inside himself ... through the work of mourning, [he] is reinstating that object as well as all his loved internal objects which he feels he has lost'.

196. Light and breath are traditionally associated with the Holy Spirit. The candles, which figure in the titles of parts one and three, transmute themselves into stars later in the poem, 'moving forward meaningfully' (18).

197. His state echoes that of Wordsworth's Lucy: 'No motion has she now, no force; / She neither hears nor sees; / Rolled round in earth's diurnal course, / With rocks, and stones, and trees' ('A Slumber did my Spirit Seal').

198. Romantic literary texts, like Wordsworth's *The Prelude* and Shelley's 'Ode to the West Wind', invariably associate breath and air currents with art's animating, restorative powers.

199. The poem's female speaker in this and in many other poems in Part One clearly sees herself as the inheritor of male power, whose task it is to amplify the suppressed male voice.

200. Murphy identifies Osip Mandelstam's 'Journey to Armenia' (*The Collected Prose and Letters*, trans. Jane Gary Harris and Constance Link (1991), pp.344–378) as McGuckian's source text. In this essay, Mandelstam describes the tombs of the monks beside Lake Sevan 'scattered so as to resemble flowerbeds' (p.344).

201. Murphy detects a note of uncertainty in the speaker's optimism because of the use of the word 'ought', and previously 'somehow' ('Roaming Root of Multiple Meanings: Intertextual Relations in Medbh McGuckian's Poetry', *Metre*, 5, Autumn–Winter, 1998, 103). It is equally possible, however, to read McGuckian's words in the light of Romantic ideology, in which the artist has a responsibility not just to project the world as it is, but as it *should* be.

202. Mandelstam, 'Journey to Armenia', p.345, describes the Sevan peninsula as 'Homerically studded with yellow bones', left by local picnickers visiting the monastery.

203. 'These people *jangle the keys of* their *language* even when they are not unlocking any treasures', ibid., p.349 (my emphasis).

204. Related references in other poems suggest that this is another acknowledgement of her parents' contribution to her own music-making. At the beginning of her interview with John Brown (*In the Chair*, p.169), McGuckian states that her father did not in fact play the piano, though 'he was musical'. There are allusions to music in 'The Appropriate Moment' where she associates her father's mouth with music (20); 'Constable's *Haywain*' ends with 'four hands (ours) at one piano' (36); while repeated musical references occur in 'Black Note Study' (39–40), prompted by an early image of locks and a key.

205. This term is deployed by Viktor Shklovsky, in 'Art as Technique' (1917), rptd in Rice and Waugh, pp.17–21.

206. Interestingly, the poem that immediately follows celebrates the father as 'an Irish speaker', though in reality Hugh McCaughran 'never spoke Irish' ('Comhrá', p.608).

207. Her father's middle name was Albert.

208. Judas in Dante's *Hell* Canto XXXIV, line 57–60 (trans. Dorothy L. Sayers, 1968) endures a similar fate: 'claws that flayed his hide / And sometimes stripped his back to the last flake'.

209. *Dialogue*, p.6.

210. McGuckian's repeated assertions of his innocence (*Dialogue*, pp.6–7) legitimise this latter reading, which clearly conforms to a traditional nationalist assessments of British justice. The latter surfaces as an issue again in 'White Windsor Soap' (*Captain Lavender*, p.81), a poem inspired by the case of the Guildford Four.

211. In *Dialogue*, p.6, McGuckian compares the prisoner's writing to her father's 'flailing under the morphine'. She continues: 'I was not able to give him the freedom to walk but only to bare his feet as with my father's corpse, a sort of ceremony'.

212. McGuckian admits to Rand Brandes that her poem, 'White Windsor Soap', is 'a very selfish one ... using the innocent Birmingham Six or Guildford "bombers"' as a means of addressing her own feelings of bereavement (*Dialogue*, p.8).

213. Speaking of poetry as a form of transfiguration ('Comhrá', pp.595–7), she repeatedly refers to Catholic practice in order to articulate her strongly

feminised, aesthetic beliefs. One of the most astute readers of her work, Clair Wills, suggests that McGuckian aims to create 'a new symbolic order' in which she can operate as both 'mother and priest' ('The Perfect Mother: Authority in the Poetry of Medbh McGuckian, *Text and Context*, 3, Autumn 1988, 109).

214. *Word of Mouth*, ed. Ruth Carr, Gráinne Toibin, Sally Wheeler and Ann Zell (1996).

215. An image drawn perhaps from the opening of Tennyson's 'Mariana'.

216. Eilish Martin, *slitting the tongues of jackdaws* (1999).

217. A subject discussed in Neil Corcoran's 'A Languorous Cutting Edge'. In this, he cites Medbh McGuckian's description of Heaney as 'a wonderful mediatrix'.

218. Gráinne Tobin, *Banjaxed* (2002).

219. At the time of her co-editorship of *HU* and *The Female Line* she was Ruth Hooley.

220. Ruth Carr, *There is a House* (1999).

221. 'Feeling Small', p.18.

222. Carr recalls in one interview how she started writing at the age of 16. See Gillean Somerville-Arjat and Rebecca E. Wilson, eds, *Sleeping with Monsters: Conversations with Scottish and Irish Women Poets* (1990), pp.165–72.

223. Carr's trope of a new birth can be found also in other contemporaneous literary texts from Northern Ireland, such as Anne Devlin's *After Easter*, Deirdre Madden's *One by One in the Darkness* and Bernard Mac Laverty's *Grace Notes*, all written during the time of the 1994 August ceasefire.

224. See below, pp.127–8.

225. Interview with the author, 12 November 2003. Jennifer's husband received a five-year sentence for the crime.

226. *Poetry Ireland Review* 64, 37–40.

227. Interviewed by Annamay McKernan, *Tatler Woman*, 24 June 2002 http://www.carcanet.co.uk/cgi-bin/reframe.cgi?app = cipher& index = author

228. There may be an echo here of Ted Hughes's 'Crow's Account of the Battle', which similarly envisages a nuclear apocalypse. See *Crow* (1970), pp.26–7.

229. This image linked to nuclear war occurs once more in 'Thoughts in a Black Taxi', p.19.

230. Later in the volume, in 'My New Angels', she returns to this theme: 'My new angels are howling, hard,/ ... /For every snuffed out light on a back road' (52).

231. The word appears at a critical moment in 'The Juggler', p.56.

232. Earlier evidence of this unease about language comes in 'If Words' (p.55), which depicts words as 'unfortunates'. Their lack of fixity is commented on later when she describes how they 'spill like sewage and dismay'.

233. MacNeice, *Autumn Journal*, IX, in *Collected Poems*, p.119.

234. Note from Michael Longley to the author, 1 December 1998. The date of publication coincided with the anniversary of the outbreak of the Second World War.

235. That such acts of magnanimity are possible can be seen in Gordon Wilson's actions after his daughter's murder at Enniskillen. See above, pp.115–16 and 134.

236. Born 1947 in Enniskillen, Ormsby is one of many Northern Irish writers whose work is too little known outside Ireland. A highly-respected anthologist and editor – his stint as editor of *The Honest Ulsterman* is by far the

longest in the magazine's history – he has to date produced only three full collections, *The Ghost Train* (1995) being the third.

237. Ormsby's delicate metaphor contrasts with Milton's image of the Holy Spirit: 'with mighty wings outspread / Dove-like sat'st brooding on the vast abyss'(*Paradise Lost*, I, 19–20).
238. Heaney, *The Cure at Troy*, p.77.
239. Heaney, *Door into the Dark*, p.56.
240. Nobel Citation, 5 October 1995, http://nobelprize.org/literature/laureates/1995/press.html
241. Kavanagh, 'The Great Hunger', VII, *Collected Poems*, p.42.
242. Heaney, 'Mint', *The Spirit Level* (1996), p.6.
243. Bernard O'Donoghue, in *The Tablet,* 11 May 1996.
244. Tom Leonard, 'Unrelated Incidents, 3', *Intimate Voices: Selected Work 1963–1983* (1984).
245. Although not identified in the poem itself, Vendler, p.155, states that Heaney was visiting Denmark with his wife, Marie, at the time of the ceasefire.
246. www.bbc.co.uk/history/timelines/ni/rise_sinn_fein.shtml
247. Significantly 'open' is the last word in *The Spirit Level*'s final poem.

3   A Longer Road: 1995–2006

1. Qtd in Bew and Gillespie, p.306.
2. ibid., p.308.
3. A report published on 31 March 1995 cited 51 incidents of beatings carried out by republicans.
4. Bew and Gillespie, p.311.
5. Feeney, pp.414–5.
6. Bew and Gillespie, p.321.
7. Taylor, *Loyalists*, p.241.
8. Bew and Gillespie, pp.333–4.
9. An extremely gifted forerunner of the younger satirists is John Morrow, whose novel *The Essex Factor* (1982) and short story collection *Sects and Other Stories* (1987) are of considerable merit.
10. Bernard Mac Laverty, *Grace Notes* (1997), p.4.
11. The mirror motif has, of course, been a commonplace in Irish and other postcolonial literatures, ever since Stephen Dedalus's reference to 'the cracked lookingglass of a servant' (*Ulysses*, p.6).
12. Cate's journey home and the unborn baby represent a rejection of the anonymity, transience and purposeless energy which London now seems to embody for her.
13. Cate's decision is not dissimilar to that of Helen Flynn in Anne Devlin's *After Easter* (1994). Another successful, London-based professional, Helen similarly creates a new persona for herself. Though Helen's sisters – like Cate's – object to what they see as at worst a betrayal, at best an affectation, she merely observes that 'London isn't a good place to have an Irish accent right now. I find when I'm buying or selling an American accent gets me through the door. Whereas an Irish accent gets me followed round the store by a plainclothes security man' (9).

14. The novel follows closely key moments in the narrative of the recent Troubles, from the early civil rights marches (64–6) right up the negotiations which led to the peace process (149).
15. In Chapter Nine, we learn how in the 1950s for a Catholic woman teacher the decision to marry meant the end of her career. Emily Quinn rails against this injustice and the commodification of women within her own community (pp.121–2).
16. *The Birds of the Innocent Wood*, p.22.
17. This minor affliction, referred to on pp.61, 65, 70, is set up as an ironic contrast to the blood-letting that will haunt the sisters' adult lives.
18. The fact Madden gives greater prominence to this atrocity than to Bloody Sunday reflects changing nationalist perspectives in the 1990s.
19. The graduation photograph becomes an object of focus again on p.87, when Cate studies a copy of it in Helen's flat.
20. The Ormeau Road is, in fact, a fiercely contested site, divided into nationalist and loyalist sections.
21. When Cate returns to London, pp.91–2, following her father's murder, she learns that similar assumptions are made about his guilt..
22. From the outset (see p.7) Brian's home is ominously associated with the colour red.
23. cf. 'He tried to fix the picture, to snap the shutter' (*Cal*, p.92). Cate's observation on the frequency with which trees and telegraph poles are decked with religious texts – 'Where is your Bible?' and 'Repent!'(p.6) – recalls *Cal*'s opening paragraphs where we meet the Preacher.
24. A phrase used by George O'Brien, 'Capturing the Lonely Voice', *Irish Times*, 12 May 1995.
25. All references will be to the 1997 Vintage paperback edition. My interpretation of the text owes a great deal to discussions with Liam Harte in 2000.
26. Heaney, *Redress*, p.6. Taking a more critical stance on this tendency, Edna Longley makes a similar point in her review of Deane's novel, 'Autobiography as History', *Fortnight*, November 1996, 34.
27. Linden Peach, in *The Contemporary Irish Novel* (2004), pp.45–54, usefully applies insights from psychoanalytical theory to the text, in particular Freud's concept of *Nachträglichkeit* which Derrida revisited.
28. In the early phases of his quest, he is anxious over what might be disclosed and its impact: 'I said to him inside my closed mouth, keep your secrets ... But, at the same time, I wanted to know everything. That way I could love him more' (46).
29. Alongside the narratorial 'doubling', we are confronted with innumerable contrasts between characters, such as Eddie/McIlhenney, the narrator/his father, the narrator's mother/Katie (60).
30. Oscar Wilde, *The Importance of Being Earnest* in *Plays, Prose Writings and Poems* (1972), p.352.
31. A haunting literary presence in Deane's novel is Henry James, and in particular two of his stories, 'The Figure in the Carpet' and 'The Turn of the Screw'. 'Katie's Story' in *Reading* is a clearly a re-working of the latter Gothic tale.
32. For a discussion of *Reading in the Dark* as 'a novel about space', see Gerry Smyth's *Space and the Irish Cultural Imagination* (2003), pp.130–58.
33. T.S.Eliot, 'Little Gidding', *Four Quartets*, in *Complete Poems*, p.193.

34. A counterpoint to this moment of non-contact comes at the novel's close, after his mother has asked him to leave. The chapter ends, 'I moved away just as she put out her hand towards me' (224).

35. At the close of 'Feet', pp.17–18, he glimpses his sister's ghost in the church-yard.

36. Foster, in *Modern Ireland* p.282, states that the 'logical consequence of the 1798 rebellion' was the Act of Union between England and Ireland, which offered 'a structural answer to the Irish problem'. Deane's novel, like other nationalist texts, addresses the continuing consequences of that answer.

37. By persisting in his reading in the dark, the narrator quickens his mother's guilt and grief, and thus inadvertently contributes to her later dementia.

38. Deane edited Joyce's novel for Penguin Classics in 1992. *Portrait* appears as the first suggestion for 'Further Reading' in a guide to *Reading in the Dark* produced by Deane's publishers.

39. Joyce, *Ulysses*, p.17. Stephen Regan's review of *Reading in the Dark*, in *Irish Studies Review*, 19, (Summer 1997), 35–40, picks up strongly the Joyce connection.

40. Regan, p.40.

41. Interviewed for *English and Media Magazine*, 12 May 1997, 2–3, Deane states that he heard this story directly from his mother. When he showed his mother this section, she praised the writing, but denied being the source of the story.

42. The priest's anecdote provides an early instance of the text's many mis-recognitions.

43. See Volume 1, Chapter 1, pp.37–45. Liam Harte, in 'History Lessons: Postcolonialism and Seamus Deane's *Reading in the Dark*', *Irish University Review*, 30:1 (Spring/Summer 2000), 152, cites this episode as one of several instances of 'Official attempts to interpellate' the boy 'as a loyal, acquiescent citizen'.

44. 'When I was much younger and lay on the landing at night listening ... [I] leaned over the banisters and imagined it was the parapet and that I was falling, falling down to the river of the hallway' (26).

45. Peter Brooke's statement in 1990 that in the wake of the collapse of the Soviet Union Northern Ireland was no longer of strategic importance to Britain had a major impact on republican thinking and the peace process (see above, pp.135–8).

46. The date when the English established a garrison as a base from which to attack Hugh O'Neill and the O'Donnells.

47. Echoing the chaplain's talk of 'family quarrels' and McAuley's of 'internal disputes', the narrator wonders whether the conflicts in his own life might simply be the residue of 'a petty squabble'.

48. Harte's comment, 'History Lessons', p.53, fn 16, arises out of a conviction he and I shared that the reason may have been principally political.

49. The privations of the 1920s and 1930s, economic decline and unemployment in the 1950s, affected the whole province, though they were at their worst in Derry and Belfast.

50. Edna Longley, 'Autobiography as History', 34. She emphasises repeatedly the particularity of the Derry location, and most usefully outlines continuities running through Deane's critical and creative project.

51. The narrator's mother central role in this and many of the novel's other most important confrontations leads one to query Edna Longley's claim that the women in the text are 'mostly sobbing and speechless' ('Autobiography as History'). Three sections later her anger seems directed not just at her son, but at patriarchy in general, when she recites the following: '*If you want to, you can tell / If you don't that's just as well. / Get it over, get it done, / Father, lover, husband, son*' (217).

52. See Volume 1, Chapter 1, pp.71–3, Chapter 2, pp.72–81.

53. He claims that his colleague, Billy Mahon, was not responsible for the death of Neil McLaughlin, her father's friend (22–5).

54. One recalls Hugh's aphorism from *Translations*: 'To remember everything is a form of madness' (p.445).

55. Four extracts from the novel appeared in *Granta*, 'Haunted' in edition 18, Spring 1986, 'Feet' in *Granta* 23 (Spring 1988), 'Craigavon Bridge' in 37 (Autumn 1991) and 'Ghost Story' in 49 (Winter 1994).

56. Harte, 'History Lessons', p.155, speaks of the 'double oppression' suffered by the family, 'an aphonia conditioned by the ideologies of both unionism *and* nationalism' (original emphasis).

57. For additional examples of clerical cruelties, see 'Maths Class', pp.90–6, and the fleeting reference to Brother Collins's blows, p.227.

58. Unlike that anonymous pair, the novel's ghosts are always named. Deane himself has referred to his narrator as 'a young child who never earns a name', 'who never achieves sufficient identity' (Carol Rumens, 'Reading Deane, *Fortnight* July/August 1997, 30).

59. Harte, p.151, notes how Crazy Joe calls the narrator 'a little savage' and 'young Caliban' (82). The gypsy boy may be the narrator's alter ego, one capable of bypassing obstacles and the debris of history. Kennedy-Andrews characterises the gypsy boy as 'an ancestral figure of itinerant, rural freedom' and as 'a fugitive yet defiant spirit of place' (*Fiction*, p.223).

60. Deane, introducing the 'Autobiography and Memoirs' section of the *Field Day Anthology*, p.382, comments on how 'the local drags, in its retarding fashion, on the aspiration to transcend it'.

61. See *Lost Lives*, pp.1405–6.

62. McKittrick and McVea, p.215.

63. *Lost Lives*, p.1408, quotes at length Seamus Heaney's moving tribute to Brown, his family and work, published in the *Irish News*.

64. ibid.

65. Qtd in Feeney, p.419.

66. See Feeney, p.416.

67. Hennessey, *Peace Process*, p.110.

68. ibid., p.109.

69. *Report of the International Body on Arms Decommissioning*, 22 January 1996, drawn up by George Mitchell, John de Chastelain, Harri Holkeri.

70. English, p.296.

71. Bew and Gillespie, p.352.

72. See *Lost Lives*, pp.1423–5.

73. Tony Blair, March 1998, qtd in McKittrick and McVea, p.306.

74. George Mitchell referred to the killing in his address of 10 April, announcing the Belfast Agreement.

75. *Guardian*, 5 March 1998, 1. 'Death Across the Divide' was the lead front-page article on that day.
76. Qtd in Bew and Gillespie, p.355. One of those arrested for Allen and Trainor's murder, 23-year-old, LVF member David Keys, was found hanged in his cell on 15 March 1998; his wrists had been slashed and there were signs that he had been tortured before his death. Subsequently a dozen LVF prisoners faced charges for their involvement in the murder.
77. George J. Mitchell, *Making Peace* (1999), pp.143–4.
78. David Trimble, interviewed for *Endgame in Ireland*, directors Mark Anderson and Mick Gold (BBC 2, 2001) praises Ahern's dedication in returning to the talks.
79. Mitchell, p.175.
80. 'Loyalists jeer Paisley', *Guardian*, 11 April 1998, 2.
81. Interviewed in *Endgame*, Clinton states that he persuaded Adams to drop his demand that paramilitary prisoners be released one year after the Agreement.
82. *The Good Friday (Belfast) Agreement*, 'Constitutional Issues', I ii, in Elliott, *The Long Road to Peace*, p.224.
83. ibid., 'Constitutional Issues', 2.
84. ibid., 'Policing and Justice', 3.
85. ibid., 'Decommissioning', 3.
86. Fintan O'Toole, 'A Radical Deal', *Irish Times*, 13 April 1998, 16.
87. See Hennessey, *Peace Process*, p.192. Here he draws attention to the massive slippage in unionist support for the Good Friday Agreement in the period leading up to the referendum. In mid-April, 70 per cent of UUP voters endorsed the Agreement, but by mid-May this had fallen to 52 per cent; the drop in approval from DUP voters was even more dramatic, slipping from 30 per cent to 3 per cent over the same period.
88. McKittrick and McVea, p.223.
89. *Lost Lives*, p.1434.
90. ibid., p.1441. RIRA called a ceasefire three days after the Omagh bombing, yet 'continued to recruit and train' (English, p.318).
91. ibid., p.1443.
92. McKittrick and McVea, p.225.
93. *Lost Lives*, p.1467.
94. *The Good Friday (Belfast) Agreement*, 'Policing and Justice', 1.
95. *The Patten Report* (1999), paragraph 15.11.
96. Qtd from a statement by the Secretary of State for Northern Ireland, Peter Mandelson, to the House of Commons, on the implementation of the Patten Report, 19 January 2000.
97. *The Patten Report* (1999), paragraph 17.6.
98. *Statement by the Ulster Unionist Party in response to the Patten Report*, Thursday, 9 September 1999.
99. McKittrick and McVea, p.226.
100. Stephen Grimason, in 'Trimble's Strategy, Step by Step', BBC News, 27 November 1999, reports how Trimble managed to gain 58 per cent backing from the UU council partly as a result of a clever ploy. He had earlier that week handed the UU party president, Josias Cunningham, a post-dated letter of Resignation, which would be activated if republicans failed to deliver on decommissioning.

101. Stephen Grimason, 'Sectarianism Raises its Youthful Head', BBC News, 10 December 1999.
102. Qtd on cain.ulst.ac.uk/othelem/chron/ch00.htm
103. Hennessey, *Peace Process*, p.208.
104. Qtd in English, p.329.
105. At the end of Act One of Gary Mitchell's *The Force of Change*, the UDA's Stanley Brown tries to get information on the home, phone number and car of Dt. Sgt. Caroline Patterson.
106. Qtd in English, p.330.
107. A report in the *Irish Times*, 10 August 2001, stated that there had been 134 loyalist pipe-bomb attacks in Northern Ireland so far that year. The RUC's Assistant Chief Constable believed that the UDA were responsible for almost all these attacks.
108. 12 July 2001 witnessed some of the worst rioting for years in the Ardoyne, around the Short Strand, and in Portadown.
109. On 17 October 2001 a loyalist bomb exploded close to the school at 3 p.m., seriously damaging a house nearby.
110. Liam Kennedy, 'They Shoot Children, Don't They?: An Analysis of the Age And Gender of Victims of Paramilitary "Punishments" in Northern Ireland', prepared for the Northern Ireland Committee against Terror (NICAT) and the Northern Ireland Affairs Committee of the House of Commons, August 2001 (cain.ulst.ac.uk/issues/violence/docs/kennedy01.htm)
111. Gerry Adams, 'Looking to the Future', 22 October 2001, (cain.ulst.ac.uk/events/peace/docs/ga221001.htm)
112. See, for example, Mick Heaney, 'Spotlight Turns to Orange', *Sunday Times*, 11 June 2000, p.22.
113. Gary Mitchell, 'Balancing Act', *Guardian*, 5 April 2003, np.
114. ibid.
115. On its website, the Women's Coalition describes itself as 'a cross-community political party working for inclusion, human rights and equality in Northern Ireland', which 'works to implement the Belfast Agreement and address the every day concerns of women, men and children in Northern Ireland. We also try to widen participation in politics and make sure the voices of young people, older people, ethnic minorities, women and community and voluntary groups are heard' (www.niwc.org/aboutus)
116. The phrase is used to describe the play *The Force of Change*'s back cover (2000).
117. According to the *Prime Suspect* website, at the time it was written, 'there were only four female DCIs in Great Britain'.
118. www.pbs.org/wgbh/masterpiece/primesuspect12345
119. Caroline, unlike Tennison, is married with two young children.
120. '*BILL resents being ordered ... particularly by a woman*' (9).
121. See above, pp.203, 208. In an interview with Fiachra Gibbons ('Truth and Nail', *Guardian*, 10 April 2000, 10–11), Mitchell refers to his own participation in UDA paramilitary activity in his teenage years.
122. This emerges in his speeches from pp.68–70.
123. It is doubtful whether many members of the original London Royal Court audience would have much sympathy with Bill's political stance or, indeed, that they would have encountered the arguments against the Agreement.

124. See Volume 1, Chapter 4, p.205 and above p.57.
125. Bill's reference to 'a Protestant police force' protecting 'the Protestant people of Ulster' consciously echoes the first Northern Irish Prime Minister's famous description of Stormont as 'a Protestant Parliament for a Protestant people'.
126. Bill's nodding, pp.58, 59, replicates Stanley's.
127. David's comment half-way down p.56 suggests that he is at this point inclined to believe Bill's assertion that the phone was stolen.
128. The sequence of priorities here is telling.
129. According to Irish mythology, two chieftains were sailing in separate boats towards Ireland. They had agreed in advance that whoever touched land first could claim the land as their own. Seeing his rival was well ahead of him and about to win, one chieftain severed his hand and threw it ashore, and thus gained ownership of the land. The O'Neill clan chose the severed hand as their symbol, but in more recent times it has been appropriated by loyalist paramilitaries as their sign.

   In stylised form it had already appeared on the covers of two other recent Northern Irish plays, Friel's *Making History* and McGuinness's *Observe the Sons*.
130. Elliott, *The Long Road to Peace*, p.8.
131. In this closing section I am indebted to the compilers of the BBC website chronicling the politics of Northern Ireland (http://news.bbc.co.uk/1/hi/northern_ireland/2933949.stm) and to the CAIN website which is primarily the work of Martin Melaugh, and maintained by the University of Ulster.
132. In early 2002 the PSNI issued updated figures for 'punishment' attacks during 2001, which revealed an increase on the 2000 figure of over 25 per cent (cain.ulst.ac.uk/othelem/chron/ch02.htm).
133. 'Catholic parents said that they had faced increased verbal abuse ... and they were attacked while coming from school in the early afternoon. A Catholic mother claimed she was punched in the face as she walked home from the school with her child ... Protestant residents claimed the trouble started when Catholics removed a wreath from a lamppost' (ibid.). There were two other disturbing incidents at this time involving Catholic schools. In one an armed loyalist gang vandalised 17 cars belonging to teachers in a secondary school; in another fireworks were thrown at a the Mercy Convent Primary school on the Crumlin Road.
134. ibid.
135. ibid.
135. Qtd by Henry McDonald, in 'The Lies of Language', *Observer*, 28 July 2002.
137. Qtd in entry for 23 April 2003, http://news.bbc.co.uk/1/hi/northern_ireland/2933951.stm
138. *Irish Times*, 4 February 2003, http://international.poetryinternational-web.org/piw
139. Brian Friel, in *Irish Writers Against War*, ed. Conor Kostick and Katherine Moore (2003), p.7.
140. ibid., pp.106–7. It appears in *The State of the Prisons*, her 2005 collection, which is discussed below.
141. Gareth Gordon, 'Profile: Jeffrey Donaldson', http://news.bbc.co.uk/1/hi/northern_ireland/3091067.stm
142. David Trimble, qtd in 'NI Talks End Without Deal', BBC 18 September 2004, http://news.bbc.co.uk/1/hi/northern_ireland/3667642.stm

143. 'Raid Blame "Scuttles Disarmament"', BBC, 3 February 2005, http://news.bbc.co.uk/1/hi/northern_ireland/4231951.stm
144. ibid.
145. ibid.
146. Interview with Kevin Connolly, BBC News, 19 February 2005.
147. 'IRA expels Three after Killing', BBC, 26 February, 2005. http://news.bbc.co.uk/1/hi/northern_ireland/4299599.stm
148. ibid. See the comments by Ian Paisley Jnr and Sir Reg Empey.
149. 'Family encouraged by Bush talks', BBC, 17 March 2005. http://news.bbc.co.uk/1/hi/northern_ireland/4359491.stm
150. 'IRA "not involved" in Bar Murder', BBC, 23 March 2005. http://news.bbc.co.uk/1/hi/northern_ireland/4374177.stm
151. John de Chastelain, qtd 26 September 2005, http://news.bbc.co.uk/1/hi/northern_ireland/4283444.stm
152. Bertie Ahern, qtd 26 September 2005, http://news.bbc.co.uk/1/hi/uk/4283720.stm
153. ibid.
154. ibid. In Britain the impact of the IRA's final act of decommissioning, announced on 28 July, was lessened as a result of the Islamist terrorist attacks on London on 7 July 2005.
155. Mark Durkan, qtd 26 September 2005, http://news.bbc.co.uk/1/hi/uk/4283720.stm
156. Reg Empey, qtd 26 September 2005, ibid.
157. Ian Paisley, 27 April 2005. In the same statement he criticised the 'endless flow of concessions' the republicans had exacted as a result of British government policy and 'weak leadership' by the UUP. http://news.bbc.co.uk/1/hi/uk_politics/vote_2005/northern_ireland/4487005.stm
158. http://news.bbc.co.uk/1/hi/uk/4283720.stm
159. 'Veteran Republican's Spy Statement', 16 December 2005, http://news.bbc.co.uk/1/hi/northern_ireland/4536896.stm
160. 'Donaldson murder scene examined', 6 April 2006. http://news.bbc.co.uk/1/hi/northern_ireland/4881628.stm
161. 'Deadline for NI Devolution plan', 6 April 2006, http://news.bbc.co.uk/1/hi/northern_ireland/4881530.stm
162. ibid.
163. Qtd in 'End of the Armalite', *Guardian*, 5 October 2006, 34.
164. Owen Boycott, 'Provos have been Transformed', *Guardian*, 5 October 2006, 7.
165. Henry McDonald. 'Blair's last-ditch deal saved Irish talks', 15 October 2006, http://politics.guardian.co.uk/northernirelandassembly/story/0,,1922980,00.html
166. ibid. See also the transcript of Peter Hain's 'BBC Sunday AM' interview, 15 October 2006, on http://news.bbc.co.uk/1/hi/programmes/sunday_am/6052804.stm
167. *The New Irish Poets*, ed. Selima Guinness (2004); *Magnetic North: The Emerging Poets*, ed. John Brown (2005).
168. This section's closing title is taken from the title poem of Sinead Morrissey's *Between Here and There* (2005), p.46. Speaking of Buddha, she writes 'His crossing was a falling into light'.
169. Brown, *Magnetic North*, p.249.

170. Morrissey's money-makers have appropriated the republicans' slogan, 'Our Day will come', and altered its tense and meaning.
171. It is an Eden that is part-Blakean, part-Kavanaghesque.
172. The title of a poem in Morrissey's first collection. See Chapter 6, p.310.
173. Like James Hogg's creation, Morrissey's poem is haunted by doublings.
174. Edna Longley, *The Living Stream*, p.65.
175. A phrase of Seamus Heaney's 'A Pilgrim's Journey', *Poetry Society Bulletin* 123, Winter 1984.
176. Morrissey uses the image twice in 'My Grandmother Through Glass' (pp.42–5), once in relation to herself (II), once in relation to her mother (IV).
177. When Polonius asks Hamlet if he will 'walk out of the air', the Prince replies with this mordant quip. *Hamlet*, II, ii, line 209.
178. A further reminder of the continuing significance of the Somme within the imaginations of the preceding generation of Northern Protestants. See Fran Brearton, *The Great War in Irish Poetry* (2000), pp.27–37, 257–60.
179. Nick Laird, *Utterly Monkey* (2005), pp.16–18.
180. This image of the famous Belfast shipyard cranes, Samson and Goliath, which imagines them blessing the city is a surprising one. More typically they might be associated with masculinity, industrial might and sectarian aggression. Reference to their 'arms' serves as a reminder of what has happened to the limbs of the man who views them in this positive light.
181. Laird here makes a coded allusion to *St Luke*, 16: 27.
182. *London Review of Books*, 25:6, 20 March 2003. The American campaign began with missile attacks on various Iraqi sites in the early hours of that day.
183. In the opening chapter of *Orientalism* (1991, first published 1978), pp.42–3, 76–83, Edward Said details the massive investment in scholarship that accompanied Napoleon's Egyptian Expedition of 1798–99, 'an invasion which was in many ways the very model of a truly scientific ppropriation of one culture by another' (42).
184. Said, in *Orientalism*, p.227, maintains that westerners like Kipling, Layard and Bell fell easily into 'the culturally sanctioned habit of deploying large generalisations' in order to categorise 'reality', 'each category being not so much a neutral designation as an evaluative interpretation'.
185. Thomas Hardy, 'In Time of "The Breaking of Nations" ', *The Complete Poems* (2001) p.543.
186. The reference to 'a preacher repeating his God' may be an allusion to Palestinian leaders' claims that President Bush had told them in 2003 'that God guided him in what he should do … and led him to Iraq to fight tyranny' (news.bbc.co.uk/1/hi/world/americas/4320586.stm). See also 'Bush puts God on his Side', by BBC Washington Correspondent, Tom Carver, 6 April 2003 news.bbc.co.uk/1/hi/world/americas/2921345.stm.
187. *Jonah*, 3, v.7–9.
188. ibid. v.10. Somewhat imprudently, Jonah rebukes Yahweh for showing mercy and is subsequently taught a lesson.. Jonah's angry response, according to one leading biblical scholar, illustrates a xenophobic tendency in 'postexilic Judaism', a 'narrowness' which 'frequently expressed itself in a hate of foreign nations' and a 'desire for their destruction'. See John L. McKenzie, *Dictionary of the Bible* (1968), p.451.

189. This might be an allusion to the former Iraqi president, though Saddam Hussein's father was a shepherd, rather than a cowherd.
190. *The History Today Companion to British History* eds. Juliet Gardiner and Neil Wenborn (1995), p.73.
191. 'Signs are taken for wonders', from 'Gerontion' (1919), *The Complete Poems and Plays of T.S. Eliot* (1969), p.37. The postcolonial theorist, Homi Bhabha, appropriated the phrase for the title of a key essay in *The Location of Culture* (1994).
192. 'The Evening Forecast for the Region' (53–4) includes further allusions to the war in Iraq. At its close, the speaker decries how 'the white so loves the world it tries to make a map of it/exact and blank'.
193. Leontia Flynn, 'My Dream Mentor', *These Days* (2004), p.20.
194. ibid., p.14.
195. ibid., p.1.
196. ibid., p.14.
197. Two of Gillis's precursors in depicting reverse versions of history are Kurt Vonnegut in *Slaughterhouse-Five* (1969) and Martin Amis in *Time's Arrow* (1992).
198. Alan Gillis, *Somebody, Somewhere* (2004), p.55.

Chronology: 1975–2006

Important political events (Northern Ireland, UK, *Irish Republic*)	*World events*	*Publication dates of literary texts and cultural events*
1975		
31 Jul: Killing of Miami Showband by UVF		**Brian Friel *Volunteers***
Aug: PIRA bomb and gun attack on Shankill Road kills five		**Robert Greacen *A Garland for Captain Fox***
Death of Eamon de Valera		Trevor Griffiths *Comedians*
Tit-for-tat sectarian killings escalate	Sept: Civil War breaks out in Lebanon	**Seamus Heaney *North***
	Nov: Juan Carlos becomes King of Spain	Ruth Prawer Jhabvala *Heat and Dust*
		Primo Levi *The Periodic Table*
		John McGahern *The Leavetaking*
		Derek Mahon *The Snow Party*
		Harold Pinter *No Man's Land*
1976		
4 Jan: **Six Catholics shot by UVF**		Alex Haley *Roots*
5 Jan: **Ten Protestant linen workers murdered by Republican paramilitaries at Whitecross, South Armagh**		Maxine Hong Kingston *The Woman Warrior*
Apr: James Callaghan replaces Harold Wilson as PM		**Brian Moore *The Doctor's Wife***
Spring: NI Secretary Roy Mason's Ulsterisation policy comes into effect.	Jun: Increasing racial violence in South Africa	David Storey *Saville*
21 Jul: Murder by PIRA of Christopher Ewart-Biggs, British ambassador to *Irish Republic*		

(Continued)

Important political events (Northern Ireland, UK, Irish Republic)	World events	Publication dates of literary texts and cultural events
Women's Peace Movement founded 30 Nov: **Mairead Corrigan and Betty Williams win Nobel Peace Prize**	Sept: Death of Mao Zedong Nov: Jimmy Carter elected US President	
1977 Mar: **Death of Brian Faulkner** May: **Loyalist UUAC strike defeated** Jun: Queen Elizabeth II's Jubilee celebrations *Jack Lynch's FF wins victory in elections*		Zbigniew Herbert *Selected Poems* **Jennifer Johnston *Shadows on our Skin* Benedict Kiely *Proxopera*** Tom Murphy *Famine* **Tom Paulin *A State of Justice*** Paul Scott *Staying On*
	Jul: Army coup in Pakistan, General Zia ul-Haq seizes power	
1978 17 Feb: **PIRA bomb planted at La Mon House, Belfast, kills 12** **Apr:** Dirty Protest begins among republican prisoners at Long Kesh/ the Maze Jul: **Archbishop Tomás Ó Fiaich, the Catholic Primate, condemns prison authorities' actions** Nov–Dec: **Massive escalation in PIRA bombings and shootings in NI and mainland UK cities**	May: Intensified unrest in Iran Aug: John Paul I succeeds Paul VI as Pope Sept: Camp David summit brings together US President, PM of Israel and Egyptian President Oct: Polish cardinal, Karol Wojtyla, elected Pope. Takes the title John Paul II	Graham Greene *The Human Factor* David Hare *Plenty* **Roy McFadden *A Watching Brief*** Eugene McCabe *Cancer* **Michael Longley *The Echo Gate*** Iris Murdoch *The Sea, The Sea* Harold Pinter *Betrayal*

1979		
22 Mar: **Murder by PIRA of Sir Richard Sykes, British ambassador to The Netherlands**	Jan–Feb: Shah flees Iran. Ayatollah Khomeini returns to take power	Italo Calvino *If on a Winter's Night*
30 Mar: **Murder by PIRA of Airey Neave, Conservative MP**	Mar: Idi Amin flees Uganda	**Brian Friel *Faith Healer***
3 May: **Margaret Thatcher becomes PM**	Apr: Ali Bhutto, former Prime Minister of Pakistan, hanged by military government	**Seamus Heaney *Field Work***
27 Aug: **18 British soldiers killed by PIRA at Warrenpoint**		Milan Kundera *The Book of Laughter and Forgetting*
Bomb kills Lord Louis Mountbatten at Mullaghmore, Co. Sligo.	Jul: General Somoza ousted by Sandinista rebels in Nicaragua	Bernard Malamud *Dubin's Lives*
Sept: *Visit by Pope John Paul II to Ireland*		Peter Shaffer *Amadeus*
28 Nov: **John Hume becomes SDLP leader**	Nov: Hostage crisis in US embassy in Iran	
7 Dec: *Charles Haughey becomes leader of FF and Taoiseach*	Dec: 7-year-long civil war in Rhodesia ends	
	Soviet Union invades Afghanistan	
1980		
1 Apr: **Special category status for paramilitary prisoners withdrawn by British government**	Mar–Apr: Robert Mugabe becomes PM in independent Zimbabwe	**Mary Beckett *A Belfast Woman***
	Aug: Solidarity trade union wins major concessions from Polish Communist government	**Anne Devlin *Ourselves Alone***
		Umberto Eco *The Name of the Rose*
		Brian Friel *Translations*
		Seamus Heaney *Preoccupations*

(Continued)

Important political events (Northern Ireland, UK, Irish Republic)	World events	Publication dates of literary texts and cultural events
27 Oct: **First hunger strike begins** Dec: **Hunger strike ended before any deaths. Concessions strikers hoped for do not materialise**	Nov: Ronald Reagan wins US presidential election	Russell Hoban *Riddley Walker* **Bernard Mac Laverty *Lamb*** **Founding of Field Day Theatre Company in Derry by Brian Friel and Stephen Rea** Czeslaw Milosz awarded Nobel Prize for Literature
1981 1 Mar: **Second hunger strike begins** 9 Apr: **Bobby Sands, hunger strikers' leader, elected as MP in Fermanagh and South Tyrone** 5 May: **Sands dies on hunger strike** 12 May–20 Aug: **Nine further prisoners die on hunger strike** 20 Aug: **Provisional SF's Owen Carron wins Fermanagh and South Tyrone by-election. SF decide to contest future elections**	Jan: Iran releases US hostages 30 Mar: Assassination attempt on life of Ronald Reagan 10 May: François Mitterand elected French President. 13 May: Assassination attempt on life of John Paul II	William Golding *Rites of Passage* Nadine Gordimer *July's People* Alasdair Gray *Lanark* Nuala Ni Dhomnaill *An Dealg Droighin* Salman Rushdie *Midnight's Children*
3 Oct: **Hunger strike officially ends** 6 Oct: **NI Secretary James Prior grants many of strikers' original demands** 10, 17, 26 Oct: **PIRA bombs in London** 14 Nov: **PIRA kills UUP MP Rev Robert Bradford**	Oct: Egyptian president Anwar Sadat assassinated	

23 Nov: **Loyalist 'Third Force' rally held in Newtownards – 15 000 in attendance**	13 Dec: Martial law declared in Poland. Solidarity leadership arrested AIDS (Acquired Immune Deficiency Syndrome) identified this year as potentially a major threat to world health	Isabel Allende *The House of the Spirits* Saul Bellow *The Dean's December* Caryl Churchill *Top Girls* Thomas Keneally *Schindler's Ark* **Medbh McGuckian *The Flower Master*** **John Morrow *The Essex Factor*** Gabriel Garcia Marquez awarded Nobel Prize for Literature
1982		
20 Jul: **PIRA bombs in Knightsbridge and Regents Park, London; 8 killed** 7 Dec: **INLA bomb kills 17 people at Droppin' Well disco, Ballykelly**	Apr–June: Argentina invades Falkland Islands. British government sends Task Force which recaptures the islands June: Israel invades Lebanon Nov: Death of Leonid Brezhnev. Andropov succeeds as First Secretary	
1983		
30 May: New Ireland Forum opens in Dublin, bringing together constitutionalist parties from North and South 9 Jun: **SF's Gerry Adams defeats Gerry Fitt in West Belfast in Westminster Election** 7 Sep: *Pro-Life victory in Abortion Referendum* 19 Nov: New Ireland Forum report published. Margaret Thatcher's 'Out, out, out' speech	Mar: Reagan announces plan for 'Star Wars' missile shield May: Reagan backs Contras' fighting against Sandinistas in Nicaragua. Oct: Suicide bomb close to US Marines HQ in Beirut kills over 240 Reagan orders invasion of Grenada	**Maurice Leitch *Silver's City*** Gabriel Garcia Marquez *Chronicle of a Death Foretold* **Paul Muldoon *Quoof*** **Bernard Mac Laverty *Cal*** **Tom Paulin *Liberty Tree*** Salman Rushdie *Shame* Alice Walker *The Color Purple* William Golding awarded Nobel Prize for Literature

(Continued)

Important political events (Northern Ireland, UK, Irish Republic)	World events	Publication dates of literary texts and cultural events
18 Dec: **PIRA bomb at Harrods, London, kills six people**	Dec: Military rule ends in Chile Lech Walesa awarded Nobel Peace Prize	J.M. Coetzee *The Life and Times of Michael K* **Seamus Heaney *Station Island, Sweeney Astray*** **Ruth Hooley ed. *The Female Line*** Milan Kundera *The Unbearable Lightness of Being* Czeslaw Milosz *The Separate Notebooks* **John Montague *The Dead Kingdom*** **Stewart Parker *Northern Star*** Graham Swift *Waterland* William Trevor *Fools of Fortune* **Una Woods *Dark Hole Days***
1984 May: **John Stalker, Deputy Chief Constable of Greater Manchester force, appointed to investigate 'Shoot to Kill' incidents** 12 Oct: **PIRA bombs Grand Hotel, Brighton, during Conservative Party conference, killing 5**	Feb: Soviet leader Yuri Andropov dies, replaced by Viktor Chernenko Apr: AIDS fatalities in US reach 1758 Oct: Indian PM, Indira Gandhi, assassinated Nov: Reagan re-elected in US	
1985 28 Feb: **PIRA attack Newry RUC station: 9 killed** 1 Mar: End of year-long coal strike 13 Jul: Live Aid concert to raise funds for famine relief 15 Nov: **Anglo-Irish Agreement signed by Margaret Thatcher and Garret FitzGerald**	13 Mar: Mikhail Gorbachev becomes new leader of Soviet Union June: Israeli troops withdraw from Lebanon	Julian Barnes *Flaubert's Parrot* Angela Carter *Nights at the Circus* Doris Lessing *The Good Terrorist* **Frances Molloy *No Mate for the Magpie* Brian Moore *Black Robe***

	21 Nov: Reagan–Gorbachev meeting in Geneva	Iain Banks *The Bridge*
18 Nov: UUP Harold McCusker makes speech in Westminster denouncing AIA		**Anne Devlin *The Way Paver*** inc. 'Naming the Names'
23 Nov: Massive unionist anti-AIA rally at City Hall, Belfast		Thomas Kilroy *Double Cross*
11 Dec: First Intergovernmental Conference meeting – clash between loyalist protestors and RUC	Dec: Palestinian terrorists attack Israeli airline counters in Rome and Vienna, leaving 14 dead, 100 + wounded	**Deirdre Madden *Hidden Symptoms***
		Frank McGuinness *Observe the Sons of Ulster Marching Towards the Somme*
1986	27 Feb: Ferdinand Marcos flees Philippines. Corazon Aquino elected	Eilean Ni Chuilleanain *The Second Voyage*
3 Mar: UUP and DUP call Day of Action – rioting leaves 47 policemen injured. Portadown major site of distrurbances	21 Apr: US air raid on Libya	**Christina Reid *Joyriders***
	26 Apr: Nuclear accident at Chernobyl, Ukraine	Vikram Seth *The Golden Gate*
Mar–May: Intimidation sees RUC officers' families forced to leave their homes		**James Simmons *Poems 1956–1986***
Jun: Dissolution of NI Assembly		
Stalker suddenly recalled from Belfast to face groundless charges		
Divorce Referendum: divorce proposals rejected		
10 Jul: DUP leaders, Paisley and Robinson, and 4000 loyalists occupy Hillsborough		
12 Jul: Portadown Orangemen allowed to march down largely Catholic Garvaghy Road		

(Continued)

Important political events (Northern Ireland, UK, Irish Republic)	World events	Publication dates of literary texts and cultural events
Surge in UVF sectarian attacks on Catholics and Catholic homes 14 Oct: Republicans end abstentionist policy with regard to Dail elections Early Nov: Paisley founds Ulster Resistance prior to anniversary of signing of AIA 15 Nov: Two days of loyalist rioting in Belfast	Sept: Arab terrorists shoot 21 in Istanbul synagogue	Margaret Atwood *The Handmaid's Tale* **Mary Beckett *Give Them Stones*** Joseph Brodsky *Less Than One* **Ciaran Carson *The Irish for No*** **Brian Friel *Making History*** **Seamus Heaney *The Haw Lantern*** Brendan Kennelly *Cromwell* Toni Morrison *Beloved* **Paul Muldoon *Meeting the British*** **Stewart Parker *Pentecost*** **Tom Paulin *Fivemiletown*** **Graham Reid *The Billy Plays***
1987 Jan: Ulster Political Research Group (UDAThink-Tank) produces *Common Sense* Apr: PIRA landmine kills Lord and Lady Gibson May: SAS kill 8 PIRA members at Loughgall UUP and DUP reject any return to power-sharing Jun: Margaret Thatcher wins third successive victory in General Election Sept: UUP and DUP end boycott with British ministerial contacts Nov: **British intercept *Eksund*, carrying Libyan arms to PIRA**	Jan: Gorbachev announces need for greater democracy and openness ('glasnost') in Soviet Union Nov: Senate and House Report into funding of Nicaragua's Contras condemns Reagan administration's actions	

Enniskillen Remembrance Day bombing	7–10 Dec: Reagan and Gorbachev sign major nuclear reduction treaty	Joseph Brodsky awarded Nobel Prize for Literature
1988		**Linda Anderson *Cuckoo***
11 Jan: First of series of Adams–Hume meetings		Peter Carey *Oscar and Lucinda*
6 Mar: SAS shoot dead three PIRA members in Gibraltar		Tsitsi Dangarembga *Nervous Conditions*
16 Mar: Attack on republican mourners at Milltown Cemetery by loyalist Michael Stone	31 May: Reagan visits Soviet Union	Anita Desai *Baumgartner's Bombay*
19 Mar: Two British corporals killed after being caught up in procession at PIRA funeral	1 Jul: Iraqi government admits using poison gas against Kurds in Halabja, killing 5000	Roddy Doyle *The Commitments*.
Aug: PIRA bomb at Ballygawley, Co. Tyrone, kills 8 soldiers.	Nov: George Bush wins US presidential election	**Seamus Heaney *The Government of the Tongue***
Oct: British government introduces broadcasting ban, directed against paramilitaries	21 Dec: Bomb causes crash of Pan Am plane over Lockerbie, Scotland; 270 people killed	**Deirdre Madden *Birds of the Innocent Wood***
		Brian Moore *The Colour of Blood*
		Les A Murray *The Daylight Moon*
		Glenn Patterson *Burning Your Own*
		Salman Rushdie *The Satanic Verses*
		Wole Soyinka *Ake*
1989	Feb: Ayatollah Khomeini sentences Salman Rushdie to death for publishing *The Satanic Verses*. Riots in Bombay leave 6 dead	Roy Foster *Modern Ireland 1600–1972*
Feb: Murder of Pat Finucane by Loyalist paramiltaries		Kazuo Ishiguro *Remains of the Day*
		Janice Galloway *The Trick is to Keep Breathing*

(Continued)

Important political events (Northern Ireland, UK, Irish Republic)	World events	Publication dates of literary texts and cultural events
	Soviet troops withdraw from Afghanistan	James Kelman *A Disaffection*
	Apr: Round table talks in Poland	Maurice Leitch **The Hands of Cheryl Boyd**
	May–Sept: Opening of border crossing with Austria sees Hungarians leaving their country in increasing numbers	Peter McDonald **Biting the Wax**
		Robert McLiam Wilson **Ripley Bogle**
	June: Solidarity wins huge victory in Polish elections. Communist control ebbing away in Central and Eastern Europe	John Montague **The Figure in the Cave & Other Essays**
		Ailbhe Smyth (ed.) *Wildish Things: New Irish Women's Writing*
Sept: PIRA kills 11 bandsmen at barracks in Deal, Kent	Student activists killed in Tiananmen Square, Beijing	Matthew Sweeney *Blue Shoes*
	Aug: F.W. de Klerk becomes acting South African President	Death of Samuel Beckett
Oct: Court of Appeal in London overturns convictions of Guildford Four	Oct: Reform demands intensify in East Germany	
Nov: **NI Secretary Peter Brooke in speech urges PIRA to seek political strategy**	10 Nov: Berlin wall pulled down	
	Dec: Overthrow of Ceaucescu regime in Romania	
1990		
17 May: Stevens Report completed	11 Feb: Nelson Mandela freed in South Africa	Martin Amis *London Fields*
30 Jul: **Murder of MP Ian Gow by PIRA bomb**	Mar: Lithuania declares its independence	Eavan Boland *Outside History*
9 Nov: **Peter Brooke speech declares UK has no strategic or economic interest in NI**	May: Boris Yeltsin elected President of Russian Confederation	A.S. Byatt *Possession*
		Brian Friel **Dancing at Lughnasa**
	2 Aug: Iraq invades Kuwait	Seamus Heaney **The Cure at Troy**
		Brian Moore *Lies of Silence*
Mary Robinson elected Irish President		Roy McFadden **After Seymour's Funeral**

John McGahern *Amongst Women*
David Park *Oranges from Spain*

John Banville *The Book of Evidence*
Alan Bennett *The Madness of King George*
Angela Carter *Wise Children*
Seamus Deane (ed.) *The Field Day Anthology of Irish Writing*
Ariel Dorfman *Death and the Maiden*
Eamonn Grennan *As If It Matters*
Seamus Heaney *Seeing Things*
John Hughes *Negotiations with the Chill Wind*
Michael Longley *Gorse Fires*
Medbh McGuckian *Marconi's Cottage*
Ben Okri *The Famished Road*
Derek Walcott *Omeros*

Nadine Gordimer awarded Nobel Prize for Literature

Kamau Brathwaite *Middle Passages*
John Hewitt *The Collected Poems*
Patrick McCabe *The Butcher Boy*

(Continued)

---

3 Oct: German reunification takes place

16 Jan–28 Feb: First Gulf War. Kuwait liberated by Allied Coalition
Feb–Mar: Warsaw Pact dissolved
Apr: 120 000 lives lost in Bangladeshi floods
25 Jun: Following their declarations of independence, Croatia and Slovenia attacked by Yugoslav federal forces. Apartheid laws repealed in South Africa
21–23 Aug: Attempted coup in Soviet Union. Gorbachev held in Crimea by plotters. His return sees Boris Yeltsin assuming even greater power
Sept: Soviet Union formally grants independence to Latvia, Lithuania, Estonia
Dec: Gorbachev resigns as Soviet Union dissolved

15 Jan: Croatia and Slovenia's independence recognised by EC
Mar: Clashes follow referendum vote in

John Bruton becomes leader of Fine Gael
22 Nov: Margaret Thatcher resigns as British PM
27 Nov: John Major becomes PM

1991
Feb: **PIRA mortar attack on Major and his Cabinet in Downing Street**
Mar: **'Birmingham Six' freed after 16 years in jail**
Mar–Jul: **Brooke hosts talks involving NI's constitutionalist parties**
Jul: **Loyalist paramilitary killings intensify**

Oct: **John Hume writes *A Strategy for Peace and Justice in Ireland***

1992
17 Jan: **Eight Protestant workers killed by PIRA landmine at Teebane, Co. Tyrone**

Important political events (Northern Ireland, UK, Irish Republic)	World events	Publication dates of literary texts and cultural events
30 Jan: *Charles Haughey resigns over allegations of misconduct. Albert Reynolds becomes Taoiseach*	which Bosnia-Herzegovina announces determination to become independent state. Bosnian Serbs boycott referendum	Toni Morrison *Jazz* Tom Murphy *The Patriot Game* Michael Ondaatje *The English Patient* **Frank Ormsby (ed) *A Rage for Order*** **Glenn Patterson, *Fat Lad***
5 Feb: **Loyalist paramilitaries kill 5 Catholics at bookmakers in Ormeau Road, Belfast**	Apr: Serb forces bombard Bosnian capital, Sarajevo	Colm Toibin *The Heather Blazing*
9 Apr: Major wins General Election		Derek Walcott awarded Nobel Prize for Literature
Sir Patrick Mayhew replaces Brooke as NI secretary		
Massive PIRA bomb attack in London, £700 m in damage	Aug: Ethnic cleansing by Serbs condemned by UN	
Dec: **Mayhew speech promising 'flexibility' if PIRA end campaign of violence**	Nov: Bill Clinton wins US presidential election	
1993		
Jan–Mar: **Spate of paramilitary murders in NI**	1 Jan: Czechoslovakia splits into two states, Czech Republic and Slovakia	Roddy Doyle *Paddy Clarke Ha Ha Ha* Carol Ann Duffy *Mean Time*
Feb–Nov: **Secret talks involving SF, Hume, British and Irish governments**	3 Jan: Treaty Commitment by US and Russia to destroy two-thirds of nuclear weapons	Les A Murray *Dog Fox Field* Caryl Phillips *Crossing the River* Vikram Seth *A Suitable Boy*
20 Mar: **Mothers' Day bombing in Warrington kills two children**	Feb: Tribunal set up by UN to look into war crimes in former Yugoslavia	Carol Shields *The Stone Diaries* Tom Stoppard *Arcadia*
Massive attendance at Peace rallies calling for an end to violence	Bomb attack on World Trade Center in New York	Toni Morrison awarded Nobel Prize for Literature
Oct: **PIRA bomb Shankill Road shop, killing 10 people**	6 May: UN declares 'safe areas' in Bosnia. Bosnian Serbs attack Srebrenica	

Loyalist retaliation culminates in Greysteel shootings, in which 7 killed	7 May: Multi-party talks in South Africa result in agreement on non-racial elections to be held early in 1994	*Ciaran Carson First Language*
15 Dec: Downing Street Declaration, the work of John Major and Albert Reynolds, speaks of creating a 'new political framework'	13 Sept: Peace agreement (Declaration of Principles) signed by Israel and PLO in Washington	*Anne Devlin After Easter*
PIRA hold three-day Christmas ceasefire		*Carlo Gebler The Cure*
		Dermot Healy A Goat's Song
1994	**1994**	*Padraic Fiacc Ruined Pages*
Jan: Broadcasting ban on SF lifted	Mar: Bosnian Serbs shell 'safe areas' including Srebrenica	*Edna Longley The Living Stream*
31 Jan: Adams granted short-term visa to visit US	Apr–May: General election in South Africa, ANC victory. Nelson Mandela sworn in as President	*Medbh McGuckian Captain Lavender*
Mar: PIRA mortar attack on Heathrow airport		*Eoin McNamee Resurrection Man*
June: RAF helicopter crash in Mull of Kintyre; 25 British security experts killed	Jul: Declaration signed in Washington by King Hussein of Jordan and Israeli PM Yitzhak Rabin formally ends conflict between their states	*Paul Muldoon The Annals of Chile*
UVF shoot 6 Catholics in a bar near Downpatrick		*Edna O'Brien House of Splendid Isolation*
31 Aug: First IRA ceasefire	11 Dec: Russian forces invade Chechnya	*Joseph O'Connor Desperadoes*
6 Sept: Reynolds, Adams, Hume meeting		*V.S. Naipaul A Way in the World*
13 Oct: Loyalist paramilitaries' ceasefire		*William Trevor Felicia's Journey*
17 Nov,15 Dec: *Albert Reynolds resigns as Taoiseach, John Bruton of FG forms new coalition government. Bertie Ahern becomes leader of FF*		
Announcements of large economic aid packages to NI from Westminster and Washington		

(Continued)

Important political events (Northern Ireland, UK, Irish Republic)	World events	Publication dates of literary texts and cultural events
1995		
9 Feb: **SF cancels meeting with NIO after bugging incident**	Jan: WHO announces AIDS cases had exceeded 1million mark	Sebastian Barry *The Steward of Christendom*
Feb–Mar: **British and Irish governments publish *Frameworks for the Future*, rejected by UUP**	20 Mar: Rabin announces talks with PLO to resume	Dermot Bolger *The Journey Home*
Mar–June: **Continuous pressure on republicans to decommission arms from British government**	19 Apr: Oklahoma City bombing. Over 160 people killed	Marina Carr *The Mai*
Jul: **Drumcree clashes. Unionist delegation finally allowed down Garvaghey Road**	Jun: UN peacekeepers held hostage by Bosnian Serbs freed	Brian Friel *Molly Sweeney*
8 Sep: **David Trimble elected as UUP leader**	11 Jul: Bosnian Serbs capture Srebrenica	**Seamus Heaney *The Redress of Poetry***
Oct: **Deadlock in talks between SF and NI secretary, Michael Ancram**	Aug: Bosnian Serbs shell Sarajevo, killing 37. NATO attack Serb positions in retaliation	Jennifer Johnson *The Illusionist*
British and Irish governments announce all-party talks to begin by Feb 1996		**Marie Jones *A Night in November***
Nov: *President Clinton's visit to NI*	4 Nov: Yitzhak Rabin assassinated by ultranationalist Israeli law student	**Michael Longley *Ghost Orchid***
24 Nov: *Divorce Referendum; narrow victory for those keen to change marriage laws*	14 Dec: Peace agreement marks end of 4-year civil war in Bosnia	Patrick McCabe *The Dead School*
		Bernard O'Donoghue *Gunpowder*
		Frank Ormsby *The Ghost Train*
		Colm Toíbín *The Heather Blazing*
		Seamus Heaney awarded Nobel Prize for Literature
1996		
10 Jan: **SF submits *Building a Permanent Peace* to Mitchell commission**	25 Feb: Hamas terrorist attack kills 25 in bus station in West Jerusalem	**Seamus Deane *Reading in the Dark***
		Emma Donoghue *Hood*

Major rejects all-party talks, including SF, if there is no prior decommissioning	25 Jun: US barracks bombed in Saudi Arabia, 19 killed	Roddy Doyle *The Woman Who Walked Into Doors*
9 Feb: PIRA ends its ceasefire, bombing Canary Wharf	3 Jul: Yeltsin wins re-election as Russian President	**Michael Foley *The Road to Notown***
Jun: PIRA bomb Manchester city centre Multi-party talks at Stormont begin, excluding SF	21 Aug: South Africa's Truth and Reconciliation Committee hears testimony of F.W. de Klerk	**Seamus Heaney *The Spirit Level***
July: Drumcree crisis. Loyalists again allowed down Garvaghy Road – widespread riots in nationalist areas Major holds talks with loyalist paramilitaries' parties	Sept: US planes attack Iraq over its incursion into Kurdish territory.	Frank McCourt *Angela's Ashes*
	27 Sept: Taliban capture Afghan capital, Kabul	**Robert McLiam Wilson *Eureka Street***
Oct: PIRA car bomb attack on Lisburn British Army barracks	5 Nov: Clinton wins US presidential election	**Deirdre Madden *One by One in the Darkness***
		Graham Swift *Last Orders*
		***Word of Mouth* Poetry Collective publishes its anthology**
1997	1 Jan: Kofi Annan, new UN Secretary-General	John Banville *The Untouchable*
12 Feb: **PIRA shooting of Stephen Restorick, last British soldier to die in NI**	12 Mar: A Nigerian court charges Wole Soyinka and 14 others with treason	**Ciaran Carson *The Star Factory***
Robert Hamill beaten to death by loyalist mob	20–22 Mar: Clinton–Yeltsin summit held in Helsinki	**Bernard Mac Laverty *Grace Notes***
1 May: Labour Party win General Election, Tony Blair new PM		**Gary Mitchell *In a Little World of Our Own***
7–8 May: **Blair in talks with UUP's David Trimble, and then the Taoiseach, John Bruton**		**Brian Moore *The Magician's Wife***
2 Jun: **SDLP's Alban McGuinness elected as first nationalist Mayor of Belfast**		Eilis Ni Duibhne *The Inland Ice*
		Edna O'Brien *Down by the River*
		Arundhati Roy *The God of Small Things*
		Colm Toibin *The Story of the Night*

(Continued)

Important political events (Northern Ireland, UK, Irish Republic)	World events	Publication dates of literary texts and cultural events
26 Jun: *Bertie Ahern becomes Taoiseach, heading minority coalition*	1 Jul: Hong Kong reverts to Chinese rule	
19 Jul: **PIRA ceasefire restored**		
11 Sept: In referendum Scots vote for own parliament		
12 Sept: *Mary Robinson steps down as President to become UN Human Rights High Commissioner*		
mid-Sept: UUP, UDP, PUP arrive at **Stormont together for all-party talks, which include SF**	Sept–Dec: A series of massacres are carried out in Algeria by Islamist extremist groups	
13 Oct: **Blair meets Adams and McGuinness for talks in Belfast Formation of Real IRA (RIRA)**		
31 Oct: *Mary McAleese elected President of Ireland*		
Dec: **Four UUP MPs call on Trimble to leave talks**		
Murder by INLA of LVF's leader Billy Wright in the Maze Prison		
1998		
Jan: **Spate of sectarian murders follow Wright murder**	12 Jan: Iraqi government prevents UN weapons inspectors from visiting sites	**Ronan Bennett** *The Catastrophist*
New NI Secretary, Mo Mowlam, visits loyalist prisoners in the Maze	26 Jan: President Clinton embroiled in Lewinsky affair, denies 'sexual relations'	Ted Hughes *Birthday Letters*
		Jackie Kay *Trumpet*
		Patrick McCabe *Breakfast on Pluto*

Gary Mitchell *Tearing the Loom*
Paul Muldoon *Hay*
Joseph O'Connor *The Salesman*

(*Continued*)

12 Jan: British and Irish governments jointly submit *Propositions on Heads of Agreement*; well-received by UUP and SDLP, rejected by SF

29 Jan: Saville Enquiry set up by Blair to look into events of Bloody Sunday

3 Mar: Poyntzpass killings carried out by LVF

March–10 April: Mitchell all-party talks culminate in Good Friday/Belfast Agreement. Ian Paisley's DUP denounces the agreement

22 May: Referenda held in NI and Republic endorse Agreement (in NI an estimated 55% of unionists in favour, 96% of nationalists)

25 Jun: Elections to NI Assembly result in 80 pro-Agreement members, 28 anti

Jul: Loyalist rioting in NI following Parades Commission ban of march down Garvaghy Road

Arson attack kills three young brothers in Ballmoney

8 Aug: LVF announce ceasefire

15 Aug: RIRA plants car bomb in Omagh killing 29

10 Sept: First private meeting between Trimble and Adams

26 Nov: Tony Blair addresses Dail, first ever British PM to do so

25 Jun: Clinton makes state visit to China

4 Jul: World AIDS Conference in Geneva

34 million people worldwide infected with HIV or suffering from AIDS

25 Jul: Clinton subpoenaed to testify to federal Grand Jury over Lewinsky affair

5 Aug: Bomb attacks on US embassies in Nairobi and Dar es Salaam, killing 270 mostly local people

8 Aug: Taliban capture key stronghold, Mazar e Sharif, in Afghanistan

16 Sept: Basque separatist terrorist group ETA announces truce in Spain

24 Sept: Iran revokes *fatwa* on Salman Rushdie

296

Important political events (Northern Ireland, UK, Irish Republic)	World events	Publication dates of literary texts and cultural events
Dec: **Hume and Trimble jointly awarded Nobel Peace Prize**	16 Dec: Clinton orders air strikes on Iraq, because of its failure to permit weapons inspections	
1999		*Ruth Carr There is a House*
Jan: **Murder of ex-PIRA man, Eamon Collins, by unknown republicans**	24 Mar: NATO bombs Serbia following its violent policy towards non-Serbs in Kosovo	J.M. Coetzee *Disgrace* **Seamus Heaney *Beowulf*** *Eilish Martin slitting the tongues of jackdaws*
Mar: **Murder of lawyer, Rosemary Nelson, by loyalist paramilitaries**		**Gary Mitchell *Trust*** Glenn Patterson *The International*
Sept: **Patten Commission on Policing releases findings**	Jun: Nelson Mandela steps down as South African president	Tom Paulin *The Wind Dog*
1 Dec: **Devolved government returns to NI – Trimble first minister, Seamus Mallon his deputy**	Oct: Gen Pervez Musharraf seizes power in Pakistan	Gunter Grass awarded Nobel Prize for Literature
2000		Margaret Atwood *The Blind Assassin*
Jan: **International Commission on Decommissioning reports that no indication of when PIRA arms will be destroyed**	26 Mar: Vladimir Putin elected Russian President	Anne Enright *What are you Like* **Michael Longley *The Weather in Japan***
11 Feb: **Peter Mandelson suspends devolved government because of PIRA's failure to begin decommissioning**	3 Apr: EU and OAU leaders hold first ever European–African summit in Cairo	Gary Mitchell *The Force of Change*
6 May: **Devolved institutions restored, following PIRA statement that they would initiate decommissioning process**	15 May: Street battles break out in Janin and Ramallah between Palestinians and Israeli soldiers	

29 May: Signs that Trimble's support ebbing in UUP when only 53% of UU Council support the Executive's return Jul: Rioting at Drumcree. UDA–UVF feud intensifies	25 Jul: Middle East peace talks involving President Clinton, Israel's Ehud Barak and the PLO's Yasser Arafat end in failure Nov: George W. Bush wins US presidential election in disputed circumstances	Peter Carey *True History of the Kelly Gang* **Seamus Heaney *Electric Light*** Matthew Kneale *English Passengers* **Eoin McNamee *The Blue Tango*** W.G. Sebald *Austerlitz*
2001 Mar: RIRA attack M16 building and the BBC in London Jun: General Election in UK. UUP lose three MPs, SF overtakes SDLP in votes cast 19 Jun-23 Nov: Loyalist hostility in North Belfast focuses on Holy Cross Primary School. Trimble and SDLP's Mark Durkan negotiate an end to violence around the school 1 Jul: Trimble resigns as First Minister over PIRA's failure to decommission 6 Aug: PIRA offers to destroy weapons. UUP argues that PIRA plans do not go far enough 23 Oct: IICD confirms that it has witnessed decommisioning of some IRA weapons Nov: Police Service of Northern Ireland comes into being. NI Executive restored and resumes work	7 Mar: Ariel Sharon takes office as Israeli PM 28 Jun: Slobodan Milosevic extradited to Hague to face war crimes tribunal 23 Jul: 178 nations support Kyoto Protocol on greenhouse gas emissions US refuses to sign up to the Protocol 11 Sept: Hijacked planes used for attacks on Twin Towers in New York and the Pentagon in Washington by al–Qaida terrorists. Over 3000 fatalities	V.S.Naipaul awarded Nobel Prize for Literature

(Continued)

298

Important political events (Northern Ireland, UK, Irish Republic)	World events	Publication dates of literary texts and cultural events
John Hume steps down as leader of SDLP Dec: Killing by loyalists of **William Stobie, accused of involvement in murder of Pat Finucane in 1989** Criticism of police response to warnings about Omagh bomb by Nuala O'Loan, Police Ombudsman for NI		Dermot Bolger *The Valparaiso Voyage* Emma Donoghue *Slammerkin* John McGahern *That They May Face the Rising Sun* Yann Martel, *Life of Pi* **Paul Muldoon *Moy Sand and Gravel*** **Sinead Morrissey *Between Here and There***
2002 Jan: **Media highlight case of three republicans arrested in Colombia** Feb: **John Hume awarded Gandhi Peace Prize** 6 Mar: **DUP motion calling for SF's expulsion from Executive** 9 Mar: **Trimble speech lambasting Irish Republic** 18 Mar: **Break-in at Special Branch HQ, Castlereagh** Apr: **Announcement re Second Act of IRA Decommissioning** May–June: **Sectarian riots in North and East Belfast** 17 May: *Bertie Ahern re-elected as Taoiseach* 16 July: **IRA issues apology to families of those killed**	Jan: Euro introduced as new European currency Mar: Robert Mugabe wins election in Zimbabwe Apr: FARC rebels in Colombia bomb night club May: Jacques Chirac wins French presidential election Siege of Church of Nativity lifted in Jerusalem	

(Continued)

21 July: UDA murder of Gerard Lawlor, following wounding of Protestant youth

Sept–Oct: Allegations re republican spy-ring at Stormont

14 Oct: John Reid suspends devolved government in NI

30 Oct: Provisional IRA break off contacts with decommissioning body

Dec: *Irish government document leaks suggests PIRA still active*

Aug: FARC rebels launch mortar attacks in Colombia, 21 killed

Almost 3000 white farmers in Zimbabwe ordered to leave their land

23–26 Oct: Moscow Theatre seized by Chechen rebels. 127 killed as siege ended by security forces

Nov: Hu Jintao chosen as new leader of China's Communist Party

UN weapons inspectors return to Iraq

Irish Writers Against War anthology
Ciaran Carson *Breaking News*
Tom Paulin *The Invasion Handbook*
Glenn Patterson *Number 5*
DBC Pierre *Vernon God Little*

2003

4 Feb: **Brian Friel, Tom Paulin letter to *Irish Times* opposing new Iraq war**

Feb, May: **Opinion polls show increasing lack of confidence in Good Friday Agreement among unionists**

Apr: Suicide of David Kelly, UK weapons inspector

Apr–May: Blair and Ahern increase efforts to resolve crisis

9 Jan: UN weapons inspectors criticise Iraq regime over weapons documentation, but find no WMD

10 Jan: Crisis when North Korea withdraws from Nuclear Proliferation Treaty

Mar: In UN France, Germany and Russia oppose use of force against Iraq

President Bush announces 'road-map' to bring peace in Middle East

19–20 Mar: US-led, UK-backed invasion of Iraq begins, which later topples Saddam Hussein

Apr: President Bush claims military victory in Iraq

Ten new member states join EU

May: India–Pakistan restore diplomatic relations

J.M.Coetzee awarded Nobel Prize for Literature

Important political events (*Northern Ireland*, *UK*, Irish Republic)	World events	Publication dates of literary texts and cultural events
June: **Three UUP MPs withhold support from Trimble over policy differences** 21 Oct: **Third Act of IRA Decommissioning** Nov: **DUP emerges as largest unionist party in Assembly elections**	Jun: General strike in Zimbabwe Israeli troops leave Gaza strip following Palestinian ceasefire Aug: Bomb destroys UN HQ in Baghdad Nov: Attack on British Consulate in Istanbul	
2004		**Ronan Bennett *Havoc in its Third Year* Leontia Flynn *These Days* Michael Longley *Snow Water* Medbh McGuckian *Book of the Angel* John Montague *The Drunken Sailor***
	Increasing reports of mass killings of black Africans in Darfur, Sudan, by Janjaweed militia March: Madrid train bombings Apr: Disclosure of abuse at Abu Ghraib prison in Baghdad	Orhan Pamuk *Snow* **David Park *Swallowing the Sun* Glenn Patterson *That Which Was***
16–18 Sept: Leeds Castle discussions on future of NI	Sept: Beslan school siege, North Ossetia, carried out by Chechens, 300 killed Oct: Hamid Karzai elected President of Afghanistan Nov: George Bush re-elected President Death of PLO leader, Yasser Arafat	Colm Toibin *The Master*
20 Dec: **Raid on Northern Bank, Belfast. IRA accused**	Dec: Tsunamis in Indian Ocean kill 150 000 Asians	
2005		
30 Jan: **Murder of Robert McCartney by IRA members**	Jan: Elections lead to creation of Iraqi National Assembly	John Banville *The Sea* Sebastian Barry *A Long Long Way*

2 Feb: **IRA withdraw decommissioning offer** Mar: **McCartney sisters invited to White House, SF snubbed** 5 May: Westminster General Election **DUP and SF increase vote share and representation**	Apr: Death of Pope John Paul II May: Election of Cardinal Ratzinger as Pope Benedict XVI July: Live 8 Concerts worldwide. G8 leaders promise to cancel debts of many of world's poorest countries 7 July: Islamist suicide bombings in London kill 56 people and injure hundreds Aug: Hurricane Katrina strikes US coast, kills 1300	**Alan Gillis *Somebody, Somewhere*** **Brian Friel *The Home Place*** **Nick Laird *To A Fault*** Ian McEwan *Saturday* John McGahern *Memoir* **Derek Mahon *Harbour Lights*** **Sinead Morrissey *The State of the Prisons*** Harold Pinter awarded Nobel Prize for Literature
25 Sept: **IMC report IRA have completed decommissioning**	Oct: Suicide bomb attacks in Bali, Indonesia, kill 22 Earthquake in Kashmir leaves 80 000 dead and 3 million homeless. Riots in Paris Saddam Hussein goes on trial for war crimes	
Dec: **Collapse of spy ring trial. Leading SF figure, Denis Donaldson, exposed as RUC / British agent**	15 Dec: Iraqi elections lead to formation of government 31 Dec: US deaths in Iraq 2200	
2006 4 Apr: **Murder of Dennis Donaldson discovered** 6 Apr: **Navan Fort Summit to discuss NI's future** 15 May: **NI Assembly recalled**	Feb: Attack on Shia mosque at Samarra sparks sectarian killings in Iraq May–June: UN reports suggest around 100 civilians a day are being killed in Iraq July: Following Hezbollah raid, in which three of its soldiers killed and two	Kiran Desai *The Inheritance of Loss* **Seamus Heaney *District and Circle*** **Paul Muldoon's *Horse Latitudes***

(Continued)

Important political events (**Northern Ireland**, UK, Irish Republic)	World events	Publication dates of literary texts and cultural events
4 Oct: **IMC Report announces IRA no longer involved in paramilitary or criminal activity**	kidnapped, Israel launches massive offensive against Lebanon	
11–13 Oct: British–Irish government-led discussions result in **St Andrews Agreement**	Oct: North Korea explodes nuclear device Presidential elections in DR Congo	

Sources: Jonathan Bardon, *A History of Ulster*; Paul Bew and Gordon Gillespie, eds, *Northern Ireland: A Chronology of the Troubles*; editor-in-chief Clifton Daniel *Chronicle of the Twentieth Century*; *Encyclopaedia Britannica 2005*; W.D. Flackes, *Northern Ireland: A Political Directory 1963–83*; Thomas Hennessey, *A History of Northern Ireland 1920–1996*; Alvin Jackson, *Ireland 1798–1998*; David McKittrick, Seamus Kelters, Brian Feeney, Chris Thornton, *Lost Lives*, David McKittrick and David McVea, *Making Sense of the Troubles*; Philip Waller and John Rowell, *Chronology of the Twentieth Century*; Norman Vance *Irish Literature Since 1800*. For the most recent political developments, I am indebted to the CAIN website, BBC websites, and World Timeline, 2002, 2003, 2004, 2005, 2006. *The History Channel website*. 28 Oct 2006, http://www.history.com/wt.do?year=2004.

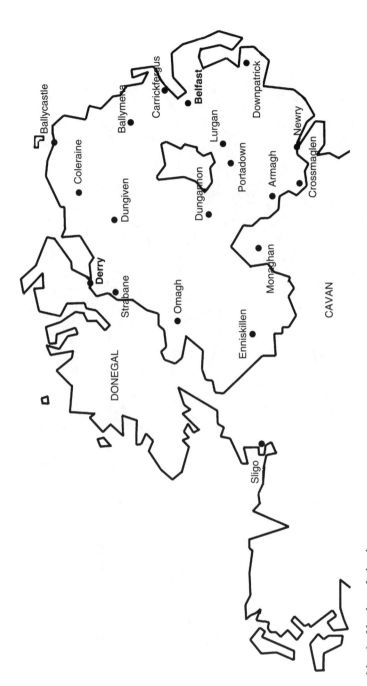

Map 1 Northern Ireland

Map 2   Belfast

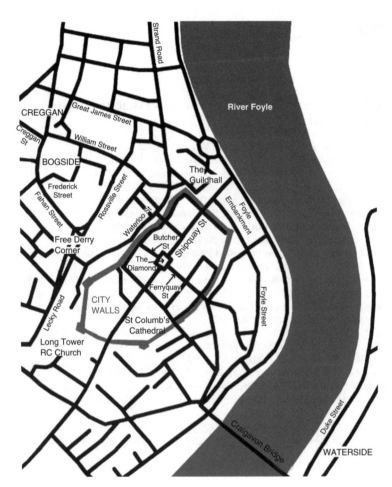

Map 3   Derry/Londonderry

Bibliography

A: Literary texts (including critical texts, journalism and memoirs)

Amis, Martin. *Time's Arrow*. London: Vintage, 1992.
Carr, Ruth (formerly Ruth Hooley) ed. *Word of Mouth*. Belfast: Blackstaff, 1996.
—— *There is a House*. Kilcar: Summer Palace Press, 1999.
Carson, Ciaran. *The Irish for No*. Oldcastle: Gallery Press, 1987.
—— *Belfast Confetti*. Newcastle-upon-Tyne: Bloodaxe, 1990.
Dangarembga, Tsitsi. *Nervous Conditions*. London: The Women's Press, 1988.
Deane, Seamus. Introduction to *Selected Plays of Brian Friel*. London: Faber, 1984.
—— ed. *Field Day Anthology*. Derry: Field Day, 1991.
—— *Celtic Revivals: Essays in Modern Irish Literature*. London: Faber, 1985.
—— *Reading in the Dark*. London: Faber, 1997.
—— 'Seamus Deane Talks about *Reading in the Dark*', *English and Media Magazine*, 12 May 1997, 2–7.
Devlin, Anne. *The Way Paver and Other Stories*. London: Faber, 1986.
—— *After Easter*. London: Faber, 1994.
Eliot, T.S. *The Complete Poems and Plays of T.S. Eliot*. London: Faber, 1969.
Fiacc, Padraic ed. *The Wearing of the Black*. Belfast: Blackstaff, 1974.
—— *Ruined Pages*. Belfast: Blackstaff, 1994.
Flanagan, Thomas. *The Year of the French*. London: Arrow, 1979.
Flynn, Leontia. *These Days*. London: Cape, 2004.
Friel, Brian. *Translations* (1980) in Deane ed. *Selected Plays of Brian Friel*. London: Faber, 1984.
—— *Making History*. London: Faber, 1987.
—— *Essays, Diaries, Interviews 1964–1999*, ed. Christopher Murray. London: Faber, 1999.
—— Preface to *Irish Writers Against War*, eds, Conor Kostick and Katherine Moore. 2003.
Gillis, Alan. *Somebody, Somewhere*. Oldcastle: Gallery Press, 2004.
Harrison, Tony. *Selected Poems*. Harmondsworth: Penguin, 1984.
Heaney, Seamus. *Wintering Out*. London: Faber, 1972.
—— *Stations*. Belfast: Ulsterman Publications, 1975.
—— *North*. London: Faber, 1975.
—— 'Unhappy and at Home', interview with Seamus Deane, *The Crane Bag*, 1:1, 1977, 61–7.
—— *In Their Element*. BBC Radio, 1977.
—— *Field Work*. London: Faber, 1978.
—— *Selected Poems 1965–1975*. London: Faber, 1980.
—— *Preoccupations: Selected Prose 1968–1978*. London: Faber, 1980.
—— *Sweeney Astray*. Derry: Field Day, 1983.
—— 'Pilgrim's Journey', *Poetry Book Society Bulletin*, 123, Winter 1984.
—— Letter to the author, 30 October, 1985.

—— *The Haw Lantern*. London: Faber, 1987.
—— *The Government of the Tongue*. London: Faber 1988.
—— *The Place of Writing*. Atlanta: Scholars Press, 1989.
—— *New Selected Poems 1966–1987*. London; Faber, 1990.
—— *The Redress of Poetry*. London: Faber, 1995.
—— *Crediting Poetry*. Oldcastle: Gallery Press, 1995.
—— *The Spirit Level*. London: Faber, 1996.
—— *Opened Ground: Poems 1966–1996*. London: Faber, 1998.
Hewitt, John *The Collected Poems of John Hewitt* ed. Frank Ormsby. Belfast: Blackstaff, 1992.
—— 'No Rootless Colonist' (1972), rptd in *Ancestral Voices: The Selected Prose of John Hewitt*, ed. Tom Clyde. Belfast: Blackstaff, 1987, 146–57.
Hooley, Ruth. ed. *The Female Line: Northern Irish Women Writers*. Belfast: Northern Ireland Women's Rights Movement, 1985 (see above, Ruth Carr).
Hughes, Ted. *Crow*. London: Faber, 1970.
Johnston, Jennifer. *Shadows on our Skin*. London: Hamish Hamilton, 1977; rptd Flamingo, 1986.
—— 'Q & A with Jennifer Johnson', *Irish Literary Supplement*, 3:2 (1984), 25–7.
Joyce, James. *A Portrait of the Artist as a Young Man* ed. Seamus Deane. Harmondsworth Penguin, 1992.
—— *Ulysses*, Harmondsworth: Penguin, 1986.
Kavanagh, Patrick. *Collected Poems*. Dublin: Brian and O'Keeffe, 1972.
Kiely, Benedict. *Proxopera*. London: Gollancz, 1977; rptd Methuen, 1988.
—— Interview in *Irish Literary Supplement*, 6:1 Spring 1987, 10.
Kostick, Conor and Katherine Moore eds. *Irish Writers Against War*. Dublin: O'Brien Press, 2003.
Laird, Nick. *To a Fault*. London: Faber and Faber, 2005.
Leitch, Maurice. *The Liberty Lad*. London: MacGibbon and Kee, 1965; rptd Blackstaff, 1985.
—— *Poor Lazarus*. London: MacGibbon and Kee, 1969; rptd Blackstaff, 1985.
—— interviewed in *Banned in Ireland: Censorship and the Irish Writer*, ed. Julia Carlson. London: Routledge, 1990, 99–107.
—— interviewed by Richard Mills, 'Closed Places of the Spirit', *Irish Studies Review*, 6:1 (April 1998), 63–8.
Longley, Michael. *The Echo Gate*. London: Secker and Warburg, 1979.
—— *Poems 1963–1983*. Edinburgh: Salamander, 1985.
—— *Gorse Fires*. London: Secker and Warburg, 1991.
—— *Tuppenny Stung: Autobiographical Chapters*. Belfast: Lagan Press, 1994.
—— *The Ghost Orchid*. London: Cape, 1995.
McCabe, Patrick. *The Butcher Boy*. London: Picador, 1992.
McDonald, Peter. *Biting the Wax*. Newcastle-upon-Tyne: Bloodaxe, 1989.
McFadden, Roy. *Last Poems*, ed. Sarah Ferris. Newry: Abbey Press, 2002.
McGuckian, Medbh. *Captain Lavender*. Oldcastle: Gallery Press, 1994.
—— 'Comhrá', a conversation with Nuala Ni Dhomnaill, *The Southern Review* 31:5 (July 1995), 581–614.
—— *A Dialogue with Medbh McGuckian, Winter 1996–1997*, interview by Rand Brandes, *Studies in the Literary Imagination*, Fall 1997.
McGuinness, Frank. *Observe the Sons of Ulster Marching Towards the Somme*. London: Faber and Faber, 1986.

Mac Laverty, Bernard. *Lamb*. Harmondsworth: Penguin, 1981.
—— *Cal*. Harmondsworth: Penguin, 1984.
—— *Grace Notes*. London: Cape, 1997.
—— 'Days of Grace', interview and article by Suzy Mackenzie, *Guardian Weekend*, 12 July, 1997, 25–32.
MacNeice, Louis. *Collected Poems*. London: Faber and Faber, 1966.
Madden, Deirdre. *Hidden Symptoms*. New York: Atlantic Monthly, 1986; London: Faber, 1988.
—— *The Birds of the Innocent Wood*. London: Faber, 1988.
—— *One by One in the Darkness*. London: Faber, 1996.
Mahon, Derek. *Poems 1962–1978*. Oxford: Oxford University Press, 1979.
—— *Collected Poems*. Oldcastle: Gallery Press, 1999.
Mandelstam, Osip. 'Journey to Armenia'. *The Collected Prose and Letters*, trans. Jane Gary Harris and Constance Link. London: Collins Harvill, 1991.
Martin, Eilish. *slitting the tongues of jackdaws*. Kilcar: Summer Palace Press, 1999.
Mitchell, Gary. *The Force of Change*. London: Nick Hern Books, 2000.
—— 'Balancing Act', *The Guardian*, 5 April 2003.
Montague, John. 'The Cry', rptd in *The Hurt World: Short Stories of the Troubles*, ed. Michael Parker. Belfast: Blackstaff, 1995.
—— *The Rough Field*. Dublin: Dolmen, 1972.
—— 'Beyond the Planter and the Gael', interview in *The Crane Bag*, 4:2, 1980–81, 85–92.
—— *The Dead Kingdom*. Dublin: Dolmen, 1984.
—— *The Figure in the Cave*. Dublin: Lilliput, 1989.
—— *Collected Poems*. Oldcastle: Gallery Press, 1995.
Morrissey, Sinead. *There was Fire in Vancouver*. Manchester: Carcanet, 1996.
—— *Between Here and There*. Manchester: Carcanet, 2002.
—— *The State of the Prisons*. Manchester: Carcanet, 2005.
Morrow, John. *The Essex Factor*. Belfast: Blackstaff, 1982.
—— *Sects and Other Stories*. London: Black Swan, 1987.
Muldoon, Paul. *Why Brownlee Left*. London: Faber, 1980.
—— Interview in John Haffenden, *Viewpoints*, 1981.
—— *Quoof*. London: Faber, 1983.
—— *Meeting the British*. London: Faber, 1987.
O'Brien, Flann. *An Beal Bocht*. Dublin: Dolmen Press, 1941, rptd Paladin, 1988.
Ormsby, Frank ed. *Poems from the North of Ireland*. Belfast: Blackstaff, 1979.
—— ed. *A Rage for Order*. Belfast: Blackstaff, 1992.
—— *The Ghost Train*. Oldcastle: Gallery Press, 1995.
—— 'Poetry', in *Stepping Stones: The Arts in Ulster 1971–2001* eds. Mark Carruthers and Stephen Douds.
Parker, Stewart. 'An Ulster Volunteer', *Irish Times*, 6 March 1970, 11.
—— 'The Tribe and Thompson', *Irish Times* 18 June 1970, 11.
—— *Dramatis Personae*, John Malone Memorial Lecture, Belfast: Queen's University, 1986.
—— *Pentecost*, in *Three Plays for Ireland*. London: Oberon Books, 1989.
Patterson, Glenn. *Burning Your Own*. London: Abacus, 1989.
—— *Fat Lad*. London: Minerva, 1993.
—— *Celebration*. Granada Television, first broadcast, 12 September 1993.
—— *The International*. London: Anchor, 1999.

Paulin, Tom. *Ireland and the English Crisis*. Newcastle-upon-Tyne: Bloodaxe, 1984.
—— *Poetry, Language and History* (television documentary). Open University, 1986.
—— *Fivemiletown*. London: Faber, 1987.
—— *Writing to the Moment: Selected Critical Essays 1980–1996*. London: Faber, 1996.
Reid, Graham. *The Billy Plays*. London: Faber, 1987.
Shakespeare's Sonnets, ed. Stephen Booth. New Haven: Yale UP, 2000.
Sidney, Sir Philip. *An Apology for Poetry*, ed. Geoffrey Shepherd. London, 1965.
Simmons, James. *Poems 1965–1986*, Oldcastle: Gallery, 1987.
Synge, J.M. *The Playboy of the Western World* ed. Anne Saddlemyer. Oxford: Oxford University Press, 1995.
Thompson, Sam. *Over the Bridge,* ed. Stewart Parker, Dublin: Gill & Macmillan, 1970.
—— *Over the Bridge and Other Plays* ed. John Keyes, Belfast: Lagan, 1997.
Tobin, Grainne. *Banjaxed*. Kilcar: Summer Palace Press, 2002.
Toibin, Colm. *The Heather Blazing*. London: Picador, 1992.
Vonnegut, Kurt. *Slaughterhouse Five, 1969*. New York: Dell, 1991.
Wilson, Robert McLiam. *Eureka Street*. London: Minerva, 1997.
Woods, Una. *The Dark Hole Days*. Belfast: Blackstaff, 1984.
Wordsworth, William. *Poetical Works*. London: Oxford University Press, 1967.
Yeats, W.B. *Collected Poems*, London: Macmillan, 1950.

B: Secondary material on literary texts

Allen, Michael, ed. *Seamus Heaney*. Basingstoke: Macmillan, 1997.
Allison, Jonathan. 'Imagining the Community: Seamus Heaney in 1966', *Notes on Modern Irish Literature*, 4, 1992, 27–34.
Althusser, Louis. 'Ideology and the State', *Lenin and Philosophy and Other Essays*, trans. B. Brewster, rptd. in *Modern Literary Theory*, ed. Philip Rice and Patricia Waugh. London: Arnold, 1989.
Bakhtin, Mikhail. 'Discourse in the Novel', *The Dialogic Imagination*, trans. Caryl Emerson and Michael Holquist. Austin: Texas. 1981.
Barthes, Roland. *S/Z*. Paris: Editions de Senil,1970.
Batten, Guinn. 'The More with Which We Are Concerned': The Muse of the Minus in the Poetry of McGuckian and Kinsella', in *Gender and Sexuality in Modern Ireland*, ed. Anthony Bradley and Maryann Gialanella Valiulis. Amherst: University of Massachusetts Press, 1997, pp.212–44.
Bell, Ian A. ed. *Peripheral Visions: Images of Nationhood in Contemporary British Fiction*. Bridgend: Seren, 1996.
Benjamin, Walter. 'The Work of Art in the Age of Mechanical Reproduction', in *Illuminations*, trans. Harry Zohn. London: Fontana, 1992.
Bennett, Ronan. 'An Irish Answer', *The Guardian: Weekend*, 16 July 1994.
Bhabha, Homi. *The Location of Culture*. London: Routledge, 1994.
Brearton, Fran. *The Great War in Irish Poetry: W.B.Yeats to Michael Longley*. Oxford: Oxford University Press, 2000.
—— 'Poetry of the 1960s: the "Northern Ireland Renaissance"', in Matthew Campbell, ed. *Contemporary Irish Poetry*. Cambridge: Cambridge University Press, 2003.
Brewster, Scott, Virginia Crossman, Fiona Becket and David Alderson, eds. *Ireland in Proximity: History, Gender, Space*. London: Routledge, 1999.

Brown, Clare and Don Paterson, eds. *Don't Ask Me What I Mean*, London: Picador, 2004.

Brown, John, ed. *In the Chair: Interviews with Poets from the North of Ireland*. Cliffs of Moher: Salmon, 2002.

—— ed. *Magnetic North: The Emerging Poets*. Derry: Verbal Arts Centre, 2005.

Brown, Terence. *Northern Voices: Poets from Ulster*. Dublin: Gill & Macmillan, 1977.

—— 'Mahon and Longley: Place and Placelessness', in *Contemporary Irish Poetry*, ed. Campbell, pp.133–48.

Cairns, David and Shaun Richards. *Writing Ireland: Colonialism, Nationalism and Culture*, Manchester: Manchester University Press, 1988.

Campbell, Matthew, ed. *Contemporary Irish Poetry*, Cambridge: Cambridge University Press, 2003.

Carpenter, Andrew and Peter Fallon, eds. *The Writers: A Sense of Ireland*. Dublin: O'Brien Press, 1980.

Carruthers, Mark and Stephen Douds, eds. *Stepping Stones: The Arts in Ulster 1971–2001*. Belfast: Blackstaff, 2001.

Cleary, Joe. '"Fork Tongued in the Border Bit": Partition and the Politics of Form in Contemporary Narratives of the Northern Irish Conflict', *South Atlantic Quarterly*, 95:1 (Winter 1996).

Connolly, Sean, 'Dreaming History: Brian Friel's *Translations*', *Theatre Ireland*, 13 (1987), 42–4.

Corcoran, Neil, *Seamus Heaney*. London: Faber, 1986.

—— 'Strange Letters: Reading and Writing in Recent Irish Poetry', in Paul Hyland and Neil Sammells *Irish Writing: Exile and Subversion*. London: Macmillan, 1991, 234–47.

—— ed. *The Chosen Ground: Essays on Contemporary Poetry of Northern Ireland*. Bridgend: Seren, 1992.

—— *English Poetry since 1940*. London: Longman, 1993.

—— *After Yeats and Joyce: Reading Modern Irish Literature*. Oxford: Opus, 1997.

—— 'A Languorous Cutting Edge: Muldoon Versus Heaney?'. *Princeton University Library*.

—— *Chronicle*, 59:3, Spring 1998, 559–80.

—— *Poets of Modern Ireland*. Cardiff: University of Wales Press, 1999.

Craig, Patricia, ed. *The Belfast Anthology*. Belfast: Blackstaff, 1999.

Crotty, Patrick, ed. *Modern Irish Poetry*. Belfast: Blackstaff, 1995.

Cullingford, Elizabeth Butler. 'Thinking of Her . . . as . . . Ireland', *Textual Practice*, 4:1, Spring 1990, 1–21.

—— 'British Romans and Irish Carthaginians: Anti-Colonial Metaphor in Heaney, Friel and McGuinness', *PMLA*, 111:2, March 1996, 222–39.

Dantanus, Ulf. *Brian Friel: A Study*. London: Faber. 1988.

Dawe, Gerald and Edna Longley, eds. *Across a Roaring Hill: The Protestant Imagination in Modern Ireland*. Belfast: Blackstaff, 1985.

Docherty, Thomas. 'Ana-; or Postmodernism, Landscape, Seamus Heaney', in Allen, pp.206–22.

Dunn, Douglas. 'Longley's Metric', in *The Poetry of Michael Longley*, eds. Alan J. Peacock and Kathleen Devine. Gerrards Cross: Colin Smythe, 2001.

Foster, John Wilson. *Forces and Themes in Ulster Fiction*, Dublin: Gill & Macmillan, 1974.

—— *Colonial Consequences: Essays in Irish Literature and Culture*. Dublin: Lilliput Press, 1991.

—— *The Achievement of Seamus Heaney*. Dublin: Lilliput, 1995.

Foucault, Michel. 'The Order of Discourse', from *Untying the Text*, ed. R. Young, London: Routledge and Kegan Paul, 1981, pp.52–64.

Freud, Sigmund. *On Sexuality: Three Essays on the Theory of Sexuality*. Harmondsworth: Penguin, 1991.

Frow, John. 'Intertextuality and Ontology', in *Intertextuality: Theories and Practice*, eds. Michael Worton and Judith Still. Manchester: Manchester University Press, 1990.

Gibbons, Fiachra. 'Truth and Nail', *The Guardian*, 10 April 2000, 10–11.

Glob, P.V. *The Bog People*, London: Faber, 1969.

Gombrich, E.H. *The Story of Art*. London: Phaidon, 1972.

Goodby, John. 'Bhabha, the Post/Colonial and Glenn Patterson's *Burning Your Own*', *Irish Studies Review* 7:1, April 1999, 65–71.

Graham, Colin and Richard Kirkland, eds. *Ireland and Cultural Theory: The Mechanics of Authenticity*, Basingstoke: Macmillan, 1999.

Grene, Nicholas. 'Distancing Drama: Sean O'Casey to Brian Friel', in *Irish Writers and the Theatre*, ed. Masaru Sekine. Gerrards Cross: Colin Smythe, 1987.

—— *The Politics of Irish Drama*. Cambridge: Cambridge University Press, 1999.

Guinness, Selima, ed. *The New Irish Poets*, Newcastle-upon-Tyne: Bloodaxe, 2004.

Haffenden, John. ed. *Viewpoints: Poets in Conversation*. London: Faber, 1981.

Hart, Henry. *Seamus Heaney: Poet of Contrary Progressions*, New York: Syracuse UP, 1992.

Harte, Liam. *Contemporary Irish Fiction: Themes Tropes, Theories* ed. with Michael Parker. Basingstoke: Macmillan, 2000.

—— 'History Lessons: Postcolonialism and Seamus Deane's *Reading in the Dark*', *Irish University Review*, 30:1, Spring/Summer 2000, 149–62.

Haslam, Richard. ' "The Pose Arranged and Lingered Over": Visualizing the Troubles', in *Contemporary Irish Fiction*, eds. Harte and Parker, 192–212.

Haughton, Hugh. 'Even now there are places where a thought might grow': Place and Displacement in the Poetry of Derek Mahon', in *The Chosen Ground*, ed. Corcoran, pp.87–120.

—— 'On Sitting Down to Read "A Disused Shed in Co Wexford" Once Again', *Cambridge Quarterly*, 31:2 (2002), 183–98.

Henderson, Lynda. 'The Green Shoot: Transcendence and the Imagination in contemporary Ulster', in *Across a Roaring Hill* eds. Gerald Dawe and Edna Longley, Belfast: Blackstaff, 1985.

Herron, Tom. 'The Body's in the Post: Contemporary Irish Poetry and the Dispersed Body', in *Ireland and Cultural Theory*, eds. Colin Graham and Richard Kirkland. Basingstoke: Macmillan, 1999, pp.193–209.

—— 'Dead Men Talking: *Observe the Sons of Ulster Marching Towards the Somme*', *Eire-Ireland*, 39: 1, Summer 2004.

Hughes, Eamonn (ed.). *Culture and Politics in Northern Ireland*. Milton Keynes: Open University Press, 1991.

—— 'Representation in Modern Irish Poetry', in *Seamus Heaney*, ed. Allen, pp.78–94.

—— 'Place in Tom Paulin's Poetry', in *Ireland and Cultural Theory*, ed. Graham and Kirkland, pp.162–92.

Hyland, Paul and Neil Sammells. *Irish Writing: Exile and Subversion*. London: Macmillan, 1991.

Jarniewicz, Jerzy. 'Derek Mahon: History, Mute Phenomena and Beyond', in *The Poetry of Derek Mahon*, pp.83–95.

—— *The Bottomless Centre: The Uses of History in the Poetry of Seamus Heaney*. Lódz: Wydawnictwo Uniwersytetu Lódzkiego, 2002.

Kearney, Richard. 'The IRA's Strategy of Failure', *The Crane Bag*, 4:2, Winter 1980, 62–70.

—— 'The Nightmare of History', *Irish Literary Supplement* 2:2, 1983, 24.

—— *Transitions: Narratives in Modern Irish Culture*. Manchester: Manchester University Press, 1988.

Kendall, Tim. *Paul Muldoon*. Bridgend: Seren, 1996.

Kennedy-Andrews, Elmer, 'The Fifth Province', in Peacock, pp.29–48.

—— 'The Will to Freedom: Politics and Play in the Theatre of Stewart Parker', in *Irish Writers and Politics*, eds. Komesu and Sekine. Gerrard Cross: Colin Smythe, 1991, pp.237–69.

—— *Seamus Heaney: A Collection of Critical Essays*, Basingstoke: Macmillan, 1992.

—— *The Art of Brian Friel: Neither Reality Nor Dreams*. London: Macmillan, 1995.

—— *The Poetry of Derek Mahon* (ed.). Gerrards Cross: Colin Smythe, 2002.

—— *Fiction and the Northern Ireland Troubles: (de-)constructing the North*. Dublin: Four Courts, 2003.

Kiberd, Declan. *Inventing Ireland: The Literature of the Modern Nation*. London: Vintage, 1996.

Kirkland, Richard. *Literature and Culture in Northern Ireland Since 1965*. London: Longman, 1996.

Klein, Melanie. *Love, Guilt and Reparation*. New York: Free Press, 1984.

Komesu, Okifumu and Masaru Sekine, eds. *Irish Writers and Politics*. Gerrards Cross, Colin Smythe, 1991.

Kristeva, Julia. *Powers of Horror*. New York: Columbia University Press, 1982.

Lloyd, David. '"Pap for the dispossessed': Seamus Heaney and the Poetics of Identity', in Kennedy-Andrews, 1992.

—— *Anomalous States: Irish Writing and the Postcolonial Moment*. Dublin: Lilliput, 1993.

—— *Ireland after History*. Cork: Cork University Press, 1999.

Lodge, David. *Modern Criticism and Theory: A Reader*. London: Longman, 1988.

Lojek, Helen. 'Myth and Bonding in Frank McGuinness's *Observe the Sons of Ulster Marching Towards the Somme*', *Canadian Journal of Irish Studies*, 14, 1988, 46.

Longley, Edna. '*North*: "Inner Émigré" or "Artful Voyeur"?', in *The Art of Seamus Heaney*, ed. Tony Curtis. Bridgend: Poetry Wales Press, 1985, pp.63–95.

—— *Poetry in the Wars*. Newcastle-upon-Tyne: Bloodaxe, 1986.

—— *The Living Stream: Literature and Revisionism in Ireland*, Newcastle-upon-Tyne: Bloodaxe, 1994.

——'Autobiography as History', *Fortnight*, November 1996, 34.

—— *Poetry and Posterity*, Newcastle-upon-Tyne: Bloodaxe, 2000.

—— ed. *The Bloodaxe Book of 20th Century Poetry from Britain and Ireland*. Newcastle-upon-Tyne: Bloodaxe, 2000.

—— 'Looking Back from *The Yellow Book*', in *The Poetry of Derek Mahon*, ed. Kennedy-Andrews, 29–47.

Macherey, Pierre. *A Theory of Literary Production*, trans. G. Wall. London: Routledge and Kegan Paul, 1978.

Magee, Patrick. *Gangsters or Guerillas?: Representations of Irish Republicans in 'Troubles Fiction'*. Belfast: Beyond the Pale, 2001.

Mahony, Christina Hunt. *Contemporary Irish Literature: Transforming Tradition*. Basingstoke: Macmillan, 1998.

Matthews, Steven. *Irish Poetry: Politics, History, Negotiation.* Basingstoke: Macmillan, 1997.

Maxwell, D.E.S. *Brian Friel.* Lewisburg: Bucknell University Press, 1973.

—— 'Figures in a Peepshow': Friel and the Irish Dramatic Tradition', in Peacock, pp. 49–68.

McCarthy, Conor. *Modernisation, Crisis and Culture in Ireland 1969–1992.* Dublin: Four Courts Press, 2000.

McDonald, Peter. *Mistaken Identities: Poetry and Northern Ireland.* Oxford: Clarendon, 2000.

McGuinness, Arthur E. 'The Craft of Diction: Revision in Seamus Heaney's Poems', in *Image and Illusion: Anglo-Irish Literature and its Contexts.* Portmarnock: Wolfhound, 1979.

Morash, Christopher. *A History of Irish Theatre 1601–2000.* Cambridge: Cambridge University Press, 2002.

Murphy, Shane. '"You took away my Biography": The Poetry of Medbh McGuckian', *Irish University Review*, 28:1 (Spring/Summer 1998), 110–32.

—— 'Roaming Root of Multiple Meanings: Intertextual Relations in Medbh McGuckian's Poetry', *Metre*, 5, Autumn–Winter, 1998, 99–109.

—— 'Sonnets, Centos and Long Lines', in *Contemporary Irish Poetry*, ed. Matthew Campbell, pp.189–208.

—— *Sympathetic Ink: Intertextual Relations in Northern Irish Poetry.* Liverpool: Liverpool University Press, 2006.

Murray, Christopher, 'Friel's "Emblems of Adversity" and the Yeatsian Example', *The Achievement of Brian Friel.* ed. Alan Peacock. Gerrards Cross: Smythe, 1992: 69–90.

—— *Twentieth-Century Irish Drama.* Manchester: Manchester University Press, 1997.

O'Brien, Eugene. 'The Epistemology of Nationalism', *Irish Studies Review*, 17, Winter 1996/97, 15–20.

—— *Seamus Heaney: Creating Irelands of the Mind.* Dublin: Liffey Press, 2002.

O'Brien, George. *Brian Friel.* Dublin: Gill & Macmillan, 1989.

O'Brien, Sean. *The Deregulated Muse*, Newcastle-upon-Tyne: Bloodaxe, 1998.

O'Donoghue, Bernard. 'Involved Imaginings', in Corcoran's *The Chosen Ground*, pp.171–88.

—— *Seamus Heaney and The Language of Poetry.* Hemel Hempstead: Harvester Wheatsheaf, 1994.

Onega, Susana and José Ángel García Landa, eds. *Narratology.* London: Longman, 1996.

Opie, Iona and Peter. *The Lore and Language of Schoolchildren.* Oxford: Oxford University Press, 1959.

Ormsby, Frank. 'Poetry', in *Stepping Stones: The Arts in Ulster 1971–2001* eds. Mark Carruthers and Stephen Douds. Belfast: Blackstaff, 2001.

O'Toole, Fintan. 'The Man from God Knows Where'. Interview with Brian Friel, *In Dublin*, 14 July 1982, 22.

—— 'Keeper of the Faith', *The Guardian*, 16 January 1992, 6.

—— 'Marking Time: From *Making History* to *Dancing at Lughnasa*', in Peacock, pp.202–14.

The Oxford Companion to Irish Literature ed. Robert Welch, Oxford University Press: Oxford, 1996.

Parker, Michael. *Seamus Heaney: The Making of the Poet*, Basingstoke: Macmillan, 1993.

—— *The Hurt World: Short Stories of the Troubles*, Belfast: Blackstaff, 1995.
—— *Contemporary Irish Fiction: Themes, Tropes, Theories* ed. with Liam Harte. Basingstoke: Macmillan, 2000.
—— 'Shadows on a Glass: Self-Reflexivity in the Fiction of Deirdre Madden, *Irish University Press*, 30:1, Spring/Summer 2000, 82–102.
—— 'Changing Skies: The Roles of Native and American Narratives in the Politicisation of Seamus Heaney's Early Poetry', *Symbiosis*, 6:2, October 2002, 133–58.
Patten, Eve. 'Fiction in Conflict: Northern Ireland's Prodigal Novelists', in *Peripheral Visions: Images of Nationhood in Contemporary British Fiction*, ed. Ian A. Bell. Bridgend: Seren, 1996, 128–48.
Paxman, Jeremy. *The English: A Portrait of a People*, Harmondsworth: Penguin, 1998.
Peach, Linden, *The Contemporary Irish Novel*. Basingstoke: Macmillan, 2004.
Peacock, Alan. ed. *The Achievement of Brian Friel*. Gerrards Cross: Smythe, 1992.
Pelaschiar, Laura. *Writing the North: The Contemporary Novel in Northern Ireland*. Trieste: Edizioni Parnaso, 1998.
Pettitt, Lance. *Screening Ireland: Film and Television Representation*. Manchester: Manchester University Press, 2000.
Pilkington, Lionel. *Theatre and the State in Twentieth Century Ireland: Cultivating the People*, London: Routledge, 2001.
Pine, Richard. *Brian Friel and Ireland's Drama*. London: Routledge, 1990.
—— *The Diviner: The Art of Brian Friel*. Dublin: UCD, 1999.
Ramazani, Jahan. *Poetry of Mourning: The Modern Elegy from Hardy to Heaney*. Chicago: University of Chicago Press, 1994.
Redshaw, Thomas Dillon. 'L'exile et le Royaume Uni: John Montague's *Death of a Chieftain*', in *Well Dreams: Critical Essays on John Montague*, Omaha: Creighton University Press, 2004.
Rees-Jones, Deryn. *Consorting with Angels: Essays on Modern Women Poets*. Newcastle-upon-Tyne: Bloodaxe, 2005.
Regan, Stephen. 'Reading in the Dark', *Irish Studies Review*, 19 (Summer 1997), 35–40.
Rice, Philip and Patricia Waugh, eds *Modern Literary Theory*. London: Arnold, 1992.
Richards, Shaun. 'Placed Identities for Placeless Times: Brian Friel and Posctcolonial Criticism', *Irish University Review* 27:1, Spring/Summer 1997, 55–68.
—— ed. *Twentieth Century Irish Drama*. Cambridge: Cambridge University Press, 2004.
Richtarik, Marilynn. *Acting Between the Lines: The Field Day Theatre Company and Irish Cultural Politics 1980–1984*. Oxford: Clarendon Press, 1994.
—— 'The Field Day Theatre Company', in *Twentieth Century Irish Drama*, ed. Richards, 191–203.
Roche, Anthony. *Contemporary Irish Drama*. Dublin: Gill & Macmillan, 1994.
Rolleston, T.W. *Myths and Legends of the Celtic Race*. London: Constable, nd. first publ. 1911.
Rumens, Carol. 'Reading Deane, *Fortnight*, July/August, 1997, 30.
Quinn, Antoinette. 'The Well-Beloved: Montague and the Muse', *Irish University Review*, 19:1 (Spring 1989), 27–43.
Said, Edward. *Orientalism*. London: Penguin, 1985.
—— *Culture and Imperialism*. London: Chatto, 1993.
Smith, Stan. 'The Twilight of the Cities: Derek Mahon's Dark Cinema', in *The Poetry of Derek Mahon*, ed. Kennedy-Andrews, 249–72.

Smyth, Gerry. *The Novel and the Nation: Studies in the New Irish Fiction*. London: Pluto, 1997.

—— *Space and the Irish Cultural Imagination*. Basingstoke: Palgrave Macmillan, 2003.

Somerville-Arjat, Gillean and Rebecca E. Wilson (eds), *Sleeping with Monsters: Conversations with Scottish and Irish Women Poets*. Dublin: Wolfhound 1990.

Stallworthy, Jon. *Louis MacNeice*, London: Faber and Faber, 1995.

Storey, Michael. *Representing the Troubles in Irish Short Fiction*. Washington: Catholic University of America Press, 2004.

St Peter, Christine. *Changing Ireland: Strategies in Contemporary Women's Fiction*. London: Macmillan, 2000.

Vance, Norman. *Irish Literature: A Social History*, Dublin: Four Courts Press, 1999.

Vendler, Helen. *Seamus Heaney*. London: Fontana, 1999.

Wills, Clair. 'The Perfect Mother: Authority in the Poetry of Medbh McGuckian, in *Text and Context*, 3, Autumn 1988, 91–111.

—— *Improprieties: Politics and Sexuality in Northern Irish Poetry*. Oxford: Clarendon, 1993.

—— *Reading Paul Muldoon*. Newcastle-upon-Tyne: Bloodaxe, 1998.

C: History and politics in Northern Ireland, the Republic of Ireland, and Britain

Adams, Gerry. *Before the Dawn: An Autobiography*. New York: Morrow, 1996.

Andrews, J.H. *A Paper Landscape*. Oxford: Clarendon, 1975.

Anderson, Mark and Mick Gold. *Endgame in Ireland*, BBC 2, 2001.

Bardon, Jonathan. *A History of Ulster*, Belfast: Blackstaff, 1992.

—— *Beyond the Studio: A History of BBC Northern Ireland*. Belfast: Blackstaff, 2000.

Bell, J. Bowyer. *The Irish Troubles: A Generation of Violence 1967–1992*. Dublin: Gill & Macmillan, 1993.

Bew, Paul, Peter Gibbon, Henry Patterson, *Northern Ireland 1921–1994*. London: Serif, 1995.

Bew, Paul and Gordon Gillespie, eds, *Northern Ireland: A Chronology of the Troubles*. Dublin: Gill & Macmillan, 1999.

Bishop, Patrick and Eamonn Mallie, *The Provisional IRA*. London: Corgi, 1988.

Boulton, David. *The UVF 1966–73: An Anatomy of Loyalist Rebellion*. Dublin: Torc, 1973.

Boyce, D. George. *Nationalism in Ireland*. London: Routledge, 1991.

—— and Alan O'Day, eds, *The Making of Modern Irish History*. London: Routledge, 1996.

Brady, Ciaran, ed. *Interpreting Irish History: The Debate on Historical Revisionism*. Dublin: Irish Academic Press, 1994.

Brown, Terence. *Ireland: A Social and Cultural History 1922–2002*. London: Harper Perennial, 2004.

Buckland, Patrick. *A History of Northern Ireland*, Dublin: Gill & Macmillan, 1981.

Carlson, Julia, ed. *Banned in Ireland: Censorship and the Irish Writer*. London: Routledge, 1990.

Deane, Seamus. 'Wherever Green is Red', in *Interpreting Irish History*, ed. Brady.

Douglas, Roy, Liam Harte and Jim O'Hara, *Drawing Conclusions: A Cartoon History of Anglo-Irish Relations*. Belfast: Blackstaff, 1998.

Downing, Taylor, ed. *The Troubles*. London: Futura, 1980.

Elliott, Marianne. *The Catholics of Ulster: A History*. London: Allen Lane, 2000.

—— *The Long Road to Peace*, ed. Liverpool: Liverpool University Press, 2002.

English, Richard. '"Cultural Traditions" and Political Ambiguity', *Irish Review*, 15, Spring 1994, 97–106.

—— *The Armed Struggle: A History of the IRA*. London: Macmillan, 2003.

Fanon, Frantz. *The Wretched of the Earth*. Harmondsworth: Penguin, 1967.

Farrell, Michael. *Northern Ireland: The Orange State*. London: Pluto, 1976.

Feeney, Brian. *Sinn Féin: A Hundred Turbulent Years*. Dublin: O'Brien, 2002.

Flackes, W.D. *Northern Ireland: A Political Directory 1963–83*. London: Ariel, 1983.

Fitt, Gerry, interviewed by John Murdoch, *Sunday Press*, 30 August, 1970, 15.

Foster, R.F. *Modern Ireland 1600–1972*. Harmondsworth: Penguin 1989.

—— *Paddy and Mr Punch*. London: Allen Lane Penguin Press, 1993.

—— *W.B. Yeats: A Life*, Vol. 1. Oxford: Oxford University Press, 1997.

—— *The Irish Story: Telling Tales and Making It Up in Ireland*. London: Allen Lane, 2001.

Gardiner, Juliet and Neil Wenborn, eds. *The History Today Companion to British History*. London: Collins and Brown, 1995.

Geraghty, Tony. *The Irish War: The Military History of a Domestic Conflict*. London: HarperCollins 1998.

Hansard: Parliamentary Debates. House of Commons Official Report, Session 1971–72, Fifth Series, Vol. 830. London: Her Majesty's Stationery Office 1972: 32–3.

Hennessey, Thomas. *A History of Northern Ireland 1920–1996*. Basingstoke: Macmillan, 1997.

—— *The Northern Ireland Peace Process*. Basingstoke: Palgrave, 2001.

—— 'Sunningdale for Slow Learners', ACIS/BAIS conference paper, University of Liverpool, 16 July 2004.

Holland, Jack. *Hope Against History: The Ulster Conflict*, London: Hodder and Stoughton, 1999.

Hume, John. *Personal Views: Politics, Peace and Reconciliation in Ireland*. Enfield: Roberts Rinehart, 1996.

Jackson, Alvin. *Ireland 1798–1998*, Oxford: Blackwell, 1999.

Kearney, Richard. 'The IRA's Strategy of Failure', *The Crane Bag*, 4:2, Winter 1980, 62–70.

Kennedy, Liam. 'They Shoot Children, Don't They?: An Analysis of the Age and Gender of Victims of Paramilitary "Punishments" in Northern Ireland', prepared for the Northern Ireland Committee against Terror (NICAT) and the Northern Ireland Affairs Committee of the House of Commons, August 2001.

McCann, Eamonn. *War and an Irish Town*. Harmondsworth: Penguin, 1974.

—— and Owen Boycott. 'Memo reveals "Propaganda War"', *The Guardian* 10 November, 1995, 1, 19.

McDonald, Henry. 'The Lies of Language', *The Observer*, 28 July 2002.

McIntosh, Gillian. *The Force of Culture: Unionist Identities in Twentieth Century Ireland*, Cork: Cork University Press, 1999.

McKittrick, David, Seamus Kelters, Brian Feeney, Chris Thornton, *Lost Lives*, Edinburgh: Mainstream, 1999.

McKittrick, David and David McVea, *Making Sense of the Troubles*. London: Penguin, 2001.

Maley, Willy. 'Varieties of Nationalism', *Irish Studies Review*, 15, Summer 1996, 34–7.

Mallie, Eamonn and David McKittrick, *The Fight for Peace*. London: Mandarin, 1997.

Mitchell, George J. *Making Peace*. London: Heinemann, 1999.

Moloney, Ed. *A Secret History of the IRA*, London: Penguin, 2003.

—— and Andy Pollak, *Paisley*, Dublin: Poolbeg, 1986.

Nelson, Sarah. *Ulster's Uncertain Defenders: Protestant Political, Paramilitary and Community Groups and the Northern Ireland Conflict*, Belfast: Appletree, 1984.

Nic Craith, Mairead. *Plural Identities-Singular Narratives: The Case of Northern Ireland*. Oxford: Berghahn, 2002.

O'Connor, Fionnuala. *In Search of a State: Catholics in Northern Ireland*. Belfast: Blackstaff, 1993.

O'Malley, Padraig. *Biting at the Grave: The Irish Hunger Strikes and the Politics of Despair*. Belfast: Blackstaff, 1990.

O'Toole, Fintan. *The Bloody Protest*, BBC Radio 4, 10 April 1996.

—— 'A Radical Deal', *The Irish Times*, 13 April 1998, 16.

Pallister, David. 'Fury at Bloody Sunday Outburst', *The Guardian*. 7 July 1999: 3.

Roberts, J.M. *A History of Europe*. Oxford: Helicon, 1996.

Rose, Peter. *How the Troubles Came to Northern Ireland*, Basingstoke: Macmillan, 1999.

Ross, Nick. *We Shall Overcome*, BBC2 documentary, 27.3.99.

Secret History: Bloody Sunday, Channel 4, first broadcast 4 December 1991.

Sked, Alan and Chris Cook, *Post-War Britain: A Political History*. Harmondsworth: Penguin, 1990.

The Sunday Times Insight Team, *Ulster*, Harmondsworth: Penguin, 1972.

Stalker, John. *Stalker*. London: Penguin, 1988

Taylor, Peter. *Remember Bloody Sunday*. BBC1, 28 January 1993.

—— *Families at War: Voices from the Troubles*. London: BBC, 1989.

—— *Loyalists*. London: Bloomsbury, 1999.

The Troubles. Thames Television documentary, 1980.

Urban, Mark. *Big Boys' Rules: The SAS and the Secret Struggle Against the IRA*. London: Faber, 1992.

Waller, Philip and John Rowell. *Chronology of the Twentieth Century*. Oxford: Helicon, 1995.

Ward, Margaret. *Unmanageable Revolutionaries; Women and Irish Nationalism* London: Pluto, 1983.

—— 'Feminism in the North of Ireland', *HU* 83, Summer 1987, 59–70.

White, Barrie. *John Hume: Statesman of the Troubles*. Belfast: Blackstaff, 1984.

Wichert, Sabine. *Northern Ireland Since 1945* (second edition). Harlow: Longman, 1999.

Wilson, Andrew J. *Irish America and the Ulster Conflict 1968–1995*. Belfast: Blackstaff, 1995.

Contents (Volume 1)

Index

(Literary texts discussed in detail are in bold. The prefix 'n' followed by a page number refers to citations in the footnotes.)